Praise for *Ink In the Blood*
From reviews of Phil Vinson's 2005 Memoir

"*Ink* is a good read, filled with the history of an era in Fort Worth, brought lovingly and vividly to life through the eyes of a young boy and young man who was a keen observer of the quirks, peculiarities, tragedies, and triumphs of his fellow time travelers."

--Betty Brink, Fort Worth Weekly

❖

"And thus does Vinson succeed at relating how it felt to be there, growing up amidst a Southern culture torn between mannered civility and rowdiness — and never once losing sight of the drive to fulfill a professional heritage. If a successful long-term career has affirmed that fulfillment, then this friendly and rambunctious memoir makes for a suitable crowning touch."

--Michael H. Price, Fort Worth Business Press

❖

"It's a great read in an easily digested, short-chapter style and told with unabashed honesty, candor, humor, and insight."

--Douglas R. Clarke, Amazon.com

❖

"Told with honesty and humor through short chapters and vignettes, Vinson's story reads like a novel--a novel that has the reader nodding and smiling at the manifest truth evidenced throughout."

--Laurance Priddy, Attorney and Author, Amazon.com

❖

"Phil Vinson writes about growing up in Fort Worth in the '50s in this easy-to-read and quite honest memoir."

--Glenn Dromgoole, Cox Newspapers

"It Takes a Worried Man" by Phil Vinson. ISBN 978-1-60264-149-5 (softcover).

Published 2008 by Virtualbookworm.com Publishing Inc., P.O. Box 9949, College Station, TX 77842, US. ©2008, Phil Vinson. All rights reserved. No part of this publication may be reproduced, stored in a retrieval system, or transmitted in any form or by any means, electronic, mechanical, recording or otherwise, without the prior written permission of Phil Vinson.

Manufactured in the United States of America.

Dedicated to the memory of Robin Edwards and to Mary Kathleen Norris, two real-world "Marilyn Reeds."

It Takes a Worried Man

❖

A Novel

By Phil Vinson

Anxiety Disorders affect about 40 million American adults age 18 years and older (about 18%) in a given year, causing them to be filled with fearfulness and uncertainty.
—National Institute of Mental Health Website

*It takes a worried man to sing a worried song,
I'm worried now, but I won't be worried long.*
—Worried Man Blues (Traditional)

Prologue

❖

Fort Worth, Texas
December 1958

Greg held Suzy snugly against him as they danced, closer than they'd ever been before. She put her hand behind his head and pulled his face even tighter against hers. The Platters' classic, "Only You," drifted across the ballroom as they pressed their cheeks together. Greg breathed in the clean scent of Suzy's skin and the subtle aroma of *L'Aimant*. Loose strands from Suzy's sun-streaked dark-blonde hair, swept up in a French twist, brushed against Greg's face. He was in heaven.

The Fort Worth Elk's Club provided an old-fashioned elegance for the occasion. Suzy had invited Greg, a freshman at Trinity Valley State College, to the Eastside High Christmas dance. Suzy, two years younger than Greg and a junior at Eastside, was Greg's first real girlfriend.

Greg remained in a daze after the tune ended, but he finally reclaimed his senses and escorted Suzy off the dance floor.

He glanced toward a corner of the room, where Suzy's older sister Beverly sat slumped at a table with arms crossed in a sulky pout. Greg's best friend Eddie King sat across from Beverly, waving his arms and gesturing as if pleading a losing cause.

"What the heck's going on with Eddie and Beverly?" Greg asked Suzy. The four had come to the dance on a double date, but Eddie and Beverly had spent the evening sniping at each other.

"Beverly thought they were going steady," Suzy said. "But she thinks Eddie's cheating on her."

"If he is, he hasn't told me." Greg adjusted his necktie.

Someone announced that the next tune would be the last dance. Greg and Suzy moved back to the dance floor and again snuggled close as the phonograph played the Spaniels' popular parting ditty:

> *Dat-dada-da-da—*
> *Good night, sweetheart, well it's time to go,*
> *...I hate to leave you but I really must say,*
> *Good night, sweetheart, goodnight.*

The four of them walked outside into the cold, breezy December air and got into Eddie's '55 Chevy Bel Air. Beverly scooted as far away from Eddie as she could and scrunched herself up against the passenger-side door. She stared out the window as Eddie started the car. Scowling, he popped the clutch and burned rubber as he roared out of the parking lot.

Greg tried to ignore the chill between Eddie and Beverly as Suzy cuddled close to him in the back seat. He put his arm around her, digging his fingers into the fur of her mouton coat. *Tonight's the night,* he thought; he still hadn't kissed Suzy. The Coxes were Southern Baptists, and Greg feared Suzy was so young and proper he might lose her if he came on too strong—even though they'd been dating three months. It scarcely mattered to Greg that Eddie had always kissed Beverly goodnight. Greg felt he had to err on the side of caution.

On the way to the girls' house, the foursome passed Lucky's Drive-in, where they'd always stopped for malts or limeades or cherry Cokes when they'd double dated. But Eddie, still steaming, sped past the drive-in and pulled onto the street where Suzy and Beverly lived. He brought the car to a jerky halt in the driveway.

Beverly threw open the car door. "Don't bother to get out," she said in a huff. "It's all over with you, buster." She slammed the door and stomped toward the house before Greg and Suzy could exit the Bel Air.

"Bitch," Eddie muttered under his breath as Greg followed Suzy out of the car.

As they sauntered up the sidewalk, Beverly stormed into the house and slammed the front door. Greg and Suzy stood alone on the porch. The scene with Beverly and Eddie had so unnerved Greg, he didn't know if he could proceed with his amorous plans.

"Greg, I had a wonderful time," Suzy said, looking deeply into Greg's eyes. Her red lipstick and brown eyes sparkled in the porch light.

"Me, too," Greg said, but his knees were going weak, and his heart pounded. "I hear 'South Pacific' is showing at the Palace. Would you like to go next weekend?"

"Oh, I'd love to," Suzy beamed. "Call me."

"Okay. I hope Beverly's okay."

"She'll probably get over it." Suzy eased closer to Greg.

He retreated. "Well, I guess I'd better go check on Eddie." He watched Suzy's face go cold. "Well, goodnight, Suzy."

She looked down. "Goodnight, Greg," her voice trailed off as her shoulders slumped, and she turned toward the front door.

Greg walked back to the car, wincing and cursing his loss of nerve. He got into the front seat.

"God damn it, Spencer," Eddie said. "Are you ever going to kiss that girl?"

"I don't know what it is, Eddie; I got cold feet again," Greg said. "Besides, you and Beverly kind of spoiled the mood."

"Yeah, well, screw Beverly and the horse she rode in on."

Eddie started the car. The Chevy's V-8 engine rumbled, abetted by the twin glass-pack mufflers Eddie had installed. He reached beneath the front seat and pulled out a pint bottle of bourbon. He'd been sneaking out to his car at the dance and taking liberal swigs from the bottle when Beverly had gone to the ladies' room. Greg had begged off, fearing Suzy would smell the booze on his breath; he couldn't take the chance. Now the bottle was half empty.

Eddie turned up the bottle and guzzled as he roared out East Oakdale Avenue. Greg watched the bubbles gurgling as Eddie swigged the spirits. Greg reached across and jerked the bottle from Eddie's mouth.

"Come on, man," Greg said. "I know you're hurting, but it's starting to sleet."

"You'll get yours, Spencer; women are poison." Eddie turned up the bottle again. Again Greg pleaded with him.

Eddie ignored him and started to sing:

>   *Far across the blue waters,*
>   *Away over yonder,*
>   *On the banks of the old River Rhine. . . .*

Eddie sped past the turnoff to Greg's house.

"Hey, where are you going?" Greg said. "This sleet is getting harder. We'd better call it a night."

"Who gives a fat fuck?" Eddie said and drained the bottle. He pulled onto a narrow blacktop road that crossed the Lake Arlington dam, east of the Fort Worth city limits. As they crossed the dam, sleet piled up on the roadway and pelted the water on their right. To the left, the earthen dam sloped downward fifty yards to an open field.

"Why don't you let me drive?" Greg pleaded. "This damn sleet is covering the road. We ought to head back."

With a defiant look, Eddie stomped the gas to the floor. The tires spun on the icy pellets, causing the car to fishtail sideways.

"Look out!" Greg shouted as the car skidded across the road. Greg tried to grab the steering wheel, but the Chevy plowed through the guardrail on the dry side of the dam. The Bel Air hit the slope and flipped upside down. Then it tumbled slowly down the side of the dam.

Greg's chest smashed into the dashboard. As he tried to right himself, the car flipped again, and his head smacked the windshield below him with the full force of gravity. The car rolled to the bottom of the dam, landing upright. Greg lay wedged between the seat and dashboard. His last sight was of Eddie shaking his head and crawling out the door, left hanging by one hinge. Then, everything dissolved into darkness.

It Takes a Worried Man

❖

One

❖

Fort Worth
May 1959

Greg Spencer woke with a jolt. He felt his heart speed up. Nothing had changed.

He looked around his room. *Why bother to get out of bed?* he thought. *What's the use? I'll never feel normal again.*

He heard birds singing outside, but they seemed to be in a separate reality, as if he were dreaming them. Yet he knew he was awake and had to get up. He had to keep trying.

He threw on a terrycloth robe and stumbled to the bathroom. Looking in the mirror, he noticed how wasted he looked. Dark circles spread beneath his coffee-colored eyes. He looked ten years beyond his age of nineteen.

He shaved and dressed, every move demanding extra effort.

As Greg approached the kitchen, his father, George, headed out the front door without speaking. Greg wondered if his dad was avoiding him. But then, why would he stick around? He'd given Greg all the advice he could, and it had been little help. George went out the door, got in his car, and drove off to work.

Vivian, Greg's mother, had weeks ago stopped trying to console Greg. He'd recovered from the injuries he'd received in the wreck. But after a few weeks, he'd grown morose and lethargic, staying home from school with vague complaints of "not feeling right."

"Are you going to school today?" Vivian put a plate of scrambled eggs in front of Greg.

"I guess so." Greg looked at the eggs and felt queasy. "I've got to try to catch up. I've missed so much already."

"Well, it'll help to get your mind off yourself."

"You always say that." Greg put a slice of bread into the toaster.

"It's true. If you ask me, all that's wrong with you is just a bad case of self-centeredness." Vivian rinsed her hands in the kitchen sink.

"I'm glad you know what's wrong with me. No one else seems to."

"I don't believe in all this modern psychology." Vivian had a stern edge to her voice. "All you need is a little backbone."

"All I've been through, and you're telling me I need backbone?" Greg wadded up his napkin and threw it onto his plate. "I've got to go."

He stomped away from the table, leaving most of his breakfast untouched. He gathered his books and stomped out to his '49 Chevy in the driveway.

He cursed his mother for several blocks, then settled back into the jangled melancholy he'd been in for weeks.

His freshman year at Trinity Valley State College had turned into a disaster, and he was in danger of flunking out. He'd breezed through high school with passing grades, but had scarcely cracked a book. He hadn't adjusted to the rigors of college, and since March he'd missed so many classes, he'd fallen perilously behind that spring semester of 1959.

Greg wondered how much the accident had to do with it. But how could it? By the end of January, he'd recovered from the concussion and broken ribs, and for a while everything had looked fine.

Then his life had come unraveled.

He pulled onto Highway 80, the main route between Fort Worth and Arlington, and headed east toward the college, wondering if he'd ever feel whole again.

It Takes a Worried Man

He flipped on the car radio. The Kingston Trio sang:

It takes a worried man to sing a worried song. . . .

That about sums it up, Greg thought. *Nothing but worry. . . Never feeling right. . . Grades going down the tubes . . . Love life in the ditch. . . What have I done to Suzy?* He clicked the radio off and drove alone with his thoughts.

Greg had played football his sophomore and junior years at Eastside High, but he'd been so shy with girls, he never reaped the fruits of jockdom with the opposite sex the way a number of his teammates had.

He'd had only a few dates in high school, but the summer after he graduated, he'd met Suzanne Cox on a blind date. Greg and Suzy had dated regularly for several months.

Greg was crazy about Suzy.

Then, when things had started to come apart, he'd stopped calling her. He didn't want her to know about his sorry state; what could he tell her?

Finally, he decided he had to talk to her again. He'd picked up the phone to dial, but had such a shattering attack of nerves, he'd put the phone down and collapsed trembling on his bed.

That had been two weeks ago.

As Greg drove along the highway, he felt utterly defeated. What was the point of it all?

But such a hopeless feeling flew in the face of Greg's previous zest for life. How could things have turned so sour?

What if he were to just give up and end it all? His heart lurched at the thought.

Cars rushed past in the opposite direction. Greg gripped the steering wheel tightly to make sure he didn't lose control. He eased into the far-right lane. Suddenly his arms and hands tingled, as if charged with electricity. He shook all over.

Then, it felt as if something exploded in the pit of his stomach. Sweat popped out on his forehead. His heart raced faster than he'd ever known. His legs felt rubbery and weak, and he feared he couldn't control the accelerator or the brakes. His head swam, and his vision filled with something like snow on an old TV screen. He felt as if the very earth were dropping from beneath him. He managed to take his foot off the gas and coast to a stop at the side of the road.

All of a sudden, waves of nausea passed through him. He opened the door and vomited on the shoulder. Cars raced past, whipping him with their suction. He retched and heaved until he felt all his insides had emptied onto the pavement.

He closed the car door and slumped over the steering wheel, trembling from head to foot. He had to get to safety, but he couldn't move. He gasped for breath and couldn't seem to stop panting. Greg was convinced he was taking his last breaths.

Someone rapped on his driver's-side window; Greg rolled the window partly down.

A middle-aged police officer bent over and peered in the window. "What's the matter, son?"

Greg shook his head, but no words came.

"Have too much to drink?" The officer's Texas accent made it sound like "drank."

"N-no, sir." Greg realized he'd forgotten to turn off the ignition. He killed the engine.

"What is it?" The cop wore a concerned look. "You look terrible."

"I don't know." Greg groped for an explanation; nothing like this had happened before.

"I can call a amb'lance," the policeman said. "You look sick to me." The officer tilted his blue cap and scratched his head.

"I don't know. I don't know." Greg winced as if he were about to burst into tears.

"You're white as a sheet and shaking like a leaf. We'd better get you to a hospital, son."

"A hospital?" The thought brought Greg another wave of panic.

"Can I see your license?"

Greg fumbled for his wallet and handed the whole thing to the officer.

The policeman went to his car and made a call on his radio. He came back to Greg's car.

"Where was you headed, Gregory?"

"School."

"Where at?"

"Trinity Valley."

"Well, I've got a amb'lance on the way. Get ahold of yourself, son."

"I'm trying."

❖

The policeman and an ambulance attendant helped Greg onto a stretcher.

"Lay down, buddy," the attendant said. "Try to relax."

Greg had heard those words countless times: *Try to relax.* Didn't trying and relaxing contradict each other? But he was in no condition to quibble.

Inside the ambulance, the attendant knelt beside the stretcher. The young man adjusted a pillow beneath Greg's head. The ambulance pulled away, siren blaring.

"My mouth is so dry," Greg croaked. Bits of dried vomit caked his lips.

The attendant filled a paper cup from a thermos nearby and handed it to Greg.

Greg sipped from the cup. His trembling, along with the movement of the speeding ambulance, sloshed water onto his face and chest. He finally drank enough to relieve his parched mouth.

"Sorry, I just can't stop shaking." Greg wiped the excess water from his chin.

"Hey, don't apologize," said the crew-cutted attendant, who looked only slightly older than Greg. "Where are you hurt?"

"Hurt?" Greg looked puzzled. "Nowhere, I guess. I think my nerves are just shot."

"Hey, pal, if that's what's wrong with you, I've been there."

"You're kidding." Greg's tremors eased slightly.

"Between you and me," the young man said. "I just about had a nervous breakdown one time. I know what it feels like."

"I don't know what's the matter with me." Greg shook his head, ashamed and disgusted.

"Take it easy," the attendant said. "Something must really be buggin' you."

"Just about everything," Greg said. "You name it."

"Listen, I hope you don't have to go through what I did."

"What's that?"

"I got this little gal in trouble. Know what I mean?"

Greg managed a wan smile. "Yeah. I don't have that problem."

"Well, if you want something to tear you apart, that'll do it."

The young attendant kept up his consoling chatter as the ambulance raced across Arlington, Fort Worth's eastern suburb, to Village Creek Memorial Hospital.

The attendant and driver wheeled Greg inside the emergency room. They moved him from the gurney to a bed in the open ward. Curtains separated the beds. Most sat vacant in the early morning. Acrid hospital smells filled the air.

Greg lay back, still anxious about what doctors might find. His family physician had told him his only problem was "anxiety" and suggested, in the now-tiresome phrase, that he "try to relax."

A nurse asked if he wanted her to call someone in his family.

Greg dithered over the decision, but finally gave her the number and asked that she call his parents.

Another nurse took Greg's temperature, pulse, and blood pressure. A tall, young intern with thinning blond hair appeared and looked over his chart. He looked sternly at Greg.

"Your blood pressure is one-eighty over one hundred. That's too high. Your pulse is about one-fifteen. That's very high, too. Do you take any medication?"

"No."

"Have you been drinking alcohol?"

"Not lately."

He fired questions at Greg in rapid succession. "Taken any stimulants, like Benzedrine or amphetamines?"

"No, never."

A nurse drew a vial of blood from Greg's arm. The young doctor looked Greg over, checking his eyes, ears, throat, lungs, and abdomen. He wheeled an electrocardiograph next to the bed and placed the sensor pads around Greg's body.

After a few minutes of watching the graph, the doctor said, "I'm going to inject you with some Miltown."

"What's that?"

"It'll calm you down." The doctor drew some liquid from a small bottle, then jabbed the needle into Greg's arm. "Have you ever been treated by a psychiatrist?"

The idea jarred Greg. "No. I didn't think I was that far gone."

"Don't say that. A headshrinker might do you some good."

"Am I crazy?" Greg's pulse raced again.

"No, you're not crazy. Psychiatrists treat all kinds of nervous disorders."

"I couldn't face my friends." He closed his eyes, thinking of the shame.

"Come on, now. They help lots of people."

Greg felt his body slowing down as the drug spread through his veins.

"Okay, bub," the doctor looked over some papers. "Your lab results look normal. I don't see anything organic wrong with you. I think you just have a bad case of anxiety. I'm getting you an appointment with Dr. Simon; he can probably see you later today at his office."

There was that word again. Three months ago, Greg couldn't have defined "anxiety."

Soon his parents arrived. George Spencer wore a fretful expression; Vivian seemed irked.

"What happened?" George asked. Greg filled them in.

"They're sending me to see a psychiatrist," he said.

"Oh, Lord God," Vivian said, looking even more peeved.

Greg rolled his eyes. *That's all I need,* he thought.

❖

Dr. Daniel Simon sat in a high-backed leather chair across a spacious mahogany desk from Greg. He had dark features, wore horn-rimmed glasses, and combed his coarse, black hair straight back from his forehead.

"You look pretty agitated," the doctor said, shuffling through a stack of papers.

"I guess I am." Greg shifted in his chair. "I think that stuff they gave me this morning is wearing off."

Dr. Simon took a medicine bottle from his desk and poured a bright-red liquid into a small paper cup. He handed the cup to Greg.

"Drink this," he said.

Greg downed the liquid and felt warmth spread into his gut. His tension loosened.

"Now, Gregory, tell me what's going on." The doctor leaned back in his leather chair and sat with his fingertips touching.

"A bad case of nerves, I guess," Greg said.

"I can see that." Simon pursed his lips. "When did all this start?"

"About two months ago. I was at a basketball game with my dad. All of a sudden, I felt like I was in a dream, like nothing seemed real."

"Okay. What else?"

"Well, I told Dad about it. He said he'd had the same sensation when he was young, and I shouldn't worry about it, it would go away."

"It's a reaction to anxiety. Go on."

"Well, it didn't go away." Greg grimaced. "It's been there ever since."

"Never went away?" The doctor leaned forward slightly.

"Never. It's there right now. Has been every minute since March."

The doctor nodded. "And you've been preoccupied with worry about it."

"Yes, and the longer it went on, the more upset I got." Greg exhaled a deep sigh.

"It's sort of a vicious circle," Dr. Simon said, cleaning his glasses. "Anxiety causes this sensation, and you react to it with more anxiety. So, it just hangs around."

"Oh," Greg said. Finally someone had a clue.

Greg told the doctor he hadn't been sleeping more than three or fours hours a night and had lost his appetite, often throwing up after meals.

"And you're depressed, too." Dr. Simon said.

"Yes, very."

"Everything feels negative to you, right?"

"Sure does." Greg slumped in the chair.

"Do you ever feel that you'd like to just go to sleep and not wake up?"

"Sometimes," Greg said. "But mostly I just worry that I'm going crazy."

The doctor fixed his gaze. "You aren't going crazy."

"Then what's wrong with me?" Greg leaned forward in supplication.

"You have a case of acute anxiety with an overlay of depression. I think I can get you straightened out."

"How?"

"You'll need to spend some time in the hospital. I'm going to give you heavy doses of some medications to ease the anxiety and treat your depression. I think you'll be fine."

Dr. Simon's diagnosis seemed to clear the air of tension. "But what happened? This all came out of the blue."

"Have you had surgery or any traumatic injuries," Simon asked.

"Well, I was in a car wreck."

The doctor's attention seemed to sharpen. "Were you injured?"

"I had a concussion and two broken ribs." Greg recounted the details of the late-night crash down the Lake Arlington dam.

"Hmm." Simon glanced at the ceiling, then looked back at Greg. "Sometimes that kind of trauma can trigger anxiety episodes."

"But I was okay once everything healed," Greg said. "I felt fine for a while."

"Sometimes the physical wounds heal, but trauma can leave unseen scars—especially in more sensitive people."

"I hadn't thought of that."

"What about your personal life? You live at home, right? Do you get along with your parents?"

Greg squirmed. "I get along with Dad pretty well. Mother's another story." Greg described his frequent shouting matches with Vivian.

"What about school? Let's see," he looked at a piece of paper. "You're in college?"

"Right, I'm a freshman. A journalism major." Greg looked down at his shoes. "I'm not doing very well. In fact, I may flunk most of my courses this semester."

"Hmm. Has college been a big adjustment for you?"

"It sure has," Greg said. "I breezed through high school."

"What about your social life? You have a girlfriend?"

"I did. I quit calling her when all this started." Greg looked down again.

"You were ashamed for her to know?"

"Very ashamed. I liked her a lot."

"Did you ever have intercourse with her?"

The question jarred Greg. "That's pretty personal."

"Yes, but if you want to get well, I need to know some personal things. It's those deep feelings that sometimes cause the most trouble."

"Okay. No, I never even kissed her." Greg cast his eyes down again. "She's a Baptist, and I was afraid she'd be upset if I tried."

Dr. Simon cracked a wry smile. "Even Baptist girls like to be kissed."

"I guess I'm just out of step," Greg said, embarrassed at his backwardness.

"I'm starting to see a pattern here: domineering mother, fear of girls, lack of confidence generally. These are things we can work on, but for now, I want to get you checked into a room at Memorial. I think we'll see a big improvement in a week. You may sleep a lot, but that's okay. You need it. You're pretty run-down, low on reserve, but we can fix that."

Greg sat in the waiting room as Dr. Simon met with George and Vivian. *This means I'll be in the psycho ward,* Greg thought. *I'd rather have people think I'm in jail.*

In the car on the way back to the hospital, Vivian said, "I don't like that man."

"Now, Vivian," George said. "This isn't the time for that."

"I don't care. He said Greg was 'too moral.' How can anyone be too moral?"

"That's not all he said. Let's give this thing a try and see if it helps."

Greg sat silently in the back seat, wondering if his time in hell were ending or about to begin.

❖

Greg spent the next ten days in the hospital. As Dr. Simon had told him, he slept most of the time under the influence of tranquilizers, antidepressants, barbiturates, and muscle relaxants. Nurses awakened Greg almost hourly to give him shots and pills. His buttocks felt like a pincushion. The first week was a blur.

George Spencer came to see him daily; Vivian came only occasionally.

Dr. Simon checked on Greg every morning on his rounds, but Greg was usually asleep. After a week, the doctor started reducing Greg's drugs, and he spent more time awake; he was hungry much of the time.

On the tenth day, Dr. Simon came to his room. Greg was awake and sitting up in bed.

The doctor checked Greg's chart. "How do you feel?"

"I feel rested for the first time in months."

"You look better. I think you've gained some weight."

"My appetite is back. This hospital food is pretty bad, but my folks have kept me supplied with plenty of sweets." Greg pointed to several Baby Ruth and Almond Joy bars on his table.

"This has taken a little longer than I expected," Dr. Simon said. "But you're in much better shape than you were ten days ago. You reminded me of a skinny old man when I first saw you."

"Doctor, guess what?" Greg smiled and felt a lightheartedness he'd almost forgotten.

"What?"

"That scummy feeling, you know, where things don't seem real?"

"Yeah."

"It's gone."

"It should be; that's all part of the plan." Dr. Simon smiled and slapped Greg on the shoulder. "You're going to be fine. I'm dismissing you today."

"You think I'm ready?" Greg had given scant thought to his future.

"Yes. I'll want to see you every week for a while," the doctor said. "Maybe we can get to the bottom of some of these things."

Fall 1959

Greg resumed his life, but shame still smoldered inside him. He found it awkward to discuss his situation with his friends, who couldn't make sense of his illness. And still, he didn't call Suzy. He couldn't bear to tell her what he'd been through. She'd never understand.

He got permission to take his final exams late, but his grades still fell below the "C" average required to stay in school. He wouldn't be admitted to Trinity Valley State again in the fall.

He took the medications Dr. Simon had prescribed and had weekly sessions with the doctor. Greg poured out his inmost feelings to the doctor and got some practical advice—especially about sex—that he should have gotten from his parents. Greg was able to shed some of the guilt he'd heaped on himself for years.

Still, he worried about a relapse and fretted over every tic and twitch that didn't seem normal. He walked a zigzag path back to health. Life didn't suddenly become free of care.

Once he'd flunked out of college, he drifted for several months, hanging out with friends and drinking beer. His parents indulged him for a while, making allowances for his "condition," but their patience ran out. His father demanded that Greg get a job.

After their wreck, Greg had kept his distance from Eddie King, even though Eddie had expressed profound regret for his actions. But Greg feared Eddie, who had been a football teammate in high school, wouldn't understand his emotional troubles. He avoided Eddie for months.

But they ran into each other at the drugstore one day in late summer, and Greg learned that Eddie had gotten a job as a copy boy at the Fort Worth *News-Beacon*. The news filled Greg with envy.

Greg had planned to go into journalism since high school. Once he'd failed to make the varsity football squad, he thought writing about sports for a newspaper might be the next best thing. A nurturing teacher had encouraged Greg's writing and named him sports editor of the high school paper.

His father had spent the first part of his career as a journalist. Greg's early years had been spent absorbing the sounds and smells of newsrooms at the Childress Daily *Reporter* and at the *News-Beacon* in Fort Worth. George had been the Fort Worth paper's state editor before the pressures of the job and low pay had convinced him to go into public relations. George had become a partner in Spencer-Ross, one of the top PR firms in Fort Worth. He'd tried to discourage Greg from newspaper work, but Greg had persisted.

"You think they might need another copy boy?" Greg asked Eddie.

"I'll let you know if they do," Eddie said. "I think you'd enjoy working there."

A few weeks later, Eddie called Greg.

"I told the managing editor I had a friend who was interested in being a copy boy. There's an opening; why don't you come down and talk to him?"

Greg jumped at the chance.

Eddie broke Greg in as a copy boy, and within a few days, Greg worked the job on his own. Eddie moved up to become an assistant in the paper's reference library.

Greg started at thirty dollars a week, and within weeks, he realized he'd found his niche. He quickly made friends with reporters and editors as he ran errands for them and delivered copy from the wire-service teletype machines to the news desk.

He worked with such intensity and speed, members of the staff often asked him, "Hey, kid, where's the fire?" or, "Here comes our own Speedy Gonzalez. Oops! There he went."

Twice each day, Greg had to go to the police station, where *News-Beacon* reporter Rob Keller worked at a desk in the station's press room. Keller had been a linebacker at East Texas State College. Greg usually ran the three or four blocks to the station and arrived panting at Keller's desk.

"Damn, son," the chunky, crew-cutted Keller said. "Are you getting in shape for the Olympics?"

"I just want to make sure your copy's not late getting to the city desk," Greg said, gasping for breath.

"Hell, it's two hours to deadline. Take it easy."

Greg leaned back on the edge of a desk. "Hey, Rob, can I ask you something?"

"Sure. Fire away."

"I've noticed you write short, snappy leads on all your stories. How do you do that?"

"Well," Keller leaned back in his wooden swivel chair, "they teach you in journalism class to put 'who, what, when, where, how, and why' in the first graf, right?"

"Right."

"But you'll bore the reader to death making them wade through all that crap. So, I'll usually pick just a couple of those 'five W's' and highlight them."

"Pretty slick," Greg said. "Thanks."

"Are you planning to get into this business?"

"I think so," Greg said. "I'd like to make it my career."

"Well, that's fine if you enjoy it, but the pay is pretty lousy."

"Yeah, my dad tells me that all the time. He used to be in the business."

Suddenly, Keller held up his hand for quiet. He cocked his head toward a loudspeaker that broadcast police radio calls.

"Hear that?" Keller said. "A signal twenty-five at Eighth and Commerce."

Greg's eyes got big. "What's that?"

"A fire. Want to come along?" Keller grabbed his sport coat and a notepad. "That's just a few blocks from here. The dispatcher said three alarms."

Outside, Greg and Rob saw boiling black smoke and ran the six blocks to the fire scene. A downtown parking garage was in flames. Hundreds of cars were parked inside.

Greg watched as Keller pulled out his notepad and wrote down the essential details that he could see. Then he collared a district fire chief and got some quotes about how the blaze had started and how many firefighters were on the scene. No one had been injured.

"Let's find a phone," Keller said. "See a phone booth anywhere?"

"There's one, next to the Texas Hotel," Greg said.

They ran to the pay phone, and Keller called the city desk. He dictated a brief story about the fire. Greg listened carefully as Rob composed the story as he spoke.

"I'd better get back to the office," Greg said. "Thanks for letting me tag along."

"Okay, kid," Keller said. "Take it easy."

When Greg got back to the *News-Beacon*, he delivered Keller's earlier copy and stood near the city desk as Rob called back with several updates. A rewrite man typed Rob's dictation.

He watched as the typed copy moved from city desk to news desk to copy desk, where editors polished the story, wrote a headline, and sent it to the composing room to be set in type.

Greg marveled at the process. He was now certain he'd finish college and work for a newspaper. Ambition burned in him.

After staying out of school the fall semester, Greg re-enrolled at Trinity Valley State in the spring of 1960. At the end of the semester, his journalism professor, Harvey Edwards, called him aside one day.

"Greg, your writing is ahead of most of my students. Looks like that job at the *News-Beacon* has taught you a few things."

"It sure has," Greg said. "Thanks, Mr. Edwards."

"How would you like to work on The Trinity Valley *Voice* as sports editor?"

Greg accepted.

The fall of 1960, he worked harder at developing his craft than he ever had. He learned from his mistakes and won a statewide award for sports writing. He didn't become an honor student, but he kept all his grades high enough to stay in school.

Harvey Edwards named Greg editor-in-chief of the campus paper for the spring of 1961.

One night as Greg sat alone in the journalism building editing a stack of stories, Eddie King bounded into the college newspaper office. Eddie, who now worked as a reporter on *The Voice*, had brought in a story he'd written for that week's edition.

"Are you still here?" Eddie asked as Greg sat marking copy, a cigarette dangling from his lips and an overflowing ashtray on his desk. Greg had only recently started smoking, and already he was consuming two or three packs a day. Several empty coffee cups littered the desktop.

Greg looked up from his desk. "Look at all this crap I've got to edit," he said. "I could sure use a beer—even two or three."

"Then let's go," Eddie said. "They're gonna have to carry you out of here if you don't stop working so hard."

"You're probably right," Greg said with a sigh of resignation. "It can wait till tomorrow."

They drove a few blocks from the campus to a dive called the Tap Room. Its saving grace was that it had a good jukebox with a number of oldies from Greg's and Eddie's high school days.

They sat at a rickety table drinking draft beer from chipped mugs. The jukebox was playing the Platters:

> *Only you. . .can make this world seem right.*
> *Only you. . .can make the darkness bright.*
> *Only you and you alone*
> *Can thrill me like you do. . . .*

When the tune ended, Greg sat disconsolately. "Damn, that song gets to me," he said, shaking his head. He took a sip from his third or fourth mug of beer.

"Old Greg, the hopeless romantic," Eddie teased.

"I guess you're right." Greg sighed and pulled a cigarette from his shirt pocket. "I sure blew it with Suzy."

"Why don't you call her?"

"I don't even know where she is." He lit his cigarette. "I guess she's out of high school now.

"Hell, call her house and find out."

"Ah, I'm so damned shy, it would take a major act of courage. Anyway, she probably wouldn't want to see me after all this time. She's probably found some other guy by now."

"There are other fish in the sea," Eddie said.

"That may be, but that song sure reminds me of Suzy." Greg got a faraway look in his eyes. "We danced to it, real slow and close. You know, at that Christmas dance at the Elk's Club. It really gets to me, Eddie. "

❖

Arlington
February 1961

For the first time in two weeks, the sun shone brightly on the Trinity Valley campus after the longest cold spell of the winter. Everything outdoors had a sharp, crisp edge to it. The warmth felt reassuring.

Greg emerged into the bright day from the Student Union Building. He'd gone there after his last class to buy a pack of cigarettes and toss down a quick cup of coffee before returning to the journalism building to resume work on *The Voice*.

The balmy day felt so nice, Greg decided to bask in it a little longer. He sat down on a bench outside the Student Union.

As he looked down to open his pack of Kool Filter Kings, he noticed a pair of black-suede girl's penny loafers and white bobby socks directly in front of him. He elevated his gaze and paused on the nice pair of legs that went with the shoes and socks. As he scanned higher, he admired the shape of the tight, plaid skirt and yellow sweater. At last, his eyes reached the face of the blonde with the creamy complexion standing before him holding a stack of books. Their eyes met.

"Hello, Greg," Suzanne Cox said.

"Suzy, I. . . ." Greg sat flustered, grasping for words.

"Been a while, hasn't it?" There was a tinge of sarcasm in her soft voice.

Greg finally managed to speak. "God, Suzy. I didn't know you were a student here."

"I'm here," she said with the shy, subdued giggle Greg remembered so well. "It's my second semester. How've you been?"

Greg rose eagerly from the bench. "Listen, can we go get a Coke?"

"I don't know." She hesitated, looked down, then met his eyes again. "Okay."

Greg hadn't called Suzy after he he'd gotten out of the hospital; it had been two years. Her figure had filled out since high school, and now she wore her dark-blonde hair in a shorter "flip" style. Her brown, widely spaced eyes sparkled. She looked better than ever.

He had to explain himself. But he couldn't tell Suzy about the anxiety, the psychiatrist, the wasted year. They walked back toward the Student Union. Greg's mind whirled, trying to think of an explanation that didn't include the embarrassing details.

"Suzy, I'm sorry I stopped calling you." He paused. "I hope you didn't think I was a heel."

"Your words, not mine," she said with a shy, inscrutable smile.

"Look, there's no excuse." He paused a moment. "I wanted to see you again. But I had some, uh, medical problems."

"Oh, what was wrong?"

"Well . . . You remember the car wreck I was in that Christmas?" Greg held the door for Suzy as they entered the building.

"Yeah, you and Eddie King."

"And I got a concussion and broke several ribs."

"I remember, but I thought you got over it."

"I thought I did, too. But there were some complications." Greg dropped some coins in a Coke machine.

"What kind of complications?"

"Just feeling lousy all the time. Headaches, lightheadedness, stuff like that. The doctor thought it might be a delayed reaction to the concussion." The machine dispensed the Cokes with a rumble.

"Oh, my. How long did all this go on?"

"Quite a while. They finally put me in the hospital. When I got out, so much time had passed, I was afraid you'd be mad that I hadn't called. So, I just kind of gave up. I really felt bad." Greg handed Suzy her Coke.

"I don't know what to say, Greg." Suzy had a strained expression. "I wish you'd told me. Maybe I could have helped."

"I should have," Greg said. "On top of all that, I missed so much school, I flunked out."

"Goodness, you did have an awful time." Suzy wore a look of sincere concern.

"Yeah, but in a way, flunking out might have been a good thing; I got this great job at the *News-Beacon*. I've been a copy boy for a year, and now they want me to work part-time as a reporter."

"That's fantastic." Suzy seemed more relaxed now. "When I saw that you were editor of *The Voice*, I thought, 'Oh, that's *my* Greg.'"

They took their drinks and sat alone at a table. Students milled about. Suzy's wholesome good looks struck Greg all over again. The special something in her features grabbed him in the gut and drew him like a magnet.

"I never forgot about you." Greg took a drink of his Coke. "I still thought about you, but so much time had passed. . . . I didn't think you'd want to see me after so long. I wasn't even sure you'd remember me."

Suzy laughed. "My memory's not that bad."

Then Greg screwed up his courage. "Are you dating anyone special?"

Suzy shook her head. "Not now."

"Would you think about going out with me again?"

"I don't know, Greg; I was pretty hurt." Her furrowed brow reflected the painful memory. "It's hard to understand when a guy just stops calling."

Greg felt a sharp jab of guilt. "Let me make it up to you. I promise I'll never do anything like that again."

"I believe you're sincere." She paused. "But I just don't know."

"I've grown up a lot; give me a chance."

She looked down, then raised her eyes and met his. "I would like to go out with you."

"Then you will?"

"Yes. . . I will." She gave him a smile so sweet, he thought he'd melt.

"It means a lot to me." He heaved a breath of relief and gratitude.

"Me, too." She put her hand on top of his and squeezed.

Greg walked Suzy back to her dormitory. They strolled to the inner courtyard and stopped, facing each other. He stood a couple of inches taller than Suzy. Her bright-red lipstick glowed against her creamy skin, and her dark eyes glistened.

Greg parted his lips to speak, hesitated, then started again. His heart hammered his ribs.

Finally, he got it out: "Suzy, do you mind if I kiss you?"

She didn't say anything, but her eyes brightened, and she smiled a mischievous smile that seemed to say, *So, you finally got around to it.* She shook her head briskly.

The kiss seemed to go on forever. Where had Suzy learned such amorous skill? They lingered in the depth of the kiss, not wanting it to end. Then, he pulled her closer, held her tightly, and they kissed again, even longer and wetter this time. Her soft breasts pressed against his chest.

Finally, Greg and Suzy parted, and as Greg ambled back to the journalism building in something of a stupor, he suddenly recalled what Dr. Simon had told him on his first visit: "Baptist girls like to be kissed, too." Greg chastised himself for not figuring that out the first time around with Suzy. But now that he knew, unlimited promise blossomed before him.

❖

Greg and Eddie King both turned twenty-one that spring and moved into a rooming house near the campus. Feeling the freedom and responsibility of living away from home for the first time convinced Greg that the shameful episode of his freshman year now lay in the distant past. Life was good again.

Though she was a psychology major, Suzy became a fixture after class in the Trinity Valley *Voice* office. Her roommate, petite redhead Gail Winters, worked on the *Voice* staff, as did Eddie King. Eddie and Gail started dating, and double dated often with Greg and Suzy. They became a tight foursome.

They all enjoyed dancing, especially at Fort Worth's Araby Club, a rhythm-and-blues nightspot that featured popular guitarist Ray Sharpe and his band.

Though Suzy was a Baptist, she didn't mind ignoring the church's jaundiced view of dancing. In fact, she was a terrific dancer, and she helped Greg overcome some of his inhibitions on the dance floor. Above all, he cherished the slow dances to ballads, when they held each other close with their cheeks pressed tightly together, and he could smell her beguiling perfume and feel her soft body against his.

But true to her Baptist upbringing, Suzy wouldn't touch alcohol. Greg, Eddie, and Gail all ordered mixers at nightclubs and spiked them with vodka or rum they'd brought along. Suzy always stuck to an uncorrupted Coke.

Greg agonized over whether to tell Suzy the whole story of his freshman-year illness. But things were going so well, he didn't want to throw cold water on his and Suzy's happiness.

Greg had never been happier. He'd always felt self-conscious and anxious around other girls, but never with Suzy. Everything seemed simple and uncomplicated when they were together. He'd never trusted anyone as much or felt as close to anyone. Their relationship was free of the kinds of games so many young dating couples played. They adored each other.

Moreover, Suzy helped Greg calm some of his many insecurities, and she encouraged him in his quest to succeed in journalism.

"I never saw anyone as dedicated as you are," she told him. "But you don't have to kill yourself, you know."

"I just want to be good at what I do."

"But you *are* good. How many scholarships have you gotten? How many awards have you won? There's no doubt in my mind that you're going to make it really big."

"It means a lot to hear you say that."

"I mean it. But you'll never work on the New York *Times* if you wear yourself out on a college paper. Ease up. You don't have that much more to prove."

"My God, Suzy. How lucky I am to have you."

After six months they considered themselves, in the terminology of the day, "engaged to be engaged."

Their physical expressions went from dancing and goodnight kisses outside the dorm to "making out" in the dorm parking lot and finally to parking on secluded lanes in city parks.

Suzy's passion for kissing and petting came as a revelation to Greg. He'd been so naïve and inexperienced, he'd thought girls mainly tolerated the male urge and acquiesced to their gropings. He'd once been certain that Suzy's religious upbringing would stifle his physical advances. He now marveled that her eagerness seemed to match his own.

Suzy's heavy breathing and passionate sighs drove Greg crazy with desire. But still, they didn't go "all the way." When they got close, she'd shove him away and say, "No, Greg. Not yet." Still, their heavy petting left him believing that on the next date, Suzy would surely cave in.

Only she didn't.

Finally, on a dark lane in a park near the campus, Greg confronted her. The night sounds of crickets drifted through the open window.

"Look, Suzy, I love you. I want us to have a future together."

"Oh, I love you, too, darlin'. You know I want the same thing."

"Yeah, but if we feel that way, what's wrong with showing our love completely?" Greg's testicles ached from the short-circuited encounter.

"We're still in college," Suzy said. "We don't know what's ahead. It's just too soon, but some day. . . ."

"But it's so frustrating to hit a brick wall every time, when we're so close."

"I understand, Greg. But I'm saving it for marriage. It's the way I was raised, and it's important to me. I promised myself."

"But we've done everything but *that*," he pleaded. "What's the difference?"

"There's a difference." Suzy took out a brush and ran it through her hair. "Besides, neither one of us is ready to deal with the possibility of me getting pregnant."

"But I've got protection."

"Yeah, but it's not foolproof," she said dismissively. "It's too risky."

"You can even get birth-control pills nowadays." Greg recalled reading an article about the new pill. Its ramifications had raised his hopes.

"Married women can," Suzy said. "I know all about it. But I couldn't ask Dr. Tucker for something like that. He's known me all my life, and he sees my parents at church every Sunday."

Greg stewed, but in spite of Suzy's stonewalling, he cherished what he had with her. Everything seemed so easy and natural. Everything but sex, anyway.

Spring 1962

Greg took only a few courses now. He moved up to the part-time job he'd been promised as a reporter for the *News-Beacon*, writing obituaries and filling in for police reporter Rob Keller once a week. His editors assured him of a full-time job when he graduated in May of 1963.

Meanwhile, he and Suzy had been going steady for a year. Sex remained a sticking point. Though the decade was two years old, many of the buttoned-up attitudes of the fifties hadn't ended yet. Nor had Suzy's Baptist conditioning.

One night they parked in a wooded area near Lake Arlington. Their ardor led them once again to the brink. But Suzy bolted upright and started gathering scattered articles of clothing.

"Greg, you know how I feel about you, but we just can't," she said curtly. "I promised myself I'd save it for marriage, and I mean it. We've been over and over this. Don't you understand how important it is to me?"

"Yes, but. . . ."

"But do you really?" Suzy showed Greg a rare flash of anger. "Seems to me if we can't control ourselves, we might as well stop seeing other for a while to let things cool off."

Her suggestion blindsided Greg. After a long silence he said, "Okay, maybe we could back off, but as soon as we're alone together, we'd just start up again."

"Then we need to find a way to keep from getting so carried away. Why don't you come to church with me? Maybe we need some spiritual guidance."

Greg sat speechless. He didn't want any such guidance. He wanted Suzy.

Greg hadn't grown up in a religious home; George and Vivian had both been raised as Methodists, but they no longer attended church. They had encouraged Greg to make up his own mind about religion. He vaguely believed in some universal power, but he simply avoided the subject of God most of the time.

Suzy had kept religion out of their relationship once she understood Greg had little patience with the topic. He'd cut her off when she mentioned religion: "You're talking about questions that have no answers."

But now Suzy pushed back. Her faith entered more and more of their conversations. Finally, Greg relented and attended Sunday services with her at Eastside Baptist Church. The pastor preached a rousing sermon on the inerrancy of the Bible.

Afterward, they had lunch at a cafeteria.

"Do you really believe all that?" Greg asked Suzy.

"Sure, I've grown up believing it." Suzy picked at her food and looked off in the distance.

"But don't you question it?" Greg asked. "You're studying psychology. Surely you've run into conflicts between psychology and religion."

Suzy pouted. "I don't want to talk about it."

"But you've got to face it sooner or later." Greg struggled to keep his voice down among the Sunday diners at nearby tables.

Suzy slammed down her fork. "Oh, you just want me to be an atheist like you. You don't believe in anything."

"No, I don't want that," Greg said. "I just don't want you to close your mind. You're smarter than that. You don't have to take the Bible literally to believe in God. And I'm not an atheist. Agnostic, maybe, because some things are impossible to know."

"Let's change the subject." Suzy folded her arms and looked immovable.

They clashed more often about religion, and Greg came away from each argument exasperated. Suzy admitted she had doubts, but she refused to confront them

Greg had thought of proposing marriage to Suzy, but now he balked. He couldn't imagine living the kind of pinched, churchy existence she must have grown up with.

And he'd have to tell her about his past problems with anxiety. He still dreaded sharing that intimate detail.

That summer, Suzy told Greg she was thinking about transferring to Baylor University in Waco, a Southern Baptist school. Suzy's mother had been promoting the idea of her going to Baylor, and Suzy finally gave in to her pressure. Greg never felt Mrs. Cox had much use for him.

Greg and Suzy stopped seeing each other as often, and in the fall Suzy moved to Waco. Greg got an occasional brief letter, but by Christmas of 1962, their correspondence had ceased.

❖

Fall 1963

Greg survived. He wasn't sure how, except that he immersed himself in his work and medicated his pain with alcohol. He spent many sleepless nights and tested the friendship of Eddie King and other cohorts by crying in his beer at every chance in local watering holes. But eventually, he convinced himself that losing Suzy might be for the best. He had put all his eggs in one basket with her, and maybe he should play the field. Maybe he could find someone who'd make his obsession with Suzy seem like a passing phase in his young life.

He cautiously dated a few other girls, warily shying away from emotional entanglements, but still feeling shaky and unsure of himself. He cultivated a cynical view of women.

One night, after he and Eddie had plied themselves with several beers, Eddie talked Greg into visiting the Jackson Hotel, a legendary brothel on Fort Worth's Lower Main Street. Greg lost his virginity thinking about Suzy.

Greg graduated from Trinity Valley State in May and became a full-time police reporter in the summer of 1963 when Rob Keller got a promotion. Greg drove himself to master the beat and got a number of front-page bylines, as well as praise from his editors.

In late November, as Greg ate lunch with Eddie King, fellow reporter J. D. Sloan rushed into the Worth Hotel Coffee Shop and shouted: "Kennedy's been shot!"

The lunchtime diners gasped. Eddie and Greg ran as fast as they could back to the paper. The *News-Beacon* had devoted its front page that morning to the president's visit to Fort Worth and Dallas.

"My God, what does this mean?" Eddie asked as they rode the elevator to the newsroom. "Are we at war with Russia?"

"Must be a hoax," Greg said. "No one would shoot the president."

When they reached the newsroom, city editor Larry McGregor told Eddie to get to Dallas as fast as he could.

"What about me, Larry?" Greg asked.

"I want you here, Greg. I'm going to need some help on the city desk. Rich Wheeler is out sick." Wheeler was assistant city editor.

Deflated, Greg took a seat at the city desk and immediately started answering the ringing phones. Many of the calls came from citizens wanting information about the shooting. Greg told them all he knew: Kennedy had been shot, and his condition was thought to be grave, but there was no confirmation.

The newsroom erupted into a state of chaos. People ran around asking questions. Larry McGregor, nattily dressed with wavy, gray hair, wore a harried expression as he tried to answer the phones and keep up with the latest bulletins from the wire services.

Greg grabbed another ringing phone.

"City desk, Spencer."

"Greg, it's Rob Keller." He sounded shaky and out of breath.

"Rob, where are you?"

"I'm at Parkland." There was a pause. "Kennedy's dead."

"My God! How do you know?"

"I talked to an intern who was in the emergency room. The intern said. . .'Scuse me, Greg. . ." Keller's voice cracked. "He said. . . Kennedy's brains were blown out, and that he probably was dead on arrival."

"Jesus, Rob." Greg's heart pounded.

"I've covered a lot of bad stuff, Greg, but nothing like this."

"Hold on, Rob." Greg covered the phone a moment and tried to regain his wits. "Rob, we just got word we're printing an extra. Have you got anything else?"

"No, I'll stay here and call back when I get more details."

"Okay, you've got the lead. I'll tell McGregor."

Greg huddled with the city editor, and they worked out a plan. McGregor would handle the phones. He gave Greg a rundown of the reporters and photographers on duty, plus a general idea of where they should go and what they should cover. Greg would round up the staff members and dispatch them to the various locations where the story was unfolding.

Greg ran to the photo lab. Several photographers were gathered around a radio.

"You guys need to get to Dallas," Greg said.

"Who says?" photographer Al Mazzetti said.

"McGregor told me to tell you. We need photographers at the police station, the Texas Schoolbook Depository, and Parkland Hospital. You guys work it out and get going!"

Greg ran back to the newsroom. He went around to all the stunned reporters milling about and gave them assignments: reaction from city leaders, reaction from Congressman Jim Wright, response of the local FBI, and so on. New ideas kept occurring to Greg, and he passed them on to reporters to check out.

Back at the city desk, McGregor took a call from Eddie King. Dallas police had arrested a suspect: Lee Harvey Oswald, age twenty-four, a former Fort Worth resident. He was also suspected of killing Dallas police officer J.D. Tippitt. McGregor took another call and handed his notes to Greg.

Greg looked over the notes, then wrote a sidebar story on the suspect's arrest. He gave it to McGregor, who marked a few corrections and passed the story to the news desk.

Greg had a reporter check on Oswald's background. Oswald's mother and brother lived in Fort Worth, it turned out. Oswald had gone to school in Fort Worth. An hour later, before anyone could locate her, Marguerite Oswald called the newsroom and told a reporter she was the mother of the assassination suspect and that she needed a ride to Dallas.

The reporter arranged to pick her up and drive her to Dallas. The *News-Beacon* would scoop all the other papers with the mother's story.

By three p.m., the paper had extras on the streets, sooner than any other publication in Dallas-Fort Worth. Rob Keller had written the main story on the president's shooting and death; Eddie King had the secondary story on Oswald's arrest.

The *News-Beacon* printed updated extras until six o'clock. Greg and Larry McGregor went to get something to eat. They sat in a booth at Landers' Café, a greasy-spoon joint across the street from the paper.

"Greg, I had a hunch I could trust your news instincts," McGregor said. "After all, I've watched you practically grow up in the newsroom. I think you did a really solid job on this story."

"Thanks, Larry. I guess it was the next best thing to being there."

Greg had the weekend off. Sunday morning, the paper sent Eddie King to the Dallas police station, where Jack Ruby shot Oswald as he was being transferred to the county jail. Eddie's was the lead story in the extra edition the paper put out that day, its second extra in three days.

On Monday, Greg covered Oswald's funeral at Rose Hill Cemetery in Fort Worth and had a front-page story in the next day's edition.

As the nation mourned the events of that November weekend, Greg rode a wave of professional confidence such as he'd never known.

Greg's editors lavished praise on his work on the assassination. The *News-Beacon* opened a new suburban office in Arlington and named Greg as the bureau chief. His coverage helped the paper increase its circulation in the eastern suburbs of Tarrant County. He got a modest raise.

He hadn't seen Dr. Simon in nearly two years, and he had gradually stopped taking the drugs Simon had prescribed for anxiety and depression.

But after months of work as the Arlington bureau chief, covering suburban government and writing fluffy feature stories, Greg grew restless and bored. He had lunch one day with Matt Whitley, the public information man from Trinity Valley, his old college.

"Know anyone that might be looking for a job?" Matt asked over coffee at the Ranch House café.

"I might be," Greg said. "What's up?"

"You may have heard, the Houston *Times* has bought the Galveston *Star*. My old boss from the Abilene paper, Seth Yeager, is the new editor. That paper has been on the skids for years. He's trying to rebuild it. Yeager likes to hire young guys from bigger papers. He matches their pay and teaches them his way of newspapering. He's looking for a city editor; it might be a great opportunity for someone like you, if you're interested."

Greg drove to Galveston the next week Eddie King went along for the ride. Greg met the editor, Seth Yeager, a portly, middle-aged man with thinning dark hair parted in the middle and a warm, fatherly bearing.

"Greg, we're looking for a city editor with a solid reporting background. Looks like you have that. Your biggest challenge will be learning a new city, but with your background, I don't think you'll have any trouble."

Yeager described Greg's duties: copy editing, making assignments, supervising reporters and photographers, designing pages, working with printers, and so on. It sounded daunting, but Greg liked the challenge.

"Sounds good, Mr. Yeager. How much is the pay?"

"How much are you making in Fort Worth?"

"Eighty-five a week."

"We'll start you at a hundred a week. How about it?"

"You've got a deal. When do I start?"

"How about Labor Day? Will that fit your schedule?"

"That'll work just fine." They shook hands.

Greg met Jeff Holcomb, the *Star*'s affable city editor who was being promoted to news editor; Greg would replace him. Holcomb told Greg that there were vacancies at his apartment complex. Greg met his future landlady, Mrs. Eva Kaplan, paid a deposit, and reserved an efficiency apartment.

Greg and Eddie spent the rest of the day lying on the beach. The palm trees, the gentle sea breeze, the surf, the sailboats in the gulf bobbing to the rhythm of "The Girl from Ipanema," the fine young things in bikinis all captivated Greg. "Man, Eddie," Greg said. "This place knocks me out. It must be a fabulous place to live."

❖

September 1964

When he returned to Fort Worth, Greg gave two weeks' notice to his editors at the *News-Beacon*. A week later, colleagues threw a going-away party for Greg. The outpouring of support from his peers and bosses touched him. He hated to leave what had become an extended family.

At the party, Greg got acquainted with a foxy young female reporter from the Fort Worth *Globe* named Sharon Rogers. The *Globe* was the *News-Beacon*'s tabloid competitor. Greg and Sharon had known each other slightly but had never dated. At the party, something clicked between them. Alcohol fueled their attraction, and soon they stepped outside the house where the party was going on and fell into each other's arms. They rolled in the cool Saint Augustine grass, eagerly kissing and embracing.

Sharon invited Greg to her apartment. He'd never had such an opportunity. He followed her home, and when they arrived, she led him to the bedroom. They quickly disrobed and got into bed; this looked like a sure thing.

But when the crucial moment arrived, Greg's male powers had deserted him. His loins were barren. He couldn't perform.

"What's the matter?" Sharon said, puzzled.

"I don't know. I guess I drank too much."

She sat up. "Well, you're a fine one," she said, snatching her clothes from the floor and stomping off to the bathroom.

Greg retrieved his garments, dressed, and slunk out the front door, too ashamed to face Sharon.

The debacle in Sharon's bedroom troubled Greg greatly; he didn't know where to turn. He wanted to talk to someone about it, but the only person he felt he could trust was Dr. Daniel Simon. Unlike Greg's parents, Dr. Simon had always been willing to discuss Greg's ignorance and uncertainty about sex. The doctor had even told Greg about the local brothel where Greg had lost his virginity.

Greg still had a week left to work at the *News-Beacon*. The first thing Monday morning, he called Dr. Simon's office and made an appointment for Thursday afternoon.

Greg poured out his tale of failure to the doctor.

Dr. Simon looked bemused. "You think you're the first guy that's happened to?"

"I don't know. I'm too ashamed to talk to anyone else about it." Greg lit a cigarette.

"It's very common," Dr. Simon said calmly. "It can happen anytime to anyone, especially if you've been drinking."

"I drank too much; that's for sure." Greg sat back in his chair.

"You know you're not impotent. So, quit worrying."

"I'm just afraid of it happening again," Greg said.

"It might, but probably won't. How did the girl react?"

"Not very well." Greg grimaced at the memory. "She stomped off to the bathroom."

"Well, think of it from her perspective," the doctor said. "She was all primed, and it was a big letdown for her. Most women are more understanding. I'd say she doesn't know much about men. Why don't you try for a repeat performance?"

"Well, maybe." Greg thought of all he had to do the next few days to get ready to move. There would be little time for dating.

"Otherwise, how are you getting along?"

Greg relaxed and sat back in his chair. "I've had a pretty good life since I graduated from college."

"I've been seeing your byline in the paper; you've done well."

"Thanks." It felt nice to have Simon's approval. He'd seen Greg hit bottom.

"What happened to the girl you were so crazy about? What was her name?"

"Oh, Suzy." The loss still stung. "We almost got engaged, then she got religion and transferred to Baylor." Greg sighed, still feeling the dull ache of his loss.

"Can't win 'em all. How did you take it?"

"It was rough for awhile, but I got over it."

"Your coping skills have gotten better."

"Well, I survived."

"How are you doing with your anxiety?"

Greg didn't like the direction Dr. Simon was taking. "I'm seldom bothered by it anymore, with the exception of the things we've just been talking about."

"Any depression?"

Greg's annoyance escalated. "I still worry too much, but I rarely get depressed. If I do, it doesn't last."

"Have you thought any more about something we talked about? You know, about getting away from your family?"

"As a matter of fact," Greg said smugly. "I've taken a job in Galveston, on the newspaper there. I leave this weekend."

"You don't say? I know Galveston well. I went to medical school there. Interesting place. One of my professors still practices there. If you have any problems, give him a call. His name is Dr. Howard Brooks."

Greg's defenses rose again. "You think I'll have problems?"

"Anything's possible, especially with the kind of predisposition you have to anxiety." Dr. Simon gave Greg a supercilious look. He had been so supportive just a few minutes ago.

"But I thought I was over all that," Greg protested.

"I'm not trying to scare you. You may never have anything like you had before. But you're a personality type that's prone to overreact to things."

Greg felt deflated. "I thought I'd become pretty easygoing."

"Maybe so. I'm just giving you my professional opinion." Now the doctor seemed on the defensive. "By the way," he said. "There's a new medication for anxiety on the market. It's called Valium. I'll give you a prescription."

Greg had prided himself in getting off prescription drugs. "I'm not sure I need it anymore."

"Don't be too sure. I'd take it regularly if I were you." Dr. Simon had assumed a cold, detached air.

Greg left the doctor's office confused. He felt relieved to hear his sexual dysfunction wasn't permanent, but he wondered why Simon seemed so determined to throw Greg's past problems in his face. He wanted to forget all that. It felt more like he'd received a curse than a "professional opinion."

Then, Greg's father took a similar tack with him. The night before Greg left for Galveston, as he was packing his things, George called him aside.

"Greg, I know you think you're doing the right thing, but don't get too cocky. You know how you are." Greg knew George was referring to his anxiety.

Now it felt like he'd received a double curse.

Greg was twenty-four.

"

It Takes a Worried Man

❖

Two

❖

The words "leaving home" flashed like a blinking neon sign in Greg's mind as his red '61 Chevy Corvair sped down U.S. Highway 287 toward the new Interstate 45. From there, he'd cruise through the East Texas piney woods to the Gulf of Mexico.

Greg had lived away from home in college, but then he'd never been far away, no more than a half-hour's drive. Galveston lay 350 miles to the south, a storied island off the Texas coast, five or six hours away.

Tension clutched at Greg's body that steamy Sunday morning as he headed out of the city into the cotton country to the southeast. Waves of heat rose from the two-lane highway. The car had no air conditioner, and Greg relied solely on the breeze from the open windows for any relief.

He passed through Waxahachie and looked for a place to stop for a snack on the town's outskirts.

He pulled onto the gravel driveway of a mom-and-pop grocery. Faded white paint peeled from the clapboard front of the building. The air was still and the heat oppressive, though it wasn't yet noon.

Inside, Greg fished in a drink box filled with icy water and retrieved a Dr Pepper. He put the drink and a pack of Tom's Toasted peanut-butter crackers on the counter. An old dog with a scabbed ear lay on the rutted wood floor eyeing him suspiciously.

The store's "pop" looked out through the double screen doors at Greg's car, which was jammed full of his belongings.

"Goin' back to school?" Pop asked.

"Nope. Movin' to the coast; Galveston." Greg handed the man a dollar bill.

"Galveston, eh? Better watch out. A young fella can get himself in all kinds of trouble down there."

"Thanks. I'll be careful." Greg took his change.

He pulled back onto the two-lane highway and sped away.

Would he find trouble in Galveston? The island city once had the reputation for vice and corruption, but most of that had ended in the fifties. Greg hoped to find a new life and a springboard to greater things in journalism.

As he drove, thoughts of Suzy darted in and out. What had become of her? Baylor was considered a "liberal" university, as Baptist institutions go. Would Suzy change in that environment or become more hardened in her beliefs?

Since she'd left for Waco, she'd never been far from his thoughts. He wondered if he'd ever see her again. The memory of her stirred his senses: her wholesome good looks, her innocent, warmhearted sweetness, the diffident little giggle that followed so many things she said. How he had loved Suzy. Things had been so free and easy with her. But how could she swallow that Baptist hogwash?

All the same, maybe he should write to her once he got settled in Galveston.

As Greg drove south, tall pines appeared in the green lushness of East Texas. Near Huntsville, the late-afternoon sun blazed through the trees and painted golden stripes across Interstate 45.

Greg's thoughts turned to his new job. He wondered about his ability to manage a staff of ten or fifteen reporters. There'd be egos to contend with; he'd seen that at the *News-Beacon*. He'd have to assign and edit every local story that went into the paper, as well as write headlines and oversee the makeup of several local pages. Every aspect of his journalistic training and experience would be tested. He swallowed hard as he thought of the increased responsibility.

At five o'clock, Greg passed through Conroe and cruised into the northern suburbs of Houston. The downtown skyline shimmered in the distance. Driving with open windows, Greg smelled the acrid air, the gaseous refuse of the many petrochemical plants around the city. A dark-gray pall of smoke from the refineries hung over the sprawling city.

Labor day traffic slowed to a crawl. Emergency vehicles blocked the interstate. Greg inched forward until he pulled even with the traffic jam's source. Off to his right he saw a crumpled Dodge at the bottom of an embankment, where it had apparently come to rest after running off the road and tumbling to the bottom of the steep incline.

Greg's mind flashed to the night he and Eddie King had rolled down the Lake Arlington dam. Prickles of anxiety stung his gut. Could the invisible forces unleashed by the wreck still reach him?

"You know how you are," his father had told him. Dr. Simon had said he had a "predisposition" to anxiety. The unwelcome memories made him squirm.

Hoping to divert his thoughts, he tuned the car radio to a Houston station. The program was NBC's weekend news show, "Monitor." The show played a sound clip from that morning's "Meet the Press," which featured politicians debating the escalating hostilities in Vietnam.

"This conflict is not worth the life of a single American soldier," a senator proclaimed.

Greg had been called for a pre-induction physical a few months earlier and had been classified "1-Y," which was a notch below the prime rating of "1-A." He'd asked someone at the draft board what chance he had of being inducted with that designation.

"You probably won't be drafted unless there's a full-scale national emergency, like in World War Two," a woman at the draft board had told him. The fact that he'd had asthma as a child lowered his chances of being drafted, she'd said.

His bout with anxiety apparently hadn't caused the army doctors any concern. *Peculiar,* Greg thought. He guessed they regarded the problem as resolved. Which it was, of course.

The forty-five-mile drive from Houston to Galveston took an hour. After the evergreen woods north of Houston, the landscape to the south flattened out, and I-45 crossed several bayous. Spanish moss hung from live oak trees along the bayous' banks. Swamps and tidal pools appeared along the interstate. Seagulls glided into the stiff sea breeze from the south.

Greg's pulse quickened as he drove onto the Galveston Bay causeway, linking the mainland with the island. Near the summit of the great span, Greg saw the twinkling lights of Galveston Island across the horizon.

❖

Galveston
September 1964

The causeway fed Greg onto Broadway, Galveston's main east-west thoroughfare, lined along its curbs and center island with tall coconut and palmetto palms.

The air felt thick and heavy. He noticed the names on businesses along Broadway: Veselka, Benedetti, Saperstein, Siegfried, Radinsky. For a moment Greg wondered if he was still in Texas.

He drove to 25th Street, near the center of Galveston, and headed for Seawall Boulevard, which ran the length of the city along the beach. He wanted to get a look at the ocean before he settled into his apartment. The sea had drawn him to this place.

He parked along the curb and for a few minutes, he stared out at the vast expanse in the twilight, and felt a sense of wonder he couldn't express.

Greg drove a block north of the beach to Avenue Q. *What a name for a street,* he thought. He pulled into a parking spot next to the apartments where he'd live.

Greg unlocked his second-floor apartment. The musty air hit him in the face. The room was hot and thick with humidity. He turned on the window air conditioner and started unloading his belongings from the car. After lugging boxes up and down the stairs for half an hour, he stood in front of the air conditioner and unbuttoned his shirt, letting the frigid breeze dry his dripping torso.

He spent an hour putting his things away, then put clean sheets on the sofa bed. He stretched out for the night, and as he drifted off to sleep on this, his first night in Galveston, he heard the surf calmly splashing against the seawall a block away. Peter, Paul and Mary's popular tune faded in and out of his thoughts:

Lord, I'm five hundred miles from my home. . . .

He slept fitfully and woke the next morning with a jerk. He shaved and dressed anxiously, then spent much of the day arranging the apartment. That afternoon, he drove to the Galveston *Star* building on Mechanic Street, a couple of blocks south of the Galveston wharves. Much of the north side of downtown lay vacant or neglected. Historic buildings that once earned that part of Galveston the title of "The Wall Street of the Southwest" sat deserted. The salt air had discolored them, and some had weathered plywood covering their windows.

He nervously climbed the stairs to the second floor of the ancient, red-sandstone building, where he'd interviewed for his job. The newsroom had a cavernous look with ceilings almost twenty feet high, from which long-stemmed rotary fans dangled. The familiar newspaper smell of paper dust, ink, and molten lead hung in the air.

The room was mostly deserted. A dapper, fortyish man with coarse graying hair sat reading a paper. Greg approached him.

"Excuse me," Greg said.

"Hi, can I help you?" The man lowered his newspaper.

"My name's Greg Spencer. Mr. Yeager told me to come in at four."

"Oh, you're the new guy. I'm Jim Stephens, the managing editor." They shook hands.

"Glad to meet you." Greg groped for what to say next. "Where should I sit?"

An impish grin lit up Stephens's face. "It's Labor Day. Why don't you take the day off?"

"If you say so," Greg said. His tension eased.

"What the hell. Go to the beach. Get drunk. Come in tomorrow."

Greg headed back to his apartment, perplexed about how to spend his unexpected holiday. As he approached the complex, a white Ford Falcon pulled into a parking place. He recognized the driver as Jeff Holcomb, news editor of the *Star*. Greg had met Jeff when he'd interviewed for the Galveston job. Jeff lived in the same apartment complex and had suggested the place to Greg.

Jeff got out of his car. "Well, I see you made it back. When do you start?"

"Today, I thought," Greg said. "But Jim Stephens told me to take the day off. I thought I'd look around a bit. But this holiday crowd kinda discourages me."

"This is about as bad as it gets," Jeff said. "But there are a few places where tourists never go. I can show you around if you like." He spoke with a deep, deliberate drawl.

"Sure. Sounds good. I'd like to get something to eat." They got in Jeff's car.

Jeff was in his late twenties, but looked older. His curly blond hair had started to thin, giving him a high, pink forehead. He had an ample girth and weighed around two-thirty.

Jeff gave Greg a grand tour of some Galveston's less publicized places. They ate at a Mexican restaurant that served Menudo—

diced cow guts—and Cabrito—roasted kid goat. Jeff ordered a bowl of the tripe soup, but Greg passed in favor of a more familiar enchilada plate.

Jeff took Greg to Lafitte's, a modern-day speakeasy that stayed open all night and sold liquor by the drink, illegal in Texas at the time. Greg marveled that such a place still existed long after Prohibition. Finally, they went to Lolita's, a dim, dingy, crowded bar that featured Greek music on its jukebox. A delegation of Greek sailors on shore leave performed native dances to the throbbing Aegean music. A scruffy collection of patrons sat at wobbly tables on the edges of the dance floor.

"This place becomes a gay bar on weekends," Jeff said. "No straights allowed."

Greg gaped in amazement. He'd seen nothing like this in Fort Worth.

They finished their beers at Lolita's and got up to leave. As they approached the exit, a chubby, dissolute-looking man wearing a rumpled tuxedo came in through the door. He looked to be in his thirties. Two teenage boys accompanied him.

"Well, it's Jeff Holcomb of the daily wipe," the man in the tux said to Jeff. The man appeared to be well into his cups.

"Hello, Lester," Jeff said. "You sure look pretty."

"We just split from the most boring goddamn reception you ever saw over at the Ashton Villa. So, we decided to party a little. These boys have never been to Lolita's."

"I hope they have some ID," Jeff said. "Markos is pretty sensitive about minors."

"Jeffrey," the man said, pulling a roll of bills from his pocket. "Markos knows what's important. Who's your friend?"

"Oh, this is Greg Spencer," Jeff said. "He's our new city editor. Greg, this is Lester Hastings. His family used to own the *Star*."

"Glad to meet you." Greg grasped the man's clammy hand.

"Oh, a new city editor," Hastings said. "Well, baby, have you got a lot to learn. Haw-haw-haw!"

Greg and Jeff walked to Jeff's car.

"Who the hell was that?" Greg asked. "Is he part of *the* Hastings family?"

"Lester controls the Hastings fortune," Jeff said, getting behind the wheel. "The family had a big power struggle a few years ago, and he won. It's a pretty bizarre story."

"Are those his kids?"

"Oh, no. You might say Lester has a weakness for young boys."

"Oh, my God," Greg said. "What next?"

"Lester throws quite a party at his compound out on the West End," Jeff said. "Maybe I can get you an invitation sometime."

"I'm not sure I want one." Greg opened the car door. "You've been to some of these parties?"

"A few. They're pretty wild." Jeff put the car in gear and drove away. Back at the apartments, he pulled into a parking space, and they got out.

"Thanks for the tour," Greg said, heading toward the stairs.

"Oh, we've just scratched the surface," Jeff said with a chuckle.

Greg lay in bed, trying to assimilate his first day in Galveston. He had come here realizing he'd led a sheltered life, and Galveston might give him a stiffer dose of "reality." He'd begun to harbor fantasies of becoming a novelist or poet, and life in a seaport could mature him and give him ample material for a literary life. He'd been here only twenty-four hours, and he'd already come face-to-face with several new realities.

A part of him embraced the eccentric, surreal nature of what he'd seen so far, but another part felt an uneasy wariness. He wondered if he could adjust to Galveston.

He lay awake a long time. Finally, he got up and swallowed one of the Valium tablets Dr. Simon had prescribed.

❖

On his first official day of work at the Galveston *Star*, Greg met with editor Seth Yeager, managing editor Jim Stephens, and outgoing city editor Jeff Holcomb. They all took seats in the wood-paneled office in one corner of the ancient newsroom. Yeager sat down at his desk whose surface was free of clutter. Two framed photographs of small children stood in one corner. Grandchildren, Greg assumed.

"Greg, did you get moved in okay?" Yeager asked, lighting a pipe.

"Yes, sir, I think I'm all settled," Greg said.

"Let's get started," the editor said, puffing his pipe. "Jeff, you'll walk Greg through all the steps of his daily routine. Let's try to get him up to speed in the next week or so."

Jeff nodded.

Yeager, Holcomb, and Stephens ran through the litany of Greg's duties: making assignments for reporters and photographers, editing copy, laying out local pages, supervising page assembly by the crew of printers on the third floor.

Beads of sweat broke out on Greg's forehead as he listened to the editors describe the task ahead.

The editors all emphasized the *Star*'s new direction. In the past, the paper had danced to the tune of the island's moneyed interests, mainly the Hastings family. Under the new owners, the *Star* wouldn't kowtow to anyone, but would strive to present unbiased coverage of Galveston, regardless of anyone's station or class.

"Well, Greg," Yeager said. "Is that enough to make your head spin?" The editor smiled and chomped on his pipe stem.

"Sounds like a challenge," Greg said. "But I guess I'm ready to go." Inwardly, he wasn't so sure.

In the sixties, printers still produced newspaper text in lead type and placed it in metal frames the size of a printed page. Part of Greg's job required him to supervise each local page's layout as the makeup men inserted type into the forms. The best makeup men understood what the editor had in mind when he drew up a "dummy," a letter-sized diagram of each page's design.

Jeff showed Greg around the paper's "backshop." Linotype typesetting machines clattered, and the vast room smelled of molten lead and printer's ink. He took Greg to the area where the makeup men, most of them Hispanic, worked on the page forms.

They approached one of the "trucks"—metal tables on wheels—that held a page form. The thirtyish man assembling the type had thick, black, Indian hair and intense, bloodshot eyes. He looked menacing.

"Greg, meet Tony Rodriguez," Jeff said. "Tony's the senior makeup man."

Tony shook Greg's hand. "Greg, eh? Well, Gregorio, is this your page?"

Greg looked at the form. "Yeah. Looks like they set too much type for that one story."

"It's all fucked up," Tony scowled. "Didn't they teach you college boys how to draw up a dummy?"

Tony, as most printers, loved to gloat when he caught an editor in a mistake. The men on the third floor had dirty, grimy, low-paying jobs and got little credit for their efforts in getting each day's paper out. They felt, sometimes rightly, that they made editors look good, and they resented the editors' supervision. Under the *Star*'s previous owners, printers had a free hand to assemble the pages as they saw fit. Since the Houston *Times* had bought the paper, Seth Yeager had insisted that editors oversee the page makeup to ensure the most attractive page designs.

Greg defenses rose. "Yeah, they taught me. Just kill the type from here on down." He pointed to the lines of overset type.

Tony dumped the extra type in the scrap can—called the "hell box." "*Ay, Chihuahua!*" Tony said. "I hope you don't fuck up like that every night, Gregorio."

Greg went back to the newsroom with his tail between his legs.

During his first couple of weeks, Greg never knew on a given night whether Tony would be angry and uncooperative or a pussycat, going along with whatever Greg suggested. Greg climbed the spiral staircase to the third floor, holding his breath with a sense of foreboding about Tony.

He quickly learned to tell when Tony was in a good mood: Tony sang jingles or quoted lines from TV commercials. If Tony didn't sing or quote, Greg knew he was in for a long night. Gradually, though, Greg's initial fear of Tony faded, and they worked together smoothly.

"Hey, Gregorio," Tony would say. "You and me, we make a great team, *qué no?*"

After a few weeks, Greg took stock of his new experience as he lay back on his sofa bed at the apartment, He was blending into the flow of the newspaper's operation, he thought. He took satisfaction in his progress, but he also discovered that after work each night, he was so keyed up, he had to take a Valium to get to sleep. He seldom went to sleep before four in the morning. He convinced himself that the medication's strength was relatively weak compared to the drugs Dr. Simon had given him when he was nineteen. Also, living alone in a new place with a new job would be stressful for anyone, so what could taking a pill once a day hurt?

Greg befriended police reporter Dan Forbes, a lanky, sandy-haired young man who had also recently joined the staff. Often Greg, Jeff, and Dan dropped by Lafitte's after work for a few drinks at the all-night speakeasy. Still, Greg felt he needed the Valium to get to sleep.

Greg awoke each day slightly hung over from the combination of Valium and alcohol. His anticipation of each day's work further jangled his nerves, and he felt unsteady as he shaved and dressed. In addition to his nightly pill, he decided to start taking Valium before work, and he carried a spare in his pocket, just in case.

He kept a bottle of antacid in his desk drawer, too, and took frequent swigs during his workday. His stomach acid boiled as the stress continued to mount. Reporters proved to be the biggest tension generators.

Most reporters were courteous, but Greg was appalled at the writing many of them turned in. Greg spent much of his time rewriting stories.

Jeff Holcomb sat across the desk from Greg.

"Can't anyone here write a coherent sentence?" Greg grumbled.

"Yeah, it's pretty bad," Jeff said. "But you don't have time to rewrite every story, so you're going to have to learn to fix the worst errors and move on."

The clock was a constant enemy. Deadlines ruled the newspaper business.

Greg reported for work at three in the afternoon. Reporters turned in most local copy by six o'clock, except for stories of night meetings and late police news. Greg spent the first three hours of every day editing the bulk of the reporters' stories.

His most dreaded chore involved confronting reporters and asking them to rewrite stories or correct problems in them. Almost every day, he had to take a story back to Stan Richter, who covered the Galveston Convention and Visitor's Bureau, an important institution in a tourist mecca such as Galveston.

Richter often came to work in Bermuda shorts and thong sandals. In his early forties, he had a deep tan and often wore a yachtsman's cap. After turning in a story, he sat at his desk, feet propped up, reading a yachting magazine as he smoked a pipe.

"Stan, got a minute?" Greg said, easing into the subject.

"Hah? What's up, chief?" Richter lowered his magazine and chomped on his pipe.

"Got a small problem here in your story."

"You mean 'small,' like in nit-picking?" Richter said with a scowl.

Greg cleared his throat. "I mean, in your lead you called this new hotel 'The Flagship,' and later in the story you call it 'The Friendship.'"

"Yeah, so what?" Richter chomped on his pipe stem.

"Well, are you talking about the same hotel?"

"Ah, hell," Richter swiped the paper from Greg's hand. "Gimme the damn thing."

Richter scratched through "Friendship" and wrote in "Flagship" throughout. He thrust the story back at Greg.

"Damned constipated, nit-picking editors," he groused and returned to his magazine.

"Thanks, Stan," Greg said, his words dripping with sarcasm. "I really appreciate your help."

Irene Dubois, a coarse, bleached blonde from Louisiana, covered the Galveston school district. Almost every story she turned in resulted in an increase in Greg's stomach acid. One day, he took a story back to her desk.

"Irene, got a minute?"

"Why, sure, hon. What's the problem?"

"I had a little trouble with this part." Greg read from her copy.

>School Supt. Henry Glass said today he would follow the lead of Alabama Gov. George Wallace and 'stand in the schoolhouse door' to prevent forced integration of Galveston schools. 'We are not going to permit the mongrelization of the races here in Galveston,' he said. 'And any spade who thinks so has another thing coming.'

"Well?" Irene looked puzzled.

"Well, did he really say that?" Greg asked.

Irene had a hurt expression. "Of course, he did. I wouldn't have written it if he hadn't."

"Okay, but that's pretty volatile." Greg measured his words. "If we print that, we could have a race riot on our hands."

"Well, what do you want me to do?" Irene threw up her hands.

"I'd tone it down and just say he expressed his opposition to forced integration. Then I'd call the NAACP or someone in the Negro community and get their reaction. But let's be careful about such inflammatory language."

"What the hell?" Irene protested. "Are we a bunch of nigger-lovers?"

After Irene rewrote the story, she slammed it onto Greg's desk and stomped off.

Hilda Nadelman had worked on the Galveston *Star* since 1918. Now in her eighties, Hilda wrote a weekly column of "names and notes" about prominent Galvestonians for the Sunday paper. She came in nearly every day to work on her week's column.

The day Greg first encountered Hilda, she said, "Glad to meetcha, Spencer." She had a hoarse, screechy voice with heavy Yiddish inflections. "I know you'll enjoy being city editor. I was once city editor and also telegraph editor, ya know. But that was years before you were born. We actually got news by telegraph in those days; can ya believe it?"

Hilda was a heavy woman. She'd sit at her desk typing her column with a lighted cigarette dangling from her lips. She'd type away in rapt thought, ignoring the cigarette as it burned down and deposited its ashes all over her massive bosom. Finally, she'd stub out the cigarette butt in an overflowing ashtray and pound her breast until she'd raised a thick cloud of ash from her dress.

"If you ever have a problem on the city desk, Spencer, you just let old Hilda know."

What a lovely old woman, Greg thought; that is, until she turned in her first column to him. He had noticed that Hilda nodded off occasionally at her desk. Now, reading her column regularly, he realized she fell asleep, then woke up and started typing from a whole new train of thought. These passages read something like, "Seen at the Governor's Ball in the Bishop's Palace Friday night were Misses Candace Olson, Betty O'Donnell and Mayor Cavelli told this reporter he hopes Splash Days will be a 'splashing' success this spring."

Dan Forbes, the *Star*'s police reporter, lived in an apartment below Greg's. Dan had moved to Galveston from San Antonio, where he'd been a copy boy on one of the newspapers. Dan, thin and stoop-shouldered with short, crew-cut hair, was a year younger than Greg. Greg had never known anyone as young as Dan who could drink as much. Greg worried that Dan's tendency to overindulge was out of control.

Dan normally did a credible job as a police reporter. But one night, he attended a cocktail party for city employees, and when he returned to the paper, he weaved from pillar to wall, trying to find his desk in the vast newsroom. Greg told Dan to get some coffee and try to sober up. The deadline was near, and Dan had a story due.

Finally, Greg couldn't wait any longer and told Dan to write something; Greg would try to clean it up.

Dan sat at his typewriter and placed his fingers on the keys. His story started:

> Ynmohj yjr djrttogd fr[sty,rmy jr;f oyd smmis; vpvlyso; [styu y pgs,o;ostodr yjr [trdd eoyj yjr fr[sty,rmyd p[rtsyopm/

Then, Dan passed out at his typewriter.

Greg took a deep swallow from the bottle of antacid. "I guess our readers won't get to read Dan's story," Greg said to Jeff.

"No big deal," Jeff said. "A city hall cocktail party wasn't going to decide the future course of the island. Just be glad it wasn't a double murder."

Greg and Jeff took Dan home to his apartment and put him to bed. Then, they went to Lafitte's for after-work drinks. Greg staggered into his apartment at three a.m.

He worried that his own drinking was getting out of hand. He had to have something to calm his nerves, he reasoned. By itself, Valium wasn't doing the trick.

❖
October 1964

Greg had been in Galveston for six weeks. He welcomed his days off, but still found it hard to relax. Living alone made him jumpy, and he often felt at loose ends without the structure of work. He'd spent much of his free time exploring the island and learning about Galveston's history, which he considered fascinating as well as indispensable for doing his job as city editor. Riding the ferry from Galveston to Port Bolivar, across Galveston Bay, helped him relax.

On a Monday afternoon in late October, aboard the lumbering craft, the *R.S. Sterling*, Greg got out of his car and walked up the steps to the observation deck. The ferry's propeller churned the water as it pulled away from the landing. Greg let the wind wash over him. He breathed in the clean salt air.

But he stewed about his job. By now, he'd learned the routine and got regular encouragement from his bosses. But nothing had prepared him for Galveston and its people—especially members of the *Star* staff.

They seemed so sloppy and unkempt, coming to work in all manner of attire: Stan Richter in his yachting gear; a sportswriter who dressed in old, dirty blue jeans with his shirttail hanging out; a society writer who wore pedal-pushers to work and often had what looked like egg or mustard stains on her blouse. Were these people supposed to be professionals?

And the level of their work seemed to Greg below that of a college newspaper staff. How could the *Star* ever become a first-rate paper with the kind of sloppy people and sloppy writing he saw every day? He hoped Seth Yeager didn't plan to put up with such a motley crew indefinitely.

As the ferry chugged across the bay, Greg thought again about writing to Suzy. Could she still be single? And if so, would she have any interest in him? It had been two years since she'd moved to Waco to attend Baylor. She'd probably graduated by now. There was no telling where she lived; she might be so far away that seeing each other would be impossible. He decided to write her in care of her parents in Fort Worth and hope the letter reached her.

As Greg rode the ferry back to Galveston, a school of dolphins swam alongside, leaping in the air and plunging back into the water with the playfulness of children. Greg watched them with envy.

Back at his apartment, Greg sat at his portable typewriter and wrote to Suzy. He told her about his job and living in Galveston. Then he added:

> I've thought about you often these last couple of years and hoped you were happy.
> It seems a shame that as close as we were for so long, we should completely lose touch. It's been a hectic couple of years for me, and I'm sure you've been busy, too. But at the very least, couldn't we bring each other up to date on our lives? I'd like it very much if you could write and let me know how you're doing.
> Suzy, I hope I'm not intruding at a time when you're in a serious relationship, but I want you to know I miss you. I'm sorry if I seemed intolerant of your religious beliefs. It's possible to overcome such differences, and I'm willing to try.

❖

Irene Dubois and Stan Richter continued to turn in stories that gave Greg acid indigestion and a galloping pulse. Greg read over one of Irene's stories.

"Damn," he mumbled to Jeff across the desk. "Irene's buried the lead again."

"You'd better go show it to her," Jeff said, shuffling through a stack of copy from the AP wire.

"Oh, hell," Greg said, lighting another cigarette from the one he'd just smoked. "I just had a run-in with her yesterday."

"Don't let her get her bluff in on you," Jeff said. "She makes a lot of noise, but you're her boss. Don't let her forget that."

"Okay, I'll go talk to her," he said.

He approached her desk. "Irene, I've got a question on your story."

"Oh, you again." She gave him an icy glare. "Seems like you were just here."

"About this story..."

"Don't you get tired of being a nit-picker?" She turned red in the face.

"Here in the lead paragraph, you say...."

"I've had enough of you, Spencer." Irene was almost shouting. "You can take that story and stick it up your ass."

Irene got up, grabbed her purse, and stomped out of the newsroom.

Jeff had heard the commotion and hurried over. He summoned Seth Yeager's red-haired secretary, Kay Sweeney.

"Go check the ladies' room and see if Irene's in there," Jeff said to Kay. He turned to Greg. "What's the problem, Greg?"

"I don't know." Greg said, now thoroughly unnerved. "I was just asking Irene about her story."

Seth Yeager stood in the doorway of his office.

"Greg, Jeff, what's going on?" the editor asked.

"I'm not sure, Mr. Yeager," Greg said. "Irene's upset about something."

"Where is she?" Yeager asked.

"Kay went to check the ladies' room," Jeff said.

Momentarily, Kay and Irene emerged back in the newsroom. Irene dabbed at her eyes with a tissue.

"Greg, Jeff, Irene," the editor said. "Come into my office."

They filed in and sat at chairs around the editor's desk. Irene sniffled and wiped her eyes.

"Now, tell me what this is all about," Yeager said.

No one said anything. Finally, Greg spoke up.

"I went to Irene with a question about a story," he said with a shaky voice.

"Did Greg say something that upset you?" Yeager leaned toward Irene.

"Mr. Yeager, I just don't feel well today," Irene said, sniffling as she spoke.

"Greg has my permission to question reporters' stories," Yeager said. "I've instructed him to be courteous and diplomatic when he does so. Was he rude to you, Irene?"

"No, sir. I guess not."

"Let's get back to work," Yeager said, standing up. "Irene, why don't you take the rest of the day off?"

Irene rushed out of the newsroom and left the building. Greg went back to his desk and rewrote her story, the acid churning in his gut. He had to make several phone calls to check some of Irene's facts. When he finished, he went to the water fountain and swallowed his spare Valium.

That night, the fifty-year-old printing press broke down. For a while there was doubt it could be repaired in time to print the day's edition. Finally, the pressmen fixed the problem, but the press run didn't begin until nearly three a.m. Greg and Jeff had to wait for printed copies of the paper to check for errors. He didn't get home until five a.m.

Once in his apartment, Greg lay awake, too wound up to sleep. He took another Valium but didn't fall asleep until well after sunrise.

The next day, Greg dragged himself from bed around noon. He realized he'd told Dan and Jeff he'd join them for a 12:30 lunch at the Jack Tar Hotel coffee shop. He rushed around in a jangle, trying to dress and shave in time to meet his friends. His mind still tossed and turned with the memory of his altercation with Irene and the press breakdown. He rushed to his car and raced toward his lunch date.

As Greg neared the hotel parking lot, with no warning, he felt as though the earth had dropped from beneath him. Where had he had this feeling before?

His heart raced, and he gasped for breath. He broke out in a cold sweat. He felt as though a hive of bees swarmed inside him. His head felt light and unsteady. He gasped for breath. *My God, I'm dying,* Greg thought.

He pulled into the parking lot and tried to grasp what was happening. The only thought he could summon was, *I've got to get out of here.*

Waves of panic spread through his limbs. Shaking all over, Greg stumbled inside the restaurant and spotted his cohorts.

"Greg, are you okay?" Jeff asked with concern on his face. "You're white as a sheet."

"Something's wrong with me. I'm heading for Fort Worth," Greg said, his voice trembling. "I've got to see my doctor there." The urge to go home seemed overpowering.

"Are you sure you can drive?" Jeff asked.

" I can drive," Greg said, not feeling so sure. "Tell Yeager I won't be in today."

"Why don't you go to the emergency room at Sealy?" Dan suggested.

"I need to leave. I've got to see my doctor in Fort Worth."

As he sped away, Greg's mind flashed back to the day in 1959 when he was a freshman in college, and he had been on his way to school.

Not that, he thought. *Please; not that again.*

❖

Still shaking, Greg drove slowly back to his apartment, threw a few things into a suitcase, took a Valium, and headed out of Galveston.

By the time he passed through Houston, he felt more in control. Maybe he should turn back, he thought, but he realized the old demon had surfaced again. Dr. Simon knew his history and would be the logical person to see. The doctor had told him about a psychiatrist in Galveston, but that doctor specialized in long-term therapy. This was something sudden, and Greg needed to see someone right away, someone who knew him. This unwavering fixation kept him heading toward home.

By the time he arrived in Fort Worth at seven that evening, he felt foolish for what he'd done. George Spencer was working late, so Greg poured out his story to his mother.

"Everyone at the paper is going to think I'm nuts," he said with despair in his voice. "I thought I was coming apart at the seams."

"Oh, Greg," Vivian said. "You had a spell like that when you were nineteen and going through all that nervous mess."

"But that was years ago. I thought I was over all that."

"Don't ask me," Vivian shrugged. "I never understood that whole business."

"I'll call Dr. Simon the first thing in the morning and see if he can see me."

"You'd better call your boss and let him know what's going on."

"I told Dan and Jeff to tell him I was sick and wouldn't be in."

"You need to talk to him yourself."

"He'll think I'm nuts."

"Call him. You owe him that."

Greg called Seth Yeager the next morning. What Yeager said stunned him.

"Greg, you might be surprised to know I went through something like that when I was about your age. I understand about these things with nerves. The main thing you need to do is to take a few days, get yourself together, and come on back down here. I'm willing to bet you'll be fine."

A deep sense of shame and contrition seized Greg. "Thanks, Mr. Yeager. I'll come back today."

"No, you take a few days, talk to your doctor, and come back when you're feeling better. Thursday is Thanksgiving. Spend that time with your family. Call me back Friday and let me know how you're doing. No need to rush things. Jim Stephens can handle the city desk till you get back."

Greg called Dr. Simon's office. The receptionist told Greg the doctor couldn't see him for three weeks. She had a grating nasal voice.

"But I live in Galveston, and I have to go back to work there. Isn't there any way I can get in this week?" Greg pleaded.

"I'm sorry. Our next opening is in three weeks."

"Can I talk to the doctor on the phone?"

"Give me your number. I'll leave it for him."

Late that afternoon, Dr. Simon returned the call. Greg told him what had happened.

"What kind of physical condition are you in? Have you lost any weight? Are you getting enough sleep?"

"Lately I've had a lot of stress, and I've been having trouble sleeping. I probably have lost some weight."

"Are you taking the Valium I prescribed?"

"Twice a day at least," Greg said.

"If I were you, I'd double that and give Dr. Brooks a call. He's the doctor I told you about. Maybe he can help you get to the root of your anxiety."

"I haven't had anything like this since you first saw me when I was nineteen. What do you think caused this . . . this spell?"

"Could be any number of things. Strange environment. Stress on the job. Being run-down physically. How's your love life?"

"Nonexistent. I haven't been out with a woman since I left Fort Worth."

"Has that caused you some worry or anxiety?"

"Sure. It gets pretty lonely down here; I live alone."

"It sounds to me as though you've had enough stress to trigger a sudden anxiety episode, as tightly wound as you are. Take the medication as I suggested and try to get your mind on something you enjoy."

"I'll try."

"How's your job going?"

"Well, it's hard to say. I think my bosses are pleased with my work. But some of the people at the paper are hard to work with. There's a lot of pressure."

"Look, I don't think you have a serious problem, though I know it may have seemed that way. That's a fairly common type of anxiety reaction. You don't sound very depressed. Have some fun; get some rest, and I think you'll be okay. Remember, take your medication."

Greg felt stupid. But it was some relief to know his boss, Seth Yeager, had an inkling of what he'd been through. Maybe it was more common than he realized, and maybe he should lighten up about it. But if it were a common problem, he thought, damned few people ever talked about it. Yeager's confession seemed a breath of fresh air.

Greg spent a quiet Thanksgiving with his parents. That night, he drove to the *News-Beacon* and saw a number of his former colleagues. His old friend Eddie King was now a rewrite man on the city desk. When Eddie got off work, they went to a bar.

"Man, working on the city desk here is a grind," Eddie said. "Is it any better in Galveston?"

"It's tough," Greg said, lighting a cigarette. "I think we must have the worst reporters on the planet. I spend half my time rewriting their stories."

"Heard anything from Suzy?" Eddie asked.

"I've lost track of her. I wrote her a letter, but I didn't know where to send it. I sent it to her folks here, but I don't know if she got it. I haven't heard back."

"Such a shame about you and Suzy. I always thought y'all were made for each other, even if it took you forever to finally kiss her."

"I miss the hell out of her." Greg felt forlorn. "But it was the Baptist thing, Eddie. I didn't think I could live with that."

"Lots of people do."

Greg called Seth Yeager the next day and told him he'd return to Galveston on Sunday and report back to work on Monday. Greg spent a relaxed couple of days at home, sleeping late and eating well. He felt a new surge of energy and a desire to rededicate himself to his work in Galveston.

❖

December 1964

Greg arrived back in Galveston on Sunday afternoon. He realized his rent had come due while he'd been in Fort Worth, so he went straight to his landlady's office/apartment.

She came to the door in her housecoat, which she held bunched together at the neck. Greg told her he owed her for the next month.

"Yeah, I noticed," she growled.

He scribbled out a check and handed it to her.

Eva Kaplan, a bulky woman in her seventies who dyed her hair jet black and plastered her face with thick makeup, spoke fractured English with Russian and Yiddish cadences.

"You feeling okay?" she asked.

"I'm okay." Greg didn't know if Jeff had told Mrs. Kaplan his reason for being gone for five days.

She frowned as she scanned his face. "You look a little peaked. Where you been eating?"

"Mostly places along the seawall."

She shook her head. "Ach! No wonder. These beach places are terrible. They cheat you blind and give to you dirty meat. You want good steak? I'll take you to market where I buy meat; It's clean. You want I should cook steak for you? You look peaked. You're not eating right."

Gren nodded through the diatribe.

"You're nice boy. Some of these newspaper peoples are bums. But you, you look like you was from a nice family. You Jewish?"

"No, afraid not."

"Come in here," Mrs. Kaplan said, leading him inside her apartment. "Do you know I was born in Russia? See those silver trays? And here, samovar and furniture. My mother brought these from Russia—on the ship. People tried to steal them; they're worth a lot of money. My people were well off in Russia in czar's time. We stayed always healthy because we ate clean food. Let me cook you steak."

"I'd love for you to cook me a steak sometime, but today's not the best time." Greg marveled at the idea that Mrs. Kaplan was alive "in the czar's time."

She wagged her finger. "You pick a day and go with me to market. Get you good steak. You look peaked to me."

Greg stopped in the entry hall and retrieved several days' mail from his box on the ground floor of his building. Inside the apartment, he sorted through the letters, mostly bills and advertising. But one envelope caught his eye. The return address read:

S. Cox
P.O. Box 1278 UTMB
Galveston, Texas

S. Cox, Greg thought. *That has to be Suzy. But in Galveston? UTMB? That's the University of Texas Medical Branch. Could Suzy be sick? What the hell?*

He ripped the envelope open.

Dear Greg,
You're absolutely not going to believe this—I'M IN GALVESTON, TOO!!!!
Mother sent me your letter, and I was completely stunned to learn you're here. I tried to call you but got no answer, so I'm mailing you a letter instead.
It's a long story. I graduated from Baylor last spring with my degree in psychology. I applied and got a scholarship to nursing school at UTMB, and here I am! This is the top

nursing school in the state, and I feel really lucky that they accepted me. I started in September, and I love it!

I'm studying to be a psychiatric nurse. I'll get my R.N. in 1966.

I've missed you, Greg. I had tears in my eyes when I read your letter. I can't wait to hear from you and see you again. My phone number is 633-9998. I know just where you live; I drove by there. I'm not that far away, just across the island. Can you believe it???!!!

All my love,
Suzy

P.S. My roommate is an Episcopalian. I've been going to church with her. Imagine that!

Greg shook his head and blinked his eyes. Did he read that right? He scanned the letter again, then sat down and read it over and over.

As Greg's joy rose, he felt a vague sense of shame and dread pulling him down. Then the reason became clear: *I should be the happiest guy on earth,* he thought, *but what terrible timing! She shows up just as I'm trying to shake off my first bout of panic in four years. . . .But she's here, and it could be my last chance with her. Getting a second chance with Suzy in college was beyond belief—but a third chance. . . .*

Something else about the letter left him uneasy, and presently he realized it was the business about her studying to be a psychiatric nurse. What could that mean for him? He could no longer escape telling Suzy about his history with anxiety. Would her studies make her more understanding—or less so. Whatever the case, he had to tell her the whole story, or they simply had no future. And now he wanted a future with Suzy—more than ever. But was it too late?

He smiled as he reread Suzy's P.S. about attending an Episcopal church. He went to the phone and called her.

Suzy practically leaped into Greg's arms when they met in the lobby of her dormitory at the medical school. They held each other with great tenderness, but there was also a palpable sense of caution.

"Let me look at you," Suzy said. "You look so . . . so mature. I think you've filled out some."

"And you've cut your hair," Greg said, running his hand over the side of her head and watching the short strands fall back into place.

"It's a lot less trouble now. I don't have time to fool with it, and they require us to have short hair. So, now, it's wash and wear." They walked toward the door.

"Why don't we take the ferry over to Port Bolivar?" Greg said. "It's warm, and it's not as crowded over there. We can walk on the beach and catch up on things."

Greg drove the Corvair onto the ferry. Few other cars boarded, and they had the observation deck to themselves. Suzy wore a pair of tight jeans and a green sweatshirt with "Baylor" in gold on the front, and the sleeves pushed up to her elbows. Her figure had lost none of its alluring contours.

"Have you lost some weight?" Greg asked, slipping his arm around Suzy's waist.

"Maybe some baby fat," she said. "I could stand to lose more."

"No, you look perfect."

"You're sweet." Suzy leaned over and kissed his cheek.

"Tell me about nursing school." Greg had some trepidation about getting into the subject of psychiatry, but they'd talk about it sooner or later.

"Oh, it's great, but it's hard, too," she said. "I have to study a lot. I go to class until two in the afternoon, then work in the psych clinic until six."

"You mean they make you work, too, on top of your classes?"

"Yeah, it's for credit, but so far it's mostly just flunky work. We run errands and follow the regular nurses around and observe what they're doing—seeing how to give injections and watching how they work with the patients. They're like our 'big sisters.' Interesting sometimes, but pretty routine most of the time."

"That sounds familiar," he said, watching the breeze from the ferry blowing Suzy's short locks off her high forehead.

"Oh, come on, now," Suzy said. "I'll bet you never get bored on a newspaper."

"Well, about the only excitement so far is when I get in a fight with a reporter."

"Oh, you do not," Suzy said, with a sidelong, skeptical look.

"We haven't come to blows yet, but our reporters got spoiled under the old owners and have a lot of bad habits. I have to be the heavy and try to straighten them out. Some of them are such prima donnas, they go nuts when I correct their stories."

"Same old Greg," Suzy giggled. "Just like in college. Always the perfectionist."

"I'm not as bad as I was," Greg said. "I think you cured me of the worst of it."

They snuggled close as they stood at the railing of the observation deck. Seagulls glided alongside them in the cool, late-autumn air.

They landed at Port Bolivar and drove off onto Highway 87, which ran for miles along the coast. They kept up their small talk, feeling each other out after their long separation.

Greg drove past a couple of bait shops along the highway. They stopped briefly to admire the old black lighthouse that had been a refuge for survivors of the 1900 hurricane. They passed several clusters of beach houses on stilts, then drove off the highway onto a narrow road that passed between two large sand dunes.

They got out and walked along the deserted beach. The air had the faint, fishy-salty smell of the sea. The sun was setting over the Gulf in the southwest. High, wispy clouds turned a flaming orange.

"Oh, how pretty," Suzy said, looking at the horizon. "Let's take off our shoes and wade in the surf."

"I'll bet the water's cold this time of year, but I'm game if you are." Greg removed his loafers and socks.

They held hands and splashed along the shore, the spent waves lapping at their ankles.

"Greg," Suzy said after a few moments' silence.

"Yeah?"

"I thought I'd never see you again," she said with a tinge of sadness.

"I'm sorry I stopped writing," Greg said. "I feel like I did that time in college when I stopped calling you."

"Don't blame yourself. I stopped writing, too. I can't remember who stopped first."

"I was stupid and bullheaded," he said. "I've really missed you, Suzy."

"Oh, I missed you, too. And for such a long time." Suzy stepped in front of Greg and turned, facing him. She placed her hands on his shoulders.

"I have to tell you something," she said.

"Oh?"

"I'm so ashamed." Suzy looked down at her feet.

Butterflies fluttered in Greg's stomach. "Go ahead; I'm listening."

"Well . . . My first year at Baylor, I was dating this guy, a senior." Suzy looked down again. "He was planning to go to seminary and become a minister." She paused and drew a deep breath. "Well, he wanted me to marry him, and, Greg, I . . . I went to bed with him."

Greg's feelings fired off in several directions. First came stabbing hurt, then anger, then envy; he was dumbfounded. A few minutes ago, he'd been brimming with joy. They were finally together again; and now, this. . . .

He grasped for words. "Why are you telling me this?"

"We were always so honest with each other, Greg. I don't want to hide something like that from you?"

"Okay," he said stiffly, groping to regain his equilibrium.

"But it only happened once." Suzy's eyes filled with tears. "Then, I found out what a phony he was, that he was just using me. He'd done the same thing with other girls. I still can't believe I was so naïve."

She put her arms around his waist. He pulled her close as she convulsed with sobs. His feelings softened.

"What do you mean 'phony?'" Greg asked.

"My roommate's boyfriend lived in the same dorm with Sidney—that's his name—and she said Sidney'd been bragging all over the dorm that he'd had sex with me. Can you believe it?"

"That's pretty damned sorry." Greg's anger rose again,

"But that's not all." Suzy put her hand over her mouth and stifled another sob. "He told several guys in the dorm that he'd slept with some other girls because he 'had the system down.'"

"System?"

"He told them all he had to do was convince these girls—including me—that he wanted to marry them, and they'd jump in bed."

"Oh, my God," Greg groaned. "And this guy was going to be a preacher?"

"Can you believe it?"

"I guess he's practicing up to lay all the women in his congregation.

"I know," Suzy looked down again. "I used to think preachers were so perfect, but. . . ."

Her shoulders started to convulse again. She wrapped her arms around Greg and buried her face in his chest. "Good Lord, how could I ever let myself be so taken in? I've never been more ashamed of anything in my life."

"I'm sorry, Suzy." Greg took his handkerchief from his pocket and wiped her cheeks.

"But then, I thought about how it used to be with us," Suzy said, stifling another sob. "And I remembered how you'd always treated me with such respect. That's when I realized I'd never stopped loving you. I've thought about you an awful lot." She pressed her head into his shoulder and cried even harder.

Greg didn't speak for a moment. He realized the truth of the matter. "And I never stopped loving you, Suzy."

"Not many people know about all that. I haven't even told my sister."

"Then get it out of your system. It's okay."

They sat on the sand and put their shoes back on. Greg held Suzy close as they walked back to the car.

"I'm sorry to dump all this on you," she said. "But we could always talk about things, Greg. You were always such a good friend, as well as someone I loved; I had to tell you. I started a dozen letters to you, but I didn't mail any of them. I was so confused."

"I'm trying to understand," Greg said. "It's just that. . . ."

"I know." She stopped crying and looked earnestly at him. "After all I put you through, don't think I haven't thought about that. I'm a little older now and not as naïve as I was back at Trinity Valley."

"I guess neither one of us is." Greg opened Suzy's door and she got in. Greg came around the Corvair and sat behind the wheel. He reached over, took both her hands, and pulled her closer.

"Look," he said. "What's done is done. I did a few stupid things myself since I saw you last. We're here now, and that's all that matters."

"Oh, Greg." She put her arms around his neck and cried some more. Greg felt tears in his own eyes.

Greg and Suzy boarded the ferry for the return trip to Galveston as darkness settled over the coast. The nighttime lights of Galveston grew brighter as they approached the island.

"So, your roommate is an Episcopalian?" Greg asked, as they cuddled together inside the enclosed deck, on a long wooden bench near a window.

"Yeah. Cindy had to talk me into going. I completely lost my faith after that business with Sidney. I didn't go to church for over a year."

"I'm sorry, Suzy."

"Well, maybe it was for the best. The first time I went to church with Cindy, it was really strange," Suzy said. "The service seemed cold somehow. But it sort of grew on me. I met the priest, and he's such a dear man. He has a degree in psychology, too, and we've had some really interesting conversations about religion and psychology."

"Yeah, such as?"

"Well, like how we get so brainwashed as children. I'd never thought about it much, but I realized how dogmatic Baptists can be. How black and white they see things: 'You're either with us or against us.' I believed so many things without questioning them. I could see why it drove you crazy."

"My uncle is an Episcopal priest," Greg said. "I went to his church a few times, and we used to talk a lot. I'm not sold on all that ritual, but I like their moderate way of looking at things."

"Oh, I love the ritual," Suzy said, her eyes brightening again. "It makes it all seem so holy. But not holier-than-thou."

Greg shook his head and smiled. "Suzy, you know I don't believe in miracles, but you are surely a miracle."

"You're so sweet," Suzy said, nuzzling her face against him.

"Let's get something to eat. Ever been to Gaido's?"

"Isn't that the place with that great big crab on the roof?"

"That's it."

"I've heard it's the best seafood in Galveston. Don't we need to dress up?"

"We're fine just like this. It's a nice place, but very casual, like any other place along the seawall."

❖

Greg and Suzy sat at a table with a white tablecloth in the tasteful dining room at Gaido's, just across from the beach on Seawall Boulevard. Immaculate waiters in starched, white jackets briskly took their dinner orders without writing anything down.

"I think I'd like a glass of white wine," Suzy said. "How about you?"

"Sure, two house Chardonnays, please." The waiter walked away.

"My, my," Greg teased. "You've become quite the libertine, haven't you? I couldn't get you to touch the stuff in college. Next thing I know, you'll be cussing and gambling."

Suzy laughed. "Probably hanging around with nurses has rubbed off a little, and you know how they are."

Greg flashed an evil grin. "Yeah, I've heard."

The waiter brought their wine. Suzy held up her glass. "To us," she said. Greg clinked his glass against it. They sipped their wine.

Greg marveled at the change in Suzy. She still bore the unmistakable trace of wholesome girlish innocence, but a more mature womanhood was ripening in her.

Greg still burned inside with the residue of Suzy's confession at the beach. For the moment, he clung tightly to his own secret.

Before he could stop himself, another nagging question popped out.

"Have you been dating anyone here?"

"Oh, my. You had to ask, didn't you?" Suzy put down her fork. "Yeah, there was somebody—a med student. We went out a few times. He was pretty stuck on himself, and it was pretty clear he was after only one thing. I didn't need that."

"Oh."

"Nothing happened." Suzy took deep breath and sighed.

"Okay, I'm sorry I pried."

"No, it's okay. Now, I've told you everything. What about you?"

"What about me?" He could spill his guts now, he thought, but why spoil dinner?

"Are you dating anyone?" Suzy asked.

"No, not since I've been in Galveston. I dated a good bit in Fort Worth, but nothing serious. None of them measured up to you."

"That's sweet. I feel the same way."

"So, what's next for us? We found each other; where do we go from here?" Greg craved reassurance from Suzy.

"I don't know," Suzy smiled. "Maybe it was meant to be. I don't think our feelings have really changed." Suzy reached across the table and squeezed Greg's hand. "Let's just take it as a gift of fate and see what happens."

Their food arrived: red snapper for Suzy and stuffed crab for Greg. They filled themselves on the succulent dishes. Greg paid the check, and they walked back to his car.

Greg had a surge of desire to take Suzy to a dark, deserted stretch of beach, or better yet, to his apartment. But he didn't want to push her. She'd been hurt badly, and he realized she needed patience right now more than passion.

Indeed, when they parked on the curb outside her dorm, they kissed deeply but less frantically than during their college days. Suzy seemed to welcome Greg's reluctance to force matters, yet he'd never wanted her more.

He pulled back from a kiss and looked into her eyes. "Suzy, I want things to work out for us, this time for keeps." He shrunk inside at the thought he might lose her again.

"I do, too," she said, holding his gaze. "I've thought about it a lot." Then, she smiled. "Haven't we fooled around long enough?"

"Yeah, we sure have." he said. Now, he had to tell her. His heart pounded and his throat tightened. "But there's something I have to tell you."

"Oh?" Suzy looked startled.

He reclined behind the steering wheel, staring off into the chilly night, trying to rein in his scattered thoughts. A freighter's horn sounded from the wharves, a few blocks away.

He took Suzy's hand and looked back at her. "Today, you told me something really personal. It wasn't easy to hear, but I was touched that you trusted me enough to tell me." Greg paused and closed his eyes a moment. "Now, it's my turn to tell you something very personal about me."

"Please do." Suzy cocked her head slightly, giving him a curious look.

"God," Greg groaned, his mind still racing. "I don't know where to start."

"Just start." She sighed. "The suspense is killing me."

"Well, you remember when I stopped calling you in college?"

"Sure."

"I never told you the whole story. I said I was having some health problems."

"Yeah, I remember."

"It was a lot worse than what I told you." Greg paused again.

"Go ahead. I won't bite you." Suzy put her hand reassuringly on his knee.

"It's so damned embarrassing." He cleared his throat and felt himself trembling inside. "I guess I had what some people call a 'nervous breakdown.'"

"Oh, really?" Suzy's expression turned more serious.

"I don't know why they call it that, but anyway, I kind of fell apart."

Suzy sat back in her seat. "I'm not sure I would have guessed."

"What I told you back then about 'complications' from my wreck injuries was only partly true. Actually, I had a bad case of anxiety and depression and spent ten days in the hospital. The doctor said it was probably caused, at least to some extent, by a delayed reaction to the wreck."

"Okay," she said in a level tone. "I'm not shocked. Go ahead."

"Well, it took about a year to get over it. I flunked out of school. Then I went back and met you again. I got that job at the *News-Beacon*, and I was fine for the next four years."

"But you didn't stay that way?"

"Right, but here's the hard part. I did okay until I'd been in Galveston for three months. Then, just last week, I had another big anxiety attack and drove back to Fort Worth to see my shrink."

"Good Lord, Greg. If I'd known, I could have gotten you some help here. Did your shrink help?"

"I guess so. He convinced me I'd be okay if I'd eat right and get enough sleep. He told me to have some fun and quit stewing about my job."

"Well, there you are. Look, Greg, hold on." Suzy bit her lip and sat a moment, looking down, in deep thought.

This is it, Greg thought. *Now I've screwed up everything.*

Suzy grasped his hand. "First of all, do you know how many patients we see who have the same thing?"

"You never hear much about it," he said.

"It's more common than you think, and it can happen to anyone. I didn't know that myself until I got deeper into this field. There's a lot of new research going on, and doctors are getting a better grip on anxiety and depression."

"You think so?"

"Yeah, according to my professors, there are some new theories about cause and treatment. It's pretty encouraging."

"That's good to know." Greg sighed, relieved that Suzy's response was tempered with medical insight. "Can you ever forgive me for not telling you about it before?" Greg looked down.

Suzy thought a minute. "To be honest, I'm not sure how I would have reacted when we were in college. My aunt had a 'nervous breakdown,' and my mother acted like Aunt Gladys had leprosy. We didn't know what to make of it. But now I understand it was just a bad case of depression." She held his gaze a few seconds. "It's an illness, Greg, like polio or diabetes. A diabetic can't make his pancreas secrete insulin with will power, and you can't cure a person of anxiety or depression by just telling them to 'snap out of it.' There's plenty of help available, and I can help you find it."

"But the trouble is," Greg said. "It scares 'normal' people off."

"Well, not me, darlin', and that's all that matters for us." Suzy leaned over and kissed Greg on the cheek.

He held her tightly and shook his head. "You're amazing, you know it?" Moisture rimmed Greg's eyes. "I was afraid you'd run like hell when I told you the whole story."

"You don't do that when you love somebody," she said. "I think we can work things out. You're the same old Greg as far as I can tell."

"Yeah, I was fine for four years, but look what happened last week."

"Then, we'll deal with it." Suzy edged closer.

"I don't want you getting into something you'll regret."

"Listen." She put her arms around him. "I can promise you that loving someone and being loved is not going to make you worse. It's a risk I'm willing to take."

❖

When he awoke the next day, Greg's first thought was of Suzy. As he rubbed the sleep from his eyes, he was still uncertain whether he'd dreamed yesterday's events. But the faint scent of her perfume was still on his skin. His handkerchief still bore the lipstick he he'd wiped off after they'd parted. His mood rose as he climbed out of bed.

But he had to go to work. He'd been away nearly a week; what would his co-workers know about his absence? When he walked into the newsroom, he felt sheepish. Seth Yeager called him into his office.

"How do you feel, Greg?"

"Much better. I think I'll be okay now." Greg was thinking of the boost Suzy had given him more than the medical advice he'd gotten from Dr. Simon.

"You look better," Yeager said. "I was frankly getting a little worried about you."

"Really? Was it that obvious?" Greg asked.

"Well, don't get me wrong, Greg. I think you've been doing a fine job on the city desk. Our local copy has looked a lot more professional since you've been here. That's just what we expected from you." Yeager lit his pipe. Smoke curled around his head. "But frankly, Greg, I got the idea you were pushing a little too hard."

Greg looked surprised. "You mean with the reporters?"

"No, not that so much. I appreciate what you've done with the reporters. It just looked to me like you were pretty tense most of the time. Holcomb tells me you stayed late often and drove yourself pretty hard."

"I stayed late to write the assignments for the next day." Greg felt a sudden sense of failure in spite of Yeager's compliments. His glass was half empty.

"Let me make a suggestion," Yeager said. "As each reporter turns in a story, write his assignment for the next day then, rather than waiting until the end of the day. They won't stack up so much that way."

"Okay, Mr. Yeager," Greg said, now flushed with embarrassment. "That makes more sense."

Yeager chuckled. "Greg, when we hired you, we didn't expect you to be perfect. You're still learning the job. Ease up."

"Thanks, I'll try to."

"And Greg." Yeager puffed on his pipe. "I understand these things about nerves better than you might suspect. You remind me a lot of myself as a young city editor."

"Yeah," Greg said. "I was surprised to hear about your troubles. My dad had problems with his nerves, too, when he was a young newspaperman."

"Well, maybe it's an occupational hazard." Yeager stood up and looked at Greg with a fatherly smile. "You're young and full of nervous energy, just like I was. Relax and enjoy what you're doing. You're pretty good at it, you know. You don't have to prove yourself all at once. We have confidence in you."

"Thanks, Mr. Yeager. I appreciate that." Greg recalled getting a similar speech from Suzy in college. Maybe there was something to it.

He sat down across from Jeff Holcomb at the news desk.

"Boy, you look better," Jeff said. "Did your doctor shoot you full of drugs?"

"No, nothing like that. But when I got back to town, I discovered my old girlfriend is going to nursing school at UTMB."

"Now, that's interesting," Jeff said. "Did you see her?"

"Yeah, we spent a good part of yesterday together."

"And?"

"And . . . I must be the luckiest son of a bitch alive."

❖

Greg called Suzy every day. When he sent up his last page dummy to the printers at 10:30 each night, he had a half-hour to spare before he had to go upstairs and supervise the page makeup. Suzy had usually just finished studying for her next day's classes and was preparing for bed.

Her soft voice was like warm honey to his spirits. Jeff kidded Greg about the faraway look he got when talking to Suzy. When Greg and Suzy talked each night, they were like two teenagers lingering over each trivial phrase.

They got together on Friday nights and weekends, spending almost every free moment together. Greg gave Suzy a tour of the island's historic sites, and Suzy showed Greg around the medical school complex. He met her roommate, Cindy O'Donnell, a petite brunette with a page-boy hairstyle.

Greg invited Suzy to the *Star*'s office Christmas party and introduced her to his co-workers. Several congratulated him on his taste in women.

He took Suzy to Lafitte's and Lolita's, where Suzy ran into a group of her fellow student nurses. They shouted to each other above the throbbing Greek music, as the sailors went through their paces.

Afterward, Greg drove to a deserted beach below the seawall on the edge of town. The tide was out, and the calm surf sloshed in gently. Greg put his arm around Suzy and drew her to him.

"Well, " he said. "Are we going to make it this time?"

"How can you doubt it?" she asked. "We'll make it work. We have so much fun together; I adore being with you. I've never loved you more, my darlin'." She tugged him into a long, juicy kiss.

He pressed his forehead against hers. "And you're sure you want me with all my warts?"

"You look solid as a rock to me. I don't think we have that much to worry about. That spell you had might have been an isolated thing."

"I want you to go into this with your eyes open."

"I am. But you seem fine to me. Remember, I see psych patients every day, and you don't fit the profile. I'll bet the worst is behind you."

"You're all the medicine I need, Suzy. I love you more than I can tell you." He lowered her gently across the bucket seats.

Naturally, their physical attraction for one another hadn't waned. They were calmer now, but still intoxicated by the sense of touch. Greg tried to avoid rushing things, but Suzy resisted, and after a while he felt the some of the same frustration he'd felt in college. Suzy sensed his exasperation.

"Greg, we need to talk about this." She sat up.

"I know; I'm trying," he said.

"I know you are, and I love you for it."

"I understand what you've been through."

"I know you do. And I know how hard it is for you. And, Greg, I want to, more than you can imagine. And we will. Just give me a little more time."

"How much time?"

"I don't know. Maybe not long. Try to be patient, darlin.'"

A week before Christmas, Suzy left Galveston to go home for the school holidays. Greg would drive to Fort Worth on his days off to be with her. Meanwhile, he asked around the newsroom for advice on the best jewelry stores in Galveston. He spent hours before work shopping at the stores and found what he was looking for at Morris Jewelers, a few blocks from the *Star* building.

At work, Greg felt more relaxed and more in the flow of his job as city editor. He had no significant conflicts with reporters or photographers, though he and Irene Dubois tiptoed around each other. He was thankful Stan Richter, the yachtsman, had taken his two-week vacation at Christmas time.

Greg thought about what Seth Yeager had told him. Maybe Greg had been too intense; maybe he pushed too hard. Perhaps a more relaxed approach to the staff would be more productive; it had worked with the printers.

Greg had to work on Christmas Eve. Holidays always meant slow news, and he and Jeff put the paper "to bed" early that night. He went upstairs to check on the page assembly. Tony Rodriguez was singing, *Plop, plop, fizz, fizz. Oh, what a relief it is. . . .*

"Hey, Gregorio," Tony said. "You're late, man. We already sent the paper to the press room."

Greg looked over the finished pages he'd designed.

"Damn, Tony," he said. "You followed my dummies right down to the last line of type."

"Hell, yes, man. I know how to take care of you."

"You do, Tony," Greg said. "And you did me a big favor; I'm driving to Fort Worth after work, and now I won't be driving all night."

"Hey, Benito," Tony said "Get Gregorio some eggnog."

The young Linotype operator brought a paper cup filled with the drink. Several other printers gathered around the page trucks.

"Here's to Gregorio," Tony said. "Our editor *mas simpático.*" The others said, "Salud!" and drained their cups.

Greg blushed. "Damn, Tony. I don't know what to say."

"Jus' have a good trip home, man." Tony slapped Greg's back. "Hey, you got a girlfriend back there?"

"It so happens that I do."

"Hey, Gregorio. A little Christmas nooky, eh?" Tony asked with a salacious guttural chuckle.

"We'll see, Tony." Greg smiled and blushed a little. "You guys have a Merry Christmas."

❖

Greg had a recurring thought as he drove north: *What if Suzy tells her parents about my anxiety problems? How will they deal with that fact?* He hadn't seen them in two years, and they'd never seemed particularly warm toward him, especially Mrs. Cox. What were they going to think about Suzy being involved with him again?

But that thought faded in and out. Mostly, Greg sped along I-45 feeling several feet off the ground, thinking of Suzy and what their life might be like in the future.

He arrived at his parents' house at two a.m. Christmas morning to discover his old bedroom occupied. Vivian Spencer woke up and told him his Aunt Maggie and young cousins Jill and Josh had come from California to be with the family for Christmas. Greg grumbled and made a bed for himself on the living room sofa.

A Christmas tree filled one corner of the room. Greg lay on the sofa, breathing in the fragrance of the pine needles. He thought of the many past Christmases he'd spent here growing up. They'd always been special to him and made him feel closer to his family, a remarkable clan Greg was proud to be part of. His Aunt Sally and Uncle Will were both journalists, as his father had been. Greg often felt he was carrying on a family tradition with his choice of careers.

Memorable as those past holidays were, he thought, no Christmas could be as special as this one.

The relatives converged on the tree at eight the next morning to open presents. Greg could have used another couple of hours' sleep, but the squealing cousins tearing open their packages made that impossible. He got up, dressed, and joined the others for breakfast.

He caught up on the latest family news. His two young cousins had grown since he'd seen them last. His Aunt Maggie complained about the smog and traffic in Los Angeles, where they'd moved after leaving Fort Worth a few years earlier. His Uncle Will, now a producer for CBS News in Los Angeles, didn't make the trip because he had to work.

After breakfast, George and the guests dispersed and left Greg alone at the kitchen table. He smoked a cigarette as Vivian busied herself preparing the holiday dinner.

"I guess Suzy's in town," she said, checking on her turkey in the oven.

"Yeah, she's at her folks' house," Greg said. "I'm going over there after dinner."

Vivian stood with her arms akimbo. "Greg, when am I going to get to meet that girl?"

"I'd forgotten you'd never met her. I'll bring her over while she's home."

"I hope things work out this time." Vivian wiped her hands on a dishtowel. "I remember how hard you took it when she went off to Baylor."

"That's ancient history," Greg said. "I need to call her."

❖

Fort Worth
Christmas 1964

Greg ate Christmas dinner with his family, then drove to the Cox home in mid-afternoon. Along the way, he passed through the familiar neighborhood he'd grown up in—the drive-ins he'd haunted in high school, Collins' Drugs, Monroe's department store, the bowling alley, his old elementary school, and, finally, Eastside High, perched high on a hill overlooking Oakwood Park, with its ball diamonds, swimming pool, and miniature golf course. He looked nostalgically at the stately high school, its red-brick colonial architecture and white cupola with a weathervane on top. He recalled how he he'd felt his life was ending when he graduated from Eastside. He had driven by the school after graduation and proclaimed to himself: *There's the place where I spent the best years of my life.* That had been before he met Suzy.

All that seemed in the distant past. He shook his head as he recalled his sentimental excess. He knew better days lay ahead.

Suzy's parents lived a few blocks from Eastside High. He turned off East Oakdale onto a side street and saw the Coxes' corner house a few blocks ahead. His heartbeat quickened. He wedged his Corvair between cars parked in front of the well-kept, white brick-and-frame dwelling, a newer house than many in the historic old neighborhood.

He carried a gift-wrapped package to the porch and rang the doorbell.

A dark-haired young man holding a baby opened the door. "You must be Greg. Come in." Suzy's older brother Richard introduced himself. Richard had just been discharged from the Air Force. Greg had never met him; Richard had been overseas all the time Greg and Suzy had dated in college.

Greg stepped into a living room littered with Christmas wrappings and children's toys. A lingering scent of sage and turkey from the holiday dinner hung in the air.

"Greg, nice to see you again, young fella," Suzy's father said, pumping Greg's hand. A toddler tore at the wrappings on the floor, covered in a lime-green sculptured carpet.

Floyd Cox, a silver-haired, athletic-looking department-store manager in his fifties, introduced Greg to Richard's wife and another young man Greg learned was the husband of Suzy's sister Beverly.

Mrs. Cox sat in a large easy chair. "Hello, Greg," she said icily.

"Suzanne and Beverly are in the backyard," Floyd Cox said. "Let's go tell them you're here." Beverly, Suzy's sister, was a year older than Suzy.

Floyd Cox clasped Greg's shoulder as they went through the kitchen toward the back door. "How've you been? We've missed you around here."

"Fine. I guess Suzy's told you all about us hooking up again in Galveston," Greg said.

"Yes, yes. Wasn't that nice?" Mr. Cox said. He had a jovial, hail-fellow-well-met manner, reminding Greg of other Baptist men he'd known. "I keep promising Suzanne I'll come down and see her so I can go deep-sea fishing. Do you fish, Greg?"

"No, sir. I never could catch anything." Greg hoped that wasn't the wrong answer.

"Why, I can teach you," Mr. Cox said, stopping at the back door. "I'll bet I could have you hauling them in in no time."

"Thanks, but I think I scare fish away," Greg said chuckling.

"Well, you let me know if you want to give it a try. How about golf? Ever play golf, Greg?"

"I haven't played in a while," Greg said. "But I was on the golf team in high school. I love golf."

"Well, then," said Mr. Cox. "We've got to play. We're members at Glen Garden. Our Baptist men's group plays over there every Saturday morning. Next time you're in town, come on out. You'll be my guest."

"I'd love to. I've never played at a country club before." Greg warmed to Mr. Cox's friendliness; he'd never been this cordial before.

"Why, we'll just tee 'em up some Saturday," Mr. Cox said. "You know old Ben Hogan and Byron Nelson cut their teeth on that course."

Greg and Mr. Cox stepped down into the backyard. It was a sunny, mild day. Suzy, wearing a pair of maroon Capri pants and a pink mohair sweater, was stretched out on a chaise lounge. Her sister Beverly, an attractive brunette with stiff bouffant hair, sat in a lawn chair next to Suzy. Greg recalled Beverly and Eddie King's long-ago romance and how they'd broken up the night Greg and Eddie had tumbled down the Lake Arlington dam. Greg wondered what his life would have been like without that sequence of events.

"Suzanne!" Mr. Cox shouted. "Someone's here to see you."

Suzy sat up. "Oh, Greg's here! Remember Greg?" Suzy said to her sister.

"Hey, Greg," Beverly said. "Long time, no see. You're looking good."

"You, too, Beverly," Greg said. "How's married life?"

"Busy, especially with a baby."

"Let's go on in the house, Bev," Mr. Cox said. "And leave these kids alone." Father and daughter went back inside.

Greg pulled Suzy to her feet and into his arms. They enjoyed a lingering hug.

"What's with your dad?" Greg asked, sitting down next to Suzy on the edge of the chaise lounge.

"I don't know," Suzy said with a puzzled look. "What do you mean?"

"Well, he's never been so friendly. He treated me like a long-lost member of the family."

"Oh," Suzy said. "I think I know. We had a long talk the other night."

"You must have told him I was Prince Rainier," Greg teased.

"No, he's always liked you, but he didn't show it much in front of mother. I think he's just so relieved that you're back in my life after all that mess at Baylor."

"Maybe he can work on your mother."

"Oh, Mother's just Mother," Suzy said. "She's old-fashioned, and I'm her baby girl. She'll come around."

Greg handed Suzy the package. "Merry Christmas," he said.

She pulled off the ribbons and carefully removed the paper. Greg had packed a smaller box inside a larger one with paper stuffed all around.

"What is this, hide-and-seek?" Suzy laughed her familiar shy giggle. She finally found the smaller box and opened it, revealing a pearl necklace and matching earrings "Oh! How beautiful!" She leaned over and kissed him. "Thank you, my darlin'."

Suzy tried on the necklace and looked longingly at Greg. He put his arms around her, and they buried themselves in a long, lingering kiss. Greg wondered if Suzy felt let down by his gift, but he didn't detect any disappointment.

"Suzanne!" Mrs. Cox shouted from the back door. "Y'all come on in. We're serving pumpkin pie."

"Uh-oh!" Greg said, untangling himself. "She may put that pie in my face."

"Oh, silly." Suzy took Greg's hand as they walked back to the house.

As they ate their pie topped with vanilla ice cream, the Cox family went back and forth about their plans for the rest of the holiday. Greg tried to avert his eyes from Mrs. Cox. The upshot of the discussion was that they all planned to leave later that afternoon to visit some of Mrs. Cox's relatives in Stephenville, southwest of Fort Worth.

"Do I have to go?" Suzy protested. "I've barely seen Greg, and he has to drive back to Galveston tomorrow."

"Oh, honey. I was hoping you'd come," Mrs. Cox whined.

"Mother! Greg and I made plans for today." Greg had counted on spending the rest of the day with Suzy.

"It's okay, Suzanne," Mr. Cox jumped in. "There'll be other chances to see your kinfolks."

"Thank you, Daddy," Suzy said with a triumphant smile. "I love you."

People started getting up from the table. Suzy pulled an unopened package from under the Christmas tree and handed it to Greg.

"It's not as nice as my present," Suzy said. "But I hope you like it."

Greg unwrapped the box and took out an elegant brown suede jacket. "I'm speechless," he said. "It's beautiful, Suzy." He squeezed her hand, preferring to keep displays of affection to a minimum in front of her parents.

They said their goodbyes to the others and walked to Greg's car. He pulled Suzy to him and kissed her warmly.

"That's for the jacket," he said. "That's how I really feel."

❖

Greg and Suzy drove across town to the Fort Worth Botanic Garden, one of the most scenic parks in the city, even in midwinter. The garden featured crisscrossing walkways through wooded areas, long arcades covered in trumpet vines, sculptures, sandstone walls, and a spacious rose garden that sloped down a hillside to a fountain and pond. The Works Progress Administration had built the garden in the thirties.

Greg and Suzy walked down the rose garden steps and stood near the fountain.

"Oh, how pretty," Suzy said. "I haven't been here in ages. I hear it's a popular place for weddings in the springtime when everything's green and blooming."

"Yeah, I'll bet it is," Greg said. His attention was elsewhere. "Why don't we sit down on that bench over there?" His heart raced.

"Are you tired?" Suzy asked.

"No, I just want to enjoy the scenery," Greg said. "It's such a beautiful day." He fished in his coat pocket.

They sat on the bench. Suzy snuggled close.

"I've got another present for you," Greg said, cupping his hands around the box to hide it.

"Oh, goody." Suzy beamed.

"Hold out your hands and close your eyes."

She complied and he set the small package, gift-wrapped in white, glossy paper with thin gold ribbon, in her hands. She opened her eyes.

"Oh, Greg!" She gasped with a flash of recognition. "Is it what I think?" She removed the ribbon and carefully unwrapped the paper.

Then, she opened the box as tears welled in her eyes. Greg took the gold solitaire diamond ring and slid it on her finger.

"Oh, it's so beautiful!" She put an arm around Greg's neck and pressed her face next to his. "The answer is 'yes, yes, yes'!"

"My God, Suzy, I'm so nervous, I don't know if I can talk." Her tears ran down both their cheeks.

"Me, too." She sniffled, leaning back, holding his face between her hands and looking into his eyes. "I love you so. I've never been so happy."

Greg realized tears had filled his eyes, too. As he wiped them away, he choked, "A month ago, I couldn't have dreamed of this day. God, how I love you, Suzanne."

They sat silently for a brief moment. Greg knew their lives were changed forever.

Presently their tears dried, and as dusk settled over the Botanic Garden, Greg turned from the sublime to the more mundane.

"I wanted to take you to some swanky place for dinner," Greg said as they walked slowly back to his car. "But I just realized that most places are closed for Christmas."

"Maybe we can find a snack somewhere," Suzy said. "After that big turkey dinner, all that pie and ice cream, I'm not very hungry."

They got back into Greg's Corvair. "After we eat a bite," he said, "how about a movie? I think 'My Fair Lady's' showing at the Palace."

"I'd love to see it," Suzy said, looking conflicted over the decision. "But, Greg, are you thinking what I'm thinking?" She giggled, and a mischievous expression lit up her face.

"About what?"

"About my folks."

"Oh, yeah, they're on their way to Stephenville."

"No, not that. I don't want to sound forward or anything, but. . . ."

A light came on. "But . . . there's no one at your house."

"And there won't be till tomorrow." Greg had never seen a more seductive expression on Suzy's face.

Greg reached across and pulled her to him. Their breathing became heavy, their kisses deeper. Greg backed away.

"Then you're saying it's okay for us to . . . ?" Greg stammered, catching his breath.

"Yes, darlin', that's what I'm saying."

Greg frowned. "But, hell, there aren't any drugstores open."

"What do you need a drugstore for?"

"For, you know, protection. I don't have any."

Suzy leaned back and fixed him in her sultry gaze. "Now, here's my surprise; I was going to tell you: I'm taking birth-control pills."

A mixture of relief and delicious excitement coursed through Greg, though he realized he knew little about how the pills worked. "How long have you been taking them?"

"Well," Suzy said with a giggle. "After we got back together in Galveston, you might say I had an inkling. It's been a month."

"I'm sorry if I pushed too hard."

"You were sweet about it," she said. "And you were partly right about why I was stalling. But mainly, I wanted to wait until I was sure the pills were doing what they were supposed to do, and that they wouldn't make me sick."

"And everything's okay?"

"Couldn't be better."

"How'd you get a prescription?"

"This is supposed to be very confidential: Nurses and student nurses can get them from the hospital pharmacy without a prescription. My roommate Cindy was taking them. She told me how to get them."

"And you're sure they work?"

"I'm sure now. I'll tell you all the biological reasons sometime."

Greg got the hint. He drove hurriedly around Fort Worth's west side looking for a place to get something to eat. The only place they found open was the Blue Star Inn, a Chinese restaurant. They ordered some food to go and rushed toward Suzy's house.

"I guess you have to find a Buddhist to get something to eat on Christmas night," Greg said, impatience nagging at him.

As they drove through downtown, its buildings outlined in Christmas lights, Greg's mind flashed to the previous summer, to the going-away party and his impotent encounter with Sharon Rogers, then his subsequent visit to Dr. Simon.

Oh, please; not tonight, he thought.

❖

They hastily dropped off the bags of Chinese food on the dining-room table. Suzy took Greg's hand and led him down the hall to her bedroom. They stood next to the bed in near darkness, the only illumination coming from light in the hallway.

The years of stifled desire boiled over.

They kissed frantically and firmly ground their bodies together. Then, still standing, they slowly undressed each other. Greg reached down, pulled the bedspread back, and lowered Suzy onto the sheets.

Suddenly, Suzy rolled onto her side, away from Greg, her shoulders shaking with sobs.

His heavy breaths slowed. He felt cast adrift and groped for something to say. A hint of panic churned in his stomach.

"Suzy," he finally said. "What's the matter?"

She shook her head and wept. No words came out.

"My God. Was it something I did?"

"No, no," she said.

Greg held her shoulders as she cried. Finally, it dawned on him. "It's what happened in Waco, isn't it?"

Suzy nodded.

"The guy at Baylor?"

Suzy turned her face back toward him. "Yes, it's him."

"But I'm not him, Suzy." Greg caressed her face with his hand and wiped her tears.

"I know, Greg, but. . . ."

"Look, that's over." Greg pulled her close and held her, his face next to hers. "Suzy, I'm with you for good. I'd never do anything to hurt you."

"I know; I trust you." Suzy put her arms back around him. "I didn't think those old wounds would surface again, but getting in bed like this brought it all back."

"Did he hurt you? I mean physically?"

"He was very rough. I wouldn't say he raped me, but I felt cornered and didn't see any way out."

"You didn't tell me that."

"He was such a bastard, I've tried not to think about it."

"Suzy, it hurts me to know you've had to bear all that. I love you so much, I'd do anything to stop some creep like that from hurting you. You have to believe me."

"I do, Greg. I never felt this way about him or anyone. I love you so, my darlin'."

Suzy pulled Greg close. He kissed up and down her neck, then all over her face, her eyelids, her ears. The aroma of Suzy's perfume, mixed with the clean fragrance of her skin, filled Greg's senses.

Suzy's inhibitions collapsed, and she embraced him wildly. There was some clumsiness getting started, and Suzy giggled as Greg made a course correction.

"Are you okay?" he asked, before going any further.

"Very okay," she said.

The release of their long-bottled-up longing propelled them to a white-hot peak in no time. Greg lay spent in Suzy's arms.

"I'm sorry," he whispered. "I guess I was over-eager."

"It's okay," she said. "We both were. I'm not going anywhere."

They lay there a long time, exploring the terrain of each other's skin, relishing the depths of intimacy, holding each other gently, with a certainty nothing could separate them.

As they lay with their naked bodies entwined, pressing against each other again, Suzy sensed Greg's returning vitality.

"Hey, I have an idea," she whispered, sounding full of mischief and jabbing Greg in the ribs. "I hope you don't think I'm crazy."

"What's your idea?"

"Let's take a shower together." Suzy nuzzled at Greg's chest.

The suggestion both surprised and excited Greg. "Come on, my little Baptist trollop."

"I've been saving all this just for you," she said, giggling as she led him down the hall to the bathroom.

They stood under the warm shower, playfully exploring each other's body as they slathered each other with soap.

In college, they had touched all the private places in the darkness of Greg's car, parked along secluded lanes. Tonight, they had first made love in the dim glow of Suzy's bedroom. But now, in the full, vibrant light of the bathroom, Greg got his first unobstructed view of Suzy's fully mature body. It took his breath away.

Their lips met in long, wet, tongue-embracing kisses, and their bodies slid languorously against each other on their soapy surfaces.

"Let's rinse off," Greg said. "I can't wait any longer."

They made a half-hearted attempt to dry each other, then hurried, dripping, back to the bedroom. They were less frantic now, more deliberate, and, this time, more sure of themselves. Time seemed suspended in time as their joy rose unabated. Greg had never known such pleasure, and as they descended from their peak of delight, Suzy shook her head and sighed, "Oh, Greg. I never dreamed. . . ."

Now, exhausted and starved, they sat half-dressed at the dining table feasting on chow mein and egg foo young from the Blue Star Inn.

They ate, absorbed in each other's sight and presence, saying little as they ate but marveling at their night together.

"Did we actually do all that?" Greg said, chuckling and shaking his head.

"Can you believe it?" Suzy said. "Just think what we've got to look forward to."

"I hope we didn't spoil our wedding night by jumping the gun."

"I'm not worried about that anymore," Suzy said, sipping the iced tea she'd made. "Tonight was our wedding night. Just think of it that way."

"We've got a lot of details to think about," Greg said, hating to come back to earth but knowing they couldn't avoid reality forever.

"Yes," Suzy said, "And I want the wedding to be at the Botanic Garden, for sure."

"Couldn't hardly be anyplace else after today," Greg said, scooping more rice onto his plate.

"Is this spring too soon?" Suzy got up to rinse her plate in the kitchen sink.

"Maybe not. How about late spring?" Greg followed her to the kitchen.

"June is the month for weddings," Suzy said. "I'll have finals in May, so June might work. Of course, there's the summer semester. Maybe we could get married during the break."

"Will it be Baptist or Episcopal, or what?" Greg contemplated the obstacles.

"Oh, my," Suzy said, putting the plates in the dishwasher. "Now we're getting to the hard part."

"I'm sure my uncle would marry us," Greg said, putting his hands on Suzy's shoulders.

"Well, we'll have to think about that a little. Can you have two ministers?"

"I guess so," Greg said. "What are you thinking?"

"I was thinking of Mother and Daddy." Suzy was calculating. "They'll be upset if I don't ask Brother Armstrong, the pastor at our church. He watched me grow up."

"It's okay with me, if that's what you want." But Greg suddenly felt a surge of dread.

"It could be tricky." Suzy shook her head.

"Well, look, we have a long time to sort all that out." They walked back to the living room and sat on the sofa. "Right now, we need to think about tomorrow," Greg said. "We have to tell both sets of parents."

"Oh, that," Suzy said. "Well, you'd better not stay here tonight. Why don't I call you when my folks get home tomorrow, and you can come over? We'll tell them then."

"What about my folks?" Greg said. "You haven't met them."

"I met your dad that time he spoke at Trinity Valley."

"That's right, you were with me. Maybe we can tell your folks and then go over to my house."

"Okay. What time do you have to leave for Galveston?"

"Probably no later than five or six." Greg's mood suddenly darkened. "Do your folks know about my anxiety problems?"

"I told Daddy a little bit. I don't think he's worried about it."

"But your mother is something else."

"I don't know. I'll talk to her. Her sister's had those kinds of problems."

Greg's head sagged. "One more strike against Spencer, I guess."

"Now, come on." Suzy moved closer and hugged him. "It won't be that bad."

They kissed and soon were wrapped tightly in each other's arms. They moved back to the bedroom and made love again.

Greg drove home with a full heart. Yet, his joy was tempered by the shadows of fear and dread. He'd always cherish the day he'd just spent with Suzy, but he faced the fact that each of them would be marrying a family as well as a person, and that knowledge gave him a queasy feeling.

❖

Greg's fears weren't unfounded. After lunch the next day, he drove back to the Coxes' home. Suzy's parents had returned from Stephenville, and Suzy's siblings and their families had dispersed to their own homes in the area.

"Mother, Daddy," Suzy said, "let's sit down. Greg and I have something to tell you." She sat on the sofa and held up her left hand, displaying the ring. "Greg and I got engaged yesterday."

Floyd Cox jumped to his feet and rushed to them. "By golly, you kids have really made an old man happy." He hugged Suzy, then grasped Greg's hand in a crunching grip and pumped Greg's arm ferociously.

Mrs. Cox didn't say a word. She sat stolidly in her easy chair and stared at them in silent contempt.

"Well, Greg," Floyd Cox beamed. "Have you all set a date yet?"

"No, sir." Tension wrenched Greg's body. "We were thinking about June, when Suzy's semester is over, but we have a lot of details to work out."

"Why, of course," Mr. Cox said, sitting back down. "You let us know if we can help you, but we understand it's your wedding."

"Thanks, Mr. Cox." Greg took Suzy's hand. "I want to do whatever makes Suzy happy."

"That's what we like to hear, Greg; isn't it, Nadine?" Mr. Cox turned to his wife.

"Well," Mrs. Cox said with a sigh. "I suppose the Lord moves in mysterious ways."

"Have you kids told Greg's folks?" Mr. Cox asked.

"Not yet," Suzy said. "We're just going over there now."

"Well, we'll have to meet them, too," her father said. "When the time is right, of course."

"Maybe we can all have dinner together later," Greg said. "I have to get back to Galveston pretty soon."

"Well, God bless both of you," Mr. Cox said, his eyes rimming with moisture.

"Thanks, Mr. Cox," Greg said. "We appreciate your support." He glanced at Mrs. Cox, still sitting stone-faced.

Mr. Cox walked with Greg and Suzy to the front door. Greg opened the door for Suzy, and she went outside.

Mr. Cox grabbed Greg's shoulder. "Can I have a word with you, Greg?"

"Sure."

"You're very much in love with Suzanne, aren't you?"

"Yes, sir. More than I can tell you."

"That's all I need to know. God bless you, son."

Greg and Suzy drove to his parents' house.

"Suzy, you've got to talk to your mother," Greg said, turning onto East Winchester Avenue. "I think she hates my guts."

"She's just shocked, Greg. I didn't tell you what she thought about Sidney."

"She didn't like him, either?"

"Oh, just the opposite. He was studying to be a minister, and—Mother is very religious—she thought I'd found Mister Right, a guy studying to be a Baptist preacher. She was thrilled to death."

"Oh, God," Greg groaned.

"She had a hard time believing what a fraud he was—of course she doesn't know all the details—and I'm not sure she's gotten over it yet."

"How can we get past that hurdle?" Greg said, driving onto his parents' street.

"I'm pretty good at changing her mind. When you leave, I'll spend some time with her and see what I can do. I'll be here another week."

They went into the Spencers' house. Vivian was cleaning the kitchen stove after her holiday cooking marathon. George sat in his favorite chair reading *Seven Days in May*. George had the week off between Christmas and New Year's. Greg's aunt and cousins had left to visit other friends and relatives in Fort Worth.

"Mother, I want you to meet Suzy Cox." They stepped inside the kitchen.

"Oh, my word," Vivian said, untying her apron. "I wondered if Greg was ever going to introduce us, Suzy. I'm glad to meet you. Please excuse my mess."

"My mother is probably doing the same thing," Suzy said. "It's so nice to finally meet you, Mrs. Spencer."

"Let's go in the living room," Greg said.

George put down his book and took off his horn-rimmed reading glasses as they entered.

"Dad, this is Suzy Cox. I think you met her at Trinity Valley."

"Oh, that's right." George stood up and formally extended his hand. "How are you, Suzy? I hope you're keeping Greg out of trouble."

"Oh, I'm trying." Suzy blushed.

"Y'all sit down," George motioned toward the sofa. Vivian came in from the kitchen and sat down across from George.

After some obligatory small talk, Greg finally said, "Well, we wanted to tell you Suzy and I are going to get married."

Suzy held up her ring and beamed.

"Oh, Greg!" Vivian's jaw dropped. "You're not kidding, are you?"

"No, Mother."

Vivian grabbed her forehead. "I think I need a tranquilizer."

"Congratulations, Greg and Suzy," George said. "Now, Suzy, you really will have to keep Greg out of trouble."

"Yes," Vivian said, gathering her wits. "Congratulations, you two. Give me a hug, Suzy. Let me look at your ring."

"Thank you. I'm so happy," Suzy said as Vivian examined the diamond.

"Greg had good taste; it's beautiful."

"He bought it in Galveston, all by himself." Suzy patted Greg's shoulder.

"After looking at about a thousand rings," Greg said.

"Suzy, I love your hair," Vivian said. "You look so pretty. Greg is a very lucky boy."

"Uh, Mother, I'll be twenty-five in a few months," Greg broke in.

"Oh, you're still just boys and girls to me," Vivian said.

Greg looked at Suzy and rolled his eyes. She stifled a grin.

"Would y'all like something to drink?" Vivian asked. "Oh, and we've got some chocolate pie left over from yesterday. How about a slice?"

"Sure," Greg said. "Suzy?"

"I'd love it. Can I help you, Mrs. Spencer?"

"Sure, come on in the kitchen."

As the two women left the room, George said, "Greg," and motioned him to stay behind.

"What is it?" Greg was perturbed.

"Does Suzy know about your nervous trouble?" George said under his breath.

"My God, Dad," Greg muttered. "Is that all you can think of?"

"No, but she needs to know."

"She knows. I told her everything, okay?"

"Okay, just wondering."

"Besides, she's training to be a psychiatric nurse." Greg was angry now. "Can we just can it?"

"Okay, okay. Cool down. Let's go get some pie."

Later that day, Greg loaded his suitcase into the car. He drove Suzy to her parents' house and planned to leave for Galveston from there. They parked in the driveway and sat talking. The sky had turned blue-gray, and a light rain fell. A cold norther was blowing through Fort Worth.

"All my dad could think about," Greg was saying, "was if I'd told you about my 'nervous trouble.'"

"He cares about you, Greg," Suzy said, raindrops pelting the window behind her. "It upsets you to talk about it, doesn't it?"

"Yeah, I guess I'm pretty defensive." Greg shook his head. "And I don't know what to do about the problem."

"You mean about getting some help?"

"Yeah, Dr. Simon told me about a shrink in Galveston I should see, a Dr. Brooks. Do you know him?"

"He spoke to one of my classes. He's a psychoanalyst, from what I gathered. I got the idea he doesn't see patients anymore."

"Is there anyone at UTMB you'd recommend?"

"Well, maybe. Let me do some checking."

"Suzy, let's not dwell on it. You may be all I need, and I've got you."

"Okay, but don't be afraid to talk about it. You know I want to help."

"I'd better go," Greg said. "Good luck with your mother."
"I may need it," Suzy said, then paused. "Greg?"
"Yeah."
"I'll never forget yesterday. It was the happiest day of my life."
"Mine, too. I love you."
"And I love you. Be careful driving in this weather." Suzy got out and walked to her front door.

As Greg pulled out of the driveway, sleet pellets pinged off the car as he headed south. The glow of his feelings for Suzy slowly gave way to memories of sleet falling that December night in 1958, and of Eddie's car skidding across the Lake Arlington dam before crashing through the guardrail. His gut tightened, and he had trouble keeping his mind on the road for a few minutes.

❖

The sleet slackened and stopped as Greg drove south along I-45, but a light drizzle fell. As he neared Houston, the sky turned even darker, and heavy rain, with crackling lightning and thunder, descended on the coastal plains. Greg tried to find a weather report on his car radio, but loud crashes of static made reception difficult. He presumed the same cold front that had raked Fort Worth was just knifing into the area, lifting the humid air and igniting the boiling storms.

In spite of the gloomy weather, Greg looked forward to getting back to Galveston. He felt a renewed commitment to his job, and in a week Suzy would return from Fort Worth. They'd be together, away from the distraction of parents, and they could plan their future with a greater sense of independence.

At work that week, Greg moved smoothly through his routine, relishing the slow pace of the holidays. There was little local news: a few traffic accidents, a fire, and the threat of a longshoremen's strike. News from Washington and Saigon dominated the headlines, and Jeff took care of those stories from the AP wire.

Greg told Jeff he and Suzy were engaged, and Jeff quickly spread the word around the newsroom. Greg accepted congratulations all through the day.

"Ahh, Gregorio," Tony Rodriguez said with his throaty chuckle, "So you got a little, eh?"

Even Irene Dubois offered her congratulations when she turned in a story that afternoon. Greg appreciated her olive branch and graciously thanked her.

Seth Yeager and Jim Stephens came in for only an hour or two each day that week between Christmas and New Year's. Stephens told Greg that reporter Roy Sanger, who usually worked the city desk on Greg's days off, was on vacation. That meant Greg would have to work on New Year's Eve and New Year's Day.

Greg had hoped to drive to Fort Worth to spend the holiday with Suzy, but he had to alter his plans. Near the end of the week, he called her on the *Star*'s free, long-distance WATS line.

"Oh, Greg," Suzy said. "I was counting so much on you being here."

"I know," he said, lighting a cigarette. "It stinks. I'll have to work twelve straight days."

"And what makes it worse," Suzy said, "is that as soon as I get back, I've got to study for finals. They're the next week. We probably won't see much of each other."

"Think we're being punished for our wanton behavior Christmas day?"

Suzy laughed. "The Lord moves in mysterious ways."

"Speaking of that, have you talked to your mother?"

She sighed. "Yeah, but I don't think I made much headway."

"Can't you and your dad gang up on her?" Greg stubbed his cigarette in the ashtray and reached into his shirt pocket for another.

"I'll keep trying. Don't give up."

"Okay, I've gotta go. The printers are waiting. Love you."

"Love you, too. Call when you can."

Greg and Jeff came downstairs from the composing room. Dan Forbes had just returned from his night at the police station.

"What are you guys doing New Year's Eve?" Jeff asked, gathering up some loose papers on his desk.

"I've got no plans," Dan said.

"Me, either," Greg said. "We'll be here pretty late."

"Maybe not too late," Jeff said. "We'll probably lock up early, just like Christmas Eve."

"Nowhere much to go, though," Greg said. "I guess we can celebrate at Lolita's or Lafitte's."

"Well," Jeff said. "I got a call today from Lester Hastings, and he invited me to his New Year's Eve bash at his place. He said bring a couple of guests if I wanted to. How about it?"

"Hastings?" Dan said. "I hear he's nuts."

"He's pretty weird all right," Jeff said. "Anyway, his parties are something to behold."

❖

Galveston
January 1965

Winter fog settled over Galveston Island on New Year's Eve. Dan and Greg rode with Jeff as he headed cautiously west, then turned north to a remote part of the island Greg had never seen.

They passed along a high limestone wall. Somewhere beyond the wall, a bright light glowed in the foggy sky. Jeff pulled into a driveway. The car faced a massive iron gate. Jeff got out and walked toward the gate, then stopped and opened a metal panel. He pushed a button, and a slightly effeminate voice boomed from a speaker, "Welcome to the Hastings Ranch, sucker. Who may I tell Lester is calling?"

"Jeff Holcomb and two friends," Jeff spoke into the intercom.

"Just a minute," the voice said. Then a few seconds later, "Okay, Jeff, Lester says get your sorry ass in here."

Jeff walked back to the car, and the trio heard several buzzes and clanks coming from the gate. An electric motor made a grinding noise, and the gate slowly opened.

They drove along a narrow road, paved with brick.

Ahead, through the fog, the house came into view—if one could call it a house. It was a sprawling, three-story structure of white marble and stone, with frilly, Baroque sculpture around the windows and a mosque-like dome above the roof.

Dan and Greg gasped at the sight.

"Lester calls it his 'ranch house,'" Jeff said.

Jeff parked along the brick drive. Dozens of parked cars lined the side of the road. They had to walk a hundred yards to the house.

Once there, another intercom greeted them at the front door. The same voice as before rasped from the speaker. "Okay, Jeff, you and your entourage may enter."

A young man opened the tall oak door. He wore a starched tuxedo collar and shirtfront, a white bow tie—and nothing else.

Greg and Dan looked at each other, then at Jeff, who wore a bemused grin. Greg tried to remain cool and said nothing. But he thought, *Holy shit!*

"Come in, Jeff and friends. Lester awaits your company," the young man said. "Please get something to eat and drink. You'll find champagne in the fountains and a bar in the corner." Then, he added, "Oh, and feel free to snuggle by the fire if you wish. And when you're comfortable, please come back here and I'll take you to Lester. He'd like to speak to you."

Greg and Dan shot befuddled looks at each other again, then looked out across the vast room, sunken below entry level and packed with people, some dancing, others standing and talking. The room was dim and smoky, with only a few indirect light sources and candles burning in large candelabra spaced around the room. An acrid smell hung over the place. Greg's eyes adjusted to the low light. Waiters moved among the guests with hors d'oeuvres and trays with glasses of champagne.

Loud, piercing, rock-and-roll music boomed from a bandstand at one end of the room The group was playing "House of the Rising Sun."

"Jesus Christ," Greg shouted through the din. "Some of these people are bare-assed naked."

"Sure looks that way," Dan said.

"Let's go get a drink," Jeff shouted above the noise.

The three of them squirmed through the smoky crowd. Along the back wall, they had to navigate past several knots of people huddled around Turkish water pipes—hookahs—smoking the contents and laughing heartily.

"What's that stuff they're smoking?" Greg shouted to Jeff.

"Probably hashish," Jeff yelled back.

"What's that?"

"Cannabis. Similar to pot."

They reached the bar and ordered drinks. Several naked bodies squeezed past them. The band stopped playing and appeared to be taking a break.

A short young man in a party hat stepped to the bandstand microphone and announced:

"Five minutes to midnight. Everyone outside for fireworks!"

The crowd moved toward a set of huge wooden doors on the north side of the house. Greg, Jeff, and Dan moved with the flow out onto a wide patio overlooking Galveston Bay.

On a dock jutting into the bay, stood a brightly lit silver spire, reaching fifty feet into the air. On top of the spire was a glittering sphere, covered with tiny mirrors—the kind of orb one often finds suspended from a ballroom ceiling. Greg surmised the device was intended to replicate the ball that dropped at midnight in New York's Times Square.

Shortly, the ball started downward. The crowd cheered, and as the ball reached the bottom, rockets fired and colored fireworks exploded across the sky. People in the crowd blew noisemakers, cheering and laughing as another series of rockets shot into the air.

The fireworks display lasted fifteen minutes. The grand finale featured a billboard-sized frame along the shore that lit up in giant sparklers and spelled out:

LESTER WISHES YOU MANY ORGASMS IN 1965

Greg and his two friends headed back inside.

"All this is a little beyond me," Greg said.

"I know," Dan said. "I guess a guy could get laid, with all these chicks running around naked, but it looks like they're all spoken for."

"I guess you'd expect that," Greg said.

"Let's go talk to Lester," Jeff said. "I think the main reason he invited us was to talk about some big project he's working on."

❖

The semi-nude doorman led them up a sweeping curved staircase and down a long hallway. They entered a large, darkened room with several spotlights trained on an oversized bathtub, sitting atop an elevated section of marble floor. Three naked teenage boys stood near the tub.

"Y'all run on; I'll see you later," a voice from the tub said.

As Greg climbed the steps surrounding the tub, he could see Lester Hastings's head poking out from an expanse of white bubbles.

"Jeffrey," Lester said. "You lads come on in. There are some chairs back here. Grab a seat."

"Hello, Lester," Jeff said. "Are you comfortable?"

"Now that you ask, Jeffrey, I'm never comfortable. I'm bored out of my friggin' mind."

"But, Lester, I thought you had some big plans." Jeff pulled his folding chair closer to the bathtub.

"Oh, hell, I've always got plans. Who are your buddies? They're from the *Star*, too, I take it?"

"This is Greg Spencer, our city editor. You met him at Lolita's. And this is Dan Forbes. He's our police reporter."

"Spencer, yes, I sort of remember. Forbes? Are you related to Malcolm?"

"Afraid not," Dan said.

"Well, next time I see old Malcolm, I'll tell him I've got a boy in Galveston who might be his nephew. How's that sound?"

"Yeah, if he's got a little cash he doesn't need," Dan said. "I'll take it off his hands."

Hastings chuckled. "Okay, men. Here's what I want to talk about: You know I control my family's wealth. Only trouble is, we're not near as rich as most people think. We need to increase our cash flow to get things back on track. So, I've arranged to open a chain of luxury hotels all over the country. Our other interests just aren't enough anymore, so I had to make a big decision. I think I've made a blockbuster deal."

The three men from the *Star* looked at each other.

"So, how does that involve us?" Jeff asked.

"Ahh, you know, Jeff, I've gotten some pretty bad press these last few years, especially from the Houston papers. I just wanted to kinda feel you out about getting this story out in the *Star*. I could've met with Yeager, but I don't think the old bastard trusts me. I'd like to know if you think the *Star* could give me a good write-up about this hotel deal."

"How much money is involved?"

"I'm not at liberty to say right now, Jeff, but take my word: it's a substantial amount. We'll release a figure when we make the announcement."

"Do you have any local investors?"

"Oh, hell, yes. But let me tell you something." Hastings paused. "Now, this is off the record, Jeff. You know Jesse Sanchez, who runs the Riviera Club?"

"I know of him," Jeff said.

"Well, you know when the state cleaned out all the gambling in town, all those dagoes moved to Las Vegas. They sent Jesse down here to sort of keep the pot boiling, you might say. Well, Jesse put me back in touch with some of those guys in Vegas, and we worked out a sweet deal." Lester grinned broadly and rubbed his palms together. "Just listen to this: They need cash. We loan them money, and they kick back a certain amount from their 'off-the-books' operations. We clean up their money, it increases the value of the Hastings Corporation, and we attract more investors for the hotel deal."

"Is it legal, Lester?" Jeff asked.

"My lawyers say it is," Hastings said. "But I don't want to go into the details in the paper. You understand?"

"I don't know, Lester. Yeager would have to approve anything we wrote, and I'm not even city editor any more. Greg here is. He'd have to assign a reporter, and we'd have to check the story out."

Greg felt on the spot. His muscles tightened.

"Why, God damn you, Holcomb," Hastings exploded. "I'm trying to give you a scoop, and here you go nit-picking the best deal I ever made. Hell, I wish we'd never sold the *Star* to those bastards in Houston. Then, we could print whatever we pleased. But we needed the damn money." Hastings thrashed around in the tub and scattered the frothy bubbles about.

"Calm down, Lester. What about it, Greg? How would you handle this?"

"Like you said, we'd have to run it by Yeager," Greg said, trying to hide his nervousness. "He's the final authority."

"Well, shit! You fuckers don't recognize a good story when I drop it in your lap." Hastings puckered his face in a pout.

"When do you plan to announce it, Lester?" Jeff asked.

"Sometime this spring, we hope."

"Let's all sit tight for a while," Jeff said. "And see what we can work out."

"I don't know why I bothered you shitheads." Hastings said and swatted at the foam in front of him. "I was going to fix y'all up with some of our sweet young things, but now, I say to hell with it."

"Have it your way, Lester," Jeff said. "We don't want you getting the wrong idea. Yeager runs a pretty tight ship."

"Well, all of you newspaper fuckheads can just kiss my rusty ass."

"Okay, Lester," Jeff said. "Is that it?"

"That's it. Get lost."

Greg, Jeff, and Dan walked out into the hall.

"See these sorry bastards out, Jimmy," Lester shouted from his elevated tub. The man with the tuxedo front and dangling genitals escorted them through the crowd to the front door.

❖

They passed out the gate of the Hastings estate and made their way through the foggy night.

"Is Hastings really that crazy?" Dan asked Jeff. "That he'd tell us about pulling an illegal scam like that when he's trying to get some publicity?"

"He's that crazy," Jeff said. "Plus no telling what kinds of chemicals he had inside him tonight."

"Jesus," Greg said. "If he's that screwed up, how did he ever get control of the family fortune?"

"It was a long legal battle between him and his sister." Jeff pulled onto Seawall Boulevard. "Lester had the blessing of his aunt, who was the family power before him. She lived to be ninety-something and became very confused in her last years. Lester and his lawyers managed to get her to name him executor of the estate, squeezing out his sister Christine."

"Has the *Star* ever printed anything about what a nut he is?" Dan asked.

"I've talked to Yeager about him," Jeff said. "It's only been two years since Hastings sold the *Star* to the Houston owners, and naturally the *Star* never said anything negative about Lester as long as his family owned the paper. I think Yeager wants the current ownership to get more established before we take on the Hastings family. They still wield a lot of power."

"But, Jeff," Greg piped up. "What he's talking about could involve hundreds of millions of dollars, coming from the mob in Las Vegas." Greg paused, considering the scenario. "We can't ignore that."

"Well," Jeff said. "We'd have to get some corroboration that Lester is really planning something like that. It would take some digging, and it might be impossible."

"But shouldn't we talk to Yeager and tell him what Lester said?" Greg lit a cigarette and cracked open a side window.

Jeff sighed. "I guess we should. But Lester's such a wild man, we don't know if there's a grain of truth to what he said."

The next day, the three of them met with Seth Yeager. They told him what Lester had told them.

Yeager puffed on his pipe and sat mulling over the information.

"Could be just Lester running his mouth when he's drunk," Yeager said.

"That's possible, all right," Jeff said. "But maybe we could have Dan here sniff around some of his unsavory sources and see if he can pick up something."

"Good idea," Yeager said. "We might also see if some of our society people hear anything among the island elite."

"Some of them go back to the time Hastings owned the *Star*," Greg said. "Can we trust them to be discreet?"

"That's a good point, Greg," Yeager said. "Mary Beth McBride is the only person in women's news I hired. She worked for me in Abilene, and I trust her. Let's bring her in on this."

Mary Beth, the *Star*'s society editor, sat working at her typewriter in one corner of the newsroom. Yeager called to her and motioned her to come in. Her high heels clicked into the office. Mary Beth was a pert brunette in her early thirties.

"Mary Beth," Yeager said. "We've got a tip that Lester Hastings may try to pull off a big money deal involving luxury hotels and the mob in Las Vegas. Keep your ear to the ground when you're with some of the bigwigs in town. Greg will coordinate anything we get on this, so let him know if you hear anything."

"Wow," Mary Beth smiled. "This sounds juicy."

"Keep it under your hat," Yeager said. "For now, don't say anything to the others in your section, okay?"

"Okay, Mr. Yeager," she said.

"Greg, if anyone learns anything, you get with Dan and Mary Beth and share information. Let's keep on top of it, even though it may just be some of Lester's drunk talk." Yeager pounded his pipe on the edge of his ashtray to empty the charred tobacco remains.

The rest of the week went routinely for Greg. Numerous stories came in from city and county reporters in a flurry of activity on their beats in the first week of the new year.

The best news Greg received was that Suzy had returned to Galveston. Although she'd be preoccupied with final exams, any time he could spend with her would be like a warm breeze.

❖

Greg hardly saw Suzy for the next ten days. Studying for and taking her exams consumed her days, and Greg had no time off for nearly two weeks. But they talked on the phone at night and met for lunch a few times. He took her to a delicatessen he'd discovered across 25th Street from his apartment, run by two Polish women who had numbers tattooed on their forearms from their years in Auschwitz.

Greg told Suzy about Lester Hastings's New Year's Eve party.

"Oh, Greg!" She slapped her hand over her mouth. "People were running around naked?"

"Yes, and smoking dope. A pretty depraved scene."

"You stay away from people like that!" Suzy giggled. "Look what you get into when I'm out of town. Your dad told me to keep you out of trouble."

"This guy is the richest man in Galveston," Greg said. "And he blabbed to us about a big, illegal money deal he's involved in."

"Was he serious?"

"There's no telling; he's about half nuts. I'll bet he's been in the psych ward at Sealy. You want to play reporter and check it out? We might do a story on his antics."

"Oh, no," Suzy said, now looking serious. "I've got enough to keep me busy, thanks."

"Well, I'm sure that kind of information is well concealed, but we may want to know at some point."

"Nope," Suzy said. "But if I hear something. . . . What's the guy's name again?"

"Hastings. Lester Hastings. His family owns half the town."

"Yeah, I've heard the name," Suzy said. "There's the Hastings National Bank."

"Right, and Hastings Savings and Loan, Hastings Construction, Hastings Shipping Company, and several of the big hotels in town."

"I'd better get back to the dorm," Suzy said. "Two more finals tomorrow."

Greg dropped Suzy back at UTMB, feeling the injustice of both their lousy schedules.

After final exams, Suzy and her roommate, Cindy O'Donnell, decided to move out of the student nurses' dormitory and into an apartment adjacent to the medical school. They drafted Greg to help, along with Cindy's boyfriend, Brian Reynolds, a fourth-year medical student from Amarillo. Brian stood about six feet tall and had thinning reddish-blond hair. He spoke with a warm but slightly raspy West Texas accent.

All day Saturday, they hauled belongings from the dorm to the new dwelling, then they all collapsed from exhaustion.

Cindy broke out a bottle of wine and served the tired movers. Cindy, who was from Odessa, wore her hair short with bangs cut straight across her forehead. Like Brian, she had a homey West Texas drawl.

As they talked and joked, Greg's fondness grew for Brian and Cindy. Both West Texans, they were a friendly, down-to-earth pair who showed more interest in Greg and Suzy than in talking about themselves.

"Hey, we need to get together and double date," Brian said. "I guess you can still double date when you're engaged, can't you?"

"Why not?" Suzy poured a fresh glass of wine for each of them.

Greg liked the idea, though he and Suzy had scarcely been alone since her final exams ended.

"Brian's got a membership at the Jack Tar Captain's Club," Cindy said. "We could go nightclubbing some night. Do y'all like to dance?"

"Oh, yes," Suzy said. "Greg and I haven't been dancing since college."

"Suzy's the good dancer," Greg said. "I just let her lead me around the floor."

"Oh, you do not," Suzy said with mock indignation.

"I'm not really a paying member of the club," Brian said. "Med students get complimentary memberships. But it's a nice club. They usually have a piano trio for dancing."

"How about tomorrow night?" Greg said.

The two couples met at the girls' apartment and drove around the island for a while, allowing Greg to point out some local attractions.

"What's that huge old mansion with all the turrets?" Brian asked.

"That's the Bishop's Palace," Greg said. "You should see the gigantic timbers the builders used to hold it together. It was built in the 1850s and has survived every storm since, including the

1900 hurricane. The Catholic Church bought it when the original owner died. Can you imagine people actually living in that castle?"

"Damn, Greg," Brian said. "You ought to work for the chamber of commerce. I've driven by that place for four years but didn't know much about it."

"And there's that big white church," Cindy said. "Only it looks more like a mosque than a church."

"Yeah, Sacred Heart." Greg said. "It was modeled after a church in Spain, which had a lot of Muslim influence."

"Where'd you learn all this stuff?" Brian asked.

"Mainly just by poking around and reading what our reporters write. You pick up a lot of information when you read every local story that goes in the paper."

They pulled into the Jack Tar Hotel at Broadway and Seawall Boulevard. Heavy surf pounded the seawall as they went inside. A full moon rose over the Gulf to the east.

Greg and Suzy held each other close as they danced to the tasteful trio music at the Captain's Club. Their touch reminded them of what they'd been missing for nearly three weeks.

"Let's get out of here," Greg whispered in Suzy's ear.

"Can we leave gracefully?" She glanced over Greg's shoulder at Brian and Cindy at a table across the room.

"Leave it to me."

When the band took its next break, Greg told Brian and Cindy they were still feeling achy and tired from the move.

"Hey, Greg." Brian smiled knowingly. "We know y'all haven't been alone in a while. Why don't you get lost?"

"How will you get home?" Greg asked.

"Hell, it's only about four or five blocks to Cindy's place," Brian said. "Seems like a nice night for a walk."

"You're sure?" Suzy said.

Cindy giggled and took a sip from her drink. "Go on, beat it, you two."

Greg and Suzy headed for Greg's apartment. There, for the first time since Christmas, they made urgent love as the sounds of the heavy surf floated through an open window from a block away.

Afterward, as Suzy dressed, Greg asked, "Heard anything new from your mother?"

"I called her last night, and she broke down crying when I brought up our wedding."

"Sounds to me like a lost cause," Greg said, lighting a cigarette.

"I'm at my wit's end with her," Suzy said.

"Would it help if I tried to talk to her?"

"Maybe," Suzy said. "After all, she doesn't really know you very well. We could drive up there some weekend."

"I'm not much of a salesman," Greg said. "But I guess I can try."

❖

February 1965

Greg and Jeff sat drinking beer at Lolita's after work one night. Dan Forbes rushed into the room and yanked up a chair.

"Listen to this," Dan said, catching his breath. "I just talked to a guy who knows something about Lester Hastings's big hotel deal."

"Who is he?" Greg asked, lighting up a filter-tipped Kool.

"He used to be Hastings's chauffeur," Dan said, trying to keep from shouting over the Greek music blaring from the jukebox. They sat at a table in an empty corner.

"He knows Jimmy Diehl, who's Lester's top assistant," Dan went on. "That's the guy we met at the party; the half-naked character that let us in and took us to see Lester."

"What'd he tell you?" Jeff asked.

"He says Lester's been flirting with the mob for some time, and he wouldn't be surprised if Lester made a deal with them. Lester's desperate for money, and also desperate to prove to others in the family that he has the balls to make the kind of deals his father and grandfather were famous for."

"What else?" Greg asked.

"That's about it—so far," Dan said.

"That's a start," Greg said. "But it's not enough. It's just hearsay. Can you talk to this guy again?"

"I think so. I've got his phone number."

"Ask him if he has any first-hand knowledge of any contact between Lester and anyone from the mob," Jeff said. "You know, he might have driven Lester to pick up somebody at the airport or something. We've got to establish some contact before we can go on with this."

"And Dan," Greg added. "I know you like to imbibe, but it's important for you to stay sober when dealing with these sources. You've got to have a clear head and make damned sure you get things right."

"I know that," Dan said defensively. "You don't have to tell me."

"Good," Jeff said. "Keep after it."

Dan was unable to learn much more from his source. Weeks passed with no new developments in the Lester Hastings story.

Greg's relations with reporters improved. He seldom had to confront them anymore. The questions he'd raised with them earlier had made them more conscious of their writing and news-gathering. Now, they came to him with their own questions about their stories, seeking his opinion or stamp of approval. He had gained a modicum of respect as their first-line editor.

Stan Richter remained the exception. He still came to work in shorts and flip-flop sandals and turned in sloppily written stories. He focused most of his attention on his sailing hobby. Greg talked to Seth Yeager about him.

"I've tried to figure out what to do with Stan," Yeager said. "The head of the visitor's bureau told me he was thinking about offering Stan a job with them as their PR man. I guess we can hope."

"Anything we can do to hurry him along?" Greg asked.

"Hang in there, Greg," Yeager said with a smile. "Every newspaper has a Stan Richter or two."

❖

Greg had been in Galveston for six months. Everything about living and working on the island seemed easier now that Suzy was nearby. He felt more securely bonded in his friendships with Dan Forbes and, especially, Jeff Holcomb.

Jeff had a mothering quality about him. He had taken Greg under his wing from the start and helped him through some difficult times as Greg had learned his job. Jeff had taught Greg much about Galveston and its people, and he'd shown Greg the sometimes dark underside of island life. Greg placed a high value on Jeff's friendship.

Greg had noticed Jeff seemed to compartmentalize his friends. Jeff had his newspaper friends but had another set of mostly invisible friends he referred to occasionally. Greg met few of them.

Greg thought Jeff's tastes a little eccentric: he collected antique spinning tops and circus memorabilia, which he displayed throughout his apartment. He had a large record collection of Greek music, such as they heard at Lolita's. But Jeff's greatest passion in music was for the French singer, Edith Piaf. Jeff had every recording "The Sparrow" had ever made, and he often played her albums for Greg, especially the song, *"Non, Je ne Regrette Rien"* (No, I Don't Regret Anything).

Dan Forbes had been dating Sandra Peterson, a photographer at the *Star*. Greg liked Sandra, though she often looked as if she needed a bath. Her mousy hair often looked tousled and unkempt. Her appearance didn't seem to matter much to her, though she wasn't unattractive.

One night in late February, Dan and Sandra planned to go to Lafitte's for drinks after work. They approached the desk complex where Greg and Jeff were wrapping up their night's work.

"Let's go have a few at Lafitte's," Dan said.

"Not tonight," Jeff said. "I promised Alex I'd come by there for a while."

Greg accepted Dan and Sandra's invitation and met them at the club.

"Greg, did you and Irene ever make up?" Sandra asked, sipping a screwdriver.

"We've reached a truce," Greg said.

"I'd hate to have to deal with that old bull dyke," Dan said.

Greg's face registered surprise. "Is she, really?"

"Of course, didn't you know?" Dan had a look of disbelief.

"I'm pretty oblivious to that sort of thing," Greg said. "Maybe I've led a sheltered life. I just never put two and two together about a lot of people."

Sandra shook her head. "In Galveston, you never know who's straight and who's not. Take the news editor, for instance."

"Who are you talking about?" Greg looked bewildered.

"How many news editors do you know?"

"There's just Jeff." Greg suddenly got Sandra's drift. "You're not serious."

"It's true. You haven't figured it out yet?"

"Not Jeff. You've got to be kidding." Greg lit a cigarette.

"I'm afraid not."

"Did you know about this, Dan?" Greg asked.

"I sorta figured he might be gay."

"You knew Jeff and I worked on the same paper in San Angelo, didn't you?" Sandra took a sip of her drink.

"Yeah," Greg said. "Jeff told me he used to date you."

"My God, I was madly in love with him. He dates a girl right here in Galveston now when he needs to be seen with a woman. That was the purpose I served in San Angelo. Before I found out, we actually got engaged. Can you believe that? Engaged! Then, he got arrested for picking up guys at the bus station."

"My God, Sandra," Greg leaned forward. "Jeff is the best friend I've got in Galveston."

"Sure. He wouldn't proposition you. He keeps his straight friends and gay friends separate. Alex is Jeff's regular lover. That's where he was going tonight."

"I think I met Alex one time," Greg said. "I went to Jeff's apartment to borrow something, and this guy was asleep in Jeff's bed, in his underwear. It seemed strange but didn't register. I know Jeff has some weird friends, but this is hard to grasp."

"Imagine how I felt when I found out," Sandra said with an edge of bitterness.

Greg sat silently for a few moments, trying to absorb the revelation. He recalled how his attitude toward homosexuals had become more tolerant since high school in the fifties, when "queers" were outcasts. But still. . . .

"I've never known many gay people," he said. "I don't quite know what to make of all this."

"Live and let live," Dan said.

"I guess," Greg said. "But it makes me a little nervous about how I should act around him."

"Why do you have to act any different?" Dan asked.

"I know what Greg means," Sandra said. "I've never felt the same around Jeff since I found out."

"I suspected he was gay when I first met him," Dan said. "But I just treat him like anyone else. His sex life is his business. I stay out of his as long as he stays out of mine."

"That's true, but still. . . ." Greg shook his head. He wondered if this knowledge might affect his dealings with Jeff. He'd come to depend on Jeff's friendship, and he didn't need a new source of stress at work.

❖

March 1965

After some weeks of stalling, Greg agreed to drive to Fort Worth to talk to Suzy's mother.

"What can I say that she hasn't already heard from you?" he asked as they drove north on I-45.

"Good question," Suzy said. "Just let her know how you feel about me. Tell her what a good husband you plan to be."

"Boy," Greg said, shaking his head. "That's a tall order. Should I get into the anxiety business?"

"I'd be careful. But if she asks, you should be honest about it. She knows something about that from her sister."

"The real hangup is religion, isn't it?"

"That's a big deal to her. You'll have to be careful with that, too."

"God almighty, Suzy. I won't have a prayer. If she asks me what I believe, no answer I can give will satisfy her unless I say I've found Jesus."

"Don't lie to her," Suzy said. "Just try to show her some understanding and be nice."

"Oh, great. 'Be nice.' This whole trip is going to be a fiasco."

"You sure are grouchy today." Suzy slouched in her seat and folded her arms.

"Think of trying to sell yourself to one of my parents. It's not a very comfortable spot to be in."

"I know, and I'm proud of you for trying."

They pulled into Fort Worth around noon and had lunch at the Wheeler Inn, a diner on East Winchester that featured food "Like Mom Used to Fix." Greg was a nervous wreck and had trouble forcing down his meal of chicken-fried steak and mashed potatoes.

They drove to the Cox home with Greg fighting a case of heartburn.

"Suzy, I don't know if I can go through with this," Greg said, trying to conceal his nervousness.

"You'll do fine," she said. "You're so sincere, she can't doubt your intentions."

Nadine Cox let them in. Floyd Cox hadn't returned from his Saturday golf game.

"You look tired, Suzanne," Mrs. Cox said in her nasal drawl. "Are you feeling all right?"

"I'm fine, Mother."

They chatted a few minutes about Suzy's siblings. Mrs. Cox hadn't acknowledged Greg's presence.

"Mother," Suzy said finally. "Greg would like to talk to you alone. Is that okay?"

"Well, I don't know what for." Mrs. Cox fumbled with a dishtowel. "Don't you have anything to say?"

"I've said it all before. It's such a pretty day. Why don't I go out in the backyard? You and Greg can talk in the living room."

"Well, my stars," Mrs. Cox said, taken aback by the proposal and groping for words.

Greg's heart pounded. He stuffed his hands into his pockets to hide the tremors. Suzy went out the back door.

"Mrs. Cox, I guess we haven't had a chance to really get to know each other," Greg said, taking a seat on the sofa.

"Maybe not," Mrs. Cox said, sitting down in her easy chair.

Greg wasn't sure where to start. "Well, Suzy tells me you're not too happy about us being engaged."

"No, I'd hoped Suzanne would find someone to marry who's more like her."

"We have a lot in common," Greg said. "And I love Suzy very much. I want to make her happy."

"That may be," Mrs. Cox said. "But there are some fundamental things you don't have in common." She stared daggers at Greg.

"Like what?"

"Well, she was raised a Baptist. She accepted Jesus Christ as her personal savior. She was baptized by total immersion. She was taught that the Bible is God's infallible holy word. I don't think you share any of those things with her."

"That's true." Now Greg was on the defensive. "I went to church as a kid, but my parents weren't very religious. They wanted me to find my own way with religion."

"And I think that's outrageous." Mrs. Cox threw up her hands. "What kind of country would we have if everyone raised their children that way?"

"Well, that's a matter of opinion. My folks are good people, responsible members of society. I can't see that not going to church has hurt them. They were both raised in the Methodist Church but aren't active anymore."

"Hmph. That sounds like Methodists." Her words dripped with contempt.

"Look, Mrs. Cox, Suzy has sort of altered her views about religion. She's no longer active in the Baptist Church."

"I know, no thanks to you."

"I had nothing to do with it." Greg raised his voice. "Suzy made that decision before we got back together in Galveston."

"Yeah, but I think you planted some blasphemous ideas in her head when y'all were going together before."

"You think so? Like what?"

"I just saw a change in Suzanne. I don't think she ever took her faith seriously after you came along."

"Look," Greg pleaded. "Suzy's a grown woman. Doesn't she have the right to make her own choices in life?"

"Yes, but I don't have to countenance them." She set her mouth in a tight, firm line.

Greg was getting nowhere. "Then, you're dead-set against her marrying me, and nothing will change that. And no matter how much I love her or how much Christian charity I show to her and the world, you still think I'm the wrong guy for her?"

"Yes, I do." She snapped a quick nod of certainty.

Greg felt defeated. He went to the back door and called Suzy. She hurried to the back door.

"So, did y'all settle everything?" She wore a sunny smile as she stepped inside.

"We settled the fact that you're not going to marry Greg, if I have anything to say about it," Mrs. Cox said sternly.

"Oh, Mother. How could you?" Suzy's cheery face collapsed.

"Suzanne, I have my principles," Mrs. Cox said, "and I'm not about to change them."

"Let's go, Suzy," Greg said. "I can see I'm not welcome here."

"Oh, Greg!" Suzy burst into tears.

Greg put his arm around her waist and led her toward the front door.

"Mother, you're being a monster!" Suzy shouted between sobs. "How could you be so mean?"

"'Unless one is born again, he cannot see the kingdom of God,'" Mrs. Cox quoted firmly as they went out the door.

"Well, here's one for you Mrs. Cox: 'Judge not, that you be not judged,'" Greg said and slammed the door.

❖

Suzy bawled all the way to Greg's parents' house. Vivian answered the door. George, like Floyd Cox, was playing golf on a Saturday afternoon.

"Suzy," Vivian said. "What's the matter?"

Suzy dabbed at her eyes with a tissue.

"Suzy's mother just condemned me to hell," Greg said. "She doesn't want Suzy marrying a heathen."

"Oh, no," Vivian said. "I didn't realize religion was an issue."

"It seems to be *the* issue," Suzy sniffed.

"Well, y'all might just have to elope," Vivian said, leading them to the living room.

"We haven't talked about it yet," Greg said, sitting down on the sofa. "But you may be right."

"It would be a lot better, of course," Vivian said, "if you could bring her around. I was looking forward to a big church wedding. I have all sorts of great ideas."

"Well, it's our wedding, Mother," Greg said, now feeling put upon by his mother as well.

"Oh, I know that, Greg," Vivian said. "I just want to help. Suzy, you feel free to ask if there's anything I can do."

"Thanks, Mrs. Spencer." Suzy spoke softly, still sniffling.

The phone rang. Vivian went to answer it.

Greg looked at Suzy. "Maybe we'd be better off living in sin than getting married."

"Oh, phooey," Suzy said, halfheartedly slapping at him.

"Suzy," Vivian said from the hall. "It's for you. It's your dad."

Greg stopped Suzy as she got up. "You can spend the night here if you don't want to go back over there," he said. Suzy nodded and went to the phone.

"Greg," Vivian said, sitting back down in the living room. "What did Mrs. Cox say?"

"She said we'd never get married if she had a say because I put blasphemous thoughts in Suzy's head."

"Oh, my." Vivian whispered behind her hand, "I wish I could give you some advice, but I don't know how you deal with religious fanatics."

Suzy talked on the phone a long time. When she hung up, she came back into the living room.

"Well, Daddy said we shouldn't worry," she said. "He said he'll take care of everything."

"I've heard that before," Greg said.

Greg took Suzy to the Fort Worth Press Club that night, where Greg's friend Eddie King joined them when he got off work. They had a pleasant, but somewhat subdued, visit.

Greg put away several drinks, and he was surprised to notice Suzy matched him drink for drink. He'd never seen Suzy consume this much alcohol before. Nowadays, she usually limited herself to a glass of wine or a single drink. They were both getting bombed to escape the the day's disappointments.

"We'd better go," Greg said. "Somebody's got to drive home."

Greg and Suzy said goodnight to Eddie and left the club on the twentieth floor of the Blackstone Hotel. Driving to his parents' house Suzy nuzzled close to Greg.

"Hey, you," she said.

"Yeah?"

"What if I sneak over to your bedroom tonight?" Suzy slurred her words. Sharing a bed in a parent's home was still mostly taboo in 1965 Texas.

"Fine with me, only we'd probably wake my folks up. We make a lot of noise, you know."

"Oh, we could be real quiet." Suzy giggled.

"You think so?"

"I'll bet we could if we tried real, real hard."

Greg drove deliberately along the turnpike, straining to keep the car from weaving. "We're both three sheets to the wind," he said. "You know what Shakespeare said about liquor and sex, don't you?"

"What?"

"'It provokes the desire, but it takes away the performance.'"

"Oh, he did not." Suzy slapped Greg playfully on the arm.

"He sure did. It's in *Macbeth*."

"Maybe he was just talking about men."

"That may be." Greg recalled his disaster with Sharon Rogers the previous summer.

"Well, we could try, couldn't we?" Suzy giggled again.

"Just make sure my folks are snoring. Mother's a light sleeper."

"Okay."

When they got to the Spencers' house, Greg stumbled to his old bedroom and put on his pajamas. He went across the hall to check on Suzy. She had passed out with all her clothes still on. Greg pulled a blanket over her and went to bed across the hall.

The next day, they had a late breakfast with the Spencers and left for the return trip to Galveston. Both were nursing headaches, and neither said much for miles.

"Cat got your tongue?" Suzy said.

"Well, I feel like crap from last night, and I'm even more depressed about yesterday."

"I know," Suzy said. "Mother was awful. I'm going to talk to my brother and sister. I know they don't feel that way about you."

"And now there's my mother," Greg whined. "She wants to plan the wedding for us. Jesus Christ. Maybe we should elope."

"She was very sweet, Greg. She just wants to help." Suzy looked in the visor's mirror and ran a brush through her hair.

"You don't know my mother," Greg said. "She's very good at manipulating people. Before we know it, she'll take over and run the whole damned wedding."

"Oh, you're looking on the negative side of everything."

"Am I? I'm being realistic." Greg drove silently for a while. "And all this comes right on top of my finding out my best friend in Galveston is a homosexual."

Suzy flipped the visor up. "Jeff?"

"Yes, Jeff. I was too stupid to figure it out. Dan and Sandra told me the other day. Not that it's such a big deal, but it took me by surprise."

The landscape along 1-45 got greener as they drove south. Wildflowers had started to bloom around Huntsville.

"I was brought up to believe that being gay was a mortal sin," Suzy said. "Baptists are very adamant about that, you know. It took several psychology classes for me to see it a different way."

Greg looked over at Suzy. "You mean teachers at Baylor don't think it's a sin?"

"This professor I had didn't. He explained it in a way that made a lot of sense. I always thought people were 'queer' because they wanted to be, because they were just evil perverts. Now, I think it's just the way they're wired; I don't believe they have a choice."

"I don't, either, but I'm afraid I'll feel awkward around Jeff now."

"No reason to," Suzy said. "He's a human being just like you; he's just put together a little different."

Greg pulled Suzy close and kissed her cheek. "You're pretty smart," he said, squeezing her hand. "You know it?"

"I think my folks would call it 'overeducated'," she giggled.

❖

Back at work Monday, Greg learned Dan had uncovered some new information about Lester Hastings.

"I think we're onto something," Dan said, thumbing through his notebook. "First, Friday night I was shooting the bull with a detective down at the cop shop, and he told me Lester had beat the crap out of a sixteen-year-old boy at his 'ranch house' last week. The kid has brain damage and may not live. Lester is scot-free."

"Wow," Greg said. "You say this was last week?"

"Tuesday or Wednesday," Dan said.

"Did you see a police report on this?"

"I went back and checked, and there was no report."

"Did you ask anyone about the report?"

"I told this detective I hadn't seen a report, and he just said, 'Hell, we never make a report if it involves a Hastings.'"

"Come on," Greg said, "let's go tell Yeager."

Jeff joined them in the editor's office. Dan repeated what he'd told Greg.

"Sons of bitches," Yeager said. He didn't often curse, but now his face was flaming.

"There's even more," Dan said.

"Let's hear it," Yeager puffed his pipe intensely.

"I spent a good part of Saturday night hanging out at the Riviera Club. I'd never been there, but I met a guy at Lafitte's who agreed to take me to the place." Dan flipped through the pages of his notebook. "I lost fifty bucks playing blackjack, but I got in a conversation with another guy at the table, and he told me Lester Hastings was in with the Vegas mob up to his teeth."

"Now, we've got another source," Greg said. "What else did he say?"

"He said Lester was laundering money for the mob, and he'd use it to finance some big project."

"Okay, hold on," Yeager said. "We've got two stories here. Let's go back to the kid Lester beat up. Have you checked the hospital? Do we have the kid's name?"

"I talked to the nursing supervisor," Dan said. "And she claimed she didn't know anything."

"They probably hush things up involving the Hastings family just like the cops do," Jeff said.

"My fiancée's roommate works in the emergency room," Greg said. "Maybe she could find out something."

"Good idea, Greg," Yeager said. "See what you can come up with." The editor cleared his throat and went on. "Okay, let's give priority to the beating; the money-laundering story is still shaky and may never pan out. Let's try to get something in the paper right away on the beating. If we can get the victim's name, maybe we can talk to his parents and get their take on what happened. But let's go slow and make sure we've got as many hard facts as we can get. It's your story, Dan. Let's get to work."

❖

Greg drove along The Strand toward the medical school, a mile east of downtown Galveston. The street ran along the edge of the city's wharves. Greg watched a pair of tugboats as they nudged a giant merchant ship away from the dock.

The coming of spring had brought an explosion of pink oleander blossoms on the shrubs that lined streets all over the island. A sweet floral scent drifted in the humid air.

Greg had arranged to meet Suzy and Cindy for dinner in the cafeteria of John Sealy Hospital, the city's premier medical facility, also the teaching hospital for the University of Texas medical and nursing schools.

Cindy and Suzy both had night duty at the hospital and, like Greg, took their dinner hour at six in the evening.

Greg got lost in the maze of hallways in the vast facility. Finally, he asked a nurse for directions. He found Cindy near the end of the cafeteria line.

"Suzy's running a little late," Cindy said. Her dark bangs stood out against her white nurse's cap.

"Should we wait for her or get in line?" Greg asked.

"Let's wait a few more minutes," Cindy said.

Shortly, Suzy appeared. Greg realized he'd never seen the student nurses' uniforms. They featured crisp cotton blouses with blue-and-white pinstripes. The blouses had white collars and white cuffs on their short sleeves. Over the blouses they wore white, bibbed pinafores. And, of course, white shoes and caps.

The three got their food and sat down at a table.

"Those are sure snazzy uniforms," Greg said.

"They stand out like a sore thumb." Suzy took the food off her tray.

"They want to make sure nobody mistakes us for real nurses," Cindy said.

After some more small talk, Greg broached the subject. "Cindy, Suzy tells me you work in the ER."

"Mostly I just watch, but, yeah, that's my assignment."

"Were you working last Tuesday or Wednesday night?"

"Yeah, I'm there all week."

"There was a young guy, maybe fifteen, sixteen years old who got beat up pretty bad one of those nights. Know anything about it?"

A look of recognition crossed Cindy's face. "Yeah," she said slowly. "Yeah, he had brain damage."

"That's him," Greg said. "We're working on a story about how that happened. Do you know any details?"

"Not really, I was mostly in the background, just observing, but I heard the doctors talking. They said he'd been beaten up, maybe with a tire iron or something heavy."

"Okay," Greg said. "Here's the main thing: we need his name. The nursing supervisor wouldn't even admit they had a case like that. So, it's very hush-hush."

Cindy looked wide-eyed. "Oh, my gosh. I hope I'm not in trouble for telling you that."

"Don't worry." Greg tried to sound soothing. "I won't reveal who told me. Is there any way you could find out his name?"

"Greg," Suzy broke in. "I think that boy is in the neurology wing on my floor. I might be able to find out his name, if you don't think it'll get me kicked out of school."

Greg tensed at the thought. "No one will know where we got his name, I promise. But I don't want to put you two on the spot. If it's too big a risk, we can try something else."

"Let me think about it," Suzy said.

Cindy frowned. "Why all the secrecy, anyway?"

Greg lowered his voice. "Not a word to anyone, okay?"

They both nodded agreement.

"We think Lester Hastings beat this kid up. Lester likes young boys. We saw several of them naked at his New Year's Eve party. Every time I've seen him, he's had teenage boys with him."

"Where are the police in all this?" Suzy asked.

"They know about it; that's how Dan found out. But they didn't make a report. They've always protected the Hastings family."

"I'll call you tonight when I get off duty," Suzy said. "I'll wait till I get back to the apartment, so I can talk."

"Okay, but be careful. Don't stick your neck out."

At eleven-thirty, after Greg had returned from the composing room, his phone rang.

"Greg, the boy's name is Curtis Wayne Warren." Suzy sounded tense and spoke in a hushed tone.

"What's his condition?" Greg asked.

"Still critical; he's in a coma."

"Bless you, Suzy." Greg said. "How hard was it to find out?"

"Not hard at all." She sounded more relaxed. "It's on his chart. The duty nurse handed it to me so I could see his vital signs. All I had to do was remember the name till I could write it down."

"Fantastic." Greg felt relieved to have the name, but also anxious about the next steps. "I'll give it to Dan. He's going to try to find the parents."

"Oh, I got that name, too," Suzy said smugly. "That was on the chart under 'parent or responsible party.'"

"And?"

"James K. Warren. I'm glad they weren't hard names."

"That's great," Greg said. "I can't tell you how much help you've been."

"Okay, but I don't want to make this kind of thing a habit."

"But you have such a good nose for news," Greg teased.

"I'm serious, Greg, I don't like sneaking around like that."

"Okay, I understand. But thanks a bunch. This ought to be worth dinner at Gaido's."

"It's a deal," she said. "But I'm worn out. Let's talk tomorrow."

Back at his apartment, Greg was too keyed up to sleep. After a couple of hours, he got up and walked to the medicine cabinet. He took out the bottle of Valium tablets and looked at it for a moment. He had gradually stopped taking them and hadn't had one in more than two months. But it was nearly four in the morning; his nerves were still in a tangle. He filled his water glass and swallowed a tablet in a gulp.

❖

Greg passed on the information Suzy had given him to Dan. The next day, Dan called the boy's parents. Greg listened on an extension.

"Is this Mrs. Warren?"

"Yes."

"This is Dan Forbes at the Galveston *Star*. Are you the mother of Curtis Warren?"

"Yes," she said hesitantly.

"Is your son in the hospital at John Sealy?"

"That's right. What do you want?" The woman had a flat, nasal voice.

"We'd like to find out what happened," Dan said.

"I can't talk about it right now. You'll have to talk to my husband."

"Is he there?" Dan flipped ashes from his cigarette.

"No, he's at work."

"Where does he work?"

She hesitated. "Todd Shipyards."

Dan scribbled down some notes. "Could I call him at work?"

"I don't think that would be a good idea."

"What time does he get off?" Dan asked.

"He should be home pretty soon. He works from seven till three."

"Would it be okay if I called back, or could he call me when he gets in?"

"Give me your number," Mrs. Warren said. "I'll have him call you."

A half-hour later, Dan rushed over to Greg's desk.

"I've got him on the line," Dan said, excitement in his voice.

Greg pushed a button on his phone and picked up the receiver.

Back at his desk, Dan grabbed the phone. "Are you there, Mr. Warren?"

"Yeah."

"About your son," Dan said. "We just learned he was in critical condition at John Sealy. Is that right?"

"Correct."

"Can you tell me how he was injured? There was no police report. Do you think a crime was committed?"

"Yes, sir, a crime was damn sure committed." Warren spoke in deep, burly, working-class tones.

"Who do you think committed it?"

"I know who committed it: that goddamned Lester Hastings."

Dan looked around at Greg and raised his eyebrows. "Did you sign a complaint against him?"

"I sure did."

"Have the police contacted you since the night it happened?"

"Hell, no," Warren said with bitterness.

"Mr. Warren," Dan said. "There's something funny going on here. The police either didn't make a report, or they withheld it. Can you tell me what happened?"

"I don't have time. I've got to get to the hospital to see my son."

"Could I talk to you at the hospital?"

"All right. I guess so."

Dan arranged to meet the father in the parking garage. Greg had taken notes, too, and when Dan left, he summoned Jeff. They went into Seth Yeager's office.

"What's up, gents?" The editor puffed his pipe.

"We got the name of the kid Hastings beat up," Greg said. "And Dan has talked to the parents. He's gone to meet with the father at Sealy to get the whole story. But the father thinks Hastings is the assailant."

"Hmm." Yeager tapped his pipe on his ashtray. "We're getting close to having a story, but we can't name Hastings unless he's charged. Let's get our county man to talk to the DA's office and find out if any charges have been filed."

"Lester's probably paid them off, but we can try," Greg said. He went to the doorway of Yeager's office and called out, "Hey, Sanders, come here."

Luke Sanders, a tall, balding man in his early forties, came into the office. He had covered the county courthouse beat for a dozen years. He was one of the most affable and reliable reporters Greg had worked with.

"What's up?" Sanders asked, taking off his dark-rimmed glasses and wiping them with his handkerchief.

"Luke," Yeager said. "We've got a story working you might be interested in."

"Sure, what have you got?"

"There's a kid at Sealy in a coma," Greg said. "His father thinks Lester Hastings beat the crap out of him. Has the DA filed any charges against Hastings that you know of?"

"Oh, man," Sanders said, shaking his head. "No. But you know the Hastings family has always been treated with kid gloves."

Yeager leaned forward. "Can you talk to the DA or one of his assistants and see what they know?"

"Yeah, but we have to be careful." Sanders put his glasses back on. "You're talking about the biggest fish in town."

"We know," Yeager said. "But it's time we started acting like a newspaper. That bastard has been getting away with murder for too long."

❖

Seth Yeager's words took on a more literal meaning that night: Suzy called Greg at ten o'clock and told him Curtis Warren had died of his injuries.

"Oh, my God," Greg moaned.

This new dimension left Greg in a quandary about how to proceed. Seth Yeager had told him to let him know anytime he needed guidance on a story. Greg called Yeager at home.

"The kid Lester beat up died," Greg said. "And Dan got the father's version of what happened."

"Oh, boy," Yeager said. "How did we learn of his death?"

"Suzy—my fiancée—called to tell me, but Dan has a confirmation from the justice of the peace. The JP signed the death certificate. He's ordered an autopsy. But the hospital nursing supervisor still isn't talking."

"Okay, let's go at it this way: Let's lead with his death and say he died of head injuries at John Sealy. Then, let's say the nursing supervisor declined to comment, but an autopsy is pending. Have Dan call the police chief, and if he won't comment, let's say so. Let's try to get something from the DA. If we can show all these officials are covering something up, then maybe we can smoke them out."

"Okay." Greg lit a fresh cigarette. "How about the father's story?"

"What did he tell Dan?"

"He said Curtis—the kid—had recently gone to work for Hastings at his mansion, and that another kid, whose name Dan has, said Hastings made sexual overtures to Curtis, but Curtis rebuffed him. Hastings went berserk and beat the kid with a crowbar. The other kid drove Curtis to the hospital, then drove on to Conroe to stay with an aunt. He was too scared of Hastings to stay in town."

"My God, what a can of worms." the editor groaned. "Okay, let's do this: Tell Dan to go with the father's story, but don't use Hastings's name. For now, let's just say the boy worked for a 'Galveston resident.' Then, quote the father about this 'resident' beating the boy 'after an altercation.' Leave the sex out of it. I'm going to call Troy Edmonds, our lawyer in Houston. We may need to have Dan read him his story before we go to press. It's getting late, so let's get moving. How much does Dan still have to write?"

"He's written the father's account. All I think he has to do is put a new lead on it, and it's done."

"One more thing," the editor said. "Be sure to mention that law enforcement officers haven't responded to questions about the case."

"Okay. Got it."

"Okay, Greg." Yeager paused. "Come to think of it, I'll come on in to the office. I'll call the lawyer from there."

Dan spent another half-hour polishing his story. Both Greg and Jeff watched over his shoulder, and Greg made suggestions based on Yeager's instructions.

Yeager came in to the newsroom at eleven o'clock. He took Dan's story into his office and called the attorney in Houston. Greg, Jeff, and Dan sat next to Yeager's desk as he read the story.

>By Dan Forbes
>Staff Writer
>
>Curtis Wayne Warren, 16, died Wednesday night at John Sealy Hospital of severe head injuries he apparently suffered in a beating last week.
>Officials at the hospital declined comment on the youth's death. Justice of the Peace Michael Radinsky has ordered an autopsy.
>Galveston police refused to comment on the case and made no report of the incident available.
>The district attorney's office said no charges have been filed in connection with the case.
>Warren had been in a coma since the incident occurred last Wednesday night. Hospital sources said he suffered severe brain damage.
>James Warren, the youth's father, told a *Star* reporter his son had recently gone to work for a Galveston resident. He said another youth, 17, had witnessed the beating and told the elder Warren his son and the youth's employer had an altercation at the employer's residence.
>The elder Warren said the witness told him the assailant beat Curtis Warren with a crowbar and that the 17-year-old had driven Curtis to John Sealy Hospital.
>James Warren said he he'd signed a complaint against the assailant.
>The *Star* has made numerous attempts to locate a police report or a copy of the complaint, but those efforts have proved unsuccessful.

The rest of the story went on to list funeral services, survivors, and so forth.

Yeager hung up the phone.

"Edmonds says we're good to go," he said. "Let's run this as the banner. Greg, let me see the headline you write. Let's make it six columns, seventy-two point, two lines, okay?"

Greg went to his typewriter and tried several ideas. He had to shuffle words and shorten others to make the headline fit the required space. After a few minutes, he took it to Yeager's office:

Galveston Teen Dies in Beating;
Police, D.A., Hospital Are Mum

"That's the ticket, Greg," Yeager said. "I don't normally like 'to be' verbs in a head, but I think it's appropriate here. Let's get it upstairs."

Greg and Jeff finished their last-minute details and went to the third floor to oversee the makeup of the front page.

Tony Rodriguez met them with a TV jingle: *Oh, I wish I were an Oscar Mayer weiner....*

"Hey, Tony, get ready to play newspaper," Greg said.

"Ah, fuck that shit," Tony growled. "I already got Page One ready to go."

"How'd you get all that type up so fast?" Jeff said.

"Hell, man, Benito can set type like Speedy Gonzalez. Look, it's *terminado,* man."

Sure enough, the page, complete with Dan's story and Greg's headline, sat glistening in the page form.

"Send it in," Greg said. "We're done."

"Don't I always take care of you, Gregorio?"

Greg went back to the newsroom with a queasy feeling.

"Okay, Dan," he said. "Let's sit back and see what happens when the shit hits the fan tomorrow."

Back at his apartment, Greg paced the floor, too geared up to go to bed. He couldn't stop thinking of what Lester Hastings might do, even if Lester's name didn't appear in Dan's story. Greg tried to think about something else, but the only other thought that came to mind was of the depressing exchange he'd had with Suzy's mother. The knot tightened in his solar plexus.

He took a Valium and fell into bed.

❖

Greg slept fitfully and awoke the next day with his nerves still raw. He took another Valium before work and put a spare into his pocket. When he got to the newsroom, Seth Yeager's office door was closed. Two men in suits sat outside the door.

Jeff worked at his desk. Greg got his attention.

"What's going on?" Greg said under his breath.

"Yeager's in there with Dan and the hospital administrator. He said to tell you to join them when you got here."

"Oh, shit," Greg said. "Who are those guys outside the door?"

"The DA and the police chief."

"Jesus Christ," Greg said and walked to the door of Yeager's office. He knocked, and the editor let him in.

"Have a seat, Greg," Yeager said. "Greg, this is Homer Davies, the administrator at John Sealy."

Greg shook the man's hand. Davies, a red-faced, balding, middle-aged man, looked bereft of good humor. Acid burned in Greg's stomach, and his pulse accelerated.

Yeager filled his pipe from a tobacco pouch. "Greg, Homer and I were talking about the attempts we made to get information from the hospital about the young man who died last night."

"Yes, sir," Greg said.

"Dan," Yeager said. "How many times would you say you tried to get information from the nursing supervisor?"

"I think it was five times," Dan said.

"And did you talk to the same nurse each time?"

"No, they rotate shifts. I talked to a couple of different ones."

"And do you have their names?"

"Sure. Rose McNeil and Jane Whitney. I know them both and talk to one or the other every day."

"And what did you ask them?" Yeager went on as if cross-examining a witness.

"I asked if they had a teenage boy who'd suffered head injuries in a beating."

"And they said what?" A cloud of smoke rose from Yeager's pipe.

"They said, 'I'm sorry, but hospital policy prevents us from releasing that information.'"

"Homer, that's what we were up against," Yeager said, re-lighting his pipe.

"Look, Seth," Davies said. "I just took this job last August, and I didn't approve any policy like that. Maybe the Hastings family put pressure on my predecessors, but you and I have discussed this before. I want to move John Sealy into the twentieth century and get rid of all that Hastings baggage."

"Yes, I think you and I have a similar approach." Yeager tapped his pipe on his ashtray. "It's time we loosened the Hastings grip on Galveston, wouldn't you agree?"

"Absolutely. I'll get a memo out today telling our people to fully cooperate with the press unless the situation is extraordinary. And I'll make the decision about that."

"Very good, Homer. Did you have any other questions of me or of Dan and Greg?"

"Well, yes. Just curious, you know," Davies said. "Who was this 'source' at John Sealy you mentioned in your story?"

"Sorry," Greg said. "We don't reveal anonymous sources. I hope you understand." Greg's palms sweated as he thought about Suzy and Cindy.

"Exactly so, Greg," Yeager added. "Well, Homer, I'll look forward to seeing you at the next chamber of commerce meeting."

As Davies left, Greg turned to Dan and whispered, "That was too easy."

"I'll bet the next two guys won't be," Dan whispered back.

Greg tensed as the police chief and district attorney entered the office. Yeager introduced the two men to Greg and Dan. They all took seats in front of Yeager's desk.

Angelo Conti, the DA, had flowing gray locks and wore an expensive charcoal-gray suit. He spoke first.

"Mr. Yeager, my office has always had good relations with the *Star*," he said. "Mind if I smoke?"

"No, go ahead," Yeager said.

Conti lit a cigarillo and took a couple of puffs. "There must be some misunderstanding regarding the story in today's paper."

"What sort of misunderstanding?" Yeager asked.

"Your story said my office has filed no charges in this beating case."

"That's correct," Yeager said. "Luke Sanders talked to a couple of your assistants, and they said they knew of no such case."

"Well, that's because I didn't tell them about it. I know about the case, but we have no suspect to charge."

"What?" Yeager's face reflected incredulity.

"That's correct," the DA said. "The police report we received mentioned no suspect. Only that the boy had shown up at the hospital badly beaten. There was no suspect, no arrest."

Yeager turned to Bill Casey, the hefty police chief with pink cheeks and thinning gray hair. "Is that right, Bill? No suspects, no arrest?"

"That's right, Mr. Yeager," the chief said. "We had a boy fatally beaten, but we don't know how it happened."

"But, Bill, our reporter has a source who told him Lester Hastings was the beater, and the boy's father told Dan the boy worked for Lester Hastings, and a witness saw Lester beat him with a crowbar."

"Well, now, Mr. Yeager," Casey said. "You can't believe everything you hear. We've investigated the incident, and we have no such information."

"Was the father lying?" Yeager pleaded, getting red in the face.

"Let's just say he's not a credible subject," Casey said. "He's been in and out of trouble for years. Has a long criminal record. He used to work at one of the Hastings hotels and was fired. I suspect he has an ax to grind."

Greg and Dan looked at each other.

"Then, why in the hell was there no police report?" Yeager was livid now.

"Well, just a little administrative foul-up," Casey said. "If you'd like to see a report, have your man come by the station and we'll give him a copy."

"Gentlemen," Yeager said, the veins in his neck bulging. "There's a turd in the punch bowl here. I think you're protecting Lester's ass. Every word in Dan's story is accurate. I'll stand behind it, and the Houston *Times* lawyer stands behind it. Now, if you don't have anything further. . . ."

"Well, hell, Yeager, no need to get salty about it," the DA said. "Let's go, Bill."

❖

"Dan, we need to talk to that other boy," Greg said after the DA and police chief left.

"I was thinking the same thing," Dan said. "I'll see if I can find out where his aunt lives and drive up to Conroe today."

"Good," Yeager said. "We may have to get a private police force to protect us, but by God, if Lester Hastings killed that boy, we're going to nail him."

Greg's nerves were raw. He bought a Coke from the drink machine and swallowed the spare Valium he'd put into his pocket.

He worked through the pile of local stories that had accumulated from other reporters. He had trouble concentrating and had to get up and walk around several times in an effort to clear his head. He sat back down and took a swig from his antacid bottle.

At eight o'clock, as Greg drew up the dummy sheets for his local pages, an ear-splitting crash of breaking glass exploded behind him, followed by a hard thud on the time-worn wooden floor.

Greg looked at his arm. Blood oozed from several small cuts. Shards of glass lay on top of the papers on his desk. He looked behind him and saw broken glass all over the floor.

"I saw it." Jeff rushed around Greg's desk, where a rust-colored brick lay on the floor among the broken glass. Jeff picked up the brick. "My God," he said. "Look at this."

He turned the brick around for Greg to see. Written in jagged letters with what appeared to be red fingernail polish were the words, "Lay off."

"Jesus H. Christ," Greg said, now shaking all over.

"Are you okay?" Jeff asked.

"It scared the hell out of me," Greg said. "And I've got cuts on my arms."

"Go get a wet paper towel. We'd better call the cops." Jeff grabbed a phone.

Greg went to the restroom and wiped his arms with several towels. None of the cuts was deep, and the bleeding stopped quickly.

When he returned to the newsroom, he saw the opening where the brick had shattered the central pane in a large, arched window facing Mechanic Street.

"Better call Yeager," Jeff said. "This is getting too weird."

Shortly two uniformed officers arrived and looked over the scene.

"Do you know who might have done this?" one of them asked.

"We can't say for sure," Jeff told the officer. "But it's hard to avoid the idea that it had something to do with a story in today's paper."

"What story?"

"About the boy who got beaten to death," Jeff said.

"So, who would have a problem with the story?" the cop asked.

"We didn't name anyone but the victim," Greg jumped in.

"Well, I'll turn this over to the detectives," the officer said. "They'll be in touch with you."

Yeager rushed into the newsroom a few minutes later. Shortly, managing editor Jim Stephens arrived. They huddled with Greg and Jeff in Yeager's office.

"Okay, we've got our tails in a crack," Yeager said. "But we've got to see this thing through. So, for tonight, let's do our main story on the fact that someone attacked the *Star* building. Then, we'll go with a sidebar story on the kid in Conroe when Dan gets back. Have you heard from him, Greg?"

"No, he left here about five o'clock. I think he got the address of the boy's aunt from Mr. Warren. I don't know if he found the boy."

"By the way," Yeager said. "Did somebody check to see if Mr. Warren was the criminal the police chief said he was?"

"Yeah, Luke checked his record with the state," Greg said. "And he had a DWI arrest in 1956. He told Luke he quit his job at the hotel and didn't get fired. Nothing else we could find."

"Okay, let's get busy," Yeager said. "Jim, why don't you finish laying out Greg's pages so he can concentrate on editing copy?"

"Sure," Stephens said. Greg handed him his incomplete page dummies.

Ten-thirty came and went, and still they had heard nothing from Dan. Greg busied himself writing a story about the brick-throwing incident. Jeff notified the composing room that there would be two late stories for the front page. Greg went upstairs to make sure Tony left empty columns in the page where the late stories would go.

"Hey, Gregorio," Tony said. "How about a nice Hawaiian Punch?"

Greg smiled for the first time all day.

The phone on Greg's desk rang a little before eleven. Dan was calling from Houston.

"I had a hell of a time finding this kid," Dan said, trying to catch his breath. "I finally did, but I realized I couldn't get back to Galveston in time to write the story."

"Can you dictate something?" Greg asked.

"I think so," Dan said. "Let me get my notes organized."

After a few moments of silence, Dan said, "Okay, you ready to type?"

"Go ahead."

"I guess we put a Conroe dateline on this."

"Let's not say where the kid is," Greg said. "Just say another city."

"Oh, okay. Well, here goes:

> A 17-year-old Galveston youth remained in hiding Friday night after he witnessed the fatal beating of his friend Curtis Warren on March 17.
>
> "I'm scared to death," the Ball High senior told a Galveston *Star* reporter Friday. "I saw something I wasn't supposed to see."
>
> The youth said he was working with Warren at a Galveston man's home on the night of March 17, when the man made unwelcome overtures to Warren.
>
> Warren resisted the man's suggestive comments and went on about his work cleaning the man's garden. The employer "flew off the handle and grabbed a crowbar from a utility room," the youth said, and began to beat Warren with the tool. He struck Warren in the head several times, according to the 17-year-old. He said the man then went back inside his house. He said Warren lay unconscious, so he dragged the boy to his car and drove him to John Sealy Hospital. Warren lay in a coma for a week before he died of his injuries Wednesday night.
>
> After leaving Warren at the hospital, the youth said he feared for his safety and left Galveston to stay with a relative in another city.

Dan went on for a few more paragraphs. Greg sent the story in short "takes" or sections up the pneumatic tube to be set in type.

Then, Greg wrote the two main headlines for the front page:

**Brick Shatters Window at Paper
After Story About Teen's Death**

And:

**Youth Recalls Beating
That Killed His Friend**

After all the type was set and the page assembly completed, Greg called Suzy. It was two a.m.

"Did I wake you up?" Greg had little doubt he did.

"Oh, I was dozing." Her voice was thick from sleep.

"I've had one hell of a day," he said.

"You sound tired."

"I wouldn't normally ask you at this hour, but can I come over?"

"Sure. I'll throw on some jeans."

"Don't bother. I just need to see you."

"Sounds serious."

"I'll be there in ten minutes."

❖

Greg knocked softly on Suzy's door, fearing he'd wake Cindy. Suzy let Greg in. She wore a flowered flannel nightgown over a pair of jeans. Her eyes were puffy from sleep.

"Sorry to bother you so late," Greg whispered.

"It's okay. Cindy's not here," Suzy said. "She and Brian went to a ball game at the new Astrodome in Houston."

"My God, has baseball season started already?"

"I think it's an exhibition game. The Yankees are playing the Astros. Brian wanted to see Mickey Mantle."

"And they're spending the night?"

"They're spending the weekend. Brian's brother lives in Houston."

Greg put his arms around Suzy and pulled her close.

"Greg, you're so tense," she said, rubbing her hands over his neck and shoulders. "And look at your arm. What's going on?"

Greg told her about his day: the irate DA and police chief, the brick through the window, and Dan's interview with the boy in Conroe.

"No wonder you're stressed out," Suzy said. "Who wouldn't be?"

A look of alarm crossed his face. "Suzy, I've got to do something. I feel like I'm sliding backward."

"But you survived today. Don't you think that matters?"

"But I've been like this for a week. It hasn't turned to all-out panic yet, but I'm scared it will."

"Okay, let's get you some help." Suzy had a look of decisive determination. "I checked on Dr. Brooks." Brooks was the psychiatrist Dr. Simon had recommended. "He doesn't see patients anymore; he just teaches. But he refers patients to Dr. Hoffman. I've met her, and she's very nice."

"She?" Greg raised his eyebrows.

"Yeah, something wrong with that?"

"Nothing. I just never heard of a female shrink."

Suzy looked combative. "Better get used to it; there are a bunch of women psychiatry students at UTMB."

"Okay, that's fine." Greg thought of his fifties upbringing, when men dominated the professions. "It just surprised me a little."

"Well, I'll get her number, and you can make an appointment."

"Okay, I'll call her Monday."

"How about a glass of wine?"

"Sure," Greg said, stretching out on the sofa. "I guess we should take advantage of Cindy's absence, but I'm exhausted."

"I'm tired, too," Suzy said, handing Greg the wine. "But we've both got tomorrow off, so why don't you stay here tonight, and we can sleep till we wake up."

Greg took a few sips of wine and drifted off.

"Come on," she said, tugging on his arm. "Stay awake till I get you in bed." She led him, stumbling, to her bedroom and helped get his shirt and trousers off. He collapsed in the bed and slept until noon on Saturday, with Suzy snuggled next to him.

Late the next morning, Suzy brought Greg a mug of coffee as he sat on the edge of the bed.

"Damn!" he growled and shook his head in disgust.

"What is it?"

"I forgot to have somebody check on the autopsy. We should have had that in the paper today."

"Are they closed on Saturday?"

"Yeah, all city and county offices are." Greg sipped the hot coffee. "I need to talk to Dan. Where's the phone?"

Suzy handed him the white Princess phone. Greg dialed Dan's number.

"Dan, this is Greg. You were in Conroe yesterday, and I forgot to ask you about the autopsy."

"The JP won't rule till Monday," Dan said. "A pathologist at UTMB is doing the autopsy this weekend."

"Thank God," Greg said, relief coursing through him. "I completely let it slip yesterday. I was afraid you didn't have time to check."

"I called the JP before I left," Dan said. "You can relax."

"Do you think we'll get any cooperation from the JP?"

"He's pretty independent," Dan said. "Luke says he's always been straight with him."

"Okay, buddy. Thanks."

"Take it easy," Dan said. "Enjoy your days off."

"How do you feel?" Suzy asked as she rinsed his coffee cup in the sink.

"Much better," Greg sat down at the dinette table. "Especially after talking to Dan. Why don't we get out of here? I'd like to get as far from Lester Hastings and the *Star* as I can."

"It's a beautiful, warm day," Suzy said. "We could go lie on the beach."

"That sounds perfect." Greg buttoned his shirt. "Let's get some lunch and drive up the coast."

Suzy browsed through Greg's bookshelves as he showered and shaved at his apartment. They had pastrami sandwiches at the 25th Street Deli, then headed out of Galveston. They took the ferry to Port Bolivar and drove farther up the coast than either had ever been. Greg found a deserted stretch of beach and drove off the highway between the dunes.

The temperature was in the mid-eighties, and the constant, stiff sea breeze raked across them as they spread a blanket on the beach. Suzy wore a pair of khaki shorts, a sleeveless, low-cut knit top, and sandals. She had let her hair grow longer again and now rolled it in an abbreviated twist in the back. As Suzy bent to smooth out the blanket, a wave of desire shot through Greg.

He wore a pair of Madras-plaid Bermuda shorts and a knit golf shirt. He anchored the blanket with a Styrofoam cooler containing a bottle of wine and several soft drinks.

Not a soul was in sight in any direction.

Something caught Greg's attention. He walked behind the blanket, then headed toward a large sand dune fifty feet away.

"Hey, where're you going?" Suzy shouted over the roaring surf.

"Come here," he said. "Look back there."

"What is it?" She came up beside him.

"That dune," he pointed. "There's sort of a cave. Looks like somebody dug out a private little sanctuary."

"Oh, my," Suzy said. "That looks interesting."

"Yeah, doesn't it?" Greg said with a suggestive grin.

❖

The indentation in the dune faced toward the surf, guarded by tall grass in front. Greg and Suzy snatched up the blanket, cooler, and Suzy's transistor radio and tromped through the sand toward the opening.

"You think we can both get in there?" she asked, sizing up the cavity.

"Looks like some couple didn't have any trouble," Greg said, pointing to a spent condom in the sand near the opening.

Suzy giggled and crawled inside with the blanket. Greg followed with the cooler and radio.

They smoothed the blanket, but had to brush away the sand that fell on it as they bumped the sides of the cave. There was just enough room for two people to stretch out and get comfortable, but with a snug sense of privacy. Someone had planned well.

They dusted the sand from their hair. Suzy unpinned her hair and shook her head. Her dark-blonde hair fell over one eye. As she brushed it back, her eyes met Greg's, and they moved into each other's arms.

He put his hands beneath her knit blouse and undid her bra. She kissed around his ear as he caressed her breasts. Suzy finished removing her top and pulled Greg's shirt up over his head.

Now both topless, their torsos pressed tightly together, they found each other's lips. They rolled on the blanket, feeling the gritty sand against their skin, but scarcely noticing the discomfort as they shed the rest of their clothes.

Soon, Greg's pleasure surpassed that of any previous time they'd made love. The freedom of the outdoors, the smell of the salt air, the sound of the surf, and an exciting new position all built and blended to drive them to new heights.

They lay tangled in each other's arms and legs. Suzy reached over and turned on her portable radio.

She gives me ev'rything
And tenderly
The kiss my lover brings
She brings to me
And I love her

A love like ours
Could never die
As long as I
Have you near me

"Who's that singing?" Greg asked.

"Who is it?" Suzy looked shocked. "Don't you know? Seriously?"

"No, I'm asking you."

"Didn't you see 'A Hard Day's Night'?"

"No, I walked out."

"Walked out? What's wrong with you?"

"I went to a double feature. It was the second feature. I stuck around just long enough to know I didn't want to see the whole thing."

"What have you got against the Beatles?"

"They're okay, I guess. But I just hate all the mass hysteria. I hated Elvis, too, for the same reason."

"Oh, Greg. You sound like our parents."

"It's getting hot in here," Greg wiped his brow with a towel. "Let's go outside and let the wind cool us off."

"You think we dare?" Suzy giggled. "Like this?"

"I will if you will."

They stepped outside the cavelet's opening and let the stiff breeze wash over their naked bodies. Greg marveled at the sight of Suzy standing there with the hazy sun bathing her creamy white skin, with the sea breeze whipping her blonde hair, with the tumbling surf and its unending roar, and at the freedom Suzy had come to embody.

They went back inside their hideaway in the dune and made love again.

Afterward, Greg ran his hand over Suzy's face, brushing sand from her cheek as they lay together.

"Could you have ever imagined," Greg asked, stroking Suzy's hair, "when you were sixteen, back at Eastside High, a solid member of the Eastside Baptist Church, that some day you'd be standing in your birthday suit in the sea breeze on the Gulf Coast?"

"Heavens, no," she said. "Could you?"

"Well, I had some pretty wild fantasies, but that wasn't one of them."

"What kind of fantasies?" Suzy cocked her head in prurient curiosity.

"Oh, the kind boys have. You know, making love to movie stars, Marilyn Monroe, that sort of thing."

"Girls do, too." She blushed a little. "They just don't admit it. Tony Curtis, for instance."

"And the prettiest girls in school," Greg said.

"Girls have those, too. The football stars."

"So, you were really a horny little teenybopper in spite of all that Baptist brainwashing."

"Couldn't you tell?" Suzy gave him a sultry pout.

"Not at first. I was afraid to kiss you. I thought you were too proper."

"I know. I thought you'd never ask."

"But then, you drew a line in the sand."

"That was part of the Baptist thing. But you know, I'm kind of glad we waited. I think it makes it a lot sweeter now."

"But we had to wait so long."

"Yes, but your patience was rewarded, wasn't it?"

Greg smiled, then leaned over and kissed Suzy's neck.

She flipped her radio back on.

An autopsy report is due Monday in the apparent beating death of sixteen-year-old Curtis Warren. No one has been charged in the case.

Suddenly, Greg's mood darkened. He recalled the brick crashing through the window and the grinding pressure of his job the past few days.

"Get some music," he snapped. "I thought we came out here to get away from all that."

"Hey, take it easy," Suzy said.

"Well, dammit, why did you bring a radio, anyway?" Greg wiped more sweat from his face. His cheeks and forehead felt flushed. He had a throbbing headache.

"Greg," Suzy said quizzically. "What's going on?"

Greg started getting dressed. His hands trembled as he fumbled with his shorts and shirt.

"I just want to leave," Greg said. "Get dressed and let's go."

"You don't look so good. What's the matter?"

"I don't know." Greg pulled his shirt on. "I'm about to burn up." Sweat poured off him and soaked through his shirt. His skin felt prickly all over.

"Don't take this the wrong way, but have you been taking some kind of drug?"

"Well . . ." Greg hesitated. "I hadn't mentioned it, but I have a prescription for Valium."

"And you took some?"

"I took it all week."

"How much?"

"Two or three a day. Five milligrams each."

Suzy started getting dressed. "When did you take the last one?"

"Last night, after they threw the brick." Sweat gushed from Greg's face, and his shaking worsened.

"And none since?"

"No."

"Greg, you're in withdrawal. Do you have any pills with you?"

"No, they're at the apartment."

"Let's go back there." Suzy wore a look of deep concern. "You're hooked. Didn't anyone tell you how addictive that drug is?"

"No, I assumed tranquilizers weren't addictive."

"Oh, these doctors!" she said. "There are all sorts of things they never tell you. Let me drive."

Greg got into the front seat and gave Suzy the keys.

"Get the cooler," she said. "I just thought of something."

"The cooler?"

"Get the wine and take a good swig."

"Are you kidding?"

"No, something else doctors don't tell you is that benzodiazepines, like Valium, have chemical properties similar to alcohol. Take a drink, you may feel better."

Sweat dripped from Greg's face as he gulped the wine. He felt his jaws trembling, then the warmth of the wine going down. Suzy steered the car onto Highway 87 and sped away.

Back in Galveston, Suzy stopped at the Dairy Queen on Broadway and picked up a couple of hamburgers.

"How do you feel now?" She put the takeout bag on the Corvair's floor.

"Better," Greg said. "Not as shaky. Not as hot. My head still hurts."

Suzy drove to Greg's apartment. Inside, she put the burgers on the dinette table.

"You need to eat something," she said. "Then, take a Valium. I don't think you ought to mix it with the wine on an empty stomach."

"Whatever you say, nurse."

"Yeah, I thought I had a day off, too." There was a bite to her sarcasm.

Pangs of shame ran through him. "I'm sorry, Suzy."

"Oh, don't worry about it. I had a rough week, too. I was scared to death Cindy and I would get some kind of reprimand for talking to you about that boy."

165

"Did you get a memo yesterday?" Greg took a bite of his cheeseburger.

"Yes, I saw it. I think those old nurses are still living in the fifties. If the cops told them to clam up, they did without asking questions."

"Did anyone talk to you or Cindy?"

"No, nobody said a word." Suzy said around a mouthful of burger. "I think they thought one of the older nurses talked to the *Star*."

"I'm sorry I put you through all that."

"Nobody made me do it." Suzy wiped her hands on a napkin. "It just seemed so silly, keeping a patient's name secret. And I wanted to help."

"Patients have some privacy rights," Greg said. "But admission to a hospital isn't one of them, especially if a crime is involved."

"I'm just glad it's over," Suzy said. "At least for me. I know it's not for you."

"I hate to feel so shaky when all this is going on. I hope it doesn't get worse next week."

"Go take a Valium," Suzy said, cleaning up the table. "And if you're going to stop taking it, taper off. You can't go up and down with that stuff. Once it gets in your system, it's a shock if you quit cold turkey."

"Did you make an 'A' in pharmacology?"

"Yeah, only I didn't know I'd get my own private patient so soon."

"I'm glad I have you." Greg felt a catch in his throat. "But I don't want to be a burden."

"Oh, Greg. Don't say that." She put her arms around him. "I don't love you so I can nurse you; I love you for so many other reasons. But I'm here if you need me."

❖

Suzy snuggled next to Greg in his bed. It wasn't an ideal arrangement; he had only a narrow single bed. Yet, it was room enough for two people in love.

But their blissful sleep came to an abrupt end around three in the morning when a loud crash jarred them both awake.

"Did you hear that?" Suzy said.

"Yeah. What the hell?"

A car raced its engine, tires screeched, and it sped off. Greg parted the blinds just in time to see a dark sports car round the corner of Avenue Q and 25th Street. The building blocked his view as the car raced away.

Greg pulled on his pants and ran down the stairs. Dan Forbes stood at the door of his apartment, just below Greg's.

"What happened?" Greg said.

"Come on in," Dan said. "Take a look."

A rust-colored brick lay in the floor. Broken glass covered Dan's bed.

"Oh, Christ," Greg said. "Now they're going after you. Are you okay?"

"I think so." Dan picked up the brick. "I was under the covers, so none of the glass hit my bare skin."

They examined the brick. Its message appeared to be scrawled with nail polish, similar to the one at the *Star*. "You too," it read.

"You think we should call the cops?" Dan asked.

"Yeah, we have to," Greg said. "Even if they don't do anything, we have to get it on the record."

"Unless they destroy the record." Dan studied the broken glass on the floor.

Greg said, "Probably the uniformed cops who take the call will do their job. I'd call them."

Dan went to the phone. Suzy, now dressed, came into the apartment. Greg showed her what had happened.

She put her hand to her mouth. "Oh, Greg, not again."

"I'm afraid so."

"Why would somebody do this to Dan?"

"His byline is on all the stories."

She nudged him with her elbow. "Don't you dare put your byline on any stories."

"City editors almost never have bylines. But Lester knows who I am, if he's behind all this. That's scary enough."

She grasped his arm. "Are you okay?"

"I think so. I'm barely awake."

Dan hung up the phone. The three chatted for a few minutes. Shortly, the police car arrived, and an officer sauntered into Dan's apartment.

After surveying the scene and asking a few routine questions, the officer, a short, chunky young man with blond hair and a light-gray uniform, got to the heart of the matter.

"You know anyone who'd want to throw a brick through your window?" He took out a notebook.

Dan shrugged. "Probably the same person that threw one through the window of the *Star*."

"How come?" The cop scribbled in his book.

"We've been running stories about that kid that got beat to death. Apparently, it pissed somebody off. That's all we can figure."

"But why would somebody single you out at home?"

"Because I wrote most of the stories," Dan said. "They have my byline."

The officer looked toward the front window. "Did you see or hear anything outside?"

"I did," Greg spoke up. "I saw a dark sports car turn the corner of 25th and Q."

"Did you see the make or the license number?"

"No, it was gone too fast," Greg said. "It could have been a Triumph or a Porsche, but I couldn't tell."

"Okay, I'm going to turn this over to the detectives." He closed his notebook.

Just then, there was a clatter at the front door. Eva Kaplan, the landlady and owner of the apartment complex, stumbled into the room, her dyed black hair in rollers.

"What's happened here?" She clutched at her robe. "At three in the morning?"

Greg explained the situation to her.

"Dear God!" she groaned. "Throwing bricks at my apartments. What have we come to? These newspaper peoples bring nothing but trouble."

"Are you the landlady?" the officer asked.

"I own these apartments," Mrs. Kaplan growled.

"Do you know any reason why someone would do this?"

"No." Mrs. Kaplan said brusquely. "I run a clean place."

"Have you evicted anyone lately?"

"No, no problems. These newspaper peoples make enemies."

"Okay, call us if you have any more problems or see anything suspicious." The officer made sure he recorded everyone's name correctly.

"Okay, thanks," Dan said.

The cop went to his car and drove away.

"You put some cardboards in that window," Mrs. Kaplan said. "I'll call a glass man Monday. I should add the cost to your rent, you know?"

"I didn't do it," Dan pleaded.

"You're pretty good boy." Mrs. Kaplan softened. "I'll take care of it this time. Insurance may cover it."

Mrs. Kaplan started for the door. She paused when she saw Suzy, who had been standing silently in the background.

"Who's this?" Mrs. Kaplan sounded suspicious.

"Oh, this is Suzy Cox, my fiancée," Greg said. "I think I told you I'd gotten engaged."

"Ahh. So this is her?" Mrs. Kaplan eyed Suzy up and down. "Nice blonde *shiksa*."

"Glad to meet you, Mrs. Kaplan," Suzy said.

Mrs. Kaplan wagged her finger at Suzy. "You see this boy gets enough to eat. Fix him a steak. He looks peaked to me."

❖

Greg and Suzy went back upstairs to Greg's apartment.
"I don't think I can go back to sleep," Greg said.
"Let's go to my place," Suzy said. "I don't think I could sleep here, either."

They drove across the island to Suzy's apartment. Inside, Greg paced around in a knot of tension. Would he be the target of Hastings's harassment again? Was the police chief behind it?

"Greg, you need to get some sleep." Suzy came out of the bathroom in her pajamas.

"I can't stop thinking about the bricks," he said. "What if they come after us with guns or bombs?"

"I know it's scary. But you're safe here."

"Unless we were followed." He lit his third or fourth cigarette since they'd arrived.

"Come on. You're borrowing trouble." Suzy fanned the smoky air with her hand. "And you're smoking way too much."

"Yeah, I know." Greg stubbed out the cigarette. "This is embarrassing. I don't like for you to see me like this."

"It's normal to be scared, darlin'."

Greg felt deflated. "Since I had that bout of anxiety in college, I've never been normal. I've always had the jitters. But except for the worst attacks, I think I've done a pretty good job of making people believe I was calm."

Suzy managed to get Greg to sit on the couch. "I've always known you were high-strung," she said. "You don't have to pretend with me."

"But it's a curse. Why can't I be normal?"

"Oh, a curse." She gave him a tap on the arm. "You sound like my mother."

"Gee, thanks," Greg said. "I just wish someone would figure out what causes this crap and what to do about it. I'm not convinced anyone knows."

"Greg, you're just torturing yourself. We're here. We're safe. Did you take a Valium before we left your place?"

"Yeah."

"It should be kicking in pretty soon. But in the meantime, there's a certain natural tranquilizer, you know." Suzy started to unbutton her blue polka-dotted pajama top.

"I think I get your drift," Greg said.

Around noon the next day, Suzy brought in her copy of the Sunday *Star*. Greg scanned the front page over coffee. A headline caught his eye:

**Beating Death of Youth
Still Shrouded in Mystery**

Dan had written the story, summarizing the previous week's events and again mentioning the claim that the victim's teenage friend had accused a "Galveston resident" of the crime.

"Who could have thrown those bricks other than Hastings or one of his lackeys?" Greg asked as Suzy came into the dinette.

"I don't know," Suzy said. "Unless it was the cops."

"It had to be Hastings." Greg folded the newspaper. "Surely the cops aren't that dumb."

"But this is Galveston." Suzy poured herself some coffee. "They don't play by the same rules everyone else does."

"Let's go get some lunch." Greg got up from the table. "I want to stop by the paper afterward."

"Can't it wait till tomorrow?"

"I just want to check something. It'll only take a minute."

They ate lunch at the Golden Greek, then drove to the *Star* building. The newsroom was almost deserted; few of the staff had yet arrived. But editor Seth Yeager sat in his office talking on the phone.

Greg and Suzy walked to the Associated Press teletype printers in a corner of the room.

"Have you seen these things?"

"In the movies, maybe." Suzy stopped in front of one of the machines.

The printers clattered as they typed the latest news from AP. Suddenly, bells started ringing on one of the printers.

"What's all that?" Suzy asked.

They leaned closer to the national wire and read as the keys typed:

BULLETIN
Washington (AP) – President Johnson announced today that two U.S. Marine divisions have landed on beaches outside Da Nang in South Vietnam.
The force has been ordered to seize the airport at Da Nang, which has been under Viet Cong control, the President said.

"Oh, that stupid war." Suzy had a pained expression. "What's Johnson doing?"

"If this keeps up, I may be over there before you know it."

"Don't say that. It scares me."

"I'm safe," Greg said. "Unless he mobilizes the whole country. But he seems determined to keep pouring troops in."

Seth Yeager came out of his office. "Greg, what are you doing here on your day off?"

"Hello, Mr. Yeager," Greg said. "I just wanted to check my notes about the autopsy. Did you hear what happened to Dan last night?"

"No, tell me about it."

"Another brick through the window at his apartment."

"You don't mean it?" Yeager looked at Suzy. "I'm sorry, Suzy. I haven't seen you since the Christmas party. I don't think I've seen you since you two got engaged. How are you doing?"

"I'm fine, Mr. Yeager," she smiled. "Just trying to keep Greg out of trouble."

"Suzy, we're awfully proud of Greg," Yeager said, shaking her hand. "You're getting a dedicated young man."

"Oh, I know," Suzy beamed.

"Now, Greg, what about the brick?"

"It was about three in the morning," Greg said. "It was the same M.O.—a message written with nail polish that said, 'You too.'"

"Did you call the police?"

"Yeah, a cop came and got the information. I saw a sports car driving away, but I didn't get a license number."

"Greg, you and Suzy come in my office." Yeager motioned them toward his door. "I've been on the phone with Houston, and we have some ideas about how to deal with this mess."

The three went into Yeager's office. Yeager fired up his pipe. Greg lit a cigarette.

"A lot of people here," Yeager said, "still want to believe this is the 'Free State of Galveston,' the way they did before the state cleaned the place up in the fifties."

"Outside the law and normal way of doing things," Greg said.

"That's right," Yeager went on. "We've got a serious situation here, Greg. The police and DA are covering up a crime to protect a rich, powerful man. People who should know tell me the JP is an independent old guy. He's got to rule on this kid's death tomorrow, and if he rules it a homicide, it's going to put the cops and the DA in a tight spot."

"What do you think they'll do?" Greg asked.

"There's no telling. But when a city or county refuses to act in the public interest, it's the state's job to do so. Our lawyer in Houston has been in touch with the attorney general's office in Austin, and they're sending an investigator and a couple of Texas

Rangers down here to look into this whole thing—the cover-up, the bricks, Hastings—everything."

"Wow," Greg said. "Finally some good news."

"We won't have anything about the case in Monday's paper," Yeager said. "But Tuesday, assuming the JP rules a homicide, we're going to put it all over the front page, along with an editorial I'm working on."

"Sounds like we've got our work cut out," Greg said.

"We sure do," Yeager said. "By the way, let's not say anything about the AG's investigation until it's complete."

"I understand," Greg said. "Thanks for filling me in."

"I wanted you to know what's coming, but you and Suzy enjoy the rest of Sunday and don't worry about it for now."

"Thanks, Mr. Yeager."

"Suzy, we've been putting this boy through the mill, and I know it's been tough. How's he holding up?"

"He's been feeling the stress," Suzy said. "But I think he's doing fine."

"Good. You're a nurse, aren't you?"

"Not yet. Just a student nurse."

"Well, you take good care of him. He's done a fine job for us. We don't want anything to happen to him."

"No, we sure don't," Suzy said, taking Greg's arm as she and Greg left the editor's office.

❖

April 1965

On Monday, Justice of the Peace Michael Radinsky ruled Curtis Warren's death a homicide, caused by blunt trauma to the head and skull. Dr. Ralph Cole, chief pathologist at UTMB, had performed the autopsy and reported his findings to the JP.

Dan called the police chief to ask how the department planned to proceed in the case in light of the autopsy. The chief refused comment, as did the DA when Luke Sanders contacted him.

Seth Yeager worked all afternoon polishing his editorial for Tuesday's front page. It read in part:

> Our island city was once known as the "Free State of Galveston." That reputation died in the 1950s when the state of Texas forced Galveston to join the rest of the state and world at large.
>
> Today, a more progressive Galveston seeks to put the past behind it and move forward.
>
> We regret that apparently not every public servant on the Island agrees with that goal.
>
> Two weeks ago, a 16-year-old boy, Curtis Warren, was brutally beaten and died later in the hospital. Another youth witnessed the beating, but police have shown little interest in interviewing him.
>
> The *Star* has convincing evidence that Galveston police and the district attorney's office are refusing to pursue the beating case in order to protect a resident of the city.
>
> Last week, someone threw a brick through the window of the *Star*'s newsroom. Over the weekend, a brick of the same type tore through the window of a *Star* reporter's apartment.
>
> We at the *Star* believe this sort of harassment may be the result of our coverage of Curtis Warren's beating death.
>
> The *Star* will not tolerate such intimidation tactics. We have taken legal measures in order to protect ourselves from these criminal acts.
>
> On Monday, a justice of the peace ruled Curtis Warren's death a homicide.
>
> The police chief and district attorney refused comment on the ruling.
>
> We believe the chief and the DA are shirking their duty to investigate a brutal crime in order to protect an influential resident.
>
> We urge right-thinking and progressive citizens of Galveston to demand that these officials do their jobs and bring this case to a conclusion.

The *Star* prominently displayed Yeager's unsigned editorial near the top of Page One, next to the main story about the JP's ruling, co-written by Dan and Luke. The headline, which Greg wrote in ninety-six-point type, read:

TEEN'S DEATH RULED A HOMICIDE

After the Tuesday edition of the paper came out, things became strangely quiet. There were no new developments in the story, no more bricks thrown, no storming of the editor's office by irate officials. The paper's production once again returned to a routine footing.

The *Star* received a couple of letters to the editor praising the paper's call for more responsible law enforcement, but little else of note.

Greg sat at his desk late one night that week. He asked Jeff if he wanted to have a couple of beers after work at Lolita's.

"Better not," Jeff said. "I promised Alex I'd drop by his place."

Alex, Greg thought. *Jeff's lover.* Jeff's sexual preference hadn't crossed Greg's mind in weeks. That knowledge had gotten lost next to everything else going on. The very fact that Greg hadn't given it a thought now resolved the matter once and for all: It was irrelevant.

Once things quieted down at work, Greg called Dr. Liesl Hoffman, the doctor Suzy had suggested. He went to see her the next Monday. Her office was in the medical school complex.

"Come in, Mr. Spencer," the doctor said with a noticeable German accent. "Have a seat." It sounded like, "Haff a zeat."

Greg had expected a plush office with a couch. Instead, Dr. Hoffman's office was small and spartan, composed of only the doctor's metal desk set and a hard wooden chair for one guest. Several diplomas hung on the light-green, institutional wall.

Greg sat in the chair.

"So, tell me," the doctor said. "What's been bothering you?" She was a thin, plain-looking woman in her forties with short, brown hair and narrow, plastic-rimmed glasses.

"I guess you'd call it chronic anxiety." Greg's heart pounded as it always did in the presence of a doctor.

"Yes, and how long have you had this anxiety?"

"Well, the first time was when I was nineteen. A doctor in Fort Worth put me in the hospital for ten days and gave me a lot of medication. This was after I'd been in a car wreck, with a concussion and two broken ribs. But I gradually got better and haven't had any problems until I moved to Galveston last fall."

She scribbled in a notebook. "And how old are you now?"

"I'll be twenty-five later this month."

"Yes, well, how does this anxiety manifest itself?"

Greg told the doctor of his panic episode in November and the stress in his job, especially since the Lester Hastings story broke, including the brick-throwing retaliation.

Dr. Hoffman didn't comment on what Greg had just told her. "Are you married?" she asked.

"No, but I'm engaged."

"And you're having sexual relations?"

Here comes Dr. Freud, Greg thought. "Well, yes, for the past three months."

"And how is it going?"

"You mean how is the sex?"

"Yes, any problems?"

"No, it's just fine, except our schedules have kept us apart more than we'd like."

"And what was your sex life like before?"

"Pretty barren. Lots of frustration. Before Suzy, my only sex was with a couple of prostitutes in Fort Worth and some backseat petting."

"I see," the doctor deadpanned. "Well, you grew up in America in the fifties, so that's not so unusual."

"I guess not." Greg wondered what this conversation had to do with anxiety.

"Does your fiancée live in Galveston?"

"Yes, she's a student nurse here at UTMB. She's talked to you before."

"Oh, what's her name?"

"Suzanne Cox. Suzy."

"Oh, yes. She's in psychiatric nursing. I see her on rounds. A very sweet and lovely girl."

Greg suddenly thought of Suzy's ex-boyfriend in Waco, and his blabbing about going to bed with Suzy. What if this got back to Suzy? "What I just told you is confidential, isn't it?"

"Oh, of course."

"Thank you," Greg said. "Sex is not a problem for us. But Suzy's mother is."

"Oh? Tell me about it."

Greg went through the whole saga with Mrs. Cox.

"Yes, and how does this make you feel?"

"I get depressed when I think about it. I mean, we don't need her permission to get married, but it would certainly be a dark cloud over our lives if she hates my guts."

"So maybe that's been nagging at you for some time."

"Yes, definitely."

"Okay, so you're under a lot of pressure at work, you're suffering from spells of anxiety. You have a history of anxiety episodes with some depression. Now, in order to understand this problem, I need to know as much about your past as possible. You may have a deep-seated subconscious conflict, and we need to find it and inspect it closely. So if you could relax and tell me the earliest thing you remember."

Greg paused, searching his memory. "Building a snowman, I think."

"Tell me about this snowman. Where were you? How old were you? Who else was there?"

Greg told of the time when he was two years old: His father and several friends were in the front yard of his grandmother's house. The snow was deep, maybe half a foot.

"And how did you feel about this snowman?"

"Well, it was big." Greg didn't have a clue how to answer such a question, but the doctor went on like this for another half-hour.

"Okay, that's enough for today," Dr. Hoffman said. "Let's try to do this once a week. Can you come that often?"

"I guess so," Greg said, wondering what he was getting into. "I can come before work. I have to be at work at three."

"How about next Tuesday at one?"

Greg agreed but left the doctor's office bewildered.

❖

That night when he took his break around ten, Greg called Suzy.

"I saw the shrink today." He lit a cigarette and exhaled a cloud of smoke.

"What'd you think?" Suzy sounded cheery and upbeat.

"She seems nice enough," Greg said. "But she's really big on dredging up the past."

"Yeah, that's how analysts work."

Greg hesitated, unsure if he should bring it up. "She seemed awfully interested in our sex life. I guess that's part of the Freudian scheme, too."

"What do you mean *our* sex life?" Suzy's voice suddenly had an uneasy edge.

Greg sighed. "Well, I told her I was engaged, and she asked me if I was having intercourse with my fiancée. I couldn't very well lie to her."

"What'd you tell her?" Suzy demanded.

"Just that we'd been getting it on for three months with no problems."

"I hope you didn't use those words." There was a hint of amusement in her voice now.

"No, of course not." Greg chuckled quietly.

"I'll still see her when she's on her rounds." Suzy sighed. "I hope I can look at her without blushing."

Greg put out his cigarette. "She's supposed to be above it all, isn't she?"

"Yeah, but she's human, and I'm someone she knows. Behind the scenes, doctors are a pretty raunchy bunch."

"Okay, but what was I supposed to tell her?"

"You said the right thing." Suzy seemed more at ease now. "It just kind of touches a raw nerve to have someone talking about my private life."

"I know. I thought about what happened in Waco."

"Well, we're all adults, but I still have some of that old Baptist shame, I guess."

"As she said, we grew up in the fifties. I felt pretty awkward, too."

"Do you feel any better after talking with her?"

Greg was relieved to change the subject. "To be honest, I don't feel any different. Things have calmed down here this week, so naturally I'm not as tense as I have been. I'm still pretty depressed about your mother."

"Oh, that." Suzy's voice turned serious again.

"Every time I think about her, I feel like a ton of bricks just fell on me."

"Greg, you'd be abnormal if you didn't. After all, she's rejected you, and that goes right to your sense of self-worth."

Greg frowned. "Now you sound like a shrink. Doesn't it depress you?"

"Sure, but more than anything it just makes me furious."

"Have you talked to her lately?"

"No, I called Daddy to tell him I wouldn't be home for Easter."

"Oh, my God. When is Easter?"

"It's this Sunday, darlin'," Suzy said with sweet reproach.

"And you're not going home?"

"No, I'm still so mad at Mother, I could scream." The anger vibrated in Suzy's voice.

"How did your dad take the news of your staying here?"

"He was decent about it. I think he understands. I've got finals coming up soon and several papers due. That's part of it, too."

"Your father deserves a medal." Greg picked at one of the remaining scabs on his arm.

"I know. I'm sure Mother would be even more upset if she knew I was going to Easter services at an Episcopal church."

"With Cindy?"

"Cindy and Brian."

"Is Brian an Episcopalian?"

"No, I think he's a Presbyterian, but there's not much difference. Why don't you come with us?"

A red flag from the past went up. "Uh-oh, trying to save my soul again?"

"No, I'm not. You might enjoy it. We could go to lunch afterward. Besides, when was the last time you went to church on Easter?"

"Probably in high school. What time?"

"Eleven o'clock. That's not too early for a night owl."

"Yeah, I was afraid it might be early. Okay. I'll pick you up about ten-thirty."

Greg no longer owned a suit. He hadn't put on a tie since his days as a reporter for the Fort Worth *News-Beacon*. He still had a couple of Oxford-cloth dress shirts, but they had grown yellow from disuse in his closet. Maybe his sport coat would conceal the shirt's sad state. He donned coat and tie on Easter morning and drove to Suzy and Cindy's apartment.

Brian Reynolds was already there. Brian and Cindy squeezed into the tight back seat of Greg's Corvair, and the four of them headed for church.

Trinity Episcopal Church was one of Galveston's oldest structures, built in 1857. It had survived a Civil War battle and numerous floods and hurricanes, including the great storm of 1900.

Greg had passed the church on his way to and from work, but had never before looked closely at its exquisite stained-glass windows.

The two couples walked inside and took seats in the ancient pews. Greg was surprised at his reaction to the service. He still didn't buy the miraculous theology, but the grandeur of the church, the sanctity of the ceremony, and the stirring organ and choral music left him with a sense of sacred mystery that went beyond words and theological concepts.

The foursome walked through the floral spring air back into Greg's car and drove to Gaido's for lunch.

At the restaurant, Brian and Cindy announced some news.

"First and foremost," Brian said. "I gave Cindy an engagement ring yesterday. We'll get married next May, after she gets her nursing degree."

"And there's more," Cindy said.

"Yeah," Brian said, "I got accepted for my internship and residency at Amarillo General Hospital. So I'm off to the Panhandle as soon as I get my M.D. next month. I'll finally get to go home after four years in this hellhole."

"Shouldn't we order some champagne?" Greg asked. They all agreed, and when the bottle arrived, they drank a toast to the couple and their good fortune.

After lunch, Suzy and Cindy excused themselves to go to the ladies' room.

"Are you going into private practice when your residency is over?" Greg asked Brian.

"I sure hope to," Brian said. "I want to stay in Amarillo if I can."

"I don't know if Suzy or Cindy has said anything," Greg said, debating whether to bring it up. "But I'm seeing Dr. Hoffman at UTMB. Do you know her?"

"Oh, sure. She's one of my professors." Brian paused. "As a matter of fact, I assist her sometimes. I saw your name on her schedule. I didn't want to break confidentiality and mention it."

"Thanks, I appreciate that."

"Yeah, I had a vague idea from what Suzy's told Cindy that you've had some problems with anxiety."

Shame trickled through Greg. "Right. I hope she can help me, but based on my first session with her, I'm not so sure."

"Let me tell you something, Greg," Brian leaned closer. "I'm not sold on psychoanalysis as a treatment for anxiety. I've been hearing about a doctor in Australia, who's changing a lot of thinking about anxiety disorders. I think she may have the right idea."

"Suzy told me about her," Greg said. "What does she say?"

"Basically, it's a matter of understanding and controlling the release of adrenaline in the body. I haven't read a whole lot, but some of my professors have talked about her. She doesn't think a person's past has much to do with most anxiety problems."

"That's pretty revolutionary, isn't it?"

"It is. It may start a war with the Freudians. But if it's effective—and it seems to be—it could have a big impact."

"Hey, maybe you can get her methods down, and I can come see you in Amarillo. I have relatives not far from there."

"Where?"

"Hereford, just southwest of Amarillo."

"Oh, hell, yes. I know Hereford well. I'd love to see you. If you're ever out that way, be sure and look me up."

❖

Greg attended his weekly sessions with Dr. Hoffman. She probed his past, but still offered little concrete practical help with the current state of his anxiety. The extra expense put a strain on his monthly finances.

He fretted about his upcoming marriage to Suzy. Time was running short. Suzy's mother had shown no sign of relenting in her opposition to the wedding. A constant tension gnawed at Greg, and low-grade depression colored his thoughts.

There had been no new developments in the Lester Hastings beating case. Moreover, Dan talked to some reliable sources who'd squelched the theory that Lester was about to spring a big hotel deal with help from the mob. Hastings had apparently floated the idea to people around him, but there seemed to be little substance to it.

An investigator from the state attorney general's office and two Texas Rangers had been in and out of Galveston looking into the beating death of Curtis Warren, but the *Star* had agreed to keep quiet about the probe until it was completed. No one knew how long the investigation would take.

Suzy remained at the center of Greg's world, but his sour mood now spilled into their relationship.

"I'm wasting my time with Dr. Hoffman," Greg said, sipping a glass of wine near the pool at Suzy's apartment complex.

"I know you're impatient," she said, rubbing suntan lotion on her legs. "But these Freudian shrinks take a long time getting to the bottom of things. That's just how it works."

"And that's time we don't have," Greg snapped. "We've got a month or six weeks to plan this damned wedding, and we haven't done anything."

"What do you mean, 'this damned wedding'?" Suzy shot back. "Is that what it's become to you?"

"You know what I mean. We haven't lined up a church or a minister. We haven't put together a guest list. We haven't talked about a honeymoon. Nothing."

"We can talk about those things, but I don't want to talk to you when you're so negative about everything."

Greg lit a cigarette and slumped in the patio chair. "I feel like nothing is going right. How can I feel so crappy when I should be happier than I've ever been?"

"Have you told Dr. Hoffman about your bad mood?"

"Sure, but it doesn't seem to matter. She's only interested in digging in my past. What good does that do when I'm messed up now?"

"Maybe she could put you on some kind of antidepressant."

"Oh, great." Greg snuffed out his cigarette. "Do you want to marry someone who's held together with drugs?"

"It would be temporary, till you get things figured out."

"Sometimes I wonder if I'll ever get things figured out. Maybe I was born this way and can't expect to ever be any different."

"Cut it out!" Suzy slammed her hand on the patio table. "You're just feeling sorry for yourself. You're better than that."

There was a long silence. Greg lit another cigarette and finished his glass of wine. He was so wrapped up in his misery, he'd scarcely noticed how voluptuous Suzy looked in her yellow two-piece bathing suit.

"Maybe you're right," he said. "I'm sorry."

Suzy gave him a conciliatory look. "I could use some lotion on my back." She handed him the bottle. He stood behind her on the chaise lounge and applied the slippery Coppertone to her shoulders.

"Mmm, that feels good," she said. "Down a little lower."

Greg slathered on more lotion and moved down Suzy's back. He slid his hands up her waist and nudged the sides of her breasts.

"Careful!" she giggled.

"Why don't we get in the pool?"

Once in the water, Suzy playfully splashed water in Greg's face.

"Hey, cut it out," he shouted. "What are you doing?"

"I'm seeing if a little water will cool off an old grouch."

"Oh, yeah? Take this," Greg said, smiling for the first time. He carved out a wave with his arm and sent it spraying across Suzy's head and upper body. Then, he grabbed her shoulders and dunked her under the surface. She came up spewing water and giggling with childlike glee.

They moved closer, and he felt the wet silkiness of Suzy's skin. He pulled her to him and slipped a leg between her thighs.

"You look really hot in that suit," he said. "It's all I can do to keep from pulling it off of you right here."

"Think anyone would notice?" Suzy gave him a seductive look. No one else was in or near the pool.

"I'd say let's go inside," Greg said. "But I don't think I can get out of the water right now."

"What's the matter?"

"Can't you tell?" He guided her hand to the bulging front of his bathing suit.

"Oh!" She giggled. "You're afraid someone might see you in heat?"

"Yeah, I'm bashful that way."

"Just wrap a towel around you, and let's run for the stairs."

They both grabbed towels and dashed up the steps, dripping water. In Suzy's bedroom, they hurriedly peeled off their wet suits, then fell into bed without drying off.

Greg's cloud of despair lifted, at least for the time being.

Greg's fingers glided over Suzy's back as they lay in each other's arms

"Hey," Suzy whispered.

"Yeah?"

"Let's elope."

He rose up and looked at her. "I've been thinking the same thing," he said. "Are you sure that's what you want?"

"It's not my first choice," she said. "But I don't see any way around it. Things are just too complicated."

Greg mulled over the idea for a moment. "We could get a justice of the peace here, or we could drive to Denton. I'm sure my uncle would do it."

"How about Father Shilling?" Suzy sat up and leaned against her folded knees. "I've gotten to know him pretty well; I think he'd marry us." Shilling was the rector at Trinity Episcopal.

"But when?" Greg asked.

"After finals," Suzy said. "They're two weeks away. Let's talk to him."

Greg and Suzy met with Shilling the next week. He graciously agreed to officiate at a small ceremony. Greg and Suzy would have one attendant each and no one else present. They agreed on Tuesday, June 8, at one in the afternoon.

Afterward, they stopped at the Dairy Queen on Broadway for a celebration with frozen treats.

"Who do you want for best man?" Suzy asked as they sat down at a booth.

"Eddie King's my first choice," Greg said. "He's known us longer than anybody. If he can't make it, I'll ask Jeff. How about your maid of honor?"

"I'd like to ask my sister Beverly." Suzy paused and wrinkled her brow. "But getting my family involved might cause problems."

"You're probably right." Greg carved at his banana split.

"Then it has to be Cindy."

Greg told Dr. Hoffman about his wedding plans.

"Yes, let's talk about your parents' marriage," she said.

Depression crept back over Greg. Would he ever get any real insight into his anxiety problem?

❖

On Monday, the team of Texas Rangers and investigators from the state attorney general's office announced that they'd hold a news conference at three p.m. on Tuesday.

The team notified members of the Galveston County press, as well as reporters from the Houston television stations and newspapers. Dan Forbes and Luke Sanders covered the conference for the *Star*, along with photographer Sandra Peterson. Greg, Jeff, and editor Seth Yeager walked the few blocks from the *Star* building to the county courthouse on 25th Street.

The attorney general himself, Weldon Williams, was on hand to present the team's findings. A small, wiry man with crisp black hair, Williams stepped to a lectern and unloaded several bombshells.

"Ladies and gentlemen, we've concluded an investigation of some five weeks, and here are our findings:

"We find that the Galveston police department and district attorney's office have been severely derelict in their duties in regard to the death of Curtis Warren on March 17 of this year."

A buzz went up from the gaggle of reporters and onlookers.

"Further," the AG went on, "we have impaneled a special grand jury, and that jury has returned a bill of indictment against one Thomas Lester Hastings Junior, age thirty-four, of Galveston, on a charge of first-degree murder in the death of Curtis Warren."

Gasps of disbelief ricocheted around the room.

Williams went on: "That same grand jury also returned indictments against Police Chief William J. Casey and District Attorney Angelo P. Conti on charges of official misconduct.

"As you know, those offices exist under the charter of the State of Texas. The state has the power to enforce any abuse of those offices, and the grand jury has heard overwhelming evidence that such abuse has occurred.

"Those indicted have been placed under arrest, and bond has been set at $100,000 for each of the three.

"That concludes my statement. I'll be glad to take your questions."

Some of the reporters rushed from the room to find telephones. Those who stayed fired questions at the AG. He expanded on his prepared statement, but added few new facts.

Greg felt relief that justice, at last, was being served. But walking back to the newspaper office, he and Jeff discussed some lingering misgivings.

"That's all well and good," Greg said. "But who knows what kind of crooked connections Lester still has with the chief and DA?"

"You mean even if they're indicted, what's gonna stop them from still trying to get even?"

"Right," Greg said, getting more agitated. "Who'll stop them from burning down the *Star* or worse?"

"They ought to realize the AG is keeping a close eye on them, and if they screw up, it just means more trouble for them."

"Sure, but who says these creeps are rational? They might try anything."

"Let's talk to Yeager and see what he thinks," Jeff said, climbing the steps back at the *Star*.

Yeager came into his office shortly. He knew the attorney general personally and had had a brief private audience with him after the press conference.

"Well, I guess we get to play newspaper again," the editor cracked, lighting his pipe.

"Mr. Yeager," Greg said. "Jeff and I were just talking about retaliation. Did you get any assurance from the AG about our safety?"

"Yes, Greg," the editor said between puffs. "We discussed that in some detail. He said they've advised the acting chief to be on the lookout for anything that smacks of retaliation against us or anyone else. He's promised the AG increased patrols around the Warren home, the home of the boy who drove him to the hospital, and the justice of the peace's home and office. The Rangers and a lawyer will remain in town to make sure that extra protection takes place."

Greg was still wary. "And the *Star* and our employees?"

"That, too, of course," Yeager said.

"But how do we know the acting chief won't be loyal to Casey?"

"We don't," Yeager said. "But if I were the acting chief and had the AG's office breathing down my neck, I think I'd be damned careful. The state could put everyone on that force in jail after all this. They're surely feeling the heat."

"Maybe you're right," Greg said.

"Try to relax," the editor said in his fatherly tones. "We may be nearing the home stretch. Things are going our way now."

Greg went back to his desk. *Try to relax,* he thought. Some consolation.

Dan and Luke came back to the office in an hour. Both sat at their typewriters, furiously pounding out their stories for the next day's edition. Sandra Peterson brought Greg several glossy prints of the pictures she'd made at the news conference. Greg chose two photos, one an overall shot of the news conference and the other a closeup of Attorney General Williams with a stern expression.

"We'll use these two, Sandra," Greg said. "By the way, do we have any recent shots of Lester Hastings?"

"I think so," Sandra said. "I made some shots of him at a reception a couple of months ago that ran on the society page."

"How about printing them and letting me see them?" Greg said. "Try to make sure they show his face nice and clear—looking as depraved as possible."

Sandra laughed. "You got it, boss," She headed back to the photo lab.

When Greg returned from dinner, he found a stack of photos Sandra had printed of Hastings. Greg chose one showing Hastings holding a plaque that named him the Galveston Historical Society's "Man of the Year." He wore a broad, self-satisfied grin. Greg thought it perfect for Page One.

The staff spent the rest of the night assembling stories for the front page and the local section.

Greg went upstairs to check on the page makeup. Tony Rodriguez worked doggedly to make all the stories fit.

"Hey, Gregorio, you got brick insurance?" Tony asked.

"We may need it, Tony," Greg said.

"What's this 'we' shit?" Tony said. "I got no problem with Hastings or the cops, either."

"Well, just keep it that way, Tony. You'll have a happier life."

Tony chuckled from his gut. "Hey, Gregorio. You're okay, man. You know that?"

"Send the page in; we're done."

Greg called Suzy. She'd fallen asleep studying for final exams and sounded groggy when she answered the phone. He gave her the day's big news.

"That's great, isn't it?" she said.

"Well, maybe." Greg was still unconvinced of his safety.

"What do you mean, 'maybe'? The bad guys are under arrest."

"Well, yeah, but they posted bond and got out right away."

"You want to come over?" she asked, around a yawn.

"No, you need the sleep. Is Cindy still up?"

"Yeah, she's at the kitchen table with books all around her."

"Well, don't stay up all night," Greg said. "I'll talk to you tomorrow."

"Okay, I'm ready to call it a night."

"Suzy," Greg paused.

"Yeah?"

"I love you, more than anything."

"And I love you, too. Sleep tight, darlin'."

Greg drove home. Inside his apartment, he went to the medicine cabinet and reached for the Valium bottle. He'd gone all afternoon without one.

Before he could open the bottle's lid, someone banged on his door. It was nearly two a.m.

Greg put down the bottle and went to the door. He cracked it open.

"Police. Open up."

Greg threw the door open. Two men in dark suits rushed in.

"What's going on?" Greg said.

"Gregory Spencer?"

"That's right." Greg's heartbeat surged.

The men flashed badges. "We have a warrant that says we have probable cause to search your apartment." The man held out a paper for Greg to see. It looked official.

"Search for what?" Greg pleaded, his voice now trembling.

"Possession of an illegal substance," the man said.

The other man walked into Greg's kitchen and opened a drawer in the cabinet. He returned with a hand-rolled cigarette and a plastic bag filled with what looked like tea.

"Are these yours?" the man asked.

Greg, now shaking uncontrollably, said, "No, I've never seen them."

"Oh, a little nervous, eh?" The man said. "Come on. We're going downtown."

The floor seemed to collapse from beneath Greg, as if a trapdoor had opened under his feet. His head swam, and he gasped for breath. He felt squeezed into a tight, crowded space filled with only terror.

"I said come on, Spencer."

Greg bolted for the door. The two men grabbed him and pinned his arms behind him. One of them clamped a pair of handcuffs on him.

Greg gagged and threw up on himself as the two men hustled him down the stairs.

"Probably a junkie that missed his connection," one of the men said. The other laughed heartily.

They threw Greg into the back seat of an unmarked car. The world spun. Greg was certain he was dying. Everything suddenly got very bright, then faded into the darkness of the Galveston night.

❖

When Greg regained a semblance of his senses, he was lying on a concrete floor in a pool of his own vomit. The sight and smell made him gag. He raised his body to escape the filth, only to be assaulted by more sickening smells in the air: urine, feces, sweat, and more vomit.

He lay in a narrow cell, containing only a grimy commode and metal cot suspended from the wall on chains. He looked down the row of cells. Men snored on other metal cots. A black man in the next cell paced back and forth, reciting what Greg took to be some kind of prayer.

Greg then saw the bars surrounding him, and he fully realized there was no escape. Panic seized him again. He shook violently and struggled to breathe. He stood at the front of his cell and grabbed the bars.

"Hey!" he shouted. "Get me out of here!"

He repeated his cries until his throat hurt. He pounded his fists against the bars.

Finally, a slovenly jailer with a protruding gut and several days' growth of beard sauntered along the row of cells.

"Finally sobered up, I see," he drawled to Greg.

"I'm not drunk," Greg pleaded. "I'm sick. I need a doctor."

"So they all say," the jailer said. "Try to sleep it off."

Greg's head swam. He tried to understand what had happened. Among the noxious thoughts, one coherent notion gradually came into focus: *No one knows I'm here.*

"Hey," he shouted as the jailer walked away. "Don't I get a phone call?"

"You was out cold when they brought you in," the jailer said. "You missed your chance."

"That's bullshit!" Greg shouted. "Prisoners have a right to one phone call. Do you know who I am?"

"I didn't see your ID." The jailer turned away. "You're just another drunk as far as I'm concerned."

"I work for the Galveston *Star*," Greg said. "And we have some high-powered lawyers who'll nail your ass if I ever get out of here."

The jailer studied Greg a moment. "Okay, pal, let's go. I'll give you one call."

The jailer unlocked the cell door and led Greg to the booking room. A phone sat on a desk across from another uniformed officer asleep in a chair, his head lolling backward.

"Dial nine for outside," the jailer said.

Greg's hand shook so, he had trouble dialing Suzy's number. She answered, sounding logy from sleep.

"Suzy, it's me. I'm in jail." His voice was desperate and tremulous.

"What? Are you trying to be funny?"

"No. They planted some marijuana in my apartment and brought me here. I passed out. Call Jeff or Dan. Tell them to get in touch with the AG's men."

"What's the AG?"

"The attorney general's investigators," he said, speaking hurriedly. "They're supposed to put a stop to this crap. I've got to go. Call them now."

"Greg, I'll come get you."

"No. Get Jeff Holcomb or Dan Forbes. I've got to go." He hung up the phone.

Back in his cell, Greg drew himself up into a knot, still shaking uncontrollably. He vomited again, but only foul-tasting bile came up. His head ached, and he could barely manage short, shallow breaths. He felt dizzy and lightheaded. Bright flashes of light appeared in his vision.

He sat this way for what seemed like hours. *What if Suzy can't get hold of anyone? What if I have to stay here? What if I die here?* He couldn't stanch the waves of panic that convulsed him with each toxic thought.

Greg heard noise outside, and shortly several people appeared in front of his cell. Jeff stood behind the slob of a jailer. A man in a sport coat and open-collared shirt stood next to Jeff.

"Hey, Greg," Jeff said. "We're here to get you out. This is Mr. Fleming from the AG's staff."

The jailer opened the door. Greg walked over and shook Fleming's hand. He was a well-groomed man in his forties with dark, close-cropped hair.

"Let's go, Greg." Fleming said. "I think we can guess what happened."

Greg retrieved his wallet and watch from the booking room and followed Jeff and Fleming up the stairs of the ancient, crumbling police-station basement. It had been built at the turn of the twentieth century and had been in disrepair for years.

"Where can we talk?" Fleming asked. "I want to get your version of this, Greg."

Jeff suggested they go to the *Star* building. They got into Fleming's car and drove the few blocks to the paper. Greg couldn't stop shaking. Sweat rolled down his face.

"Jeff, did Suzy call you?" he asked.

"Yes," Jeff said. "She's pretty worried. You better call her when we get to the newsroom."

They climbed the stairs to the second floor. The teletypes in the newsroom sat silent. Greg looked at a clock. It was nearly six a.m.

"I need to stop in the men's room and wash up," Greg said.

"Go ahead," Jeff said. "I'll get you some coffee."

Back in the newsroom, Greg sipped his coffee and asked if Fleming could give him time to call his fiancée. Fleming agreed.

"Suzy," Greg said into the phone. "I'm out."

"Are you okay?"

"Not exactly," Greg said. "I can't stop shaking."

"Have you taken your Valium?"

"No, it's at the apartment."

"Be sure you take one when you get home," she said. "Where are you?"

"At the *Star*. This guy from the AG's office wants to interview me."

"Greg, I'm coming down there."

"No, Suzy. You've got exams. I'll be okay."

"Are you sure?"

"Yes. Try to get some sleep."

Greg poured out his story to Fleming, who took notes as Greg answered his questions.

"Did these two cops give you their names?" Fleming asked.

"No," Greg said. "They showed me badges, but never identified themselves."

"Something's funny here," Fleming said. "Do you remember being booked at the jail?"

"No, all I remember is passing out in the car and coming to in the cell."

"I checked with the acting chief," Fleming said. "And he swears he doesn't know anything about a drug arrest last night. I checked with the vice detectives, and they claim they don't know about it, either. There's no record that you were booked."

Greg squinted and tried to clear his head. "You think they may have been some of Hastings's goons?"

"It's possible," Fleming said. "But on this island, almost anything's possible."

"But how could they put me in jail if they were fake cops?"

"Good question," Fleming said. "Unless someone paid off the jailers."

"This place is like some little country in Central America," Greg said, at last showing his anger. "A goddamn banana republic, with Lester Hastings as the dictator."

"It's one hell of a mess," Fleming said, putting his notes in a pocket. "Okay, Greg, that's enough for now. Go home and get some sleep."

"Oh, Greg," said Jeff, standing nearby. "I don't think you know what else happened last night."

"No, what?"

"Dan had his tires slashed, and somebody cut all the wiring in Yeager's car."

"God almighty," Greg groaned. "I'm afraid to go home."

"I'll take you," Jeff said. "We can look things over."

When they arrived, Jeff walked upstairs with Greg to his apartment. They looked around inside for anything suspicious, Greg's panic quivering just below the surface. But they found nothing unusual.

"Call me if you see anything strange," Greg said.

Jeff left and went to his apartment across the complex's inner courtyard.

When Jeff had gone, Greg went to his medicine cabinet and swallowed a Valium, as Suzy had suggested. Greg waited for the pill to take effect, but after a half-hour he felt no relief. Instead, a vile cloud of depression seized him. His gut churned. Sweat popped out again on his forehead, and his limbs again shook. Then, a single thought gripped him.

Gasping for breath, he dialed Suzy's number.

"I've got to get out of here," he said when she answered the phone.

"What do you mean?"

"I mean, I can't take this place any longer." He paused to draw in a labored breath. His voice quavered. "I'm going back to Fort Worth."

"Greg, what are you talking about?"

"I'll see Dr. Simon and see if he can help me. He's the only doctor who knows my history. Dr. Hoffman was no help at all."

"But there are lots of doctors here who could help you," she pleaded. "Don't run away."

"I can't explain it, Suzy." The compulsion gripped him even harder. "I've got to leave. I can't stay in this town another hour."

"Greg, please." Suzy was practically sobbing. "You're having what's called the 'fight-or-flight' response. Let me help."

"I know you want to. But I've got to get out of here. This is how I felt in December when I had that spell. I feel like I'll go crazy or die if I stay here."

"Let me come over, Greg. Please." Suzy now wept audibly.

"No, Suzy. I'm leaving. I love you, but I can't stay here." Greg hung up the phone.

He got his suitcase out of the closet and threw some clothes inside. He gathered his toiletries from the bathroom, put them in his travel bag, and closed it inside his suitcase. He locked his door and took his suitcase to the Corvair, parked along the curb.

In five minutes, he was speeding northward across the Galveston Bay causeway.

Fuck you, Galveston! he thought. *I hope I never lay eyes on you again.*

❖

Greg drove with a fury. The hard, glaring light made him squint as the sun climbed higher. But he sped onward with a single-minded obsession.

In some part of his mind, he knew he'd probably never work for the Galveston *Star* again. He also knew he was putting his upcoming wedding in jeopardy. But those thoughts lay far back in his consciousness. The only thing that mattered was getting to a zone of safety: He had to get home. That impulse drove him forward. His panic had transmuted into a searing compulsion to keep going, to get as far from Galveston as he could.

He passed through Houston during the morning rush. He impatiently crept northward on the Gulf Freeway, cursing the slowdowns. Once he passed downtown, the traffic moved again. Greg stomped the accelerator and sped ahead.

The adrenaline gushed, and Greg's heart thumped at a furious pace as he passed through first one town, then another: Conroe, Huntsville, Madisonville, Corsicana. Sweat streamed down his face and soaked through his shirt.

At Ennis, he turned westward on Highway 287; he'd reached the home stretch. He passed through Waxahachie and Midlothian and finally entered Tarrant County. He was almost there.

Suddenly, he heard a loud thump in the Corvair's rear engine compartment. White smoke poured from the exhaust. He pulled onto the shoulder of the two-lane highway.

The fan belt had broken. Greg normally kept a spare on a clip next to the engine, but he'd forgotten to replace the spare the last time the belt had broken.

His doggedness now reverted to fear, and panic again surged through him. He remembered that he'd driven for short distances without a fan belt before. Maybe he could make it to Mansfield, the next town just outside Fort Worth.

He looked around. He was on a lonely stretch of road. There were no other cars or buildings in sight. He'd have to chance it. He got in the car and turned the starter. The engine coughed smoke, but finally started. Greg heard clanks and clatters, but the car was running. He pulled back onto the highway.

He tried driving slowly, but the engine ran more roughly and then died again. He coasted to the shoulder and turned off the ignition. Maybe he could let the engine cool and then drive for only a few miles at a time.

Tension gripped his arms and shoulders. His head felt as if a tight band were squeezing it. His eyes burned from the strain and lack of sleep.

He tried the starter. The engine wouldn't fire. He tried and tried until finally the battery went dead. Tears of anger and frustration filled Greg's eyes. He got out of the car and opened the rear engine compartment. The engine hissed and sizzled. Smoke seeped out of its seams.

"God damn you!" Greg shouted and kicked the rear fender. "God damn you, you sorry-assed piece of shit!"

Then, he crawled back inside and lay across the bucket seats. His body convulsed, and the visible world faded.

Greg's consciousness darted in and out. He heard voices from outside the car.

"When I stopped, I seen him just like that. I thought he was dead, but he was breathin'."

Another voice said, "Okay, thanks, Mr. Bodiford. I've called an ambulance."

Greg turned his head. Through the driver's side window, he saw a tall man wearing a white Stetson hat and a gray uniform with a black tie and patches on his shoulders.

The man opened the front door and shook Greg.

"Sir," the man said. "Sir, can you hear me?"

"Yeah," Greg croaked.

"Can you get up, sir?"

Greg raised himself, shaking all over.

"Are you sick?" the man asked.

"Yes," Greg said.

"I've called an ambulance. Do you think you need medical attention?"

"Yes," Greg said in almost a whisper. "Take me to Village Creek Memorial Hospital and call Dr. Simon."

"Can you show me some ID?"

Greg pulled his driver's license from his wallet.

"Okay, Mr. Spencer. I'm Officer Craft of the Department of Public Safety. Can you stand up?"

"I don't know," Greg said.

"Why don't you try? Here, I'll help you."

Greg put one foot on the ground, then the other. He wobbled as he tried to stand. The officer helped him to stay on his feet. Greg's head spun, and he had to grab the car door to keep from falling.

"You haven't been drinking, have you?" the trooper asked.

"Hell, no," Greg said. "I mean, 'no, sir.' Smell my breath."

The officer put his nose inches in front of Greg's mouth and sniffed.

"What about drugs? Do you use drugs?"

"I have a prescription for Valium. I took one this morning before I left Galveston. I'd been driving nonstop all morning until my fan belt broke. I couldn't start the car."

Greg heard a siren in the distance. Shortly, an ambulance from Moore's Funeral Home pulled to the shoulder.

The trooper and an attendant helped Greg into the back of the ambulance. He lay down on the stretcher.

"Take him to the ER at Village Creek Memorial," the officer told the attendant. "And call Dr. . . . What was his name, Spencer?"

"Simon. Dr. Daniel Simon."

"Right," the officer said. "I'll have your car towed to the city auto pound in Fort Worth."

The ambulance sped away. Greg's thoughts flashed back to the day almost exactly six years earlier when an ambulance had taken him to the hospital for his first serious encounter with anxiety.

"You're shaking pretty bad," the attendant said.

"I've a got a nervous condition," Greg said.

"You're not epileptic, are you?"

"Not that I know of." Greg said. "I could use a drink of water. My mouth is dry."

Just as in 1959, the attendant filled a cup and handed it to Greg. "Try to relax. We'll be at the hospital in a few minutes."

There it was: *Try to relax.*

In the emergency room, Greg went through an examination similar to the one he'd had when he was nineteen. An intern gave him a shot of Valium and a muscle relaxant. Greg's breathing slowed, and he sank into a semblance of calm.

A nurse brought a telephone to his bed, and he called his parents' house.

"Greg, we've been worried to death," Vivian said. "Suzy called us at seven this morning to tell us you were on your way to Fort Worth."

"I'm here," Greg said with a thick tongue from the drugs. "They're calling Dr. Simon. I guess they'll keep me here."

"Your dad and I will be right over." Vivian said.

Suzy, Greg thought. *What have I done to Suzy?*

It Takes a Worried Man

❖

Three

❖
Arlington
June 1965

Greg fell into a drugged sleep before his parents arrived. He awoke late in the afternoon with George and Vivian at his bedside in a private room. He told them about being jailed and his car breaking down.

"It all came crashing down on top of me," he said. "I guess I just cracked."

"Okay," George said. "Try not to think about it. Let's concentrate on getting you well."

"I wish I understood you, Greg," his mother said. "You had everything going for you, and then this."

"Okay, Vivian," George said. "Not now. Let's see what the doctor says."

A nurse brought Greg his dinner. He nibbled at a few things, but had no appetite.

A slender man in a dark suit appeared in the doorway.

"Gregory Spencer?" he asked.

"That's him." Vivian gestured toward the bed.

"I'm Dr. Green," the doctor said. "Dr. Simon is out of town, and I'm seeing his patients."

The doctor stood next to Greg's bed. "Sounds like you had a bad anxiety episode."

"The worst." Greg told the doctor what had happened and about his past history with anxiety.

"And you've been taking Valium?" The doctor looked over some papers.

"Yes, I've been taking five-milligram tablets, and they gave me a shot of it here."

"Greg, I make it my business to stay on top of the latest advances in medication." The doctor wore a self-satisfied look. "I don't think Valium is the right drug for you. I'm going to put you on Haldol. You should feel better right away."

Something didn't sound right to Greg. "Whatever you think, but I've had withdrawal symptoms from stopping Valium too suddenly."

"Hogwash," the doctor said. "Valium isn't addictive."

When the doctor left, Vivian walked back to the bed. "Greg, you should call Suzy. She must be worried sick."

Depression sank deep into Greg's gut. "I don't know if I can talk to her after all this."

"For heaven's sake, you're engaged to her," Vivian said. "You have to talk to her."

"Okay, but I want some privacy."

"We need to get home," George said. "You call her. And call us if you need anything."

Greg ached at the thought that he'd hurt Suzy, maybe irreparably. Their wedding was three weeks away. What could he say to her now? How could he possibly get married?

He hesitantly dialed the operator and asked for a person-to-person call to Suzanne Cox in Galveston. He gave the operator her number.

"Suzy, it's me."

"Greg! Where are you?"

"I'm in the hospital."

"My God, I've been going crazy." The strain in her voice was palpable.

"Suzy, I'm so sorry. What have I done to you?"

"You haven't done anything to me," she practically shouted. "Tell me what happened."

He told her how his car had broken down and how he'd come to the hospital in an ambulance.

"I finished my last exam today," she said, sounding more collected and determined. "I'm going to drive to Houston and catch a flight to Dallas. I'll be there as soon as I can."

"Are you sure?"

"Of course, I'm sure. I have to."

"Do you want my folks to pick you up at the airport?"

"That's probably simpler than getting my folks involved."

"You have their number, don't you?"

"Yes."

"They just left, but I'll call them and tell them you're coming. You can tell them what time to be at Love Field."

"Okay, darlin'. I'll be there no later than tomorrow morning. You sound kinda groggy."

"They've given me a lot of drugs. I'm pretty doped up."

"You can tell me all about it when I get there. I'd better start packing."

Greg felt relieved, but guilt still gnawed at him. "Okay, but don't push yourself too hard. You've been through a rough time, too."

"Don't worry, I'm fine." She paused. "I love you, Greg. Very much. Don't ever forget that."

❖

A nurse brought Greg his nighttime medication. He took the pills from the tiny paper cup and swallowed them.

"What are these?" he asked the nurse.

"Haldol, Triavil, and Orphenadrine."

"What are they for?"

"They'll help you get some rest."

Greg lay on his back, staring at the ceiling. Remorse and depression shot through him. How could the basket case he'd become get married and support a wife in nursing school? He'd spent the past month with a psychoanalyst, and he had no more insight into his anxiety problem than before. He'd tried to work through the stress of his job, much as he'd played football in high school with a broken wrist, but he'd failed utterly. How could he hold a job with this illness always lurking and ready to strike?

He wondered if Suzy were kidding herself in thinking they could make a life together with such a plague hovering over them. The thoughts spun more slowly as he felt himself getting heavier from the drugs.

Greg suddenly noticed his arms and legs twitching, then the muscles around his face. The weight of the drugs made him struggle to form thoughts. With muscles jerking all over his body, he closed his eyes, hoping he'd fall asleep.

But instead, outlandish apparitions appeared. With closed eyes, he saw bright black-and-white images of Felix the Cat and other cartoon characters. He remembered having seen these cartoons on early TV when he was a kid. They swarmed and frolicked and ran across his field of vision. He forced his eyes open again. His arms and legs jerked and twitched.

He grabbed the alarm button and pressed it. Shortly, a nurse arrived.

"What's the problem?" she asked.

"I don't know," Greg said, barely able to form the words. "Look at me."

"You're having some muscle spasms," the nurse said. "It may be a side effect of some of the medication."

"Can't sleep," Greg slurred. "Seeing things."

"Okay, we'll give you something else to make you sleep."

The nurse left and returned with a huge needle that looked more suited to livestock. Greg turned over and she jabbed the needle into his buttocks.

"Okay, honey, you'll be fine now." The nurse sounded full of self-assurance.

After a few minutes, Greg plunged into a miasma of blackness.

Dreams appeared, first more cartoon characters, and then Greg found himself lying on a beach. Suzy was in the water up to her waist, crying for help as a school of sharks circled her. Greg lay in a cave alive with poisonous snakes. The snakes hissed and coiled, striking at Greg's arms and legs. He jerked with pain as each set of fangs pierced his skin. He tried to rise to go to Suzy's aid, but he couldn't move his limbs.

That dream faded, but others followed. He and Suzy were riding on a bus through the mountains of Mexico. The bus traveled over what appeared to be a mountain road with hairpin turns and switchbacks. The road was littered with rocks and boulders, and the bus bounced up and down and side to side as it passed over the debris.

The dreams came one after the other; each one seemed more painful and distressing than the last. This pageant of terror seemed to go on endlessly.

Finally, Greg opened his eyes. Suzy stood next to the bed, wiping his forehead with a wet washcloth.

"Suzy, is it you?" He had trouble focusing.

"It's me, darlin'. I'm here."

"Suzy, what have they done to me?"

She straightened his cover. "They made quite a mess. I'm trying to get it fixed."

"What happened?"

"I've had to piece it together from what the nurses told me, but it sounds like the guy that's filling in for Dr. Simon is a complete fool."

"I didn't like that guy," Greg said with a heavy tongue.

"First, he had no business taking you off of Valium. You were in withdrawal. Then he gave you Haldol, which is mainly for schizophrenia. I have no idea what he was thinking. It caused all those muscle spasms."

"What about the cartoons?"

"Cartoons?"

"Yeah, when I closed my eyes I saw cartoons of Felix the Cat."

"Oh, no," Suzy managed a weak laugh. "That was probably the Triavil doing that. It can cause hallucinations, not to mention what all that stuff does mixed together."

"What are they going to do with me?"

"I got the head nurse, and we went to one of the staff residents. I told them your history, and they agreed to put you back on Valium. Here's your dose. Open up."

Greg swallowed two light-blue tablets. "God, Suzy, you're a wonder. You should be a doctor, not a nurse."

"No, thanks. We're just lucky Dr. Green's gone for the weekend. The resident agreed with me and changed your meds. Dr. Simon will be back Monday."

"How much Valium are they giving me?"

"Twenty milligrams. That's a big dose, and you'll probably go back to sleep. But we're done with the rest of that stuff they were giving you."

Tears filled Greg's eyes. "My God, what have I put you through?"

"I'll be okay." There was a long pause. "At least I hope so."

❖

Greg slept until late Sunday afternoon. When he awoke, Suzy sat on the edge of a cot she'd brought into the room. She yawned and stretched, then walked over next to Greg's bed.

"Finally get some rest?" he asked her.

"Yeah. How about you?"

"I feel like I've been asleep a week."

George and Vivian came into the room. All three stood at Greg's bedside.

"I've sure let everybody down," Greg said.

"Don't talk like that," Suzy said. "A lot of people love you, no matter what's happened."

"But the paper . . . I really left them in the lurch," Greg said, trying to raise himself up. George turned a crank to raise the head of the bed.

"You need to call Jeff Holcomb," Vivian said. "He called the house today, and I told him what happened."

"How did he take it?"

"I think he understood as well as anyone can," Vivian said. "But I told him you'd call him when you felt like it."

"I'll call him." Greg shook his head. "But I dread it."

"How do you feel today?" Vivian asked.

"A little more rested, but I'm pretty depressed and still nauseated. I don't feel like eating."

"You need some nourishment," Vivian said.

"Well, I'll try," Greg sighed. "After last night, I think my whole system is wrong side out."

"What happened last night?" George asked.

"Oh, you didn't know? Suzy, you tell them. You know the details better than I do."

Suzy filled in the Spencers on the substitute doctor's instructions and the rough night Greg had spent. She explained how she'd gotten Dr. Green's orders reversed by the staff resident.

"Suzy, I don't know what we'd do without you," Vivian said.

"I just did what I've been trained to do," Suzy shrugged. "But I think we're on the right track now. Dr. Simon'll be back tomorrow."

After his parents left, Suzy approached the bed.

Greg looked at her with a doleful expression. "I don't see how we can go ahead with the wedding now. God, I feel awful."

"Well, darlin'," she said, taking his hand. "If we have to postpone it, then we postpone it. Nothing was set in stone, anyway."

Greg squinched his face in anguish. "I've screwed everything up," he moaned.

"No, you haven't. Now, stop it. We'll work things out."

Greg turned over and buried his face in his pillow. Suzy ran her hand along the back of his neck and massaged his shoulders. "Oh, Greg," she said. "My dear, darlin' Greg."

A nurse's aide brought Greg's dinner. He gagged at the thought of food, but after another round of Valium, his stomach settled enough for him to eat some soup and Jell-O.

"I'd better call Jeff," he said. "I hope I still have a job."

"Of course you do." Suzy removed Greg's food tray. "Do you want me to wait outside?"

"Stay here." Greg looked at Suzy's face. She wore no makeup, and her eyes looked hollow from the strain. "I'll bet you're exhausted."

"I'm okay, but I think I'll lie down while you call."

Greg dialed the phone on the bedside table. Jeff had weekends off, so Greg called him at his apartment.

"Greg, you had us worried," Jeff said. "How are you doing?"

"Not so good."

"Are you still in the hospital?"

"Yeah," Greg said. "Thank goodness, Suzy's here to keep these people straight." Greg recounted his problems the first night.

"But you're doing better now?" Jeff asked.

"I don't know. I see my regular doctor tomorrow."

"Okay, I wanted to fill you in on what's going on here." Jeff's tone sounded grave.

"Doesn't sound good." Greg's nerves stood on edge.

"It's not." Jeff paused. "Yeager's in the hospital with a bleeding ulcer."

"My God, him, too?"

"Yeah, he's in intensive care, and Jim Stephens is running the paper. He's pretty tense about your situation. You need to let him know what your prognosis is."

"Hell, I don't know myself. Maybe after I talk to the doctor tomorrow I can tell Jim something, but not now."

"Okay, I'll tell him you'll call him tomorrow. But I wouldn't wait around too long."

Greg's heart sank. "Do you think he wants to fire me?"

"You'll have to talk to him, Greg."

"Damn," Greg said. "Okay, Jeff. I won't keep you."

They wrapped up their conversation. Suzy sat up on her cot. "You don't have a job anymore?"

"It doesn't sound good," Greg said. He repeated what Jeff had told him.

"Good Lord, Greg. What will you do if that's true?"

"I don't know. Everything's coming unraveled, Suzy." Greg fell back onto his pillow.

❖

When Dr. Simon came into Greg's room the next morning, Greg recounted the events that had led to his most recent setback.

"Seems to me a lot of people might have panicked under those circumstances," the doctor said. "But you're so tightly wound, it's no surprise all that affected you this way."

"But it's ruining my life. Suzy and I have had to postpone our wedding. I might get fired. This can't keep up."

"Did you ever see Dr. Brooks in Galveston?"

"He doesn't see patients anymore. I saw one of his colleagues, Dr. Hoffman."

"For how long?" Dr. Simon sat on the end of the bed.

"About a month."

"That's not very long. Did it help?"

"Not that I could tell. She was more interested in my past than my present."

"Yeah," Dr. Simon sighed. "That's how analysts work. But I think you could benefit from long-term therapy. I still believe you have a subconscious conflict that needs to see the light of day."

"That may be true," Greg said. "But what do I do in the meantime?"

"I want to keep you on a higher dose of Valium and give you an antidepressant. You seem pretty down."

"I am. How could my life be more screwed up?" A nurse came in and brought Greg a fresh pitcher of water.

"What about your job?" the doctor asked. "Are you going back to Galveston?"

"I don't know. My boss is in the hospital, and the guy filling in for him may not be as sympathetic as he was."

"Have you talked to him?"

"I'm supposed to call him today. My friend Jeff told me he wants to know my 'prognosis.'"

Simon looked at his watch. "Why don't you call him now? I'll give him my opinion."

Greg's muscles tightened as he placed the call.

"Greg, how are you feeling?" Jim Stephens said in a flat, emotionless tone.

"Not so hot, Jim. Jeff said I should call you."

"Yeah, Greg, we're in a hell of a spot here. This Hastings thing won't settle down. Frankly, we need you here now. But if you're not well enough to come back right away, we need to get somebody in your job we can count on."

Greg's jaw clenched. "I'm sorry, Jim. I sure as hell didn't plan it this way."

"I know you didn't," Stephens said. "But this has happened more than once. We need a city editor who can see this thing through."

Greg shrugged his shoulders in exasperation. "Okay, I understand—I guess."

"So, what do you think?" Stephens sounded impatient. "How long are you going to be laid up?"

"My doctor is right here. He can tell you." Greg handed the phone to Dr. Simon.

"Yes, this is Dr. Simon. Greg is not in any shape to return to work right away, in my professional opinion." He paused to let Stephens reply.

"Yes, yes, I understand your position, but Greg has been through a very traumatic experience, not only in Galveston, but on his way here, and also once he got here. He's had a pretty rough time." Dr. Simon paused again.

"That's right. I wouldn't recommend that he come back for at least a few weeks. He needs to rest and let some of his new medication do its job." Another pause.

"Yes, here he is." Dr. Simon handed the phone back to Greg.

"Jim, does that answer your question?"

Stephens paused a moment. "Yes, Greg, and I hate to do this. You've done a nice job for us, but this just can't go on. I'm going to have to replace you."

Greg's heart sank even lower.

Stephens went on, "Maybe when you get well, you can come talk to us about a job here. But for now, I'm going to have to let you go."

Greg's voice grew more tremulous. "Jim, can I ask you a question?"

"Sure, go ahead."

"Does Mr. Yeager know about your decision?"

"No, Greg. His doctors have told him to avoid contact with the paper. He's in pretty bad shape. He made me the acting editor, and I make the calls as I see them."

Greg's whole body burned with shame. "Okay, Jim. I guess that's it, then."

"I guess so. Do you want us to mail your last paycheck to your address here in Galveston?"

"That's okay. I guess it'll get forwarded once I move out."

"Okay, I'll take care of it. Good luck, Greg."

"Right." Greg hung up the phone.

He sat shaking his head. "He just fired my ass," Greg said, looking forlorn and feeling numb all over.

"Not a very understanding boss," Dr. Simon said. "But that's how some people view this kind of ailment." He looked squarely at

Greg. "Okay, it's done. I had to be honest with the man. Let's look ahead. Can you get a job here?"

"I'll try the *News-Beacon* and see if they have anything. Beyond that, I don't know. Maybe one of the Dallas papers."

"I don't think you need to stay in the hospital. You're not close to being as run-down as you were the first time I saw you. I think you can bounce back pretty fast."

Greg shrugged. "That's good, I guess."

"You need some time to rest awhile and get over this. Still, I wouldn't wait too long to start looking for a job."

Suzy walked back into the room. She had gone to her parents' house to change clothes and clean up. Greg introduced her to Dr. Simon.

"This is the girl you were afraid to kiss?" Dr. Simon asked with a wry smile.

"This is the one," Greg said. "But we made up for lost time."

Suzy blushed. "Glad to meet you, Dr. Simon."

"And you, too, Miss . . .?"

"Cox. Suzy Cox."

"Suzy, I just got some bad news," Greg slid out of the bed. "Jim Stephens fired me."

Suzy's face registered shock. She put her arms around Greg. "I'm so sorry, Greg. As hard as you've worked for those people, how could they?"

"Yeager didn't know anything about it. I don't think he would have fired me."

"It could be a blessing," Dr. Simon said. "I don't think you were very happy in that job."

"It's a relief in a way," Greg said. "But it's so humiliating. It blows my career plans all to hell. It'll be on my employment record."

"Just don't give that guy as a reference," the doctor said. "It may not matter that much. You've still got a long career ahead of you."

"Even if I get a job here, Suzy'll still be in Galveston; we'll be miles apart. That's going to be hard."

"I think we can make it work, Greg," Suzy said. "Don't despair."

"Better listen to her," the doctor said. "This girl has the right idea."

"Did I tell you Suzy's studying to be a psychiatric nurse at UTMB?" Greg said.

"Oh, really?" The doctor brightened. "That's my old stomping grounds. I went to med school at UTMB. I'll bet it's changed since 1952."

"It keeps growing," Suzy said. "I really like it there."

They made more small talk, then Dr. Simon said, "Okay, Greg. I'm going to release you today."

Greg looked surprised. "You think I'm ready?"

"I think the quicker you get back on the horse, the better off you'll be. Don't just sit around feeling sorry for yourself. Suzy, how long will you be in town?"

"The summer semester at school doesn't start for two weeks. I can stay here at least a week, maybe ten days."

"Good. You can keep tabs on Greg, make sure he's taking his medication, and give him moral support. I think that's important right now. You two get out and do something you enjoy. I wouldn't push the idea of trying to set a new date for your wedding. Let's just keep an eye on things for a while."

"We can deal with that," Suzy said. "Thanks, doctor."

"And by the way, Suzy. They told me what you did Saturday morning, about Greg's medication. That was good, alert nursing. I wish you well with your career."

"How nice. Thank you," Suzy said.

"By the way, doctor," Greg said. "Who is this Dr. Green, and what was he doing giving me all that weird medication?"

"Greg, some things are better not discussed outside the profession. Let's just say we have differing views on the subject of pharmacology."

"What do I need to do to get out of here?" Greg asked.

"I'll leave a release with admissions," the doctor said, then he paused. "Suzy, could you go down to the nurses' station and ask them for a release form?"

"Sure," Suzy said and left the room.

Dr. Simon turned back to Greg. "Do you have any idea how lucky you are?"

"Of course, I do. It kills me to put her through all this."

"She's going to make damned sure you get yourself well. You can count on it."

"I'll do whatever it takes," Greg said.

Suzy appeared with the form. The doctor filled in some blanks and signed it. He wrote two prescriptions and gave them to Greg.

"Call my office and make an appointment for next week," he said. "Good luck to both of you."

❖

Suzy, sleep-deprived and near exhaustion, drove Greg home from the hospital, then returned to her parents' house where she was finally able to get some rest.

Likewise, Greg spent the next two days lolling around the Spencer house, reading a little, and, for the first time in years, watching TV in the evening, seeing for the first time such popular programs as "The Andy Griffith Show" and "Leave it to Beaver." It occurred to him how sweet and simple these programs were, more reflective of a past era now seemingly being overtaken by coarser realities.

Once Suzy felt rested, she picked up Greg, and they spent easy afternoons in parks around the city, playing miniature golf, riding a miniature train, feeding the ducks in Trinity Park, and generally taking it easy.

As they walked through the Botanic Garden, Greg felt a bittersweet ambivalence that came from revisiting the site where they'd become engaged last Christmas and facing the reality that they'd had to postpone their wedding to some indefinite date in the future.

Suzy reminded Greg that his Corvair had been towed to the city auto pound. He'd had it moved to a Chevrolet dealer, where the service manager proclaimed the car's engine damaged beyond repair. A rebuilt engine would cost more than the car was worth. Greg, now virtually broke, stewed about what to do.

George agreed to float Greg a loan to make a down payment, and Suzy helped Greg pick out a '65 Volkswagen Beetle, the cheapest new car on the market. Greg groused about going into debt.

"But it's so cute," Suzy said.

Greg and Suzy met their old friend Eddie King over dinner the next night. Eddie told Greg he thought there might be staff openings at the *News-Beacon*. Larry McGregor, Greg's former city editor, had been elevated to managing editor and was making some changes in the newsroom. Eddie had been promoted to night city editor.

Greg talked on the phone with Jeff Holcomb in Galveston.

"I'll be down next week," Greg said, "to move my stuff out of the apartment. Would you tell Mrs. Kaplan what's going on?"

"I've already told her," Jeff said. "I'll tell her when you're coming."

"Have they set a trial date for Hastings?" Greg cringed, recalling the Galveston saga.

"Not that I've heard," Jeff said. "But I hear Lester has a high-powered defense lawyer from Houston who's trying to get the charge reduced to manslaughter."

"The sorry bastard," Greg said. "Okay, I'll probably be down there next Wednesday or Thursday. We can talk more then."

Greg walked into Larry McGregor's glassed-in office at the *News-Beacon.* McGregor greeted him warmly.

"I read about that mess in Galveston," McGregor said, offering Greg a seat.

"You mean the Hastings story?" Greg wondered if McGregor knew about his sudden departure from the Star.

"Yeah. I was just telling your dad a couple of months ago that if you ever decided to come home, I'd sure like to hire you." McGregor knew Greg's parents socially.

"Why, thanks, Larry." Greg felt relieved that McGregor apparently didn't know he'd been fired. "You got any jobs open?"

"Greg, we need a makeup editor and part-time copy editor. Your experience in Galveston probably taught you about both of those things."

"Yeah, I supervised the makeup of our local pages and edited lots and lots of copy."

"How'd you get along with the printers?"

"Pretty well, I think. They trusted me; I trusted them. They were a tough bunch."

"I think you'd fit in real well here. You'd come in at five every afternoon and work till one a.m. You'd oversee the makeup of each edition and work the copy desk between editions. How's that sound?"

"Great," Greg said. "I'm your man."

Greg would start work on June 8, the day he and Suzy had originally planned to get married.

❖

"I'm worried about Mother," Suzy said, walking into the living room of the Spencers' house. She had been spending nights and most mornings with her parents. "Maybe it's a good thing we put off our wedding."

"What's wrong?" Greg asked, sitting next to Suzy on the sofa.

"She has these terrible headaches," Suzy said, popping open a compact to touch up her lipstick. "She stays in bed most of the time and doesn't make much sense."

Greg thought of saying Mrs. Cox had never made much sense to him, but he held his tongue. Greg and Suzy were alone in the house that Sunday afternoon in late May. George and Vivian had gone to Dallas to visit friends.

"She has an appointment with a neurologist in a couple of weeks," Suzy said.

They were sitting side by side on the sofa. "Are you going with her?"

"No, I can't. I've got to get back to Galveston."

"When are you going back?"

"Probably Friday," she said. "How are you feeling today?"

"I'm okay as long as I'm doing something," Greg said. "But this gloom comes over me when I'm not busy."

"Is your medication helping yet?"

"Maybe a little. I've been pretty calm. The only time I get a little shaky is when I drive. I guess my car breaking down spooked me."

Suzy wore a pair of cutoff jeans and a tight-fitting knit top. For some time, sex had been far from Greg's thoughts. Now, his male juices bubbled to the surface, and he couldn't keep his eyes off Suzy. "We've got the house to ourselves, you know," he said.

Greg moved close to Suzy. "Have I told you lately what great legs you have?"

They made love for the first time in weeks, but Greg felt something wasn't right. Suzy tried to reassure him that all the medication he was taking could diminish his libido and that he shouldn't worry about it; she didn't notice a problem. Greg remained unconvinced.

❖
June 1965

Suzy left for Galveston at the end of the week. Greg felt her absence keenly and dreaded the idea of being apart from her.

The next week, he and George drove to Galveston to retrieve Greg's belongings from his apartment. Once there, they rented a small U-Haul trailer for the return trip.

At the apartment, Greg and George spent a couple of hours boxing up Greg's things.

"Why don't you go see Suzy?" George said. "I can start loading the trailer while you're gone."

"Save the heavy stuff till I get back," Greg said, wiping sweat from his face. "I'll try not to be too long."

Greg unhitched the trailer from George's Dodge Dart and drove east along Seawall Boulevard, watching the surf crash into the beach below the wall. The sea had drawn him to Galveston, but like the sailors who had answered the sirens' song in myth, Greg felt his life in Galveston lay shattered on the rocks.

He parked in front of Suzy's apartment.

She greeted him at the door, and they stood hugging as if they hadn't seen each other for months. Cindy appeared and gave Greg a hug, too.

"I've missed you," Suzy said. "And it hasn't even been a week."

"I know," Greg said. "I hate to think what it'll be like a month from now."

"You'd better just stay here," Cindy joked. "Maybe you can get a job as a lifeguard or a beachcomber."

"Oh, sure," Greg said, smiling. "Have you heard from Brian?"

"Yeah, he's started his residency in Amarillo," Cindy said. "I miss him something awful, so I know how you and Suzy feel."

"Give him my best," Greg said.

"I will. Well, I'll leave y'all alone." Cindy retreated to her bedroom.

"You look better," Suzy said. "How's it going?"

"Okay. I start the new job next week."

"Have you seen Dr. Simon?" Suzy led him to the couch, and they sat down.

"I saw him last Friday. I asked him what he thought about setting a new date for our wedding."

"And?"

"He thought I should get settled in the new job for a while before deciding anything."

"I can't say I'm surprised," Suzy said.

"I'm sorry, Suzy."

"No, there's no deadline. I want the time to be right."

"Me, too," Greg said. "If it helps any, the *News-Beacon* has one of those free WATS lines. I can call you every night if you want."

"That's nice," Suzy said. "Not like you being here, but. . . ." There was a soft sadness in her voice.

Suzy put her head on Greg's shoulder. He felt her shuddering with sobs.

"Suzy, I'm sorry I put you through all this." Greg put his arms around her. She couldn't stop crying long enough to get any words out.

"You've been through hell," he said. "Go ahead and let it go; it's my turn to comfort you for a change."

She put her head in Greg's lap and cried some more. He wiped her tears with his handkerchief and held her head in his hands as the pain and stress of the past month came gushing out.

Finally, Suzy composed herself.

"You're right," she sniffed. "I've been holding it all in. I guess the dam had to break sometime."

"You're a brave girl, and I love you more than ever."

"Greg," she said, then paused. "There's more."

"What do you mean?"

"The doctors think my mother has a brain tumor."

"Oh, no." Greg sat silently for a moment. "What are they going to do?"

"More tests. It could mean surgery."

"Could that explain some of her behavior?"

"Maybe," Suzy said. "She hasn't been herself for a long time."

"If your dad needs anything . . . I mean, if I can help in any way."

"I know. I'll keep you posted."

"I hate to go, but Dad's at the apartment. He'll think I fell in the ocean."

"I'm sorry I didn't get to see him. Please give him my best."

"I will." Greg stepped toward the door.

"When are you driving back?"

"Later this afternoon. We're going to stop at the hospital. I want to see Mr. Yeager."

"That's nice. He's such a sweet man."

"The best."

Greg and George finished loading the U-Haul and hitched it back to the car. As George carried the last box to the trailer, Greg looked around the empty apartment for anything they might have missed.

Jeff Holcomb knocked at the open door and walked into the apartment.

"I saw you over here," Jeff said.

"Yeah, I guess we've pretty well cleaned the place out."

"How do you feel?" Jeff sat on the sofa bed, now stripped down to its bare mattress.

"I'm doing better," Greg said. "But still a little wobbly."

"For what it's worth, I thought Stephens treated you like crap. As hard as you worked, you didn't deserve that."

"I don't think the guy understands my situation very well."

"Well, it's done," Jeff said. "And I'm really sorry it had to happen that way." Jeff looked out the window. "He's got me back on the city desk now. I'm working both jobs: city editor and news editor."

"Wow, that's a load. How are you holding up?"

"Okay, so far. But I'm worried about Dan."

"Drinking too much again?" Greg stood before the air conditioner, fanning his chest with his open shirt.

"Yeah, he comes in hung over and looking like hell almost every day."

"Tell him hello for me," Greg said. "I don't want to stop by the office."

"Okay. I don't blame you; Stephens is probably there."

Greg changed the subject. "What's the latest on Hastings?"

"His lawyer has managed to get the charge reduced to manslaughter."

"You're kidding."

"No; money talks."

"Well, I still have my notes on the story." Greg buttoned his shirt. "Give me a call if they can be of any help."

"Thanks, I will," Jeff said. "What are you going to do now?"

"They hired me back at the *News-Beacon* as makeup editor. I start next week."

"Good luck. Let us hear from you."

George came back into the apartment. Greg introduced him to Jeff.

"Are we done?" Greg asked.

"I think that was the last load," George said.

"Jeff," Greg said. "Thank you for everything, the moral support, the professional advice, everything." The sadness almost overwhelmed him.

"And you take care of yourself," Jeff said, clasping Greg's hand. "I hope you can keep your demons under control."

Greg went to Mrs. Kaplan's apartment and gave her his key. Jeff had told her about Greg's time in the hospital.

"You tell that blondie-girl to fix you a nice steak. You'll be fine if you just eat right and get rid of that peaked look. I could have told you that was your trouble all along. What do these doctors know?"

George parked outside John Sealy Hospital. He and Greg went inside, and Greg got Seth Yeager's room number from the information desk. They took an elevator to the fourth floor.

Yeager was sitting up in bed, finishing his evening meal.

"Greg, come on in. I've been wanting to talk to you."

Yeager looked pale and drawn. Greg introduced his father to Yeager.

"You know, George, we might have known each other years ago," Yeager said. "Weren't you state editor of the *News-Beacon* at one time?"

"Sure was," George said.

"Well, I was your stringer in Wichita Falls."

"Son of a gun. I used to take stories from you over the phone back in the late forties."

"Isn't that something? I never made the connection before." George and Yeager chatted a few minutes about past newspaper days.

"How are you feeling, Mr. Yeager?" Greg stood near the foot of the bed.

"Pretty weak," Yeager said, sipping from a cup of iced tea. "I couldn't eat for a couple of weeks. But the ulcer seems to be healing now."

"I guess you heard about what happened to me."

Yeager shook his head. "That was an awful move on Jim's part, Greg. I feel responsible. I'm truly sorry."

"It might work out okay. I start back at the *News-Beacon* next week."

"I couldn't have hoped for better." Yeager lay back against his pillows. "Let me tell you something about Jim Stephens. We've worked together since right after the war. I know Jim pretty well."

"I knew you two went back a lot of years," Greg said.

"Jim was a bombardier on a B-17 during the war. Saw a lot of action over Europe. He came down with a bad case of what they used to call 'combat fatigue' and got a medical discharge. When I first met him, he was still suffering from shot nerves and nightmares.

He drank like a fish, and he worried me to death. He gradually got better and became a successful newspaperman. But he carried a deep sense of shame about what had happened to him. I think he tried his damnedest to deny to himself that his nervous trouble ever happened. So, instead of showing sympathy for anyone in a similar fix, it only angers him. He had no patience with you, Greg, because he has no patience with that part of himself."

"Did he know about your problems with nerves?" Greg asked.

"Most of my problems were over by the time we met," Yeager said. "But when I told him about my old trouble—just trying to let him know I understood—he treated them with disdain. So, I didn't mention them again."

"That's sad," Greg said. "And I guess I should feel sorry for him. Maybe I will someday, but right now I'm still smarting from getting fired."

"I know you are, Greg. And I can't tell you how much I regret that. But I made Jim the acting editor, and with me flat on my back in intensive care, I couldn't overrule him. I only learned about it a few days ago. But I'd be glad to give you a good reference if you ever need it."

"Thanks," Greg said. "When do you think you'll be able to work again?"

"Well, Greg, my days at the *Star* are over. The folks in Houston have asked me to be executive editor of the *Times*, and I'll be moving up there as soon as I'm able."

"Looks like Lester Hastings has taken his toll on both of us," Greg said.

"Yeah, that bum. But I'm proud of what we did, and you were one of the biggest parts of that." He looked at Greg's father. "George, this boy was the glue that held our coverage of this story together."

"Oh, I'm proud of him, too," George said. "I tried to warn him against going into newspaper work. But you know how kids are."

"Yes, I do," Yeager said. "But when it's in your blood, it's hard to get out. I think Greg still has a bright career ahead if he can tame his nerves a bit."

A nurse came in and said visiting hours were over.

Greg and George said their farewells to Yeager and left the hospital. They drove west on Broadway and out of Galveston.

As they crossed the causeway to the mainland, Greg saw again the shimmering water of Galveston Bay and, in the background, the twinkling lights of early evening on the island. For a moment, Greg thought it looked like a ghost city hovering above the sea, and it flickered through his mind that maybe he had dreamed all that had happened to him there the past ten months. But the momentary spell broke, and he turned his eyes to the road ahead.

❖

Fort Worth
September 1965

Greg's first three months back at the *News-Beacon* went smoothly. He worked well with the printers, as he had in Galveston, supervising the assembly of every page in the paper, except the sports and classified sections. The *News-Beacon*'s printers were union men and a little more polished than the Galveston crew, but they were similar in their attitudes toward editors: *Editors think they know everything, but it's us printers who make them look good.*

Between editions of the paper, Greg worked on the copy desk, editing stories and writing headlines. He dreaded this part of his daily routine: He liked the freedom of movement he had as makeup editor, but felt cramped and confined sitting at a desk for long periods, working under constant deadline pressure. It was all too familiar.

Greg befriended Harold "Bud" Riley, a slight young copy editor near Greg's age, who had poor eyesight and read copy with his nose almost touching the page. Greg, Bud, and Eddie King, now the night city editor, often went for a late-night snack after work at the Hotel Texas coffee shop. Sometimes they walked up Main Street late at night to a notorious nightspot called The Cellar, which featured waitresses in bikinis and illegally served stiff drinks made from grain alcohol.

Greg saw Dr. Simon monthly during that summer. The doctor still insisted Greg would be dogged by anxiety the rest of his life unless he resolved the "subconscious conflicts" at the root of his malady. Simon insisted deep analysis wasn't his specialty, and Greg would need to find another doctor for that kind of therapy.

He gave Greg the name of a psychiatrist in Dallas, who, Simon said, was having great success with group therapy, utilizing a school of psychology called "transactional analysis." Greg agreed to think about giving it a try.

Suzy drove to Fort Worth on weekends. Her mother now suffered from seizures, and doctors agreed she had a brain tumor. In late August, Mrs. Cox had an operation, and a surgeon successfully removed a benign tumor the size of a walnut from her brain.

Suzy's frequent trips to check on her mother meant Greg didn't have to drive to Galveston. It was just as well; he'd developed a strong aversion to driving. He didn't know if his phobia resulted from the harrowing experience of his car breaking down or the wreck he'd been in with Eddie. Whatever the reason, his four-mile drive to work every day caused his heart to race and his palms to sweat. Unless he was forced to drive somewhere, he avoided it.

Greg also noticed every time he saw a police car, he suddenly felt panicky and feared the police would stop him and, for no good reason, throw him in jail. He had nightmares about being in the Galveston jail. His vexations multiplied.

Greg noticed as long as he stayed busy, he felt calm and steady, but when he was alone or idle, depression crept over him. He told Dr. Simon about it. Simon increased his dosage of his antidepressant. Greg didn't notice any improvement.

He hadn't talked to anyone from the Galveston *Star* but noticed several AP wire stories about Lester Hastings's upcoming trial, which kept getting delayed by a Galveston judge. The most recent story said Hastings's lawyer had gotten a postponement until February 1966.

Suzy spent two weeks in Fort Worth during the break between summer school at UTMB and the beginning of the fall semester. She spent much of her time looking after her mother, who had been placed in a convalescent facility to recover from her surgery.

Greg resisted going to see Mrs. Cox, but Suzy pressed him.

"You might be surprised," Suzy said over lunch at Wyatt's Cafeteria, not far from the Spencers' house. "She's not the same person."

"She may hate me even more," Greg said, lighting a cigarette after finishing his meal.

"Give it a try," Suzy said. "I can promise she won't get out of bed and bite you."

They drove to the facility in the hospital district on the near south side of town. Greg tensed as they approached her room.

"Go on in," Suzy urged as Greg hung back at the door.

"Look who came to see you," Suzy said, approaching her mother's bed in a semi-private room.

Nadine Cox's head was swathed in bandages. She looked small and weak, but her pale blue eyes cut through Greg.

"Why, is that Greg Spencer?" She spoke in a soft, weak voice.

"Hello, Mrs. Cox," Greg said warily. "How are you feeling?"

"I'm weak," she said, barely above a whisper. "But I'm getting stronger every day."

"That's good." Greg was taken aback by her friendliness. "I guess Suzy's been taking good care of you."

"Yes. Everyone's been been awfully good to me. Suzanne's going to be a good nurse; she already is."

Suzy spoke up. "Mother wants to tell you something, Greg. About us."

"Come here, Greg," Mrs. Cox said. Greg stepped closer to the bed.

"Greg, did I say some ugly things to you?"

"Well, I. . . ."

"You don't have to answer. I know I did. I barely remember it, but I know I wasn't myself for a long time. I was pretty crazy, to put it bluntly."

"The tumor did that to you," Greg said.

"Yes, and for some reason, I was confused about you. I don't even know why, but I do know I said some hateful things about you marrying Suzanne."

"Yeah, well. . . ."

"Greg, I realize Suzanne loves you, and nothing I can say is going to change that. I pray for your happiness."

Greg couldn't believe his ears. "And you don't mind that I'm not a Baptist?"

"Well, of course I mind." She managed a feeble laugh. "I wish everyone in the world was a Baptist. But my other kids didn't marry Baptists, and I love them all."

"That's sure nice to hear, Mrs. Cox. Thanks for saying those things. I hope you're feeling better soon."

"Thank you, Greg. You take care of yourself."

❖

Greg and Suzy celebrated Mrs. Cox's blessing with dinner at the House of Molé, one of Fort Worth's nicest restaurants.

"Did it ever occur to you something like that was wrong with her?" he asked, polishing off the last of a bottle of wine.

"Sure," Suzy said. "We've studied brain-tumor cases in school, and I thought about it. But she wouldn't go to the doctor. I told Daddy it was a possibility, but he refused to believe it."

"I never thought she liked me, even when we first started dating, but she was never that hostile."

"Mother is pretty shy," Suzy said. "She probably gave you that idea because she didn't say much then. But what you're seeing is what she was always like before. She's pretty much her old self again."

"Well, it wasn't unconditional," Greg said. "But she did soften quite a bit. At least that cloud hanging over us isn't quite as dark as it was for so long."

"I'm so happy," Suzy said with a rosy glow from the meal and wine. "I can think of another way we could celebrate."

"Yeah, but where?" Greg asked. "I think our choices are limited to a motel room or the back seat."

"Daddy will be with Mother. He always stays until visiting hours are over at ten-thirty. And it's only seven."

"You talked me into it," Greg said.

Back at the Coxes' house, Greg and Suzy rushed to her old bedroom with an eagerness approaching their first time the previous Christmas.

They undressed and got into bed, but Greg could tell something was wrong. As Suzy's passion mounted, Greg backed away.

"What's wrong?" she asked.

"Nothing's happening."

Suzy's gentle efforts to help out proved frutiless.

"It's no use," he said. "It's not working."

"Okay, maybe you're trying too hard. Let's take our time, and maybe it'll be all right."

But Greg knew nothing was going to happen. Depression knifed into him. He lay there disconsolately.

"Hey," Suzy whispered. "It's probably the medication, like I told you before. Didn't you say Dr. Simon increased your antidepressant?"

"Yeah."

"And you've had half a bottle of wine. Remember Shakespeare."

"It's not funny."

"Okay, but it's not permanent."

Greg rolled away from Suzy and sat on the side of the bed, staring down at the floor.

"It's not the end of the world, Greg." Suzy reached over and put her arms around his waist. He flung them off.

"What's wrong with you?" Suzy sat up. "I'm trying to help."

"It's no use," Greg moaned. "I don't see how we can plan to get married if I'm on drugs that make me impotent."

"Stop it! You're making too big a deal of it."

"I'd better go." Greg started getting dressed.

"Greg!" Suzy shouted. "You're acting like an asshole."

He'd never heard Suzy use that word. "Well, maybe you'd better find you a stud," he snapped. "Obviously, I'm not right for you."

Greg stomped toward the front door, tucking in his shirttail. Suzy stood naked and speechless as he went out the door.

Greg drove home in a cloud of despair. Driving along Beach Street, he noticed a black-and-white police car behind him. Sweat popped out on his brow, and tremors overtook him. His foot slipped off the accelerator as his legs trembled. He tried to stay within the speed limit. The car followed him as he turned onto East Winchester. His arms ached from the tension of gripping the steering wheel. The police car followed him for about a mile, then finally passed him and sped ahead.

He shook all the way home. His parents were in bed. He went to his room, shut the door, and fell face down, still shaking, onto the bed. He buried his face in the pillow and lay awake most of the night, finally falling asleep after sunrise.

"Greg," his mother's voice called. "Get up. Suzy's here."

Greg sat on the edge of his bed for a moment, then got up and threw a robe around him. He went into the living room, where Suzy sat on the sofa.

"I'm going to the grocery store," Vivian said going out the door, leaving them alone. Greg was grateful for the privacy.

"What time is it?" he asked.

"One o'clock," Suzy said with a grave expression. "We've got to talk."

"I'm not awake yet," Greg said.

"Quit acting like a baby," she snapped. "At least you got some sleep. That's more than I can say."

"Okay, what?"

"Greg, we got the best news yesterday we could have hoped for from my mother. And yet last night, you threw cold water on everything because your male ego couldn't take a little disappointment."

Greg cringed. Suzy had never spoken to him like this. She sat fiercely glowering at him on the edge of her chair. Greg had never seen her so incensed.

"It's more than that," he said weakly.

"Oh, I know. Poor Greg. You're depressed. You're frustrated." she said bitterly. "The world has ganged up on you, and you have nothing to feel good about."

"Of all people," he said weakly. "I thought you understood."

"Will you shut up with that crap? I'm not going to put up with your whining. And I'm damned sure not going to put up with any more stunts like you pulled last night."

Greg sat speechless. After a long silence, he said, "Suzy, I've tried everything, and nothing works. I don't see much hope that I'm ever going to be any different."

"And that's giving up," she said, a little more calmly. "There are plenty of things you haven't tried. Didn't Dr. Simon tell you about a guy in Dallas who does group therapy?"

Greg winced. "Yeah, but it just sounds like more of the same old BS to me."

"How will you know unless you try it?"

"Okay, I'll call him," Greg snapped. "Will that make you happy?"

"What'll make me happy is for you to get off your butt. Sitting around feeling sorry for yourself won't accomplish anything."

"I've made your life miserable, I know."

"Will you stop it?!" Suzy's face turned red. "Quit whining! I can take care of myself."

"But, Suzy, we can't get married with things as screwed up as they are."

"We can't get married before spring, anyway. Now that you're back here and I'm in Galveston, it would be foolish to get married before I graduate. Just quit all this damned pissing and moaning and decide you're going to fight."

Greg winced. "Where'd you learn that kind of language?"

"You haven't been around nurses much, have you?"

"I guess not."

"Well, don't change the subject." Suzy leveled her gaze at him. "Greg, I fell in love with a guy who fought like hell to succeed in his profession. What's happened to that fight?"

"It's hard to find right now. I feel like my world crumbled in Galveston."

"Greg, you have to want to get well. No one can do it for you."

Greg sighed and sat silent for a moment. "You've been so patient. . . .Okay, I'll call that shrink in Dallas Monday."

"I've got to go," Suzy said. "I'm going back to Galveston tomorrow. I need to pack."

"You're going back already?"

"I have to. The fall semester starts in a week, and I've left a million things undone."

Greg got up and walked with Suzy to the door.

"Don't give up on me," he said. "I owe you everything."

"You don't owe me anything," she said firmly. "But you owe yourself the rest of your life. I'd like to be part of it."

"I love you, Suzy."

She looked at him a moment. "I know," she said softly and gave him a dry, lifeless kiss. Then, she went to her car and drove away.

❖

Greg made an appointment with Dr. Joseph Cochran at his office in Dallas's fashionable Oak Lawn neighborhood. The doctor, a tall man in his fifties with a pasty, cadaverous face and flowing white hair, ushered Greg into a spacious room that contained a dozen leather-covered Ames chairs arranged in an oval around the room's periphery. The doctor wore a black turtleneck sweater, which revealed a protruding belly.

"This is where our groups meet," the doctor said, anticipating Greg's question. "Have a seat."

"Thanks."

"So, Greg, what brings you here?" The doctor assumed a concerned expression.

"Well, Dr. Daniel Simon in Fort Worth suggested that I see you."

The doctor sighed with seeming disapproval. "Yes, I've met Simon. What's troubling you?"

Greg went through his history of trouble with anxiety. The doctor folded his hands and extended his two index fingers so they touched his nose as he listened.

"Sounds like a pretty clear-cut case," Cochran said. "I think I can help you—probably pretty quickly."

"What's with group therapy?" Greg asked. "All I've ever heard about it has been from comedians on TV, mostly debunking it."

"Just remember, Greg, people will debunk anything if they don't know much about it. Have you heard of a book called *Games People Play?*"

"I think I've heard of it, but I don't know much about it."

"It's written by Dr. Eric Berne, who has developed a method of psychotherapy called Transactional Analysis. TA throws out much of the technical jargon of conventional psychoanalysis and describes neuroses in very simple, understandable terms."

"That sounds like a positive step," Greg said, becoming more interested. "Tell me what I need to do."

"We have weekly group sessions, right here in this room. We've found that our patients get better faster when they interact with each other, rather than just meeting with a therapist alone. I moderate the sessions and keep us on track. I can assign you to a group, and we can get started right away."

Greg felt uneasy but thought the pros outweighed the cons. "Okay, when can I join a group?"

They discussed the fee, and Greg agreed to start attending sessions the next week.

Greg drove the thirty miles back to Fort Worth on the Turnpike at rush hour with a thumping pulse and sweaty palms. He dreaded having to drive to Dallas every week, but if the group therapy sessions worked, he might get some relief from his driving phobia.

When he got to work that evening, his nearsighted colleague, Bud Riley, approached him.

"Did you hear the news about McGregor?"

"No, what's up?"

"He had a heart attack this morning and died around noon."

The news hit Greg hard. Larry McGregor, the paper's managing editor, had hired Greg and had been a mentor when Greg was a cub reporter. McGregor had trusted Greg to help direct coverage of President Kennedy's assassination and recommended him to head the Arlington bureau. "My God," Greg said. "He wasn't that old."

"Fifty-nine," Bud said. "Nelson is moving into his job."

"Oh, shit," Greg said.

"What's the matter? Nelson's a great guy." Ben Nelson was the paper's Sunday editor.

"I know everyone likes him," Greg said. "But I've never gotten along with him, going all the way back to when I was a copy boy. He chewed my ass out over the most trivial things. I've never thought he trusted me."

"Well, he's kind of a sloppy dresser and doesn't radiate the elegance McGregor did, but I think we'll be fine with him in charge."

The next day, Ben Nelson called Greg into his office. Nelson stood more than six feet and weighed around two-fifty. His profile resembled that of a bear. News editor Cliff Clifton called him "Smokey."

"Greg, I'm putting you on the copy desk full-time." Nelson had a gruff, direct way of speaking.

Greg's heart sank. "Did I do something wrong?"

"No, you did fine. It's just that we're losing people on the copy desk, and I need your experience there."

"Who's leaving?"

"We've already lost Fanning. He came to work drunk one time too many, and I fired him. Now, Massey has given notice."

"Who's going to work makeup?" Greg asked.

"I've hired a couple of part-timers to do makeup. Both have regular PR jobs, but they want to earn some extra bread."

"Okay, when do I make the move?" Greg's anger simmered.

"I've got the part-timers coming in next week, so you'll move to the desk on Monday."

Greg stomped out of the office. He told Bud Riley of the change.

"I guess that doesn't enhance your opinion of Nelson," Bud said, adjusting his thick glasses.

"You've got that right," Greg said.

❖

Greg attended his first group-therapy session the next week. Most in the group were in their twenties and thirties.

Dr. Cochran introduced Greg and asked him to tell the members why he was there.

"I've had problems with anxiety since I was nineteen," he said. "I take medication for it, and I've been to a psychoanalyst, but the problem keeps getting worse."

"Greg, we don't deal in shrink-talk here." Cochran wore a smug grin. "I'm sure that's what you got from the analyst."

"There was plenty of that," Greg said.

"Okay," Cochran said, "Let's have some comment from the group."

"Sounds like a case of Greg playing 'Poor Me,'" a young man named Steve said. Members were instructed to use only their first names.

"Yeah," a red-haired girl who looked to be in her late teens said. "Sounds like Greg is really hung up in his 'Child.'"

"What do you mean, 'Child'?" Greg asked.

Cochran produced a blackboard and drew three circles. He labeled them "P," "A," and "C."

"Since Greg is new, I'll go over this again. These three circles represent the ego states from which we operate. Dr. Berne's studies have shown we basically function from three ego states: Parent, Adult, and Child. When we operate from our Parent state, we are either nurturing and protective or harsh and judgmental. When we're in our Child state, our feelings are childlike; we're either happy and carefree or scared and vulnerable. The Adult state is our rational, mature state. But often the negative aspects of the Child or Parent states bleed over and corrupt the Adult; then we feel bad or make bad decisions."

"Yeah," said Norma, a fortyish woman. "My husband and I were getting a divorce, and I stayed in my Scared Child state most of the time. Once I got rid of that infantile fear, I got into my Adult and was able to deal with the situation."

Ego, superego, and id, Greg thought. Hadn't he heard all that before from Dr. Hoffman? How was this different?

The session went on like this for an hour. Greg came away scratching his head. Could the complex human mind be so easily reduced to a few parts?

He called Suzy on the *News-Beacon*'s WATs line late that night and told her about the session.

"I've heard a little about Berne and TA," she said. "It's mainly new labels for Freud's ideas. But my professors seem to think Claire Weekes in Australia and Aaron Beck at the University of Pennsylvania are doing the most hopeful research on anxiety and depression."

"TA sounds a little goofy to me," Greg said. "But I'll stay with it. I don't want another tongue-lashing from you."

There was a moment of silence. Then Suzy said distractedly, "Oh, Greg, hold on. Someone's at the door."

Greg's heart sank. Who would be calling on Suzy at that late hour?

She sounded harried. "Greg, I need to go. Someone wants to see me."

"Who is it?"

"Just someone from school."

"I love you, Suzy."

"Gotta go. Call when you can."

At home in bed that night, Greg lay awake thinking about Suzy. When she'd left for Galveston, she hadn't said she loved him. She went back earlier than she had to. Now, some mysterious stranger appears at her door at eleven at night, and she won't say who it is.

Visions arose in his mind of some handsome a med student or doctor taking her to bed after she hung up with Greg. She hadn't replied when he'd said he loved her. What the hell was going on?

Most of the night, he tortured himself thinking of what he and Suzy once had. He imagined someone else touching her and feeling the joy he'd felt with her. He pictured her returning someone else's kisses and caresses. Could she be sharing a shower with someone else these days? He fell into a deeper funk.

Greg started work in his new job as a full-time copy editor. The copy desk was now short three of the usual six people who worked there each night, editing all the news stories that went into the next day's paper.

A chief copy editor or "slotman" sat in the center of the horseshoe-shaped copy desk and dealt out stories to each of the editors or "rimmers." Their job was to check for errors in grammar, style, spelling, and facts, then write a headline for each story.

It Takes a Worried Man

The pressure built to a peak for each edition, and Greg sat in a knot of grinding tension, trying to get through the overload of stories. He felt exhausted and depressed at the end of each shift.

Greg called Suzy each night for a while, but she sounded distant and eager to get off the phone.

"Something's wrong, Suzy," he said. "I can tell. Are you okay?"

"Sure, I'm fine."

"How about if I come down next weekend?" Greg wondered if he could drive to Galveston without coming apart. He had to do something.

"Oh, I don't know, Greg. I've started doing weekend duty at the hospital. We'd hardly see each other."

"Dammit, Suzy, you sound a million miles away."

"My last year of nursing school is a lot harder, and we're having to work more shifts. I have to keep up, and there's a lot on my mind. Don't you want me to graduate?"

Rather than argue, Greg bit his tongue. "Of course I do. We're engaged, you know. I just want to see you again—sometime. I love you."

"Okay, darlin'," she said. "Take care."

That's it? he thought and hung up the phone.

❖

November 1965

After dinner at work one night, managing editor Ben Nelson called Greg into his office.

"Greg, I need you in the slot. Leonard Story is leaving us in two weeks."

"I'm not sure I'm qualified," Greg said. The slotman's job was one of the most pressure-filled jobs in the newsroom. Greg couldn't imagine absorbing any more stress.

"Hell, yes, you're qualified," the bear-like managing editor snorted. "You ran the city desk in Galveston during that Hastings story. I need you, Greg."

Yeah, but it nearly killed me, Greg thought. "Isn't there anyone else?"

"Bud is nearly blind, and Russell is too slow. Nobody else has near your experience. I need your help, Greg."

"Okay, I'll try," Greg said after a pause.

"By the way," Nelson said. "Did you know the Galveston *Star* has been nominated for an AP award for the stories you all did on Hastings beating up that kid?"

"I'll be damned. No, I didn't."

"Congratulations, Greg. I'm counting on you."

Greg went to his group therapy sessions weekly. He asked other members if any of them ever suffered from anxiety or had panic episodes, as he'd had. Not one of them had. Mostly these were affluent people from north Dallas who were unhappy with their lives. Some suffered from minor, periodic depression, but none was on medication. One member was gay and had come to therapy to be "cured."

The sessions often degenerated into shouting and name-calling. Dr. Cochran encouraged members to "get your anger out in the open" or "tell it like it is." The group used the TA language indiscriminately and used the names of "games" Eric Berne had described in his book, games such as "Poor Me," "Ain't It Awful," and "Now I've Got You, You Son of a Bitch."

Greg wondered where his anxiety and depression fit into this free-for-all.

By November, he had become the butt of everyone's wrath in the group. No one could understand why his symptoms seemed to get worse, but it had to be his fault. Cochran told him, "Your anxiety is just an excuse, Greg. It serves an important purpose for you."

At home, George and Vivian told Greg he looked as if he were losing weight and not getting enough sleep. Greg looked in the mirror. What he saw shocked him. His face looked drawn and his eyes hollow. He weighed on the bathroom scales. He had dropped from one-fifty to one-thirty-five.

Greg told Suzy what was happening in his group sessions.

"Don't give up, darlin'," she said casually. "I'm praying for you. Oh, did I tell you, I finally joined the Episcopal Church?"

The first week in December, Greg drove to Dallas for his weekly group session. As he crossed the long Trinity River viaduct just west of downtown Dallas, panic suddenly exploded full-blown. He slowed the car to a crawl. Drivers whizzed past him, and those behind him sat on their horns. There was no shoulder to pull onto. He struggled to reach the next exit, shaking as badly as he could ever recall. Everything in his stomach came up, and he puked out the window as drivers on the access road stared and honked.

He crept along back streets to the Oak Lawn area and went into Dr. Cochran's building. Members of the group gathered outside the office. The doctor finished with another group and came out into the hallway.

"Joe," Greg said. Dr. Cochran had asked to be called by his first name. "Can I see you privately before the group meets?"

"Not the normal protocol," the doctor said officiously. "But make it quick." They went inside.

"I just fell completely apart driving over here," Greg said, still trembling. "I thought I wouldn't get here, but I took some back streets. It was one of the worst anxiety attacks I've had. I've gotten worse instead of better. This isn't helping."

"Greg, you're just locked up in your 'Scared Child.' Until you can assert your 'Adult' and quit playing 'Ain't It Awful,' you're not going to get anywhere."

"But I don't know how. I've tried."

Cochran looked gravely at him. "Trying won't cut it, Greg. You've got to do it."

"Do it?" Greg said. "You people sit here and talk about the 'Parent' and 'Child.' You talk about games people play, but you offer damned little insight into what to do about the symptoms. I think I'm wasting my time here."

"Well, Greg, maybe TA just isn't for you. You have to want to change. You have to be willing to rewrite your 'Life Script.'"

"Goddammit, I want to change. But all I hear in this group is TA jargon. None of these other people has the kind of symptoms I have. They haven't had their lives turned upside down."

"Sounds like you just can't resist playing 'Poor Me.' Until you stop that, you won't get any help here."

Greg shook his head. "I don't think I can drive over here anymore. I'm a complete wreck, and this isn't working."

"It's clear to me you'd rather stay sick. I don't think you have the balls to do what it takes to get well. You're too comfortable in your misery."

"I think that's a load of bullshit," Greg said and stormed out of the building.

❖

Now, Greg had to drive the thirty miles back to Fort Worth, and it was four-thirty in the afternoon. Rush-hour traffic clogged the freeways. Boiling panic hovered just beneath the surface as Greg still trembled all over. His anger at Dr. Cochran made his already-raw nerves scream. His muscles ached with tension.

He drove slowly down residential streets to avoid traffic. He passed several police cars, and his head felt as if it were in a vise. Finally, he made it to the old Fort Worth highway and relaxed slightly. He could creep home without getting on a freeway.

He was finished with Dr. Cochran's group therapy. But where did this leave him? Ben Nelson had virtually ordered him to assume the slotman's job at work. He and Suzy had postponed their wedding. And he was now half-convinced Suzy was screwing around with someone else in Galveston.

These thoughts descended on Greg, one by one, as he made his way back to Fort Worth. Where was a way out? Was there anywhere left that he could turn?

On the edge of Fort Worth, he stopped at a package store and bought a fifth of whiskey. He shook as he paid the clerk.

"Anything wrong, pal?" the clerk asked.

"No, I just need a drink," Greg said.

"Yeah, you've got a pretty bad case of the shakes."

Back in his Volkswagen, Greg opened the bottle and took a long drink. Even now, taking heavy doses of Valium and Imipramine, Greg felt no blunting of his pain. He'd have to resort to his own brand of medicine.

He had the night off. As he drove toward home, he stopped periodically to take a drink. The whiskey warmed his insides and finally his entire body.

Each time he thought of Suzy, he stopped for another drink. The thought of her with another man haunted him and twisted his insides.

He reproached himself for getting drunk as he drove. He remembered the wreck he and Eddie had been in and cringed. Yet, he had to ease the pain.

He made his way toward home, still barely able to keep the car in a straight line. He saw several police cars, but managed to drive slowly and turn onto side streets to avoid them.

Finally, he reached his parents' house and went inside. No one was home. He took the bottle inside and went to his bedroom. He shut the door and drank most of the whiskey left in the bottle. The room swirled, and he passed out.

"Greg, get up." His mother shook him. "You've got to get ready for work." It was two o'clock in the afternoon.

"No way," Greg mumbled.

"What do you mean, 'no way'?"

"I can't go. I can't move."

"Are you drunk?" Vivian asked. "I saw that bottle you left on the nightstand."

"To hell with it," Greg said.

"Are you sick?"

"I was born sick."

"You're making no sense. Look, it's your life. But if you're sick, the least you could do is call your boss."

Greg didn't move from the bed. He pulled the covers up over his head and stayed there the rest of the day. He peeked out long enough to notice the gas space heater in the bedroom. What if he just turned on the gas . . . ? But he felt immobile. There wasn't enough strength in him to move a muscle.

George Spencer came in from work and went to Greg's room. He yanked the covers off Greg.

"What are you trying to pull, Greg?"

"Dad, I'm so tired." Greg spoke barely above a whisper.

"Do you think you're something special? Get up."

Greg's limbs felt like flaccid rags. "I can't."

"This is no time for games. Get up."

"No joke. I can't move. My whole body feels dead."

George's face registered alarm. "Then, we need to get you to a hospital. I'll call that doctor in Dallas. What's his name?"

"His name is Cochran, and I told him I was through with him."

"What?"

"He wasn't doing me any good, and I told him to shove it." Greg stared at the ceiling.

"Then, I'll call Dr. Simon."

"Call him. He'll just pass the buck."

"Well, we need to do something. Have you taken your pills?"

"Not since yesterday."

George went to the medicine cabinet and grabbed two bottles with Greg's name on them. "How many of these do you take?"

"Two of each," Greg muttered.

George filled a water glass and brought the pills to Greg's bedside. "Can you swallow?"

Greg made a gulping sound. "I think so."

"Open your mouth," George said, and he placed the tablets on Greg's tongue. He held the water cup to Greg's lips, and Greg swallowed them. Greg noticed his father's hand was shaking.

The telephone rang. Vivian answered it and talked a few minutes, then she stuck her head inside Greg's bedroom door.

"It's Bud Riley at the paper," she said. "He says they're all wondering what happened to Greg."

"Just tell him Greg's sick," George said. "We don't know what's the matter."

Greg soon discovered he was able to move, but he'd never experienced a greater weight of fatigue and depression. He could get out of bed, he thought, but the effort seemed so great, he just lay there.

"Greg, why don't you try to get up?" his father said.

"I just can't, Dad. I've never felt so drained."

"Okay, I'm going to call Dr. Simon first thing in the morning and see what he thinks."

"I don't know what good he can do," Greg said with a sense of utter defeat. "I don't know what good anyone can do."

George drove Greg to Village Creek Memorial Hospital the next morning. On the phone, Dr. Simon had told George he thought Greg had a case of major clinical depression and needed immediate treatment.

Greg got checked into a private room and immediately started receiving shots. He fell asleep as a cold rain fell outside.

He woke up hours later with Dr. Simon standing over him.

"Looks like you've got yourself in about the same fix you were in when I first saw you."

"It's worse than that," Greg said with a thick tongue.

"We'll treat it about the same way," Simon said. "Plan on getting a lot of sleep."

"Whatever you say."

"Things look pretty bleak to you, don't they?"

"Hopeless. I've lost everything."

"What about your fiancée?"

"Suzy's back in Galveston," Greg said. "I think she's screwing around."

"How do you know that?"

"She's been so distant. Strange people come and go from her apartment. She won't tell me who they are."

"Look, you don't know anything," Simon scolded. "It may be completely innocent. I saw how much that girl loves you. That's not something that just goes up in smoke."

"She's been patient too long; all this crap has driven her away."

"It's probably not as bad as you think."

"Whatever you say." Greg's voice was flat and lifeless.

George and Vivian came to Greg's room. Vivian told him they'd talked with Dr. Simon as he was leaving, and he hadn't sounded optimistic.

"I called Suzy this afternoon," Vivian said. "I told her you were back in the hospital."

Greg winced.

"She's in the middle of her senior-year evaluation," Vivian went on. "Apparently it's a big deal, and they get put through the wringer for a week. She can't leave now, but when it's over, she'll be out for Christmas vacation, and she's coming home."

Greg lay silently. He knew he was losing Suzy.

"Greg," George said. "I talked to Ben Nelson at the paper today and told him your situation."

"I guess he's pretty pissed," Greg mumbled.

"He's not happy. He was counting on you taking the slot job. But he's making other plans and said to tell you not to worry. He said he'll give you a leave of absence. You can come back when you feel like it."

"Okay." Greg felt a twinge of relief.

A nurse came in to give Greg more shots and pills. Outside, the rain had turned to sleet and rattled off the windows. Greg thought of the night sleet covered the road across the Lake Arlington dam. He drifted off to sleep with the memory of tumbling and crashing down the embankment.

❖

A week passed. Greg slept most of the time. George and Vivian came to see him daily, but he usually slept through their visits.

Dr. Simon also saw him every day, and on each visit got Greg awake enough to talk to him. The doctor had put Greg on a new antidepressant drug.

"I see a little progress," Dr. Simon said. "But you're still not eating much. I'll have to keep you here a while longer."

Greg felt empty. His life had become a desert. "Okay. Whatever."

"I'd like to see a little spark," Simon said. "And I'm not seeing it."

Someone knocked at the door. "Come in," Dr. Simon said.

Suzy walked into the room.

She walked slowly to Greg's bed and kissed him on the cheek without saying anything.

"I'm leaving you guys alone," Simon said. "Or do I dare?"

Greg cracked a lame smile. Suzy snickered weakly. The doctor went on his way.

"I couldn't get here any sooner," Suzy said, shrugging her shoulders dispiritedly.

"You look tired," he said. "You've lost weight."

"I've been through hell this semester," she said. "I never dreamed school could be so hard. It took a lot out of me. Your mom told me you quit the TA group."

Greg shook his head. "I couldn't take that guy, Cochran, and all of his gobbledygook. I was getting worse instead of better. I had to get out."

"I've got some news from Brian." There was a flatness to Suzy's voice.

"What kind of news?"

"You know Brian is doing his residency in psychiatry in Amarillo?"

"Yeah. How's he doing?"

"He's doing fine. He calls Cindy all the time, and I talked to him last week. He told me to give you a message." Suzy slumped against the side of the bed.

"What kind of message?"

"He said to tell you he's met a therapist in Amarillo who specializes in nothing but treating anxiety disorders."

"I didn't know such people existed."

"This woman has studied with one of the biggest names in that field."

Greg looked skeptical. "What's she doing in Amarillo?"

"I think she's from there originally. Maybe you could go see her."

"I don't know, Suzy," Greg said dispiritedly. "Amarillo is a long way from here."

"Didn't you tell me you have relatives up there?"

"My Aunt Sally lives in Hereford. It's near there."

"Maybe you could stay with her."

"But, Suzy, you know the trouble I have driving, and besides, I'm pretty beat after what happened with Cochran."

"Okay, Greg. I'm really tired, and I'm tired of fighting you. If you're going to give up, there's nothing I can do." Suzy suddenly turned and started for the door.

Her words hit him like a fist in the gut. "Wait!" He sat up in bed.

Suzy turned back toward him.

"Look," he said, "I know you must be at wit's end, but don't just walk out."

"You should talk to Brian," Suzy said, reaching for the doorknob. "He says this woman has had amazing success with her patients.

This could be a real opportunity for you, if you'll take it. I'll bet you could find a way to get to Amarillo. I know at this stage it's a long shot, but at least think about it."

"I'm on a leave of absence from work. I don't know how long I can stretch it out."

"It's just an idea. Talk to Brian, okay?"

"Okay."

Suzy walked dejectedly out the door. Greg turned over and buried his face in the pillow.

❖

When Greg had been hospitalized in June, Suzy came to stay with him every day and some nights. But now, she came only sporadically and didn't stay long. Greg fretted and heaped abuse on himself, but he knew in his heart Suzy couldn't endure much more of his downward spiral.

Dr. Simon reluctantly released him from the hospital on the Thursday before Christmas, which fell on Saturday.

"You'll probably do as well at home as you're doing here," the doctor said. "Keep taking your medication. We might see some gradual improvement."

"And if not?" Greg asked.

"If not, we'll have to look for alternatives."

"What kind of alternatives?"

"We could try some other drugs, but ultimately we might be looking at electroshock therapy."

"Oh, my God!" Greg's grandmother had been through electroshock, and he recalled that she came away much worse than before.

"It's a last resort, Greg. If we can get you eating right and sleeping normally at night, you'll be on the right path."

"But something in my life has to go right, and it's not."

"Like what?"

"Like being able to work. Above all, I think I'm losing Suzy."

"Give her some time; she's had a lot to deal with. This sort of thing can put a lot of strain on loved ones. Just call a time-out and give things a chance to level out. She might surprise you."

Greg went with Suzy to a Christmas Eve service at St. Luke's Episcopal Church, but by now, Greg had all but stopped driving, and Suzy had to pick him up and take him home. She invited him to join her family for Christmas dinner, but he begged off, saying the thought of food made him sick. He also didn't know if he could face her family in his current state. He felt like an invalid, hemmed in on all sides and barely able to move outside his house.

Greg ate a quiet Christmas dinner with his parents. They hadn't invited any family members to join them this year because of Greg's condition. After dinner, George and Vivian drove to Denton, thirty miles north of Fort Worth, to visit with Greg's Uncle Ben and Aunt Millie. Greg stayed behind.

He tried watching TV, but gave up and collapsed on his bed, staring at the ceiling and feeling certain that his life, as he'd once known it, was gone forever.

The doorbell rang. *Let it ring,* he thought. *Maybe they'll go away.* It rang several more times. Finally, his guilt overtook him. He got up and sauntered to the door.

Suzy was getting in her car to leave. Greg got her attention, and she walked slowly back toward the house.

"Were you asleep?" she asked.

"I guess I was dozing," Greg said. "Come on in."

Suzy had a grim expression. "We need to talk, Greg."

She followed him to the living room and sat in an armchair across from him. A low overcast hung over Fort Worth, dimming the light from the living room window. Greg clicked on a lamp.

Suzy pulled off her heavy coat and laid it in a chair next to her. She smoothed her dark wool skirt. "Not quite the same as last year," she said with a wistful expression.

"No, and I can't find the words to tell you how sorry I am."

"I don't know when I've felt so low, Greg."

He'd never seen her look so doleful. "I know you must," he said. "I wish I could promise you everything would be all right."

"But you can't," she said. "And that's what we need to talk about."

"I know." His insides felt gray with remorse. "I wish we didn't have to, but I know we do."

"I've done all I could to help you, and you've only gotten worse." Tears came to her eyes. The words caught in her throat. "I don't think I can take any more of this."

Greg hung his head. "I know," he mumbled.

Suzy took out a tissue and wiped her eyes. "Oh, Greg, I wish to God you could find the real you again. I know it must be there someplace."

Greg moved across the room and sat on the arm of Suzy's chair. He took her hand as tears coursed down her cheeks. "I know it's not fair to keep hoping against hope. But I've got to get better. Dr. Simon told me if I don't get better, he may have to try electroshock therapy."

"Oh, God, no," Suzy said, now crying harder.

"So, I've got to do whatever's humanly possible. I'm going to call Brian about that doctor in Amarillo."

"God bless you, my darlin'," she sniffed and squeezed his hand. "I know you're at the end of your rope, too."

"Hard as it is to say it, I know it's not fair to ask you to wait to see how that turns out. I could never live with myself if this doctor turns out to be another flop, and you're left hanging again."

Suzy shook her head, doubled her fists, and grimaced in anguish. "I thought, I really thought, that love could really conquer all. I gave you every ounce I had, but it wasn't enough."

"You gave me more love than any human could expect," Greg said with a catch in his throat. "And I thought my love for you could overcome anything, too. . . but it didn't." Greg's voice trailed off, and he slumped dejectedly. "That's my failure, not yours."

Suzy stopped crying and stared downward a long moment. "Greg, I have to tell you something: There's a guy in Galveston who's very interested in me. I like him a lot, too, and he has a lot to offer me. I put him off all last semester." There was another long pause. "I can't put him off any longer. Oh, Greg."

Suzy started to sob again, and as she did, she took the ring off her finger. She grasped his hand, put it in his palm, then closed his fingers over it. "I've got to go, my love. I'll be praying for you."

Greg sat stunned and speechless as she got into her coat and rushed to the front door. He didn't try to stop her. She closed the door and walked slowly to her car with Greg watching through the front window. She wiped her eyes as she backed her Ford Falcon out of the driveway. He held the ring in his hand and looked at it a long time. His heart was a polluted swamp.

That night, Greg called Brian Reynolds in Amarillo.

"Greg, I'm glad you called," Brian said. "Suzy told me you've been having a pretty rough time."

"You could say that. I just got out of the hospital—again."

"Man, I hate to hear that. Did Suzy tell you about this therapist I've met up here?"

"Yeah. What's the story?"

"Well, this woman is not your typical shrink," Brian said. "She's having some fabulous success treating people with anxiety and panic problems. She's studied with one of the biggest names in that field. I've seen what's she's done with people who show up at the hospital in really bad shape. She's able to get them back to living normal lives in a matter of weeks."

"That sounds too good to be true," Greg said. "Is anyone else doing that kind of therapy—like maybe closer to Fort Worth?"

"There are a few doctors like her on the East Coast and in Australia, but no one else in Texas that I know of."

"Look, Brian. I don't know if I can swing it, but I told you I have an aunt in Hereford. I might be able to stay with her for a while and come to Amarillo. What's the therapist's name?"

"Dr. Marilyn Reed," Brian said. "Hereford's about a forty-minute drive from Amarillo."

"I have to do something," Greg said. "My doctor is telling me that if I don't get better I might be facing electroshock therapy."

"Jesus, I hope not. I'll bet Marilyn can help you. By the way, how's Suzy?"

"She just broke our engagement, Brian. It looks like it's all over."

"Oh, hell, Greg. How are you dealing with it?"

"I'm just numb," Greg said. "What else can go wrong?"

"I understand. I think you need to get on up here as soon as possible. Don't sit around stewing about it. I'm pretty confident, Greg. I see a lot of patients in the same shape you're in and worse, people who are out of hope. This woman is getting them back in the groove in no time. And Greg, I'll tell you an inside secret."

"Okay, let's hear it."

"In med school, anxiety is something they sort of gloss over. The causes have never been very well understood. Dr. Reed is in the forefront of treating those disorders based on the latest research. It's one of the most positive signs I've seen in my line of medicine."

"Okay, Brian. Thanks a million. I've got a lot of things to work out, but I'll be back in touch."

"Call me anytime, Greg."

"Are you and Cindy still set for June?"

"You bet. She's lined up a job at Amarillo General, too."

A fresh spurt of sadness flooded Greg. "I wish you two the best."

❖

Over dinner, George and Vivian commiserated with Greg over his broken engagement. Nothing they said eased his despair. They turned to the prospect of his going to stay with his Aunt Sally in Hereford.

"I think it's a good idea," George said. "Sally would probably be glad to have you."

"What about money?" Vivian asked.

"Maybe I could find a job up there," Greg said.

"Oh, Greg," Vivian said, exasperated, "You're in no shape to work anywhere."

"I'll work it out, don't worry," Greg said, getting more agitated.

"And who's going to pay for that doctor in Amarillo?" Vivian asked.

"Okay, you two cut it out," George said. "I think it would be good if you and Greg were out of each other's hair for a while. I'll loan Greg enough money to get him by for a while. Besides, it's an investment. When Greg gets well, he'll have plenty of earning power to pay us back."

"George, we're not made of money," Vivian said.

"We're doing okay," George said. "Greg, why don't you call your Aunt Sally tonight?"

"Why, my stars, yes," Sally Hilliard said over the phone. "I'd love to have you as a house guest, Greg." Sally was George Spencer's older sister. She had just turned sixty and worked as the Women's Page editor for the Hereford *Plainsman*.

"Of course, you may freeze to death up here," Sally went on. "There's snow on the ground right now, but it's a small price to pay; it doesn't get as hot in the summertime as it does down there where you are."

"I've heard about a doctor in Amarillo who specializes in nervous problems like I have," Greg said. "And I thought since you're so close, it might be convenient to give it a try."

"Oh, you're still fighting that Spencer family disease, are you?" There was an edge of ironic humor in nearly everything Sally said.

"Yeah, I'm afraid so."

"Well, we've all been there in this family; just ask your daddy. This climate and higher altitude might be just what you need. Come on up anytime. I'll show you all the finer tourist attractions of Hereford."

"Sounds good, only I'm not sure how I'm going to get there." Greg hesitated. "I've developed this sort of phobia about driving."

It Takes a Worried Man

"Oh, well, it's got to be something, and I guess driving is as good as anything. The train still runs from Fort Worth to Amarillo. Are you scared of trains?"

"I don't think so. Maybe I could ride the Zephyr."

"You just let me know when you're coming, and I'll meet you at the Amarillo depot."

❖

January 1966

On the Monday after New Year's, George and Vivian drove Greg to the Texas & Pacific Railway depot on the south edge of downtown Fort Worth. This once-elegant art-deco terminal now looked dirty and neglected. Passenger rail service had been in decline since the fifties; air travel was becoming the norm.

"Let us know how things are going," George said. "Tell me if you need some money."

"Thanks, Dad. Bye, Mother."

"I sure hope that doctor can help you," Vivian said.

Greg hadn't been on a train since the age of nine or ten. He boarded the Burlington Texas Zephyr, which ran daily between Fort Worth and Denver.

The silver, streamlined, diesel-electric Zephyr had been one of the flagships of the Burlington Route from 1940 through the fifties. But, like the Fort Worth train station, its cars had fallen into a sad state of neglect. Cotton stuffing bulged through torn seats. A stale smell filled the air, and personnel moved about dispiritedly. A conductor told Greg of a rumor that the railroad planned to discontinue all passenger service the next year.

As the train pulled out of Fort Worth in the early afternoon, Greg tensed up, wondering if his driving phobia would extend to the rails. Gradually, he relaxed and took in the scenery as the rails clattered beneath him.

He passed through all the towns he recalled from his childhood: Decatur, Bowie, Wichita Falls, Vernon, Quanah, and Childress, the town where he had been born; he'd made this trip many times as a kid. He watched the green rolling prairies of North Central Texas turn to an arid and more barren landscape as the train moved west.

Beyond Childress, the train crossed the Red River and moved northwestward through Memphis and Clarendon. There the Zephyr ascended the Cap Rock, or *Llano Estacado*, a rise of several hundred feet to the flat tableland of the High Plains at the top.

The trip took nearly eight hours. Greg had ample time to reflect.

His gut churned and tightened at the thought of Suzy. Where was she now? Was she getting in bed with this other guy in Galveston? What was he like? Could he ever love Suzy as Greg did? Greg got a cup of water and swallowed two more Valim tablets.

What about his career? What about Freud's dictum that a healthy person is one who can successfully work and love?

He wasn't healthy. Did he now fail on both counts? He wondered if he would ever again have what it took to succeed in the stress-filled world of journalism. Would a newspaper even hire him with his track record? Could he ever love responsibly with his affliction?

Darkness had fallen across the Panhandle as the train pulled into Amarillo. Greg looked forward to stretching the stiffness from his muscles after the long trip.

Aunt Sally stood on the platform, wrapped in a heavy overcoat with a scarf around her head. Greg spotted her and crunched through frozen snow as he walked toward her.

"Is that the heaviest coat you brought?" she said.

Greg had on the suede jacket Suzy had given him and no hat or gloves. "It's the heaviest coat I own," he said, falling in step with her as they walked to her car. "It didn't get very cold in Galveston."

"I'm glad I didn't throw away Lloyd's old overcoat. You're going to need it up here." Sally's husband, Greg's Uncle Lloyd, had died four years earlier. They'd had no children. Greg had always held a special place in Sally's life, and she was his favorite aunt.

They climbed into her baby-blue '57 Nash Rambler. Sally turned on the heater full blast as they headed out of Amarillo. Several inches of snow still stood on the ground, but the highways were clear.

"I've never been very far outside Amarillo," Greg said. "This is all new territory for me."

"Well, the first town is Canyon," she said as they passed out of Amarillo. "West Texas State College is here. Only I guess it's called 'University' now."

As they moved along the highway Sally pointed out the little hamlets of Umbarger and Dawn, each with a monolithic grain elevator.

As they approached Hereford, an awful odor invaded the car.

"God, what's that?" Greg asked.

"That's the smell of money, boy," Sally said, chuckling. "We have two big cattle feedlots just outside Hereford, and that's one of them."

"Does it smell like that in Hereford?"

"Only when the wind is right, and it's usually not. But it helps people remember why Hereford is such a prosperous little place. They raise thousands of head of cattle in those lots."

"Boy," Greg said. "What a far cry this is from Galveston. I feel like I'm really in Texas again."

They cruised into Hereford around ten-thirty and drove along brick-paved streets to Sally's house, a neat white stucco structure in an older part of town. Sally's dog Sam, a shorthaired mutt, met them at the front door.

Greg lugged his suitcase inside. Sam followed him, sniffing at the strange new odors in the house. Greg could smell the dusty dryness in the air, the way it had smelled in Childress when he was a child. He thought of the contrast with the salty, humid ambiance of Galveston.

Aunt Sally offered Greg a cup of hot tea, but he declined. She put a teakettle on the stove for herself, and Greg sat at the kitchen table.

Sally had grown thinner since Uncle Lloyd had died. Her once-light brown hair had turned mostly gray, and she now wore it shorter in a well-sprayed puffy style she had redone on her weekly trips to the beauty shop. Sally wore a simple cotton blouse tucked into a straight pencil skirt.

Sam nuzzled at Greg's legs, begging to have his head scratched. Greg accommodated him. Sally poured her tea and sat at the table.

"I was just looking at all your books," Greg said. "Maybe I'll have a chance to catch up on my reading."

"Oh, I've got books, all right." Sally sipped her tea. "Help yourself to any of 'em. Reading's probably a good thing to do till we get some warmer weather. Then, I'll give you the grand tour of Hereford and vicinity."

"You know, I always wanted to try my hand at writing something 'serious,'" Greg said. "Like poetry or a novel, but my life has been so hectic since college, I've never gotten around to it."

"Jump in there and write, then," Sally was scratching Sam's ears now. "My typewriter's in the dining room. I gave it a whirl when I was about your age. Nothing came of it, of course, but we all have to try some time or the t'other."

"I might do that," Greg said, "But I need to go to Amarillo pretty soon."

"Well," Sally said. "I have to see my eye doctor up there, and maybe we could plan our appointments on the same day. I have Mondays off."

"That would be perfect," Greg said. "But I wouldn't mind just hanging around here and reading for a few days before I schedule anything."

"Fine. You just unwind a little and tell me when you want to go, and we'll hit the road."

Sally introduced Greg to the small guest bed she kept in the dining room. He fell asleep feeling right at home.

It Takes a Worried Man

❖

Four

❖
Hereford, Texas
January 1966

Greg spent the next several days reading. Sally's bookshelves housed a number of classic novels he'd never read, including *David Copperfield, Madame Bovary, The Red Badge of Courage,* and *Of Human Bondage.* As he read Maugham's novel, he couldn't shed the thought of protagonist Philip Carey's disablility. Wasn't anxiety Greg's own version of Philip's clubfoot?

He read some Shakespeare plays he hadn't read in school. A passage in *Richard III* caused him to pause. Was he, like King Richard:

> *Deformed, unfinished, sent before my time*
> *Into this breathing world, scarce half made up. . . .?*

Sally had anthologies of poets, such as Keats, Shelley, Byron, Browning, and Coleridge. Greg had read selected poems by them in English classes, but had never taken the time to read many of them in any depth. He started piecing together poems of his own on Sally's typewriter. He'd had a little practice in college, where a sympathetic creative writing teacher had encouraged his poetry writing. He'd written some of his poems for Suzy.

Now, he wrote letters to Suzy, but he threw them away, judging them to be too rambling and fatuous, relying too much on phrases he'd been reading of late. She probably wouldn't appreciate hearing from him, anyway.

After a week, temperatures finally climbed to the fifties. He decided to walk the four blocks to the newspaper where Sally worked, the Hereford *Plainsman.*

But after two blocks, his heartbeat lurched, and the sinking feeling that came with anxiety episodes churned in his stomach. He hurried back to Sally's house and arrived before full-blown panic had erupted. He sat on her couch and gathered his wits. Then, he went to the phone and called Brian Reynolds in Amarillo.

"Greg, good to hear from you," Brian said in his usual friendly voice. "Where are you?"

"I'm in Hereford, at my aunt's."

"Hey, man. You're here. When are you coming up to the city?"

"That's what I wanted to talk to you about." Greg lit a cigarette and pulled an ashtray next to the phone. "I'm ready to see this Dr. Reed. Can you give me some particulars?"

"Well, her office is on Adams Street, just down the block from Amarillo General." Brian paused. "Hey, you know what I'll bet I could do?"

"What?"

"I have a little cubby-hole of an office, along with the other residents, but I'll bet you I could introduce the two of you in my office. Then, you could set up a formal appointment if you like. But it would give me a chance to see you and have you meet her at the same time."

Greg was skeptical. "Would she take the time to do that?"

"I think so. We've become pretty good friends. She comes by the hospital for her rounds at eleven o'clock. I could just invite her up here before she goes to lunch."

"You're sure that wouldn't be interrupting your day?"

"Hell, no. I start work at one o'clock. I'll just come a little early and catch her when she comes by."

"How about a Monday?"

"That would be great," Brian said. "How about next Monday?"

"Sure. I'll plan to be there." Greg suddenly felt more buoyant than he had in weeks.

"Okay, Greg, I'll see you then." Brian hesitated. "Have you heard from Suzy?"

"No, I haven't," Greg said. "I doubt if I will."

"Oh, that's right. Damn, Greg, I'm so sorry."

"Yeah, me, too." Greg felt his exuberance trickling away. He was afraid to ask Brian if Cindy had mentioned Suzy to him in their phone calls. "See you Monday."

Aunt Sally made an appointment with her ophthalmologist for the next Monday. She and Greg drove to Amarillo and parked in a garage next to Amarillo General Hospital. Sally went to the professional building next door for her appointment. Greg went inside the hospital, feeling anxious and lost in the strange surroundings. He found a directory with the names of resident physicians on it. He did a double take when he came to the name: "Brian K. Reynolds, M.D." He'd seldom thought of Brian in those formal terms.

He walked down a long corridor on the ground floor and came to a row of residents' offices. He found Brian's door and knocked.

"Come on in here, Greg," said the smiling, sandy-haired Brian. He looked a few pounds heavier and a little less frazzled than he had in Galveston. "Marilyn's not here yet, but she should be any minute. Have a seat. Want some coffee?"

"Sure, I'll take a cup."

"Relax," Brian said. "You look a little jumpy."

"I guess I am." Greg sat down. "Hospitals and doctors' offices do that to me."

Brian drew a mug of coffee from a pot and handed it to Greg.

"So, this is the kind of office a doctor gets?" Greg looked around the tiny, sparsely furnished room. Pungent hospital smells filled the air.

"Residents and interns are the bottom of the barrel," Brian said. "It's like we're one notch above boot camp."

"How do you like your work here?"

"I can't complain," Brian shrugged. "This is where I want to be, doing the kind of medicine I want to practice." He sipped from his coffee cup. "How are you feeling, Greg?"

"Not too bad. I think the Panhandle agrees with me."

Someone knocked at the door. Brian opened it.

A trim, fortyish woman with hazel eyes and streaks of gray in her coarse, dark hair came in. She and Brian greeted each other and exchanged brief pleasantries.

"Marilyn, this is Greg Spencer, my old buddy from Galveston." Greg and Dr. Reed shook hands and sat in vinyl-backed chairs.

"I'm gonna leave you two alone," Brian said. "I've got an errand to run." He left the room.

"Well, Greg," the doctor said, still slightly out of breath. "Brian told me a little about you. You're having problems with anxiety?"

"Sure am," Greg said. "Seems like things keep getting worse. I've been to three different doctors in three cities: Fort Worth, Galveston, and Dallas."

"And Amarillo makes four," the doctor smiled. "Are you on medication?"

"Yeah, Valium and Norpramin."

"Okay, tell me some of your symptoms."

"The main one is panic that just comes out of nowhere. And lately, I've developed a phobia about driving. And even going places alone."

"Are you tense and anxious much of the time?"

"Oh, yes." Greg wondered if Dr. Reed would be like all the other doctors. But her words and manner reassured him. She seemed to go to the heart of things.

"Okay, just judging from what you're telling me, it sounds like agoraphobia and panic disorder. Are you depressed?"

"Yes, it's a little better now, but I went through a terrible time last month."

"Do you blame yourself for all your problems?"

"Yes."

"That's very common. Tell me about the doctors who treated you before."

Greg ran through his experiences with Drs. Simon, Hoffman, and Cochran.

"What we're finding, Greg, is those Freudian theories usually don't apply to anxiety disorders. Your past may determine your personality and behavior to a great extent, but the anxiety itself has more specific causes."

"What kind of causes?"

"You become sensitized to certain things that trigger the anxiety, and when those triggers appear, you get anxious. Then you overreact to the adrenaline your body produces. You start trying to avoid those triggers, and your world shrinks until you're hemmed in."

"Like my driving," Greg said. "I was in a bad car wreck when I was nineteen. Most of my panic attacks were when I was in my car. It's gotten so bad, I can't drive without fear of panic."

"That's it. 'Fear of panic.' Something to work on." She pulled an spiral-bound book from her purse. "Do you think you'd like to make an appointment with me?"

"Oh, yeah, if Monday is okay," Greg said. "My aunt can bring me on any Monday, her day off."

Dr. Reed flipped through the appointment book. "I'm pretty booked up for a few weeks," she said, "but I have an opening at one o'clock on Monday, the fifth of February."

"I'll be there," Greg said.

"Good." She scribbled in the book. "Now, let me suggest something regarding your driving: Do you have a car?"

"It's in Fort Worth, but my aunt has a car."

"All right. I want you to go sit in the car a few minutes every day for three days. Just sit behind the wheel, don't do anything but take some deep breaths and relax as much as you can. Let the anxiety come and go. Don't resist it, just let it come and go. Then, for three days, put the key in the ignition and sit there. Then, start the engine, but don't put the car in gear; just sit there. Do that for three days. Finally, I want you to start the engine and back the car out of the driveway. Don't go anywhere; just pull back in the driveway."

"Is that it?" It sounded too easy. Greg's skepticism surfaced again.

"Yeah, and it sounds simple. But what you're doing is desensitizing yourself to being in the car. If you get too anxious at any point, go back to the previous step and work back up. And don't rush or try to skip ahead. Take two or three days for each step."

"Okay, it just sounds like common sense."

"It is. You'll find that much of what we'll be doing is common sense. But common sense works."

"That's encouraging," Greg said, feeling a renewed determination.

"I have to meet someone for lunch," she said. "I'd better be going."

"It was awfully nice of you and Brian to do this for me. I really appreciate your stopping by, Dr. Reed."

"Glad to do it for a friend of Brian's," she said. "And, by the way, everyone calls me Marilyn."

❖

February 1966

The worst storm of the winter struck the Texas Panhandle in late January. Amarillo recorded a foot of snow; eight inches fell in Hereford, forty-five miles to the southwest. Winds of fifty miles an hour dragged the snow into five-foot drifts along fences and buildings.

Greg helped Aunt Sally dig her car from a drift, but she decided against driving to work; temperatures in the teens left the snow-covered streets mostly impassable, so Sally put on her overshoes and heavy layers of clothing and walked the four blocks to the Plainsman office.

An eerie quiet settled over the Hereford as traffic ceased to move. An occasional train could be heard passing through town, and a sporadic dog's bark punctuated the stillness. Greg stayed inside and read, occasionally going to the typewriter and pecking out some attempts at poetry.

And he thought about Suzy. Her face burned in his brain, and memories of their time together stabbed him hard: her blend of warmhearted sweetness and mischief, her playfulness and earnest passion, their explorations of each other, the secure feeling of just being with her.

He hadn't mailed any of the letters he'd tried to write to her. Surely she thought about him and had some curiosity about how he was doing. But if she was involved with someone else now, she probably wouldn't want to hear from him. The thought left him despondent.

He sat at the typewriter and tried to express what he felt, six hundred miles away from her now:

> *Look out at the ocean,*
> *The one outside your door.*
> *The one that alone*
> *in all this tragic world*
> *bore silent witness*
> *to the tenderest moments*
> *we shall ever know.*
>
> *Look out at the waves:*
> *Does my face leap up*
> *then crash down again*
> *in the unceasing wash*
> *of the perpetual surf?*
>
> *The tides creep near*
> *then draw silently away.*
> *Do thoughts of me*
> *lap like the sea*
> *at your memory?*

Greg put on his coat, went out to Aunt Sally's car, and got inside. He sat there, freezing, surrounded by snow, thinking of Suzy in the balmy, subtropical breezes of Galveston.

Over the next days, the snow melted. Aunt Sally drove her car to work once the streets were clear. But every afternoon when she came home, Greg went to her Rambler and sat quietly inside for five minutes, as Marilyn Reed had suggested. When time came to start the engine, he felt a rush of anxiety, but he sat still until it passed. Finally, he backed out of the driveway with a stronger spurt of fear, but he again sat still until his body calmed down.

He met Dr. Reed—Marilyn—for his first official appointment in early February. Aunt Sally drove him to Amarillo on a Monday and went shopping while he met with the therapist.

He sat in a stylishly decorated waiting room, and promptly at one o'clock, she opened her office door and ushered him inside. He sat on a cushy sofa, decorated in a pattern of tiny yellow flowers on a field of blue. She sat across from him in an easy chair. A north-facing window provided a view of downtown Amarillo and the level plains beyond.

"You look scared, Greg," she said.

"I am," he replied.

"I know it's foolish to tell you to relax," she said. "But once we get started, maybe you'll feel more comfortable"

At last, Greg thought. *She didn't say, "Try to relax."*

"Why don't you tell me a little more of your history?" she said. "How long you've had anxiety problems, what happened in Galveston, that sort of thing."

Greg told her about the wreck, his first bout with panic in college, how things had stabilized for several years, came unraveled in Galveston, and spiraled downward from there. He told her about Suzy and how she'd broken their engagement little more than a month ago. Finally, he told her about Dr. Simon's threat of using electroshock therapy if he didn't improve.

"First off," Marilyn said firmly, "Forget about electroshock therapy. I'm adamantly against it. I've never seen any convincing evidence that it does any good, and I've seen plenty that suggests it does harm. You don't need anything that draconian, Greg, so put it out of your mind."

Greg relaxed and exhaled a sigh of relief. "I'm glad to hear you say that."

"Okay, let's start where you are," she said. "You're still having some pretty strong bouts of anxiety, right?"

"Yes, and depression. I feel like I'm backed in a corner and can't get out."

"I want to go slow, Greg," Marilyn told him, "but pretty soon it'll seem fast to you. Let's start with the driving fears you have."

She suggested he now start driving to the end of Aunt Sally's block—no more and no less—and he should do that every day for five days. Then, they'd discuss driving farther. He felt a pang of dread.

"I don't want to pile too many things on you at once," she said. "But I want you to get off your medication."

A chill went through Greg.

"I want you to reduce your Valium from two tablets a day to one and a half tabs a day this week and see how you feel."

Greg squirmed in his chair. "But I've been on Valium a long time."

"I know, but some studies have shown Valium actually makes depression worse. You don't need that, having just lost someone you loved."

"But it helps my anxiety," Greg said. "It's kind of damned if I do and damned if I don't."

"Actually, it's more like damned if you do." Marilyn smiled. "Those same studies show that if you take it as long as you have, your body adjusts, and it doesn't really ease the anxiety anymore. So, really, you're just putting a lot of chemicals in your body that aren't helping you and are actually doing harm."

"Are you against drug therapy?"

"Not at all. Medication can help in certain situations, but I think most people do better without it, and I think you're one of those people."

"That's scary," Greg said. "I've had withdrawal symptoms when I quit taking Valium."

"That's exactly why we're going slow. I want you to taper off slowly. You can do it. Trust me."

"I'll try." His palms felt damp.

"Okay, now I want you to spend a few minutes filling out some tests. I want to get a more definitive diagnosis."

Greg went into the small waiting room outside Dr. Reed's office and filled out the forms. He knocked on her door when he finished and handed her the tests.

She spent a few minutes looking at them. "Okay, I have a clearer picture now."

"Don't you have to run those things through a machine?" Greg asked.

"Not anymore." Marilyn took off her reading glasses. "I've done so many, I can just look at them and know how someone scores."

"How'd I do?"

"Well, you have a complex of problems. Let me ask you, do you have a lot of 'what if'-type thoughts?"

"Oh, yes. All the time."

"I call that 'horribleizing.' Does that describe your thoughts?"

"Exactly: What if I grab a knife out of the kitchen drawer and go on a killing spree?"

"Yes, that's what I mean. And those thoughts add to your anxiety, right?"

"Definitely."

"Greg, everyone has irrational thoughts, but a sane person doesn't act on them. You never have and likely never will. Can you see that?"

"Well, I'd hope so."

"Okay," she said, stacking the papers in front of her. "Here's what we have to work with: you have a generalized anxiety disorder with panic attacks. That much was obvious." She looked at him and nodded. "You have agoraphobia; that's the business about driving and the cops and fearing to be alone out in the world. Okay?"

"No surprise there," Greg said.

"And this isn't so clear-cut," Marilyn said, "but I believe you have a borderline case of obsessive-compulsive disorder—that's the 'what-if' stuff. Of course, you have the type of depression that's causal, meaning all these other things cause you to be depressed, including your loss of Suzy."

Greg sighed. "That's quite a list. Is there any hope?"

"Most people with anxiety or phobia disorders have a combination of several of those things. You're not unique by any means. Of course, there's hope. Let's get to work, shall we?" Her tone of voice was so self-assured, Greg's doubts dissipated as she talked.

"Okay, what's next?"

"Well, you've got plenty to work on for now. Except for one other thing. Have you ever tried meditating?"

"Never. I don't know much about it, but I always thought of it as contemplating your navel—sort of being wrapped up in yourself and shutting out the world." Greg recalled some students in college who'd taken up Eastern religions and sat cross-legged in campus flowerbeds. He'd dismissed them as pseudo-beatniks seeking attention.

"It's really the opposite if it's done right," Marilyn said. "More like opening yourself to the world."

"Hmm. I'm not sure I'm ready for that."

"Still, I want you to consider trying it. Just think of it as breathing exercises, if you prefer. I want you to take some breaths, and let me see you breathe."

Greg inhaled and puffed his chest out.

"Yes, you're breathing from the waist up, sucking air into your lungs, but tightening your belly and shoulder muscles."

"I've always breathed that way."

"Most people do, but try this: Relax your diaphragm and your shoulders and let your abdomen expand, along with your chest."

Greg tried it. "It feels strange."

"At first it does, but watch a baby sometimes. That's how infants breathe. It's completely natural. The older we get and the more stress we encounter, the shallower our breathing gets. It makes it hard to relax. Breathing from the belly promotes calm. Try it, and see if I'm not right."

Greg agreed to try, though still skeptical.

"When you're doing your breathing, it helps if you have some image in your mind to help you relax. For starters, pretend you're a pebble that's been thrown into a stream, and think how it feels to fall slowly through the water."

Greg thought the idea sounded flaky, but he agreed to try it.

He changed the subject to the thing that had dominated his thoughts and feelings since he'd left Fort Worth.

"Nothing gnaws at me more than what happened with Suzy," he said, growing somber and feeling fluttery in his gut. "I try not to think about it, but it's hard. It keeps me depressed most of the time."

She sat back in her chair and sighed. "There's nothing worse than ending a love affair—especially one that results in a broken engagement," she said with a look of understanding. "I've been through a divorce, and it really flattened me. You'd be pretty unusual if you weren't devastated by what happened with Suzy. Look at it this way: We're not working to cure just one or two parts of you; we're looking at the overall person. The more progress you make in other areas, the better able you'll be to cope with that situation. Who knows? Suzy may change her mind and come begging for you to take her back."

"I can't imagine that." Greg looked down at his shoes.

"But you don't know. Greg, part of the practice I do is called 'cognitive therapy' with a few other wrinkles thrown in. It's about learning to get rid of irrational, emotion-based thoughts. That's the kinds of thoughts you're having, do you see that?"

"Yeah, I guess so."

"That gives us a lot to work on. You could be right about Suzy, of course, but we'll take those thoughts apart and look at them. It's time to quit for this time. You're doing great. Let's pick up there next time."

Greg left the office wondering if he was getting a crush on Marilyn Reed. Already, she seemed to know him better than he'd ever known himself.

❖

That night, Greg paced around his bedroom at Aunt Sally's house thinking of what seemed to be a colossal task ahead of him. Could Marilyn Reed really help him, or were her encouraging words just soothing shrink-talk that would come to naught in the end? Might his condition indeed be so intractable that he might face shock therapy? Marilyn had calmed those fears some, but they still lingered.

More than anything, memories of Suzy shot daggers through him. Each thought of her brought the sensation of his gut being twisted and pulled into a dark pit of despair.

He had disdained Marilyn's idea of meditation as some counter-culture notion that probably had some connection to illegal drugs. His first attempt at deep breathing left him still agitated, and he stopped after five minutes. His feeling of hopelessness bore down on him harder.

He lay on his bed and tried to sleep, but he couldn't turn off the images of Suzy with another man. After an hour or so, he sat on the edge of the bed and began taking deep breaths again. This time, he kept on, and he watched what had been short, labored breaths gradually start to slow down. The image of a pebble falling through water helped. He realized that every muscle in his body was tense, and as his breathing slowed, his arms, legs, and shoulders started to soften and relax. After twenty minutes, his mind felt emptied, and no longer scattered and out of control. He stayed that way for another ten minutes, then lay back in bed and went to sleep convinced that Marilyn Reed knew what she's talking about.

The next week, Marilyn broadsided Greg with a suggestion he wasn't prepared for.

"I have a monthly support group that meets on Saturday mornings," she said. "I'd like for you to think about coming sometime."

Up to now Greg had shown little resistance to Marilyn's approach. But, recalling his disastrous experience with Dr. Joseph Cochran in Dallas, he drew the line.

"No way," he said, growing tense all over. "I've seen all I need to see of group therapy. You know what I think of it; it's bullshit."

"I do understand. What happened with Cochran is regrettable. But I'm not asking you to 'join' in any formal sense. It's an opportunity for you to meet other people who've had similar experiences to yours, so you won't feel so all alone in having this problem."

Greg's temper cooled a little. "All the same, I don't think so."

"Look, just try it out. You don't have to say anything. Just sit there and listen a few minutes. You can leave if you think it's bullshit."

"Well. . . ."

"Come on, Greg. You're doing so well, you'd have a lot to share with some of these people who are worse off than you are. Don't you think you'd feel better if you could help someone else?"

"Yeah, I guess so." Greg recalled his mother scolding his "self-centeredness."

"Okay, it's at ten Saturday morning."

"Well, all right. Aunt Sally doesn't work Saturday morning."

Greg's watch showed exactly ten o'clock. He didn't want to get there a minute early. He walked tentatively into Marilyn's office, dreading the thought he'd find the kind of people he'd encountered in Dallas.

Marilyn met him at her office door. Several people had gathered around the waiting room.

"Okay, I'm going to leave the room for awhile and let you folks talk to each other. I want you to say hello to Greg Spencer, who hasn't been with us before."

Greg looked over the group as members came to shake his hand. Most were female, varying in age from their teens to elderly. Some dressed stylishly, others casually or in work clothes.

"Hey, Greg," said a skinny, weathered man in his fifties, wearing jeans and scuffed cowboy boots. He pronounced Greg's name "Graig" in his Texas drawl. "Come on in here, boy and join the rest of us inmates." He told Greg his name was Hiram Oates, and he was the foreman on a ranch near Dimmitt. He pronounced his first name "Harm." His manner put Greg more at ease.

Greg took a chair and listened as the group members described their experiences with anxiety.

An attractive, well-dressed woman in her thirties had sold her travel agency because she'd had panic attacks driving to work. She'd stopped driving a car and had a crippling fear of flying. With Marilyn Reed's help, she said, she'd defeated her driving phobia and hoped to restart her business.

A shy teenage girl with mousy brown hair, dressed in faded jeans and T-shirt, described how she'd dropped out of school because she was overcome with fear of having an attack of diarrhea once she was in class. The thought so troubled her, she had panic attacks when she went inside a classroom.

A man about Greg's age told of having what Marilyn described as "depersonalization"—the sensation that he was dreaming or that nothing seemed real. Greg recalled the feeling as his first serious symptom of anxiety when he was nineteen.

A prim gray-haired woman in her sixties told how she'd been in and out of hospitals since she was forty-five because doctors had misdiagnosed her problem as schizophrenia. She'd had electroshock therapy, she said, which had little effect except to obliterate her memory. She'd had such a bad case of agoraphobia, she had become housebound for four years before she heard about Dr. Reed. Now she had resumed a productive life and had started training to become a nurse's aide.

But nothing prepared Greg for Hiram Oates's story: He'd developed a fear of horses.

"And, by God, there ain't nothin' worse on a ranch than bein' skeered a' horses. I got to where I'd walk up beside ol' Rags and start to tremblin' and shakin' to beat the band. My knees got so damn weak I couldn't even mount 'im. Made me so blue, I'd set in the bunkhouse cryin' my eyes plumb out. Went on like that for a month, before this ol' boy in town told me his wife had them kind of nervous jeebies, and Dr. Reed helped her out. So, here I am."

"Did you ever fall off a horse, Hiram?" Greg asked.

"Why, hell, I've fell offa horses a thousand times. I done what everbody always says: 'Git back on the horse.' Always worked before. But not with this here bidness. It plumb come at me out of the blue."

Most of the group agreed that their trouble started "out of the blue" or "came from nowhere." But after some discussion, most revealed that there had been some traumatic event in the months before the onset of their problems, things such as major surgery, divorce, loss of a loved one, or an accident involving injury. Sure enough, Greg thought, it usually takes some kind of trigger, such as his wreck on the Lake Arlington dam.

"Come on, Graig," Hiram said. "Le's hear your story."

Greg recounted his seven years of ups and downs, starting with the car accident when he was nineteen. Group members punctuated his story with remarks such as, "I know just what you're saying," and, "Happened to me exactly that way."

After an hour, Marilyn came back into the office and took Greg aside.

"Well, was it really so bad?"

"I had no idea, Marilyn. I'm sorry I acted like such a jerk."

"Okay, you owe me one."

"I owe you plenty," he said.

❖

By the end of February, Greg was driving Aunt Sally to work every day and cruising around Hereford in her Nash Rambler. But he had setbacks, as Marilyn had warned him.

"Recovering from an anxiety disorder is almost always two steps forward and one step back," she'd said.

He had a panic attack driving in Hereford one afternoon waiting for a train to pass at a railroad crossing. Cars lined up in front and behind him and boxed him in; there was no escape route. The ear-splitting sound of the train added to the tension, and after a few minutes panic exploded as it had in the past.

At first, Greg choked on the fear that all his progress was lost. But he remembered to look at an index card Marilyn had given him to carry in his shirt pocket. He pulled out the card and read:

Face your panic. Do not run away.
Accept. Do not fight. Breathe normally.
Be patient. Let the panic run its course.

The urge to flee back to Sally's house overpowered Greg; he felt he had to get to a safe haven. But he gritted his teeth and tried to apply all of Marilyn's slogans. He started focusing on his breaths and letting the panic dissipate.

Gradually, the worst passed. He drove around for another half-hour with little further anxiety. Another of Marilyn's methods was working.

For the next month, Greg had similar ups and downs. He walked a zigzag path, but each panic episode was less severe. Day by day, he felt calmer. He ate and slept well and spent his days writing poems. He gained back his lost weight. His depression lightened but still knifed through him when he thought of Suzy.

After six weeks, he drove alone to Amarillo alone for the first time. He went to Marilyn's office.

"Hey, I did it," Greg beamed when she opened her door.

"Bravo, Greg," she said. "For that you get a big hug." She wrapped her arms around him and squeezed.

Greg felt a thrill run through him at her touch. Marilyn was a handsome woman with a lovely figure. He realized how much he'd missed that kind of physical contact. She was divorced, he thought, but this wasn't the time or place for such feelings. He stepped back, feeling a spritz of embarrassment and guilt.

"So, how did it go?" She looked approvingly at him, still holding his shoulders.

"A little scary at first, but I floated through it."

"Wonderful. Now that you're off those drugs and driving freely, the sky's the limit." She'd had him reduce his medications slightly each week until he was free of them completely. He'd found the process easier than he expected.

"I haven't felt this good in months, even with the setbacks. Now I know they're temporary."

"Heard anything from Suzy?"

"Nothing." Greg looked down. It still hurt him to the core.

"So, have you thought about dating someone else?"

"Not really. I haven't met anyone close to my age in Hereford."

"Hereford's not far from Canyon, and it's a college town." Marilyn moved from her desk to an easy chair. She crossed her legs.

"Maybe I need to explore a little more." Greg's juices still buzzed from Marilyn's hug. He tried to resist noticing her short skirt resting just above the knees and her perfectly shaped legs.

"Have you thought about looking for a job?"

Greg forced his attention back to the conversation. "Yeah, I have, as a matter of fact."

"In Amarillo or Hereford?"

"Maybe the newspaper in Amarillo."

"Okay, Greg, I think it's time to spread your wings some more. There's no reason you couldn't work now. And there's no reason you couldn't meet someone you'd like to date."

"You think so?" A charge of excitement hummed in Greg's stomach. "I've noticed I've been thinking about sex a lot more lately," he confessed.

"Well, of course," Marilyn smiled. "You're a normal twenty-five-year-old male, free of all those drugs and starting to feel your oats again. What did you expect?"

Greg laughed. "Well, it's nice, but it's a little scary, too."

"Tell me what you feel right now?"

"Anxiety, right in the gut."

"Okay, what have we talked about that's causing that?"

"Adrenaline and those other chemicals that are released with fear."

"Right. With fear and excitement. That's normal. Just experience that, in the present moment, and remind yourself: 'That's just my body reacting.' Don't add more anxiety to that. Just let the adrenaline burst peter out. Because it will."

Greg relaxed and sat back on the sofa. "Okay, I'm doing better at understanding that."

"Yes, I can tell. Now, I want to ask you to consider something else."

"Okay, shoot."

Marilyn leaned forward. "Since you were nineteen, you've been ashamed of your anxiety problem, and you've done everything you could to keep it from being common knowledge, right?"

"Right. Only the people closest to me knew about it." Greg recalled how tightly he'd kept his secret, especially from Suzy.

"Are you still doing your breathing thing?"

"Yes. Every day. Sometimes several times a day. I finally learned to be that pebble falling through the water. Afterward, I'm more focused, and I can think clearer."

"When you sit down to meditate, I want you to keep this thought in mind: 'I am who I am, and that's just fine.'"

"Well, I see what you're getting at," Greg said. "But a minute ago, we were talking about my looking for a job. Do I just go in and announce: 'I've got anxiety problems, hire me'?"

"No, but if it comes up, don't run from it. You don't have to tell your employer about it unless it's relevant. But you don't have to be ashamed, either. It's who you are."

"Suzy used to tell me that, but people are so squirrelly about someone with 'nervous' trouble."

"Yes, and that's too bad. But you know, about one in twenty people has some kind of anxiety problem, and I'll bet you'd be surprised at how many people suffer from it or know someone who does."

Greg thought of Seth Yeager. "My boss in Galveston had that problem, but I can't expect that every boss would understand."

"No, but you can accept yourself as you are. And you'll always have the disorder—just like an alcoholic's always an alcoholic."

"Oh, hell." Some of Greg's old shame shot through him.

"No, it's okay. You happen to be wired with some extra sensitivity. But that cuts two ways: sensitivity can be creative, and anxiety can lead to purposeful action. That's the upside. You can use that energy in a positive way once you're aware."

"I guess it takes practice," Greg said.

"Of course, anything worthwhile does, but your disorder needn't disrupt your life. If you can learn to accept yourself, you'll be amazed how free of stress your life can be."

It had never occurred to Greg that his illness had a positive side.

Two weeks later, after his appointment with Marilyn, Greg drove by the offices of the Amarillo *Journal.*

Fear crawled up his gut as he looked at the building. He parked across the street and sat in the car, watching people come and go from the newspaper. He breathed deeply, and after a few minutes, his anxiety settled.

Greg thought about going inside, but then he saw a young man about his age come out the front entrance. Greg recognized him immediately: Larry Chambers. Greg had known Larry and his wife Sharon in college at Trinity Valley. Greg had heard Larry worked in Amarillo, but he'd forgotten. He got out of his car and crossed the street.

"Hey, Larry!" Greg shouted, catching up with the young man.

Chambers turned around. About Greg's medium height, Larry had fierce brown eyes and dark, wavy hair. He'd grown his hair longer, skimming his collar in back.

"I'll be damned. Greg, what are you doing in Amarillo?"

"Oh, just bumming around. Looking for a job." They shook hands warmly.

"Are you really?" Larry spoke with a nervous intensity.

"Yeah, I came up to visit my aunt in Hereford and decided I might stick around a while."

"Listen, if you want a job, we're looking for a night city editor. The guy in that job just gave notice."

"Hmm. You don't say?" Greg felt another flurry of anxiety. Did he want that kind of responsibility again?

"Weren't you city editor in Galveston?" Larry asked.

"Yeah. I left there last May." Greg didn't see any cause to bring up the reason. He had plenty of work to do on his self-acceptance project.

"Where've you been since?"

"Back in Fort Worth," Greg said. "The *News-Beacon* copy desk. Ugh."

"That's tough work."

"You said it."

"Man, we'll have to get together. Sharon and I live in Canyon."

"Oh, yeah, just down the highway. How is Sharon?"

"She's great. She's in grad school there at West Texas State."

"Oh, really?" Greg said. "Well, I could drive up from Hereford sometime."

"Some Friday or Saturday night would be cool. Let me give you my phone number." Larry took out a business card and wrote a number on it. He handed it to Greg.

"How about this weekend?" Greg asked.

"Great," Larry said. "Hey, come on inside and I'll introduce you to Neal Douglas, the managing editor."

Douglas, in his mid-thirties, stood a thin six feet tall. He wore glasses with clear plastic rims and lenses that made his eyes appear smaller, the mark of nearsightedness. His mousy brown hair looked plastered down with a greasy tonic.

Greg gave Douglas a rundown of his newspaper experience.

"Greg, I feel pretty lucky. Our night city editor Clyde Inman just gave me two weeks' notice today. And a few hours later, you walk in the door. You sound like just what we're looking for. I can pay you $135 a week. How about it?"

"Sounds good." Greg hesitated, then realized it was time to take the plunge. "When do you want me to start?"

"Well, a week from today is the sixteenth. You could spend a week with Clyde before he leaves. He could break you in. How about that?"

"Okay," Greg said. "I'll need a little time to learn the city, too. I think I'm ready to go."

"Great. We'll look for you then."

They shook hands to seal the deal; that's all it took in the newspaper world in those days. Douglas walked Greg to the personnel office to fill out some paperwork.

"By the way," Douglas said. "How did you like working for Seth Yeager in Galveston?"

"Great. Best boss I ever had."

"I worked for him in Abilene. He taught me most of what I know."

"Me, too," Greg said. "Not just about journalism, either."

When Greg got back to Hereford, he sat at Sally's typewriter and wrote to Ben Nelson at the *News-Beacon*.

> Dear Ben:
> This is my letter of resignation from the *News-Beacon*.
> I've found a job in Amarillo and will be starting in a week. Thank you for the courtesy you extended me by putting me on a leave of absence without pay. I've gotten my life and health in better order now. I'll always remember the *News-Beacon* as the place where my journey began.
> Best Regards,
> Greg Spencer

As Greg addressed and sealed the envelope, he'd never felt a greater sense of closing a chapter in his life and starting a new one.

❖
March 1966

Aunt Sally dropped Greg off at the train station in Amarillo, where he caught the Zephyr and rode it back to Fort Worth. There, he'd reclaim his Volkswagen and drive it to the Panhandle.

His parents met him at the Fort Worth depot.

"Greg, you look a lot better," Vivian said.

"I am, Mother. And I expect to stay that way."

"We're going to miss you, Greg," George said. "But I'm glad to hear you'll be able to make car payments."

"I feel good about that, too, Dad."

"What do you hear from Suzy?" Vivian asked as they got into the Spencers' car.

"Not a word," Greg said.

"What do you make of that?" Vivian looked distressed.

"I'm afraid it's over. She's got a boyfriend in Galveston." The old pain wasn't quite as sharp, but it was still there.

Greg loaded his Beetle with belongings from home. As he rounded up the smaller items from his room, he came across the jewelry box where he kept his senior class rings from Eastside High and Trinity Valley State College. He opened the box. Next to his large rings he'd placed Suzy's engagement ring. He had to stop what he was doing and sit down. He allowed the rush of feelings to pass and resumed his packing.

The drive back to Hereford was accompanied by the arrival of spring across most of West Texas. Redbud trees exploded with deep-pink blossoms, and bare limbs on trees along creek bottoms sprouted new leaves of light green. Winter wheat stood out across the countryside against the barren stubble of the previous growing season.

Greg drove for eight hours, stopping for breaks along the way. He had dinner at a roadside cafe in Childress, but he drove on without looking around. All of his relatives and friends who'd lived in Childress had either died or moved away.

He smiled as he listened on his car radio to some of the small-town Panhandle radio stations. They all seemed locked in the fifties, playing music by Eddy Arnold and Lefty Frizzell. They promoted church suppers and 4-H Club events, paying little heed to the popular culture or music of the day. It was a refreshing change from city life.

He arrived back in Hereford at eleven.

"How was the trip?" Aunt Sally asked.

"Nice," Greg said. "I felt a little shaky a time or two, but I enjoyed the scenery. It was pretty."

"Boy, when West Texas looks pretty to you, you must be feeling good. You sure you didn't have a snort or two along the way?"

"Cold sober," Greg said. "High on life."

"Oh, fiddlesticks," Sally said.

That Saturday afternoon, Greg drove north out of Hereford on U.S. 60 toward Canyon, named for nearby Palo Duro Canyon, a prominent gash in the High Plains that's one of the Panhandle's few tourist attractions.

The weather was unusually warm for March. As he drove, Greg watched a cluster of springtime thunderstorms building to the northwest above the uniformly flat horizon. Lightning flicked at the ground among several thunder-gray shafts of rain. *Looks like Amarillo might get a shower,* he thought.

He pulled off the divided highway in Canyon and drove past the clean, orderly campus of West Texas State University, the school where Sharon Chambers was a graduate student. Larry and Sharon lived in an apartment complex a few blocks beyond the campus.

Greg found a parking space between two apartment buildings and located the Chambers apartment on the ground floor. Sharon answered the doorbell.

"Greg! It's so good to see you. Come on in." She grabbed Greg and hugged him.

"Larry'll be back in a few minutes," she said. "He went to the store to pick up some oregano. I ran out, and dinner wouldn't be worth eating unless the tomato sauce had enough oregano. How about a beer?"

"Sure."

Sharon had short black hair, turned up in a "flip" on each side of her face. She wore a pair of tight, plaid Capri pants.

"You want to watch TV? There's probably a basketball game on."

"No, thanks. I haven't been following sports much lately."

"Well, why don't you get comfortable while I finish dinner?"

"Sure," Greg said. "Mind if I look through your record collection?"

"Go right ahead. Put a record on if you find something you like." Sharon went to the kitchen and brought Greg a chilled longneck bottle of Schlitz.

As Greg thumbed through the stack of LPs, he recalled Sharon from their undergraduate days at Trinity Valley State. She and Larry had both been drama students until Larry changed his major to journalism. They'd often gone to parties thrown by the journalism crowd. Greg had always enjoyed Sharon's company. She had a bubbly, outgoing personality that always put Greg at ease. Larry and Sharon had double-dated with Greg and Suzy a few times.

Greg pulled out an LP by Miles Davis and scanned the liner notes. The doorbell rang.

Sharon came out from the kitchen and answered the door. A strikingly attractive girl with a compact build and light brown hair stood in the doorway. She wore cutoff jeans and a sleeveless sweatshirt with "West Texas State" on the front. Her hair was on rollers the size of beer cans.

"Hi, Jessica," Sharon said. "Come in."

"I didn't know you had company," the girl said. "Do you have some typing paper? I've got an assignment due, and I just ran out."

"I think so," Sharon said. "Come on in."

Greg stood awkwardly next to the stereo trying to decide whether to play the LP. The girl named Jessica looked at him as though she didn't quite know whether to speak.

"Oh, I'm sorry," Sharon said from the hallway. "This is Greg Spencer; he just got hired at the *Journal*. Larry and I knew Greg in college. Greg, this is Jessica Taylor."

"Hi, Greg Spencer," Jessica said, jauntily cocking her head to one side.

"Hi, Jessica." There was a pause. Greg cleared his throat. "I take it you go to West Texas State."

"Yeah, I'm a senior." She had a high, throaty, little girl's voice.

"What's your major?" A trite question, Greg thought, but a safe one.

"Journalism."

"Oh, really?" Greg brightened. "Are you thinking about newspaper work?"

"Maybe, if a newspaper will hire me. I'm, like, editor of the paper at WT."

"That's good experience," Greg said. "I was editor of my college paper."

"Maybe you could get me a job at the *Journal*. I applied, but I never, like, heard back from them."

"Well, I haven't started yet, so I don't know anything about their hiring practices. But I'll look into it."

"Would you? That would be so cool." Jessica's face lit up, and she grasped Greg's arm.

"Sure," he said, a little nonplussed.

"Thanks." She squeezed his arm. "What will you do at the *Journal*?"

"Night city editor. I start next week."

Sharon returned with a handful of typing paper.

"Thanks, Sharon," Jessica said. "You're an angel."

Jessica looked back at Greg and stared a few seconds, as if she were studying him.

"Good luck, Mister Editor. Don't be, like, too mean to the reporters." She closed the door and left.

"Me? Mean?" Greg chuckled and gave Sharon a puzzled look.

"Oh, Jessica just says whatever's on her mind. She probably heard in her journalism classes that city editors are mean."

"Where's she from, anyway?"

"Amarillo. She's homegrown." Sharon headed back to the kitchen.

Larry returned with oregano, and before long the three sat down to their dinner of lasagna and mixed vegetables.

"Excellent, Sharon," Greg said, finishing the last bite on his plate.

"It's my grandmother's recipe. She came here from Italy."

Afterward, they sat talking at the table over coffee.

"Say, Greg, where do you stand with the draft?" Larry asked.

"I'm safe, I think," Greg said. He hadn't thought about his draft status in months. "I'm classified 1-Y, which means I'm among the dregs after all the 1-A's are taken. I had asthma as a kid."

"I'm 4-F," Larry said. "Heart murmur; I had scarlet fever. But if I were 1-A, I'd be a conscientious objector."

"Really? I don't know if I'd go that far."

"Well, hell, this war is immoral and probably illegal. We have to resist it any way we can."

"We feel very strongly," Sharon said. "Have you heard of Students for a Democratic Society?"

"SDS? Yeah. They've made a lot of noise at the University of Michigan."

"They started there, but they're spreading all over. There's a chapter at UT in Austin. Jessica and I have talked to a couple of professors about trying to start a chapter at WT. We have to let people know Vietnam is not America's problem."

"Jessica's a war protester?" Greg asked.

"Oh, yes. She's editor of the WT newspaper and writes some scathing editorials against the war."

Greg didn't want to debate the war. He'd heard all the arguments, but he'd been fighting his own personal war for so long, he hadn't formed a firm opinion. Sometimes he felt old and out of touch at twenty-five. He managed to steer the conversation to less global matters.

The three spent the rest of the evening recalling their college days and updating each other on mutual friends and what they'd been doing since college. Sharon finally asked Greg about Suzy.

"She's in nursing school," Greg said. "In Galveston."

"Didn't I hear y'all were engaged?" Larry asked.

"We were," Greg said. "But we broke up last Christmas."

"Oh, that's too bad," Sharon said. "I remember how close you two were at Trinity Valley. I thought sure you'd be married by now."

"I thought so, too," Greg said, then sat silently for a moment. Larry and Sharon seemed to sense that he didn't want to pursue the subject.

"Greg, we're having a party next Saturday," Sharon said, shifting gears. "There'll be some friends from the college there, plus some newspaper people. Come if you can."

"Thanks," Greg said. "I'll try to make it."

They chatted a while longer. Greg thanked Larry and Sharon for the dinner and their hospitality. He said goodnight and walked to the parking lot.

He got into his VW and started the engine. He noticed Jessica Taylor cutting across the parking lot carrying a basket of clothes from the laundry room. He sat for a moment, admiring her shapely legs and a bosom that jounced freely beneath her sweatshirt, unencumbered by a bra, he thought. He rolled down his window.

"Hey, do I look mean?" he shouted.

Jessica looked up with a startled expression. Then she smiled. "Aren't all editors mean?" She walked over to his car.

"Not me," Greg said. "I'm easy." He couldn't remember the last time he'd tried to flirt. He never thought he was much good at it.

"Oh, I'll bet," Jessica said, leaning against the car, leaning one arm above the window. Jessica had taken the rollers out, and her long, straight, brown hair cascaded over her shoulders and down her back.

"I haven't had a chance to be mean yet," Greg said.

"Okay, I'll, like, reserve judgment."

"Mighty big of you. Thanks."

"Did Larry and Sharon tell you about their party?" Jessica pushed back a strand of hair that covered one eye

"Yeah, are you going?"

"I plan to," she said. "Are you?"

"Yeah, I'll be there." Greg hadn't thought much about the party until now.

"Oh, good." Jessica picked up her laundry basket. "I can find out if you're mean or not."

"Well, I'd better be going. You've got a paper to type."

Greg watched her walk back toward her apartment and considered the new possibilities. He put the Beetle into gear and drove away.

❖

Greg walked into Marilyn Reed's office on Monday afternoon for his weekly appointment.
You look a little rattled," Marilyn said. "Are you okay?"

"I don't know," Greg said, fidgeting on the couch. "I report for my first day at the *Journal* in a couple of hours. I guess I've got the jitters."

"How very human," Marilyn said. "Want to talk about it?"

"I guess it's part fear, part excitement. I'm eager to get started, but there are all these doubts."

"What kind of doubts?"

"Oh, just thinking about Galveston and whether I'll get involved in anything like that scandal again." Greg recalled the bricks, the jail, the overwhelming panic.

She smiled. "In Amarillo? Fat chance."

"You're probably right, but the scars are still there."

"But Greg, that was then; this is now. You might as well be on a different planet."

"True enough," he said. "Amarillo feels like a different world from Galveston. But I'm also looking for a place to live in Amarillo. I dread living alone again."

"Your main fear of being alone was your lack of self-acceptance. You were so at war with yourself, you couldn't stand being alone. You're doing a lot better in that respect."

Greg relaxed a little. "There's something else."

"Okay, let's hear it." Marilyn raised her chin and gave him a knowing look.

"I've met someone that's got me a little off-balance."

"You mean a girl?"

"Yeah. She's a journalism student at WT."

"And you've gone out with her?"

"Well, not yet. But I think there's something going on there."

"Are you going to ask her out?"

"We're both going to a party," Greg said. "I'll probably spend some time with her and ask her out."

"So, what's the problem?"

"I still don't have Suzy out of my system." The old wound arose in his gut.

"And you feel guilty about being attracted to this other girl?"

"Yeah. It doesn't feel right. Suzy's the only girl I ever really cared about or spent much time with. I'm not sure I know how to act around someone else."

"How is this girl different from Suzy?"

"She's a few years younger; part of the anti-war, counter-culture crowd. Makes me feel like an old man. I'm not part of that scene. I've never used illegal drugs, I don't have long hair, and I don't even listen to rock and roll anymore."

Marilyn laughed. "An old man at twenty-five. I really feel sorry for you. Seriously, aren't you playing 'what if' again?"

"I guess so. It's just so unusual to have these kinds of feelings about another girl besides Suzy."

"Not all bad feelings, I take it."

"No, just strange."

"Greg, you're a healthy young man again. Can you accept that?"

Greg's first day at work went smoothly. He was struck by the contrast with the reporting staff in Galveston. There, he'd had an uphill battle against older reporters with entrenched habits. At the *Journal*, most staff members were younger and looking for direction from someone with more experience. They treated Greg with more deference and respect.

Still, Greg spent a tense first week learning the city desk routine as he became more familiar with the staff and the paper's operation.

And there was the stress of finding a place to live in Amarillo. He didn't know the town well, so he asked for advice from colleagues. He settled on a place in the southwestern part of the city, just off Highway 60, about halfway between Canyon and downtown Amarillo.

Aunt Sally helped Greg pack his belongings. He crammed them into his Beetle and hauled them to his one-bedroom unit in the Canyon Oaks Apartments, a typical sixties "luxury" complex with swimming pool, laundry room, and thin walls that did little to keep out sound from adjacent apartments.

He spent most of Saturday moving in, lugging belongings up the stairs to his second-floor apartment. By late afternoon, he was so tired he'd almost forgotten about Larry and Sharon's party in Canyon.

He pondered whether he even felt like going to the party. But then he remembered that Jessica Taylor would be there. Maybe he wasn't too tired after all.

Greg stood under a hot shower in the new apartment with a kind of anticipation he'd almost forgotten. But he had to temper his giddiness; after all, he didn't really know Jessica. What if she showed up with another guy? And there was Suzy. Was his interest in Jessica a way of getting even with Suzy? Still, a pleasant buzz ran through him and energized his tired body. He cut himself shaving in two places, then bolted down a McDonald's hamburger as he drove toward Canyon.

❖

April 1966

Greg looked out across the open farmland for a few miles along the highway to Canyon. Spring was in full flower, and fresh farm crops painted the level landscape a bright green. Irrigation sprays spread like giant spiders across the fields, tapping the vast underground aquifer that made the High Plains such a rich agricultural land. The air smelled light and clean.

Greg pulled off the highway at Canyon and navigated the few blocks to his destination.

The front door was open, so he walked into the living room of Larry and Sharon's apartment. Guests gathered in bunches. Laughter occasionally burst forth from the clusters of people. The pungent aroma of beer filled the place. Greg recognized a couple of people from the *Journal*.

He looked around, but didn't see Jessica anywhere.

Larry and Sharon greeted Greg and directed him to the kitchen, where a keg of beer awaited his thirst. He filled a plastic cup from the tap.

Greg walked through the apartment again. Still no sign of Jessica. Oh, well. She probably had a date and went somewhere else.

Sharon came in and took Greg around to the various groups, introducing him to a number of the people. One of them was Dr. James Harwell, chairman of the philosophy department at WTSU.

"Ah, another misinformant." The man literally looked down his nose at Greg.

"What?"

"You're an editor on the newspaper, aren't you?"

"Sort of."

"Well, I call anyone in the news media a 'misinformant.' You spread misinformation, in other words."

"Not deliberately." *What an arrogant bastard*, Greg thought.

"Oh, come now," The professor dripped with scorn. "Your newspaper is owned by the Richburg family. They're the greatest reactionaries in the Southwest. Do you think they'd let you tell the truth about things like Vietnam, civil rights, nuclear weapons?"

Greg shrugged. "I've never even seen the Richburgs. I've only been here a week, so I can't say what their influence is."

Harwell shook his head. "You've got a lot to learn, my boy."

Somebody tapped Greg on the shoulder. He looked around.

It was Jessica. She wore a tight, blue dress, cut low in the front and revealing just enough cleavage to suggest the round contours of her breasts. Her makeup accentuated her deep blue eyes. The sight of her momentarily took Greg's breath away.

"Hey, I didn't know if you were coming." He guided her to a more private spot across the room.

"Yeah, I had to finish a paper for class. Now, I'm free the rest of the weekend."

"My, but you're conscientious."

"Just trying to keep my GPA from, like, falling through the floor."

"Aw, I bet you're a four-pointer."

"Well, three point six. I'll take it." She flashed a cocky smile.

"You want to dance?" Greg asked. Music from the stereo wafted across the apartment.

"Oh, Spencer, I'd love it."

Greg pulled Jessica close to him, and they moved around the floor. Her hair brushed his cheek, then their faces touched, then pressed close. Her soft breasts burrowed into his chest.

It Takes a Worried Man

They glided slowly to the sound of Billie Holiday singing "These Foolish Things." As the song ended, Jessica said, "I have that album. I think there's a song on there just for you."

"Huh?"

"Just a minute. Why don't you get me a beer while I find what I'm looking for?"

Jessica went to the turntable and moved the needle to another track. Greg returned and handed her a cup of beer.

"This is dedicated to you, Spencer."

Billie's soulful voice sang:

> *Mean to me,*
> *Why must you be mean to me?*
> *Gee, honey, it seems to me*
> *You love to see me cryin'. . . .*

They laughed at their private joke. Others looked at them, puzzled.

"I've been kidding Spencer about being a mean old editor." Jessica spoke loudly enough for nearby guests to hear. They laughed at her joke.

A mischievous urge seized Greg. "Come outside, Jessica," he said. "I'm taking you to the woodshed."

"Oh, boy!" Jessica giggled.

He grabbed her arm and pulled her toward the back door.

"You weren't kidding, were you?" Jessica said with a big smile.

"No," Greg said, closing the door. "And you weren't, either."

They stepped into the darkness of the backyard. They kissed frantically. And they kissed slowly and tenderly. And then they kissed some more. Greg kissed Jessica's forehead, her cheeks, her ears, her neck. Finally, they separated and took deep breaths.

"Let's go over to my place," she said.

Jessica led Greg across the courtyard and unlocked her apartment. She closed the door, and they stood kissing furiously in the living room. Greg unzipped her dress in back and let it fall to the floor. He grasped her buttocks and pulled her against him. She stepped back, breathing heavily.

"Wait for me in there," Jessica nodded toward the bedroom.

Greg stood next to the bed, taking off his shirt. He felt fully whole again.

Jessica emerged from the bathroom naked and walked toward Greg slowly enough for him to savor the sight. She ran her hands over Greg's chest and kissed along his middle. She unfastened his pants and pulled them to his ankles.

She guided Greg onto the bed and straddled him as he lay on his back. She took control of everything and, like a seasoned pro, led Greg to a stunning finale.

They lay together, relaxing and caressing.

"Oh, Spencer," she whispered. "You were *fantastic!*"

"Think so?"

"Oh, it just doesn't get any better."

Flattered but flummoxed by her comments, Greg gave her a long, wet kiss. "You're pretty good yourself," he said.

Suddenly, a disturbing thought jarred Greg. He'd let himself be swept away in the moment's passion.

"Jessica," he whispered. "You are on the Pill, aren't you?"

"Of course, silly." She buried her face in his neck. "Who's not?"

He exhaled relief.

"Spencer?" Jessica nuzzled below his ear.

"Yeah."

Jessica nibbled his earlobe. "Do you really think you could, like, help me get a job at the *Journal*?"

❖

Greg and Jessica spent a night of wild, uninhibited lovemaking. He came back the next night, and the following weekend they shared two more free-spirited nights together.

Yet Greg couldn't escape the thought that sex with Suzy had been a deeper, more intimate experience. With Jessica, the phrase "style over substance" occurred to him.

Between their escapades in the bedroom, Jessica pulled out several scrapbooks that contained clippings of her work on the newspaper at West Texas State.

Greg found her work passable, but she obviously needed seasoning. He complimented her better stories and columns, but soft-pedaled the problem areas.

Jessica's praise for Greg seemed to have no limits. She showered flattery on his prowess in bed and raved about his past newspaper work.

"Wow, you covered the Kennedy assassination?"

"Not really. I worked the story from the city desk."

"Still, you were, like, in the middle of it." She ran her finger down his chest.

"Yeah, we put out an extra."

"And you covered Oswald's funeral?"

"Yeah. Quite a scene."

"Tell me about the murder case in Galveston." She massaged his shoulders.

"It got me thrown in jail. This rich guy beat a teenage boy to death. He and the cops tried to cover it up, and we exposed them."

"Oh, man. Spencer, you've done it all." She leaned over and kissed him, rubbing a bare breast against his shoulder.

"Well, not quite." Greg had trouble concentrating on her words.

"I want to work for you. Did you talk to anyone about, like, hiring me at the *Journal*?"

"Yeah, I mentioned it to our managing editor."

Jessica stood up and threw a nylon robe around her. "Neal Douglas?"

"Yeah."

"He interviewed me last fall and said he'd be in touch, but he never called back."

"Well, Jessica, it seems that when he showed your resumé to the editor, the editor said, 'Isn't that the girl down at West Texas State who's been writing all those anti-war editorials?'"

"Oh, shit," Jessica said.

"Our editor is the brother-in-law of Chase Richburg, and you probably know about the Richburgs' politics."

"I know. Fascist pigs." She scowled.

"That may be, but if you're going to work for them, you have to understand they probably aren't going to change."

"I wouldn't sell my soul just to work for their crappy paper."

"You don't have to, but you do have to do things their way as long as they're writing the checks. You have to be subtle about trying to change things. Either that or get off the bus."

"You make it sound so awful, Spencer. If everyone just cowers before all that power, the world will always be screwed up. Someone has to raise hell."

"All I'm saying is, you have to go slowly and pick your battles."

She gave him a hateful look. "I didn't realize you were so, like, conservative."

"I don't think I am," Greg said. "But if you have so much faith in my experience, you might take my advice and not try to save the world right out of the box."

"So, they don't want to hire me because I'm too radical?" She folded her arms and sat cross-legged on the bed in full pout.

"No, I didn't finish. Neal said he might be able to use you part-time to begin with. Go talk to him and try not to scare the crap out of him. I think he'll hire you."

"Oh, Spencer!" Jessica said. "You're wonderful!"

Jessica Taylor appeared at the *Journal* office later that week. She came dressed in a conservative blue suit. She'd pulled her long, dark hair into a tight bun and wore dark-rimmed glasses.

"Hey, Spencer," she said leaning on the city desk. "Where you been, stud?"

"Working, as usual," Greg said, smiling. The sound of teletypes and typewriters clattered in the background.

"Yeah, but I thought you might come down after work some night."

"I don't get off until one a.m."

"Well, I could, like, wake up for you." Her voice oozed seductiveness.

"Hmm. You don't say," Greg said. "Did you come in to see Neal?"

"Yeah, are you going to introduce me?"

"I thought you'd already met him."

"Well, it's been a few months." Jessica straightened her suit coat. "How do I look?"

"You look great; very professional," Greg said. "Come on. I'll go with you."

Greg showed Jessica into Neal Douglas's office.

"Neal, this is Jessica Taylor. I think you two might have met."

"Thanks Greg," Douglas said. "Come on in, Jessica and have a seat."

Greg excused himself and walked back to the city desk. He lit a cigarette and stared off across the newsroom. *What to do about Jessica?* The more he thought about it, the more he thought she was using him. But so what? Maybe it wouldn't last, but it felt good to be with a woman again. Greg knew it wouldn't be the same as it had been with Suzy. Maybe Jessica laid on her compliments a little thick, but surely she wasn't faking her pleasure. Or was she? Anyway, why not ride the wave of passion while it lasted? After all, Suzy could be out of his life forever.

He stubbed out his cigarette as the telephone on his desk rang. He took dictation from a reporter, and had just hung up the phone when Jessica reappeared.

"Well?" He looked up at her.

She wore a triumphant smile and looked as if she were about to explode with glee. "He hired me, Spencer!" she said. "All because of you." She took off her glasses and put them away in her purse, then undid the bun and let her hair fall to its natural length. She leaned over close to Greg and whispered, "I can't wait to pay you back."

Greg looked around to see if anyone was looking. "I can't, either," he whispered back. Then, in his normal voice, "Congratulations. When do you start?"

"Tomorrow," Jessica said. "He wants me to work, like, Friday through Sunday. Three to eleven. General assignments. It's perfect with my class schedule."

Greg got up and walked with Jessica toward the *Journal*'s front entrance.

"Well, since I work the desk Sunday through Thursday, I guess you'll work for me on Sundays."

"How cool," she said. "But it kinda, like, screws up our weekends together, doesn't it?"

"I'm off on Fridays and Saturdays. If you're up for a late date on those nights, we could see each other then."

"I'm game if you are." Jessica kissed Greg on his cheek and walked to her shiny, red Ford Mustang in the parking lot across the street.

Greg met Jessica at her apartment after she finished work on Friday night. Her passion seemed more subdued, and Greg saw a more tender, needy side of her. After they made love, she held him tight, as if he might escape.

"Spencer, I'm scared to death." She turned on a bedside lamp.

"What's the matter?"

"I don't know what the hell I'm doing at work. You're going to have to help me."

"What's wrong? I thought you said it went fine."

"They sent me to cover a real estate convention. I don't know batshit about real estate. I didn't know what to ask those people. I just froze. I was afraid I'd sound dumb."

"Just find some official who likes to talk," Greg reassured her. "Salesmen love to tell you how great they are. Just ask how the real estate business is these days. Get them talking and take good notes."

"Well, I got enough for a story," Jessica said, leaning on her elbow. "But when I turned it in, Pete Kirkland cut it down from two pages to just four paragraphs."

"So what? Haven't you ever been edited before?"

"Not like that." She pulled the sheet around her.

"Jessica, it was your first day. All cub reporters get edited a lot. It's how you learn. He probably had a small hole to fill in the paper. Did you notice what he cut out?"

"No, I was so shocked, I just left."

"Okay, I'll dig out the carbons and go over them with you Sunday."

"You're a sweetheart." She kissed his cheek.

Greg pulled her close. He ran a hand up her ribs and caressed her breast.

"Hey, Spencer," she whispered.

"Yeah?"

"Wanta smoke some weed? I got some."

Greg lay silently for a moment, turning the question over. Marijuana had proliferated since his college days, and he'd previously taken a dim view of anyone who smoked it. But he was curious enough that he wanted to find out what made it so attractive. *No,* he thought. *Not now.*

"Jessica, you know in Texas you can go the penitentiary for simple possession, don't you?"

"Yeah, but who's gonna look for it here? It makes for great sex."

"One thing I've learned in a short time is that cops around here are really hard-assed about drugs. They could raid anywhere. You've got a reputation for being outspoken in the college paper. I saw one of your columns that argued in favor of legalizing pot. Don't think cops don't pay attention to stuff like that."

"You really think so?" Jessica's body suddenly felt tense.

"Yeah, I do. There are undercover agents on every college campus. I might try the stuff some time, I guess, but not now. If I were you, I'd get rid of it."

"Damn, Spencer," she said, taking a plastic bag from her chest of drawers. "You sound like my daddy sometimes." She went in the bathroom. Greg heard the commode flush.

She came back to bed, and they made love the old-fashioned way.

Saturday night, she came to his apartment after work, and they spent the night in his bed. She again clung to him with a sense of desperation.

"I'm really discouraged, Spencer. Kirkland is ripping the crap out of everything I turn in."

"Everybody feels that way at first," Greg said. "Just be glad they're giving you stories that aren't very important. Then, when a big story hits, you're ready. You get better by making mistakes."

"Nobody ever tore my stories apart like that on the school paper, not even the faculty adviser."

"You're not working on a school paper any more." Greg smiled. "Welcome to the real world."

"Oh, you're such a mean old bastard." She pinched his buttocks.

"Only with prima donnas," Greg said and tickled beneath her ribs.

Jessica squealed, then nuzzled close to him.

Greg drove to Hereford on Easter Sunday to visit with Aunt Sally and retrieve any mail that might have come for him at her house.

Driving down the level highway, he watched the puffy cumulus clouds swelling over the Plains in the afternoon heat. Maybe they'd get some rain. The farmers had been complaining about the dry Panhandle spring.

He tried again to sort out what he'd gotten himself into with Jessica. She was obviously on the front lines of what was being described as the "sexual revolution." He'd never come across a more aggressive and sexually charged female. And, being a male who grew up in the repressed fifties, he found her hard to resist. Wasn't she the answer to many of his adolescent fantasies? And yet, recently he'd seen a more tender, vulnerable side of her. Maybe that was the real Jessica, not the brash, aggressive radical he'd first encountered. The more he thought about it, the more the "radical" thing seemed more and more like an act. She came from a well-to-do Amarillo family and seemed to be enjoying her season of rebellion. She might aspire to being a hippie, he thought, but most hippies he knew about didn't drive '66 Mustangs or dress as stylishly as Jessica. Her habit of saying "like" all the time seemed an affectation and grated on his nerves. Still, her softer side appealed to him and he hoped to get to know it better.

Jessica's driving ambition unsettled him. She wasn't much of a writer, he thought, although she could probably be trained out of her worst habits. She was smart and seemed to have a vast reservoir of energy. Those were good qualities in a reporter. He admired her idealism, yet he didn't need the stress of trying to mold someone into a seasoned reporter. Didn't he have enough to deal with? Six months ago, he was in the hospital for panic attacks and major depression. Was he tempting fate by getting involved with Jessica? He recalled an old newsroom adage: "Don't get your pussy where you get your paycheck."

Suddenly, he recalled where he was on Easter Sunday a year ago: with Suzy, Brian, and Cindy, at church in Galveston, then at Gaido's, where Brian and Cindy had announced their engagement. It seemed a universe away, in another lifetime. The thought lingered of how lovely Suzy had looked that day. Where was she now? Did she go to church with her new lover this Easter?

Greg arrived at Aunt Sally's as the clouds continued to boil above the Plains.

"I wondered when you were coming by," Sally said. "You've been getting more mail than I have." She handed him the stack she'd saved for him.

He thumbed through the letters. Still nothing from Suzy, as he'd come to expect. Maybe it was finally time to declare Suzy a lost cause and concentrate on Jessica. But he didn't love Jessica. He felt more tenderness toward her now, but he doubted he could ever love anyone as he had Suzy.

He visited with Aunt Sally awhile and drank a cup of tea with her. She told him about the Easter service she had attended at the First Methodist Church and how she planned to spend the afternoon setting out tomato plants in her backyard garden. Greg scratched Sam's ears as he told Sally about his job and new apartment. Then, he left for the return trip to Amarillo.

❖

The sky had darkened as Greg drove out of Hereford. Big drops of rain pelted his windshield, and a chilly wind blew out of the west, pushing sand, trash, and tumbleweeds across the highway. The sparse trees bent their branches to the east as the wind scoured the flat landscape.

The farther northwest he drove, the darker it got. Rags of low-hanging scud raced across the sky. Hail the size of peas started to pepper Greg's Volkswagen.

Off to the west, dark, the low scraps of cloud seemed to be circling in the sky like hungry vultures

Greg realized he was looking at a "wall cloud."

As a reporter for the Fort Worth *News-Beacon*, Greg had attended a training class for storm spotters. An old high school friend, Todd Franklin, was an amateur radio operator in Fort Worth. Local "hams" served the National Weather Service as its eyes and ears on the ground during the spring storm season, reporting on weather conditions over their mobile radios. When Todd had told him about the training class, Greg thought it might make a good story for the paper. He had attended the class, written the story, and in the process, learned to recognize the early signs of a developing tornado. He'd never had to put that knowledge to use before.

He'd learned that wall clouds signaled rotation in a thunderstorm. Wall clouds drooped ominously beneath the main cloud base. When they started to swirl, there was a good chance a funnel would soon appear.

What Greg saw to his west, perhaps five miles away, was exactly what photographs and motion picture film had shown in the training course. Sure enough, a ragged, gray snout dropped from the wall cloud and hovered over the open land.

The funnel moved northeast. Greg realized he was on a collision course with the twister. It was headed directly toward U.S. 60, the highway to Amarillo.

The storm grew more intense. Hailstones grew larger and covered the highway. Greg could barely see the pavement in front of him. Finally, he saw the faint outline of the white grain elevator in Umbarger just ahead.

He pulled into a service station in Umbarger, joining some other motorists who had sought shelter under the station's awning. His heart pounded, but he remembered to let it hammer, without fueling his body with more fear.

"Did you see that twister?" Greg shouted to a man standing outside his car and looking up the highway to the northeast.

"Damn right I did." The man wore a tan western hat and a shirt with pearl buttons. "That son of a bitch is on the ground."

A couple and two small children piled out of another car to look. The hail stopped and the rain slackened. A few miles up the highway, the swirling monster tore across the highway like a buzzsaw and ripped into roadside buildings, scattering tires, shingles, planks, paper, and all in its path.

"How far is it to Canyon?" Greg thought about Jessica; maybe he should call her.

"It's about twelve miles," the man with the western hat said. "But I think that tornader is south of Canyon. There's some warehouses out there and some other stuff along the railroad."

Greg got back in his car and sped toward Canyon. Ahead, the twister ground across the farmland to the east, spouting a cloud of dust and debris, moving away from him. It roared in the direction of Palo Duro Canyon, looking like some insane machine grinding up everything in its path.

Shortly, Greg came upon a highway patrol car blocking the road. Beyond it, scraps of sheet metal and other flotsam lay scattered across the wet highway.

Greg pulled to the shoulder and took some deep breaths. He approached the patrol car. Rain had started up again and quickly soaked through his clothes. A hawk-nosed patrolman rolled down his window partway.

"Anybody hurt up here?" Greg asked.

"Who wants to know?" The patrolman looked suspiciously at him.

"I work for the Amarillo *Journal*," Greg said.

"Don't think anybody's hurt," the patrolman said. "Good thing it's Sunday. The sheriff's men are going to search the area."

The twister had torn through several storage buildings built of cinder blocks and corrugated metal.

"Any chance I can get through here?" Greg asked. "I'm the night city editor, and I need to get to the office."

"It's a pretty big mess," the officer said. "You'll have to drive real slow and weave a lot. But if you're willing to try, you can go ahead, I guess."

Greg got back in his car and crept forward, dodging the storm's refuse. He tuned his radio to an Amarillo station.

> *. . . We have mobile units en route to Pampa, where early reports say a tornado struck a housing subdivision north of downtown. Civil Defense is reporting another twister has just passed through the Claude area. Interstate 40 has been closed due to debris west of Amarillo. At least four tornadoes have been sighted thus far in the Panhandle. The National Weather Service says conditions remain ripe for more twisters to form.*

Greg had to drive over scraps of lumber in the wet road to avoid the large sheets of metal. He passed a twisted bicycle, a smashed washtub, several tires, and a sea of tree limbs, twigs, and leaves. After a mile he reached a clear highway. He floorboarded the Beetle and raced toward Amarillo. As he passed through Canyon, he saw no damage other than twigs and leaves apparently stripped from trees by the hail. Maybe he didn't need to check on Jessica.

Rain stopped and started as Greg drove into Amarillo. It was 3:15, and he wasn't due at work until five. Most reporters had the day off. A single reporter was assigned to come in at three to answer the phone. Greg had forgotten which reporter would be on duty.

At one point, the visibility became so poor, he had to pull off the road and stop under an underpass until the rain let up.

Finally, he arrived at the *Journal* building downtown. He walked inside, pleased that he'd survived his harrowing drive without a panic attack. He pushed open the glass doors.

Jessica Taylor was the only person in the newsroom.

❖

Jessica sat at the city desk with a phone cradled between her ear and shoulder. She looked up when she saw Greg approach. She put her hand over the mouthpiece.

"It's Larry Chambers," she said.

"Let me talk to him." She handed him the phone.

"Larry, where are you?" Greg asked.

"I'm at home. We watched that tornado touch down just south of here."

"Are you and Sharon okay?" Greg emptied his ashtray and lit a cigarette.

"Yeah, but there's still some hail on the ground here. I think it beat up my car."

Greg pointed for Jessica to answer another ringing phone. She picked it up.

"Larry, is your car in good enough shape to drive?" he asked.

"Yeah, where do you want me to go?"

"Why don't you head over to Claude? I heard on the radio that same twister moved through there a little while ago."

"Okay, I'm on my way."

As soon as Greg hung up with Larry, another phone rang. Neal Douglas was on the line. He and Greg talked a few minutes about how they'd cover the tornado outbreak. Greg hung up with Neal about the time Jessica hung up her phone.

"That was Tracy Biggs," Jessica said. "She was headed for Pampa, but her car broke down. She's trying to get it towed."

"Crap," Greg said. "We need to get somebody over there fast." Greg pulled a list of reporters and photographers from his desk drawer. It had their home phone numbers. He handed the sheet to Jessica.

"Go down the list and call these people," Greg said. "I need to find out what's going on in the big picture."

"Spencer, I'm scared," Jessica said.

"So am I," Greg said. "Get on the phone."

Jessica looked at him in disbelief as she picked up the receiver.

Greg turned on the police radio scanner on his desk. He tuned to the highway patrol frequency and listened a few minutes. Numerous units were being dispatched to Pampa. A patrolman pleaded with the dispatcher that more ambulances were needed in Pampa.

"Spencer," Jessica said with frustration. "I'm not getting anywhere. I mean, like, nobody's answering their phones."

"Well, that's no surprise," Greg said. "It's Easter, after all." He paused a moment. "Do you know how to get to Pampa?"

"Sure," Jessica said. "I have relatives up there. But surely you don't want me to go."

"I don't have any choice. Maybe some of the other reporters will check in later, but for now, you're it. Apparently they've got a mess on their hands in Pampa."

"Oh, Spencer, I don't know." Jessica shook her head warily.

"Come on, it's either you or me, and I have to be here. You can do it. I'll talk you through it. Get going."

"Tell me what to do."

"Make sure your car has plenty of gas. Do you have a raincoat and umbrella?"

"I have my raincoat in the car."

"There's an umbrella on that coat rack over there. Go by McDonald's and get something to take with you to eat. Then drive like hell for Pampa; it's fifty miles up Highway 60. If you get stopped, tell the cops who you are and where you work. Be polite and don't argue with them. If they give you any crap, tell them to call me."

Jessica grabbed her forehead. "My God, I hope I can remember all this."

"Then, when you get there, try to see if there's a command post set up. Find who's in charge and identify yourself. Be polite, but persistent. Remember the 'five W's' you learned in journalism class. Get those questions answered: Who's hurt? What's damaged? When did the storm hit? Hell, you know all that."

"Well, okay, Spencer, I'll try."

"Find a phone and call me as soon as you can. I'll take you through it. Okay?"

"Okay, I hope I don't screw it up." Jessica grabbed her purse and ran out of the building dragging an umbrella and looking overwhelmed.

Greg returned to the staff list and started dialing numbers. He located two photographers and sent Dave McGee to Claude, Jerry Ragsdale to Pampa.

"And Jerry," Greg said before hanging up. "I had to send Jessica Taylor, our new reporter, up there. Keep an eye on her and try to calm her down if she needs it."

Larry Chambers called back to report six people had been injured and a dozen homes damaged on the outskirts of Claude, forty miles southeast of Amarillo.

"Okay, Larry," Greg said. "I'll start a story based on that, but get back out there and get some more details. Talk to some witnesses. Call me back as soon as you can."

Greg called the National Weather Service and typed notes as a forecaster described the atmospheric conditions that created the tornado outbreak. He told Greg he thought the worst was over, although a dozen tornadoes had been spotted across the Panhandle.

Gradually several other reporters called in, asking what they could do. Greg sent one to Vega, west of Amarillo, and another to Dimmitt, to the south. The weather service had reports of tornadoes near each town.

He dispatched two other reporters to come to the office to assist him on the city desk. Sunday was usually a slow day, and Greg normally worked the desk alone.

Neal Douglas came into the office and manned the copy desk, where stories got a final edit and a headline.

As evening fell, Greg stood up and walked to the men's room. He took a deep breath and realized his hands were shaking. His armpits were soaked with sweat. *Okay, then,* he thought, *shake and sweat, Spencer, but stay focused.* As he relieved himself, he realized Jessica hadn't called him yet. He needed to check with Aunt Sally to see how Hereford had fared.

Back at the desk, he dialed Sally's number.

"It's all quiet here," she said. "We got a good rain, though."

"Isn't the *Plainsman* out covering this mess?"

"If they are, they didn't call me; I'm the women's editor. I guess I'll find out in the morning. We only print twice a week and won't have a paper out until Tuesday."

"I'm sure they'll put your expertise to good use. I'd better get busy. Just wanted to check."

Reporters Tim Hackett and Sid Weimer joined Greg on the city desk.

"Tim, see if you can round up some of the guys from the copy desk. Neal needs some help over there."

The phone on Greg's desk rang.

"Spencer, it's me." Jessica sounded shaken.

"Where've you been?"

"Oh, God, you wouldn't believe. . . ."

"Okay, did Jerry what's-his-name, the photographer, show up?"

"Yeah, he's here. We've been all over this place. It looks like a war zone." Her little girl's voice sounded even higher and squeakier.

"Okay, tell me what you've got."

"At least five dead and, like, twenty injured badly enough to be hospitalized. The twister hit a trailer park and several new homes in the north part of town."

Greg's own reporting instincts kicked in. "Who told you that?"

"Captain Lewis of the Department of Public Safety."

"What's his first name?"

"Oh, crap. I had it." Jessica seemed to be fumbling with her notes.

"Okay, you can get it. And find out how many homes were hit. Go ahead."

"Well, the tornado covered an area two blocks wide and plowed through a half-mile of homes and trailers."

"Any estimate of damage?"

"I don't know," she said. "Like, who would tell me that?"

"Probably Captain Lewis. Maybe some city official. Try to find the mayor or police chief. Can you talk to Lewis again?"

"I think so." Her voice sounded small and weak.

"Okay, go back and try to tie up your loose ends. Have you talked to any survivors?"

"Just one guy. He was too upset to say much."

"Okay, Jessica. Here's where you have to be a real pain in the ass. Be polite, but talk to witnesses and press them for details if you have to. We need some personal accounts of what happened."

"Okay, I'll try."

"You can do it. You're no shrinking violet. Call me back in half an hour. We need to get our lead story together."

"Okay, you mean old editor."

Greg cracked a smile. "I guess you had me pegged all along. Get back to work," he growled mockingly.

"Bye, sweetie."

By ten o'clock, Greg had written a dozen stories from information he'd gotten over the phone from reporters. Jessica supplied information for the main story on the Pampa tornado. She showed her inexperience at several points, but slowly gained confidence and turned in a respectable job.

Photographer Jerry Ragsdale returned from Pampa and promptly developed his pictures in the paper's darkroom. He put a stack of prints on Greg's desk showing the devastation in Pampa.

Larry Chambers rushed into the newsroom and typed an addition to his story of the storm's damage in Claude. Ragsdale brought prints to go with Larry's story. Greg edited Larry's story and sent it to the copy desk. At least Greg didn't have to write headlines or supervise the paper's makeup, as he had in Galveston

By eleven-thirty, all the copy for the Monday morning edition had been turned in. Jessica called with a few late details. Greg typed an "add" to the main story and told Jessica to come back to Amarillo.

"Hey, Spencer," Jessica said. "How late will you be there?"

"Till the paper comes out. Probably one or one-thirty."

"How about if I, like, get us something to eat and meet you at your place?"

"Aren't you tired?"

"Yeah, and I've got class tomorrow. I won't stay long. I just thought you might like a snack."

"I 'm pretty pooped," Greg said.

"But, Spencer. I want to talk to you after all this. We made quite a team."

"Okay." Greg relaxed a little. "I guess we both need to unwind a little. Look for me around one forty-five. If you get there before

I do, you can use the pay phone outside the office to call the paper to see if I'm still here."

"Okay, sweetie," she said. "And Spencer, you know what?"

"What?"

"I think I'm in love with you."

❖

A little before midnight, Neal Douglas sat down at the desk next to Greg's. Everyone else in the newsroom had gone home, except for a lone editor on the copy desk.

"Greg," Douglas said. "I think Seth Yeager would've been proud of you tonight."

"Thanks, Neal," Greg said. "That was quite a workout."

"I've never seen anyone handle a big story any better than you did. I'll bet I can get you a raise, especially after Mr. Southworth sees tomorrow's paper." Jacob Southworth was the paper's executive editor.

"That's nice to hear, Neal, especially since I haven't been here very long."

"I think you've got a great future here, if you plan to stick around."

"No reason not to," Greg said.

"Well, I'd better get home," Douglas said. "I just wanted to let you know what a nice job you did. I'm thinking of nominating you for an AP award."

"Wow, Neal, that's awfully nice of you. But I was just doing my job."

"I know, but it was a hell of a job. Goodnight, Greg."

Greg stared across the empty newsroom, tired but satisfied. Few people could know the depth of his satisfaction. He thought of how far he'd come since he arrived in the Panhandle. Six months ago, his life had seemed at a dead end.

Greg got to his apartment sooner than he'd expected. He didn't see Jessica's Mustang anywhere in the parking spaces near his building. He went upstairs, unlocked his door, went inside, and collapsed on his sofa in the living room.

He rubbed his tired, burning eyes. What the hell had he gotten himself into with Jessica? He was so tired, he couldn't think straight. His doorbell rang, and he let Jessica in.

She put her arms around him and kissed him. He took a step back.

"What's the matter, Spencer?" she asked. "You just won my heart tonight, you mean old editor."

"I'm really tired, Jessica." He held her shoulders. "I may not be able to stay awake."

"It's okay," she said. "I won't keep you up long. I've got school in the morning. I just wanted to tell you that, like, I couldn't have done crap tonight without you."

"You done good, girl," he said. "You made it easy. I'm proud of you."

"Oh, Spencer." Jessica beamed. "Do you have any idea how that makes me feel? I'd gotten so discouraged. Now, I think I may really turn out to be a reporter after all."

"You'll be fine," Greg said. "What have you got to eat?"

"I picked up some sandwiches at Arby's. It's a new place out on I-40. You want roast beef or ham and cheese?"

Greg took the ham and cheese, and they sat in his dinette eating their sandwiches. Jessica couldn't stop chattering about all she'd seen and done in Pampa.

"I mean, it looked like an atomic bomb had hit the place," she said. "I saw them pull, like, two bodies out of the rubble."

"That's the hard part," Greg said.

"No kidding. I'd never seen a dead body in my life, except at a funeral. I didn't know people could be so mangled. One old man's head was crushed and you could see his brain falling out."

"Yeah, it can be awful. Don't ever let yourself get callous about that kind of thing. I've seen that happen to some reporters."

"I'll probably have nightmares."

"You did a nice job of interviewing those witnesses. That was the meat of your story."

"I'm so glad you gave me a pep talk about that. I think that got me over the hump. Once I got going, it was easier."

"You'll be telling your grandkids about what you just did." Greg took her hand and kissed it. "I really am proud of you."

"Well, I'd better go. Call me tomorrow. I'll be home by noon."

"You'll probably want to take a nap."

"It's okay, call me before you go to work."

Jessica kissed Greg on the lips and went out the door.

He sat on his couch staring at the ceiling. He certainly preferred the softer version of Jessica. He didn't feel as convinced she was using him now. Why would she tell him she was falling in love with him if she didn't mean it?

Greg met with Marilyn Reed early Monday afternoon.

"I saw the paper this morning," Marilyn said. "It was impressive. How much of that was your doing?"

"Quite a bit," Greg said. "I wrote most of the stories from reporters' notes and had to ride herd on the staff."

"Where was your byline?"

"City editors don't get bylines. The reporters did all the leg work."

"I guess people don't realize how much work editors do. How'd you do through it all?"

"It started off pretty scary," Greg said. "I was driving from Hereford to Amarillo, and one of those tornadoes crossed the road right in front of me."

"Oh, Lord, that would give anyone a panic attack. Did you have one?"

"No, but I was scared stiff. I just stayed focused, took a lot of deep breaths, and drifted through the anxiety."

"Greg, that's wonderful. You get a big hug for that." Marilyn squeezed him hard and patted his back.

"There's something else that's bearing down on me pretty hard," Greg said.

"Your love life, I'll bet." Marilyn walked to the window and adjusted the venetian blinds to let in more light.

"You know me too well," Greg said.

"What now?" Marilyn sat behind her desk. "Are you having problems with Jessica?"

"I guess you could call it a problem." Greg hesitated. "She's telling me she's in love with me."

"And you're not in love with her?"

"No." Greg paused again. "I'm not saying I couldn't ever be or that it's out of the question. But so far, it's mostly physical."

"But she's showed you a side of her you kind of like."

"Right. But we really don't know each other very well. I've never told her about my medical history."

"Maybe it's time to tell her." Marilyn leaned back in her chair. "How she reacts might give you a clue about how serious she is."

"Good idea," Greg said. "I'm going down there this afternoon."

"No time like the present."

Greg decided to walk down the street to Amarillo General to say hello to Brian. He hadn't talked to Brian in a while.

He passed along the corridor to the row of residents' offices. The door was open to Brian's office. Brian sat at his desk thumbing through a stack of papers. Greg knocked and stood in the doorway.

"Hey, Greg, come in," Brian said, removing a pair of glasses.

"When'd you start wearing glasses?" Greg asked.

"About a week ago." Brian took off the glasses and laid them on the desk. "I have so damn much paperwork, I got to where I couldn't read the fine print any more."

"An old man at thirty," Greg teased.

"Hell, I won't be thirty for another six months. How about some coffee?"

He drew a cup for Greg and handed it to him. "Sit down, it's been a while."

"It really has."

"How're you doing?" Brian said. "I guess you had a busy day at the paper yesterday."

Greg told Brian about dodging the tornado and the pressure of directing the *Journal's* coverage. "And you know, Brian, I don't think I've had a chance to thank you."

"For what?"

"For hooking me up with Marilyn Reed."

"Listen, I knew in very short order that she was the real McCoy, and that she was just what you needed."

"I really appreciate you thinking of me." Greg felt a lump in his throat as he recalled how far he'd come since Brian first told him about Marilyn.

"Glad to do it for a friend." Brian looked touched, then he smiled. "You really look good, Greg. I can see a world of difference in you. I remember how uptight and frazzled you were in Galveston. Seems like you're enjoying life now."

"Well, yeah. But I've still got work to do."

"Don't we all," Brian said, still smiling.

"You mean you shrinks have stuff to work on?"

"Oh, my God," Brian chuckled. "Probably more than most people."

Greg looked around Brian's office at his diplomas. "I keep wondering how Marilyn managed to jump so far ahead of most people in her field. She's amazing."

"Yes, she is," Brian sipped from his coffee cup. "She hasn't had an easy time of it. She had her own bout with anxiety when she was younger. I'm sure that's what drove her"

"Marilyn?" Greg leaned forward in disbelief. "You're kidding."

"No—and this is just between us, Greg. Marilyn was in grad school at Texas Tech. She'd married her high school sweetheart. The stress of school got so bad, she developed agoraphobia and was having panic attacks. Her husband couldn't cope with it, so he left her and ran off with another woman. Marilyn had been studying cognitive therapy, and, with help from one of her profs, she managed to work her way through her stuff. Then she went to Australia and worked as an assistant to Dr. Weekes. She even spent some time studying with a Zen master."

"I guess that's where she picked up the meditation stuff," Greg said.

"Right," Brian said. "A lot of that Eastern philosophy is leaking into psychotherapy. I think it's a good thing."

"I didn't know most of that." Greg finished off his coffee. "She did tell me she'd been through a tough divorce."

"She's a wonder," Brian said. "And she speaks from experience. I'm really glad she's been so good for you."

Greg sat a moment, reflecting on what Brian had told him. Then he remembered why he had come to see Brian. "How are your wedding plans coming along?"

"It's been pretty hectic trying to get things organized with Cindy still in Galveston. We're just now putting the wedding party together. In fact, I was going to call you; how about being an usher?"

"I'd be honored," Greg said. Then his heart dropped. "I guess Suzy's still planning to be Cindy's maid of honor."

"Oh, yeah. That's been settled for a long time."

Greg's heartbeat surged, and he bit his lip. "I don't know, Brian. Maybe it'd be better if I weren't in the wedding party."

"Okay, I know you must feel a little awkward, but let me fill you in on some things about Suzy." Brian leaned back in his chair.

"Please do. I haven't heard anything since December." Greg dreaded talking about Suzy, but his curiosity was overwhelming.

"Well, you knew that she was dating this guy in Galveston?"

"Yeah, but that's all I know. Just 'a guy.'"

"Okay, I know him," Brian said. "His name is Raúl Espinoza; he's from Venezuela. He was getting his M.D. in neurology. Suzy got to know him when she was working in the neurology wing."

"Probably when Curtis Warren was there." Greg recalled the information Suzy had given him about the teenage beating victim.

"I don't know exactly when they met." Brian leaned on the desk. "But I don't think things got serious until after y'all broke your engagement. Then, I think it got pretty intense."

"Meaning she was sleeping with him." Greg felt tight all over and doubled his fists.

"I'd guess so, from what Cindy told me. Sorry about that."

"Damn, I knew it." Greg's face was getting hotter.

"Well, hold on," Brian said. "From what you've told me, you and Jessica haven't exactly been playing jacks."

Greg let out a breath. "Okay, okay. Go ahead."

"Well, the bliss didn't last for Suzy and Raúl."

"How so?"

"It got to the point where he proposed to her, but when they started getting into the details, Suzy balked."

"Oh? What happened?"

"Raúl is a very macho kind of Latin guy who wants to run the whole show. He had it all figured out that they'd move back to Caracas, and she'd stay home and raise kids, while he established his practice. You know Suzy's had her heart set on a nursing career, and she wasn't willing to go along with his scenario. He wouldn't budge, so they split. Cindy said it got pretty ugly. He finished med school last month and moved back to Caracas. And now Suzy's free as a bird."

Greg's mind whirled. "She's not seeing anyone now?"

"Not according to Cindy," Brian said. "Cindy says Suzy's been pretty miserable, so she's sort of drowned herself in her work. They get their nursing degrees in a couple of weeks, so they're busy as hell. They have to pass a state certification exam, in addition to finals."

Greg sat stunned and didn't say anything for a minute. "I wonder if there's still a glimmer of hope?" he said. "But I think Jessica's getting serious, and that puts me in a real bind."

"I wish I could advise you, pal," Brian grinned with resignation. "I don't envy your choices."

"Did Cindy tell you if Suzy's mentioned me at all?"

"I'm taking the fifth." Brian smiled and shrugged. "You'll have to get that from Suzy."

"Then I guess I'll be an usher at your wedding."

Brian slapped Greg on the shoulder and laughed. "I thought you might see it that way."

❖

Greg drove to Canyon in a wad of tension. He stopped at a service station on the highway into town and went to a pay phone. He called Jessica.

"Spencer, I just woke up." Her voice sounded thick from sleep.

"Did you make it to your classes this morning?"

"No, I slept right through them." She yawned. "My alarm went off at, like, eight, and I rolled over and went back to sleep. I don't think I've ever been so tired."

"I'm not surprised," Greg cleared his throat. "I'm in Canyon. Okay if I come by? I can't stay long."

"Yeah, I've got to get dressed." She paused. "Or do I?"

"You'd better," Greg said. "We need to talk."

He drove to her apartment. She opened the door in a pair of jeans and a T-shirt with no bra. *Nothing is easy,* Greg thought.

"Let's sit down," she said. "What's on your mind?"

"Did you see the paper today?"

"Not yet. I'm barely awake."

He handed her a copy of the *Journal* he'd brought with him. Her face lit up as she scanned the front page.

"Man, how cool is this? I got two front-page bylines!"

"Yes, you did. You've hit the big time."

She leaned over and kissed him. "Thank you, Spencer. I mean that."

He held her for a minute, wondering if he shouldn't wait to talk with her about his past. It might sound as if he were throwing a wet blanket on her good feelings about work. He realized that her ego was more fragile than he'd first suspected, but he needed to get to the heart of the matter before things went any further.

He squeezed her shoulders and looked at her with what he hoped she'd take as tender concern.

"I'm proud of you, Jessica," he said. "I'm glad I could help." Greg paused. "But we need to talk."

"About my job?"

"No, you're doing fine. This is personal." Greg cleared his throat. "Why don't we talk about us and what you said last night?"

"Huh? What'd I say last night?" She gave him a flirty grin.

"You said you thought you were falling in love with me. I didn't know how serious you were."

"Well, I was just, like, telling you how I felt. Anything wrong with that?"

"Nothing wrong with it." Greg sat back on the couch. "I just didn't know how to take it." He paused and looked down a moment, then met her eyes. "We really don't know each other that well. We've only been seeing each other a little over a month. I don't know that much about you, and there are some things you don't know about me."

"You make it sound so heavy."

"It is." Greg cleared his throat.

"What's the deal? Things are going great."

"Yeah, but nothing's that simple."

"Well, okay, but, Spencer, we have such great vibes." Her eyes brightened. "Look at last night, at how well we worked together."

"That's work, Jessica. Not everyday life."

"Come on. You're not making much sense."

"Look, you know I'm awfully fond of you, but I don't think I've known you long enough to call it love." Greg pulled out a cigarette and lit it. "And there's something very important that you don't know about me."

"Oh? What's the big secret?"

"Jessica, six months ago, I was in the hospital in Fort Worth for acute anxiety and clinical depression. I came up here to see a doctor who specializes in those problems. I'm doing a lot better now, and the worst may be behind me. But I can't be sure."

He told her the complete history of his disorder, going back to 1959. He watched her face grow more somber as he recounted the problems, the panic attacks, the hospitalizations.

"But, Spencer," she said in a pleading tone. "How's that possible? You seem so cool, both at work and when we're together."

"Dr. Reed's been a tremendous help. But for a couple of years, I was a basket case. I hope I never go through anything like that again, but the disorder's always there, and there's no guarantee it won't resurface."

Jessica shrugged. "But you're fine now. Why not just live for today? Couldn't we give what we have to give to each other and just go with the flow? People can, like, drop dead or get hit by a truck anytime."

"That's true. I just want you to know what you might be facing with me. You're barely twenty-one. Are you sure you're ready to start thinking about married life and that whole scene?"

"Who said anything about marriage?" Jessica's shoulders dropped in exasperation. "Marriage is, like, so passé, anyway. I just know that I feel good when you're with me. I mean, you'll make sure everything's all right. That's a good feeling I haven't had very often."

"I care about you, Jessica, and I want to help you all I can. I'm just not sure either of us is ready to go to the next level."

"I'll have to give it some thought, Spencer, but I think you're, like, getting ahead of yourself." She sighed again and looked thoroughly irked. "And by the way, your timing's pretty shitty, if you ask me."

❖

Greg drove to work in a tangle of emotions. In the newsroom, his colleagues shook his hand and congratulated him on the paper's tornado coverage. Jacob Southworth, the *Journal*'s editor, called him into his office.

"Spencer, that's as good an issue of this paper as I've seen on a major story in a long time," the editor said.

Greg's mind darted in all directions as he tried to focus on the editor's words.

"Thanks, Mr. Southworth. The staff worked awfully hard."

"You know, that Taylor girl did one hell of a job up at Pampa. I hear she's only been with us a short while."

Greg wondered if the editor remembered he'd refused to hire Jessica the first time she applied.

"Spencer," Southworth said. "I'm going to raise your pay to $150 a week. You're a man we want to hang onto. How's that sound?"

"Great, Mr. Southworth. I'm really glad to be working here." He knew the editor couldn't fathom the depth of that statement.

"You all did one hell of a job. I'm more excited about our staff than I've been in a long time. I'm putting a memo on the bulletin board telling all of you what a fine job you did."

"Thank you, sir. I hope I can justify your faith in me."

Greg walked in a daze back to the city desk. Phil Jackson, the daytime city editor, went over the stories they'd be working on for the next day's paper. The tornado outbreak's aftermath still dominated the coverage.

Greg plowed distractedly through the copy his staff had turned in. He had trouble focusing. He got up and got some coffee. He worked the rest of the day stewing about what to do about Jessica and Suzy. The "what-if" scenarios multiplied.

Over the next two weeks, Greg had trouble sleeping, and he worried about losing all he'd gained with Marilyn Reed's help. He thought about calling her for advice, but decided he could wait until his next appointment.

Greg and Jessica didn't see as much of each other, what with their conflicting work schedules. Also, she was approaching graduation, and she insisted on keeping her grade-point average as high as possible. She spent most of her spare time studying for finals and completing research papers.

She made time to spend the next two Saturday nights with Greg. But she seemed distant and preoccupied, though she paid rapt attention as Greg went over the stories she'd written for the *Journal*. She seemed more blasé about sex. Their bedroom encounters had lost some novelty for him, too.

"You look pretty frazzled," Marilyn Reed said when he came to her office for their next session.

"I know it amuses you," he said, taking his seat on the couch. "But my love life is driving me nuts."

"I don't mean to make fun, Greg. I've been there myself. It always feels miserable when you're in the midst of it. It's only later that you can laugh about it."

"It feels miserable, all right."

"Okay, let's hear it. Did you talk to Jessica?"

"Yeah, and I told her my medical history. She didn't want to believe it. And she thought my timing was awful, bringing it up right after her big newspaper debut."

"Ouch!" Marilyn said. "But you didn't have much choice, did you?"

"No, she'd just told me she thought she loved me the night before."

"So, how's it been with her since?" Marilyn leaned against the couch.

"She's been pretty distant," Greg said. "Of course, she's got finals and plenty to keep her busy at the paper."

"So you don't know what effect you had."

"Hard to say. She said she'd give it some thought. But Jessica's not my only headache."

"I'll bet I can guess: You'll see Suzy at Brian's wedding."

"Bingo. How did you know?"

"Brian told me. I'll be at the wedding, too, you know."

"I guess so, now that I think about it." Marilyn and Brian were close friends, after all.

"So, how has all this romantic turmoil affected you?"

"I've had trouble sleeping, and I've been preoccupied with worry. I hope it hasn't shown on the job."

"Are you meditating?"

Greg felt ashamed. "I've skipped it more often that not."

"Okay, quit skipping it. Just sit there and become that pebble in the stream. If you're still tense, just be tense. Keep coming back to the breaths gently, and little by little, you'll gain some calm."

"You're right, of course." He sighed. "I've let all this knock me off stride."

"Greg, you know I promised you'd have setbacks. It's a bump in the road, but you're handling it well. Hang in there; you'll be fine."

"Okay, but the closer that damned wedding gets, the tighter the noose feels."

"Have you thought how lucky you are to have two women to worry about?"

"No, not really. Just the opposite."

"A lot of guys would love to be in your shoes."

"Hell, Marilyn. You can make me feel better when I'm doing my damnedest to be miserable."

Marilyn laughed. "See you at the wedding. Have you rented your tux yet?"

❖
Amarillo
May 1966

Jessica graduated from West Texas State the first Saturday in May. She didn't invite Greg to the ceremony. Several of her relatives came to Canyon to stay with her and attend the graduation. Neal Douglas gave her the weekend off, so Greg didn't see her in the newsroom Sunday.

A reporter told Greg that Jessica had been dating photographer Jerry Ragsdale.

He didn't see her the next Sunday, either. She and Ragsdale spent the day in Pampa together working on a story with pictures about rebuilding efforts there in the wake of the tornado. She didn't come by the office that night.

Greg spent the next few days working on a special section for the Sunday paper on local residents fighting in Vietnam. He plowed through mountains of copy and photographs for the section. He didn't have much time to think about the upcoming weekend.

Friday night, Greg parked outside St. John's Episcopal Church, an upscale contemporary structure, and headed for the entrance, weak in the knees and trembling inside.

He stopped before a tall metal door, his nerve endings exploding like fireworks. He stood a moment, then pulled the door open and entered the spacious amphitheater of the sanctuary. He looked toward the altar where several people were gathered.

He spotted Cindy near the front, then Brian, standing next to a priest in clerical garb. Several other young men and women stood nearby. Greg presumed they were other members of the wedding party. Their muffled voices echoed around the room, but Greg couldn't make out what anyone was saying.

He didn't see Suzy anywhere.

Greg walked toward the front. Cindy spotted him and hurried to him as he reached the front pews. "Greg, you look so good!" she said, and wrapped him in a smothering hug. Brian came up behind her.

"Good to see you, Greg," Brian said as they shook hands. "But we've got a small problem."

"Oh?" Greg said and paused a moment. "Is Suzy here?"

"That's the problem," Cindy said.

"We're worried to death about her," Brian said. "She was supposed to be here an hour ago, and she hasn't shown yet. We're supposed to start the rehearsal in fifteen minutes."

"My God," Greg said. "Was she driving?"

"Yeah," Cindy said. "She spent the night with her folks in Fort Worth and drove up here today."

A side door to the sanctuary opened. A woman stuck her head inside. "Dr. Brian Reynolds?" she called out.

"Right here," Brian responded.

"You have a phone call in the office."

"Oh, hell, probably some patient," Brian grumbled. "Only I don't know how they found me." He followed the woman through the door.

Greg and Cindy stayed behind. Greg complimented Cindy's striking appearance, then groped for something to say. "How's Suzy been?" he finally asked her.

"She's had a hard time the last couple of months," Cindy said. "Brian said he told you about Raúl."

"Yeah," Greg said. "He told me."

"I was worried about her," Cindy said. "I wondered if she'd hold up till graduation. But she did, and we're both real nurses now."

Brian hurried back through the door and rejoined them. "Damn, Greg, I'm glad you're here. That was Suzy."

"Where is she?" Greg said as a new shot of adrenaline surged through him.

"She got lost out on the north side of town." Brian panted to catch his breath. "This church is on Yucca Circle, and she went looking for Yucca Avenue, out north of downtown. She got lost and drove clear out of town. She found a gas station with a phone. She said she was completely turned around. I said I'd send somebody out there to lead her to the church. I told her you were here. She's at Broadway and St. Francis; know where that is?"

Greg knew the city fairly well by now. "Yeah, just west of Highway 287."

"Oh, I'll bet she's exhausted," Cindy said. "She's been driving all day."

"Well, we can delay the rehearsal a while," Brian said. "If you can get her back here by 7:30, I think we'll be okay. It's nearly seven, so why don't you head out there."

Greg was befuddled, but he agreed and hurried outside to his car. As he drove across town, his anxiety still barked. He hadn't seen Suzy since she'd broken their engagement. How would she react to seeing him? What would he say after all that had happened?

He found the Texaco station Brian had described and saw Suzy's blue Ford Falcon next to a phone booth near the street. Suzy sat behind the wheel nervously looking around. He pulled into the driveway and stopped next to her car. She looked at him as though she didn't recognize him right away. He got out and walked up next to the driver's side of her car.

"Oh, Greg," she said. "It's you." She looked down.

"Who were you expecting?" Greg said.

"Well," she said, clearly flustered. "I wasn't sure. Brian said you were there and that he'd send somebody. But I didn't know he sent you."

"Well, here I am," Greg said. "At your service."

"Oh, Lord, Greg." She looked down again. "I'm so embarrassed."

"Don't be," he said. "Let's get you to the church on time."

"I've been driving for eight hours," she said. She looked thinner, and the fatigue showed on her face. "I'm just exhausted. I'm not thinking too clearly. I got completely lost and didn't know north from south. I feel so stupid."

"It's okay, really." He wanted to smother her in his arms and reassure her, but he knew he couldn't; not yet, anyway. "Do you feel like following me to the church?"

"How far is it?"

"It's three or four miles, but we can go slow and stay off the freeway."

"Okay, I'll try to stay close behind you," she said. "Oh, and Greg. . . ."

"Yeah?"

She gave him a tentative smile. "Well, I don't know if I should say. . . .that is, I mean. . .," she stammered. "Oh, never mind; I'll tell you later, darlin'."

"We'd better get going," Greg said.

With echoes of Suzy's "darlin'" ringing inside, Greg got back in his Volkswagen and pulled out into the intersection. Her car lunged forward a little jerkily, and she pulled in behind him. *Are the old feelings still there?* he wondered.

It was 7:15 now. He had to hurry. He got the Beetle up to forty, but he could see that Suzy was having trouble keeping up with him. He slowed to about twenty-five to let her close the gap. As they neared downtown, he stopped at a red light, and she came to a halt behind him.

The light changed, and he pulled forward slowly. With his window down, he heard a rising roar to his left: the sound of loud mufflers and a fast-running engine. The noise got louder. A red Ford pickup barreled into the intersection. *That son of a bitch is running a red light,* Greg thought, and he stomped the gas to get out of the way. In his rearview mirror he saw the world shift suddenly into slow motion, the images burning into his psyche:

As Suzy's Falcon entered the intersection, the pickup rammed it broadside with a loud, metal-on-metal bang, accompanied by the sound of breaking glass and the hiss of a ruptured radiator. The Falcon spun around and came to rest crossways in the street. The pickup stopped dead in mid-intersection, its front end spewing steam from the radiator and the hood gaping open.

Greg felt a charge of inner energy such as he'd never known. It wasn't panic; maybe the flip side of panic. Whatever it was drove him to unthinking action. He killed his engine and threw the door open. He rushed to Suzy's car, now completely caved in on the driver's side. Suzy lay sprawled across the front seat. Greg tugged, but couldn't get the crumpled door open.

Another man ran up as Greg rushed around the car and opened the passenger door. Blood covered Suzy's left arm and chest and soaked the seat fabric.

Suzy looked glassy-eyed and moved her head from side to side, quietly moaning.

"I think she must've cut an artery," said the wiry Hispanic man, who appeared to be in his thirties. "Blood is spurting from that arm."

Greg crawled inside and grabbed her arm. "Suzy, it's me."

"Greg," she said, barely audible. "I think my arm's hurt bad."

She bore a ragged gash from just above the elbow to the inside of her forearm. Broken glass lay all about. Jagged metal from the caved-in door protruded near the steering wheel.

"I'll call an ambulance," the wiry man said.

"We're only a few blocks from Amarillo General," Greg said. "I can get her there quicker than waiting for an ambulance." He took out his handkerchief to make a tourniquet. He'd had no training in first aid, but it came to him automatically; maybe he'd seen it in the movies. Whatever it was, he knew what he had to do.

Suzy seemed to fade in and out of consciousness. She looked down at the tourniquet as Greg took a pen from his pocket and tightened the tourniquet on her upper arm.

"That's it," she whispered. "That's what a good nurse is supposed to do." She looked at him and smiled weakly. "Now, put pressure on the artery, darlin'."

"Okay, Suzy. Stay with me." She closed her eyes again.

"I'll help you move her," the man said. "Do you want me to go along and drive?"

"No, I can make it. Why don't you check on that bastard in the pickup? He may need an ambulance."

Suzy was pale. An ugly red-and-purple knot was forming along her temple.

"Suzy, we're close to the hospital. I'm going to drive you there."

She didn't answer.

Greg gently grasped her arms, and the other man took her legs. They set her in Greg's front seat. Her head bobbed loosely as they tried to prop it against the back of the seat.

Greg got behind the wheel and started the car. The man who'd helped Greg came running back toward his car.

"Hey," he shouted. "Here's her purse. You might need this."

Greg sped off with Suzy leaning limply against him. He shifted into high gear and grabbed her bloody arm. The blood was now trickling instead of spurting. He drove with his left hand and wrapped his right hand around her arm. He placed his thumb over the crook in the arm and pressed as hard as he could.

Please, don't let her die. Not now, please, he said over and over. *Stay with me, Suzy!*

He heard a siren behind him. When he looked in the rearview mirror, a police car bore down on him. The cop inside was waving him to pull over. Greg couldn't stop. He floorboarded the Beetle and drove even faster. As he approached the hospital, the police car pulled next to him and tried to force him to the curb, just as he came to the emergency room driveway. He whipped in with the police car right on his tail.

He sped across a parking lot to the emergency room entrance and stopped. The officer came running up to his car as Greg got out.

"What the hell are you doing, buster?" the cop shouted.

"What the hell are you doing?" Greg echoed. "I've got a girl in here who's been hurt real bad in a wreck."

The cop spotted Suzy in the front seat. "I'll go get some help," he said and rushed inside.

Shortly, personnel from the emergency room came outside with a gurney and lifted Suzy onto it. They wheeled her inside. Greg and the officer followed.

The ER personnel rolled the gurney through a set of double doors. Greg pushed through behind them.

"Sir, you can't come in here," a nurse said firmly and stood in front of Greg.

"But she's my. . . ." He wanted to say she was his fiancée, but he realized that label was obsolete. "I brought her in," he said. "She's a dear friend." Greg handed the nurse Suzy's purse.

"Okay, sir, if you'll just wait outside in the waiting room, we'll keep you informed." The nurse grabbed Greg's arm and pulled him toward the doors.

"What kind of place is this?" Greg pleaded.

"Sir, I know you're upset. Just have a seat and try to collect yourself."

Greg went into the waiting room. The cop was talking at a pay phone. When he hung up, he approached Greg. "Why don't you have a seat, buddy, and unwind a little?"

Greg sat in one of the orange molded plastic chairs.

"Listen," the officer said. "I apologize for trying to run you down. I didn't know about the girl, but you were about thirty over the speed limit."

"Okay." Greg exhaled a deep breath and shrugged. "I didn't know what else to do."

"Don't sweat it, pal." The cop smiled. "I'd have probably done the same thing. In fact, if I'd known what you were dealing with, I could have led you with my lights and siren."

"I need to figure out what to do about her car," Greg said, his head spinning with things to do. "Oh, hell, I need to tell Brian and Cindy."

"I talked to the dispatcher," the officer said. "They've sent a wrecker out there. We have units on the scene."

"Good," Greg said. "I've got to use the phone."

He looked up the number and called the church. The phone rang a long time; finally someone answered and called Brian to the office.

"Brian, it's Greg," he said. "Suzy had a wreck. I'm with her at Amarillo General. She's not in good shape."

"Good God, what happened?"

Greg gave him the details. Brian debated whether to cancel the rehearsal.

"No, go ahead with it," Greg said. "Can't you get one of the other girls to be maid of honor?"

"I'll have to talk to Cindy." Brian paused a moment. "Listen, we should come right over there."

"No, you can't do that. I'll let you know what's going on. Go on with the rehearsal."

Brian finally agreed. Greg hung up and sat back down. The policeman sat with Greg a few minutes and asked some questions about how the accident had happened. He offered his best wishes and left. Greg worried over whether to call Suzy's parents, but he decided to wait until he heard something from a doctor.

It was early evening and the waiting room was deserted. Greg sat alone for minutes that stretched on interminably. He got up and paced the floor, then went to the men's room, where he saw himself in the mirror. His hands, arms, and the front of his shirt were covered with blood. He washed up as best he could, then walked back to the waiting room. A young man in green scrubs stood waiting.

"Are you with Miss Cox?" the dark-haired man asked. A nametag read, *Kenneth Mitchell, M.D.*

Greg's pulse quickened. "Yeah, how is she?"

"She's lost a lot of blood," he said, grim-faced. "But somebody put a tourniquet on her. That probably saved her life."

Relief rained in buckets over Greg. "Is she awake?"

"She was, but she's had a pretty bad concussion. We've given her several transfusions. I've sutured her arm and given her a sedative. She was about to go into shock, and I want her to rest and let some fluids drip into her. I've sent her to a private room upstairs. You can go up there if you like, but don't disturb her."

"Will she be okay?"

"I think so," the doctor said. "But we'll probably keep her here a couple of days." He looked curiously at Greg. "Did you put the tourniquet on her?"

"Yeah," Greg said. "She told me what to do as long as she was conscious. She's a nurse, you know."

"No, I didn't, but you did exactly the right thing."

❖

Greg stood next to Suzy's bed. He watched a moment as she now breathed ever so peacefully—though she looked a mess. Her hair was matted with splotches of dried blood, and her head looked misshapen from the ugly knot along her temple. All her makeup and lipstick were gone, yet something of Suzy's sweet essence shone through, perhaps more than ever before. Life still surged in her, and Greg had never been more grateful for anything in his life.

He sat down next to her bed in an upholstered chair and watched her tranquil sleep for a while. Then he turned his thoughts to what else he needed to do.

He'd called Brian and Cindy. They'd wait to hear from him Saturday before deciding to come see Suzy. The rehearsal had gone well, in spite of the complications. Another of Cindy's friends from nursing school had taken Suzy's place as maid of honor. Brian had called a colleague to replace Greg as an usher. Everything seemed on track with the wedding, still scheduled for Saturday night.

Greg realized he still had other calls to make. He went to the snack bar on the first floor and got a pocketful of change. Then he went to a pay phone near the main lobby.

He called Floyd and Nadine Cox in Fort Worth. They insisted on driving to Amarillo immediately, but Greg convinced them that Suzy should be well enough to travel soon, and he'd keep them closely informed until he could drive her back to Fort Worth. They reluctantly agreed.

He called Neal Douglas at home to ask if he could give Greg some time off to look after Suzy. He explained the situation, and Douglas told him to take as much time as he needed; he'd earned it.

Greg then called the *Journal* to leave instructions for Pete Kirkland, who would fill in for him as night city editor. He dialed the number.

"City desk, Jessica Taylor."

Greg drew a deep breath. "Jessica. It's me, Spencer."

"Spencer," she said jauntily. "Long time, no see."

"Is Pete there?"

"I think he's back in the photo lab. Will I do?"

"Not really." Greg debated how much he wanted to tell her. "I've got a problem I need to discuss with him. I may be gone a few days."

"Are you okay?"

"Well, not really. I'm calling from the hospital."

"My God, is it, like, that stuff you told me about?"

"No, no," he said. "It's not me. An, old, dear friend has been in a car wreck."

"Oh, anybody I know?"

"No, she drove up here for a wedding. She was following me to the church."

"She?"

"Yeah, Suzy's an old girlfriend. I've known her since high school."

"Sounds serious."

"Well, we were engaged for a year." Greg was tired of explaining. "Look, I'll call Pete back later. I need to go."

"Okay, Spencer," she said, sounding a little petulant. "You never told me any of that."

"You never told me much about your past, either," Greg said with an edge.

"Spencer, I think we've got a problem here."

"I think you're onto something, Jessica." He hung up the phone.

Greg went back to Suzy's room. A nurse came in to check Suzy's blood pressure and temperature. She adjusted something on the IV bottle, whose tubing coiled into Suzy's right arm.

"How does she look?" Greg asked.

"I think she's doing just fine," the red-haired LVN said. "Her vitals look good. Are you going to stay with her?"

"If it's okay."

"You can stay, but if you want to sleep, you'll have to make do with that chair."

"That's fine," Greg said. "I'm so tired, my body won't know the difference."

He stretched out in the chair and fell asleep immediately.

After sleeping heavily for hours, Greg dreamed he was lying on a beach with warm surf washing over him. Beyond the beach, in the distance, he spotted a cave in a sand dune, out of which came a voice, ever so faint.

"Hey, darlin'," the voice said. "Come over here." It was so faint he could barely make it out. Suddenly, he woke with a jolt. Suzy had turned onto her side in the bed and was calling to him in almost a whisper, "Come over here, darlin'."

He shook the cobwebs and stood up. Bright daylight filled the room. Suzy took his hand as he approached the bed. She looked at him and shook her head.

"I've never been so glad to see anyone in my whole life," she said. "Come here and let me hug you."

"I don't want to hurt you," he said. "Or pull the IV loose."

"You let me worry about that; I'm a nurse, you know?" Her left arm was in a cast, but she reached for him with her right, tubing and all, and pulled him close. "My sweet darlin'," she said. "I always knew deep down that you'd be my hero."

Greg's heart rose to his throat, and he squeezed harder.

When he stepped back, Suzy held his shoulder and regarded him with an amused frown.

"You look like hell, darlin'," she said. "And so do I. Why don't you go home and clean up and maybe they'll let me do the same."

Greg rushed across town to his apartment, where he soaked under a steaming shower, then shaved and put on fresh clothes. All the while he was thinking, *Now where did I put the damn thing?*

Once dressed, he dug through every drawer in his bedroom, franctically tossing socks and underwear aside. Finally, he found the tiny box in the back corner of a bottom drawer, behind an old pair of pajamas he'd stuffed there when they'd become threadbare.

He got in his VW and drove furiously back to the hospital.

When he arrived at Suzy's room, she was sitting on the edge of her bed, fully dressed with her hair rolled into a French twist and her face gleaming with makeup.

They stood looking at each other a moment, then they embraced, then buried themselves in a long, juicy kiss. How long had it been?

"You look terrific," he said, stepping back. "I didn't even notice the knot on your head."

Suzy smiled. "Cindy came by and helped me. She loaned me the clothes and fixed my hair."

"Just like the first time we met," Greg recalled.

"But you're the one who looks terrfic," Suzy said. "That's what I was trying to tell you before the wreck. Brian told me how great you were doing, but I didn't realize it until I saw you. Then I knew."

"I've got something for you," Greg said. "Do you remember what you said when we got back together in Galveston, and I told you I wanted it to be for keeps?"

"Not exactly. That seems so long ago."

"You said, 'Haven't we fooled around long enough?'"

Suzy giggled. "Yeah, now I remember."

"Close your eyes and hold out your hand."

"Oh, Greg, darlin'." She squinched her eyes shut.

He took the box from his pocket, opened it, and slipped the ring on her finger, sticking out below the cast on her left hand. She wrapped her arms around him and squeezed.

She pressed her face tighter against his. "Do you remember what I said that Christmas day at the Botanic Garden?"

Greg felt her tear on his cheek. "Not exactly. What?"

"I said, 'The answer is yes, yes, yes'!"

❖❖❖

Acknowledgements

Great thanks to Lanny Priddy, Mike Nichols, Elizabeth Delisi, Pat Stacy, Jack Carter, and Rita Vinson for reading the manuscript and offering many helpful suggestions.

I'm grateful to Gary Cartwright's book, *Galveston: A History of the Island,* which provided much helpful information and filled some gaps in my knowledge of the Island.

Thanks to graphics wizard Kathryn Kroll for helping me get unstuck from some tricky formatting problems.

I couldn't have written this book without the assistance of Google and the World Wide Web.

And abiding thanks to Bobby Bernshausen of Vitualbookworm.com Publishing for his continued help and support in getting this book between covers.

Typography Note

The body text in this book was set in Adobe Garamond 11-point type. Hypatia Sans Pro was used for titles.

Cover photographs by the author:
Galveston Sunrise, 1978
Umbarger Grain Elevator, 1986.
Cover design by the author.